What Is This Feeling?

Also by Robby Weber

If You Change Your Mind

I Like Me Better

What Is This Feeling?

ROBBY WEBER

HARPER
An Imprint of HarperCollins*Publishers*

What Is This Feeling?

 For information address HarperCollins Children's Books, a division of HarperCollins Publishers, 195 Broadway, New York, NY 10007.
www.epicreads.com

ISBN 978-1-33-500995-1
Typography by Julia Feingold
First Edition

In loving memory of my grandmother
Geraldine Addison
1947–2024

For Hola.
Thank you for helping me find my voice.
I'll always be your shining star.

And for the kids who have ever been told they're too much.
You're just enough. Dream big, live bigger.

Tuesday

Chapter 1

Get'cha Head in the Game

"Teddy McGuire's got his head in the clouds again."

I snap to and offer a smile, but Sebastian, one of the guys on the tech crew, is checking something off on an iPad as he hands me my microphone and then walks away.

People say that sort of thing to me all the time. But I don't think there's anything wrong with a little daydreaming or an overactive imagination—in fact, I *love* having my head in the clouds.

Truly, it's what gets me through life. As an actor, I have people literally clapping for me to indulge in flights of fancy.

I most recently wrapped my run as Troy in the spring production of *High School Musical*.

Well, almost wrapped. After today.

The local newspaper called my Troy a "fresh, newly

inspired take on what already feels like a strangely classic role." I'll take it, considering I hadn't seen it before getting the part—I wasn't even born when that movie came out.

My favorite singer, Benji Keaton, has a whole song called "In the Clouds" from his *Icarus Complex* album.

And if my head weren't in the clouds,
Crafting all these wild schemes,
I wouldn't be flying toward the sun,
I wouldn't be the guy of your dreams.

Enough said.

Anyway, it doesn't matter what people think because my optimism is endorsed by the universe. Everything always works out because I have a lucky bracelet, which is—

Shit.

Nowhere to be found.

No, no, no.

It takes no time at all for me to absolutely lose my mind and nearly break out in a cold sweat.

I can't go out on that stage without it. There's no way.

No matter what anyone might think, that bracelet is good luck. It's a friendship bracelet I made with Annie, strings knotted together in a multipatterned mix of blue hues. It has practically been ordained by some universe-administered powers of positive fortune. These bracelets repel things like awkward moments, clumsiness, and fear of public speaking. They magically make grades better, too, I swear.

Obviously, I didn't always have a charmed friendship bracelet, so I know it's not just something I'm making up. The night we made the bracelets, sitting in Annie's room with the strings on clipboards and burning Bath & Body Works candles we saw some YouTuber recommend, Benji announced his *Sunrise* album after a two-year hiatus. What do you call that? A coincidence?

Of course, at the moment Annie is nowhere to be found, like my damn lucky bracelet.

I have less than two minutes before curtain to find this thing, and if I don't, I honestly am not sure what will happen. Will I puke on the audience?

And this audience, of all audiences, is . . . different.

It's one thing to perform the school musical for the people who want to see it. The people who buy tickets for the evening shows are at least interested to some degree, and they probably won't *boo* or laugh or throw tomatoes. This audience is not interested, though. This is all upperclassmen, who all just want to skip the last two weeks of school the way God intended but are instead held captive for the end-of-the-year assembly.

It's torture, and every year at least one mouth breather cracks a loud, hilarious joke at one of the actors' expense.

Luckily we're only performing one number.

I need my lucky bracelet, or I'm not going out there.

It literally goes everywhere with me. I've never gone on

this stage without it. Even when I couldn't wear it because of my costume, like when I had to wear a basketball jersey and shorts for "Get'cha Head in the Game," I'd always have it in my—

"Oh, thank you, thank you, thank you."

I pull the bracelet out of my pocket and slip it onto my wrist, pulling it tight as the nerves dissipate.

I realize this all sounds silly. Of course, it absolutely does. How can a bracelet be lucky? Maybe it is all in my head, and maybe there isn't even really any such thing as good luck or bad luck. But I just don't believe that.

Like I said, I don't think "having my head in the clouds" is a bad thing.

Microphone in hand, I exhale and step into the wings. The slideshow is wrapping up—a Citrus Harbor High year in review that is impossibly boring and feels like it needs its own intermission.

Eden Bloom clears her throat beside me, a subtle way of announcing herself. She looks forward at the stage with a fierce determination, her blindingly blond shoulder-length hair tousled into waves that appear effortless, though nobody would ever think anything about Eden is effortless.

Since it's only an assembly, we're not in costume, and this is her doing casual: white Gucci sneakers without so much as a crease in the leather, along with onyx Lululemon leggings and a soft-pink crop top.

She shifts her weight, her hip popping as she cocks her head and pokes her tongue in her cheek, deep in thought.

The small movement is enough to offer a fresh waft of a sugary vanilla perfume—sickeningly sweet and undoubtedly expensive.

"Do you need concealer?" she whispers, icy cobalt eyes darting over to give me a once-over.

I blink. "What?"

"You look green." She raises a brow, and her lip pulls up a little like she smells hot garbage. "A little pasty."

"I'm fine," I say. "But thank you for the confidence boost."

"You'd better not get sick onstage." She shoots me a look. "And try not to make that one face you do when you hit the F. We have two angles to keep in mind—Briar is filming for my TikTok and Jason is filming for the drama club account. I'm sure I can cut something together either way, but if you could keep that in mind."

I smile. "Of course."

Eden sighs and uses her hot-pink nail to flick up the power switch on her microphone.

The slideshow has finally ended and they're introducing us now—the stars of the Citrus Harbor spring production. For the next three minutes and sixteen seconds, we're not Teddy and Eden, we're Troy and Gabriella.

For the next three minutes and sixteen seconds, all I have to do is play pretend and sing.

And that's what I do. It's whatever, really. When I'm onstage, it's fun. Even playing opposite Eden—she's a great actress, after all, so her smile lacks its usual vicious, apex predator vibe, and her eyes have the sparkle of a Disney princess and not Cruella de Vil. I've learned to let myself believe she's sweet and naïve and a brainiac who got stuck singing with me after we had a chance encounter at the teen lounge on New Year's Eve.

Once Eden and I are done circling each other in duet with outstretched arms, exaggerated grins, and make-believe heart eyes, we hold hands and bow. The spotlight makes it hard to see too far past the stage, but the drama club kids are in the front row, clapping like they're watching the performances at the Tony Awards. And there's Annie—she must have slipped in at the end of the slideshow like the genius she is.

Eden blows kisses and bounces around onstage like the applause is feeding her—making her grow, even, as she rises onto her tiptoes to receive the praise. She giggles and fakes humility for a moment before bringing her hands to her chest and batting her eyelashes.

"Thank you. So much. For me? Oh my gosh."

Once the lovefest is over, we exit stage right so the band kids can do their rendition of a Taylor Swift *1989* medley that won them an award this winter.

"You did great," Eden says once we're far enough backstage. I stop at the table to get my backpack and she narrows her eyes as she sets down the microphone. "Though I did notice you kept hitting a D instead of the F. Are you tired or something?"

"No, I'm not tired." I want to groan and throw my head

back, but I also don't want to give Eden the satisfaction of knowing she's getting to me.

"You seemed tired," she offers. "You normally hit it fine. It's not a huge deal." She winces. "Only, you should know it can be really jarring to your partner. Luckily, I'm more experienced so I can handle it but . . ." She raises a brow. "Something like that has the potential to throw off the entire performance."

I nod. "Sorry, Eden."

"It's fine." She smiles. "At least you always hit the note for the shows. Just a pointer for next time."

"Thanks."

She turns on her heel and for a moment, I think that's going to be all, but I should know better. Hovering for a moment, she interlocks her fingers and pouts, stretching her arms straight out.

"You know, I actually was sort of looking forward to having some competition for the scavenger hunt," she says, eyes lowering before she shrugs. "Winning is so much more satisfying that way."

I laugh, almost too loud if it weren't for the cellist going hard on "Blank Space."

The girl can have her own head in the clouds, sure, but if there's one thing she should know, it's that Annie and I are going to win the scavenger hunt.

The seniors from drama club leave for New York City tomorrow, and Mrs. Mackenzie has scored three tickets to an absolutely amazing after-party on Friday night. The two students who win the scavenger hunt get to go with her, and normally I wouldn't care too much about something like this, but Benji Keaton is on the line.

Benji Keaton is a god among men: He's a songwriter, an actor, a window into the artistry humans are only divinely lucky enough to create so many times in one generation. After hit records and winning an Oscar for his breakout acting role in *This Side of Paradise*, he turned to the stage. They all said he couldn't do it, but now he's Broadway's darling, originating the role of Louis XVI in *Versailles*.

Annie and I live for Benji Keaton. Every album release, we stayed up together. And as long as we've been able to drive—for his last four albums—we've made it a tradition to listen together in the car for the first time, blaring it and driving along A1A with the sun rising over the ocean. We listen to Benji when we carpool, when we get ready to do literally anything, and we've drawn his lyrics in Sharpie or lipstick on just about any surface you can imagine—mirrors, scrapbooks, laptops, our own bodies.

And Benji Keaton is going to be at that after-party.

So you better believe we're winning that scavenger hunt. There is nothing more important in the entire world than Annie and I winning that scavenger hunt and meeting Benji Keaton. This isn't optional, and it's destiny the opportunity would be presented like this. Practically wrapped in a bow.

"Me and Annie are going to—"

Eden raises a hand. "You and Annie?"

"Who else? You're acting like we haven't—"

"Wait. Are you telling me you don't know?" She raises her brows and nods slowly, a small laugh escaping her lips before she catches herself and her voice goes low. "Teddy, Annie isn't going. Mrs. Mackenzie told me herself."

What the hell is Eden talking about? Is this a scare tactic? A practical joke?

"Annie is going," I say.

Eden frowns. "She isn't."

"What is this? You can't haze me again, I'm already in the International Thespian Society—"

"No, Teddy, Annie isn't going on the trip."

I'm stunned. This can't be true.

Taking a step toward me, she offers a stage-friendly sympathetic smile—one the audience would buy, but not her costar.

"If you want to back out, I think people would get it." She glances to the right. "I mean, with Annie not going and everything . . ."

And once I realize what's happening, I can't form a single thought. It takes everything I have to form one sentence in response.

"I'm not backing out," I say, a hot rush washing over my body. "I'll be fine alone—"

"Oh my gosh." Eden's voice shifts to a high-pitched tone of aggression masked in kindness—the one she uses with teachers and baristas. "Don't worry, Ted, you won't be alone."

There is sweat starting to form under my arms and on the back of my neck and it suddenly feels icy and hot in here at the same time.

"Mrs. Mackenzie says you get to room with that kid from tech," she says. "Sebastian, I think?"

My heart sinks. *Sebastian*?

Just when I thought this couldn't get any worse.

"Well, great!" Eden yanks her purse out of a swivel chair, and her overwhelming inertia will keep it spinning long after she walks away. "See you in the AM. And don't worry"—she pops her AirPods into her ears and provides a final headshot-ready grin—"we're all in this together, remember?"

Chapter 2

Omigod You Guys

"I swear, I was going to tell you," Annie says. It comes out quickly—slightly rehearsed, even—and she draws in a deep breath once we're past the double doors and settling down at a table in the palm-lined courtyard. "Really, I only thought it'd be better for you to find out after the performance. I knew how stressed you were about this one."

My best friend, Annie Taylor—don't even get her started on sharing a name with the woman who went over Niagara Falls in a barrel—looks up at me with big, sincere aquamarine eyes, an apologetic expression I recognize instantly. Though the sun plays with the iridescent specks of her fair-skinned and highlighted cheeks to maintain a vibrant glow, her glossed lips form a frown. I can tell it's sincere.

"It isn't my fault, really." She throws her head back and groans, her freshly dyed pink hair falling behind her dramatically. "Look, I know what you're thinking."

"I'm just thinking you could have done this after the trip," I offer, trying to keep calm.

Annie shakes her head. "I didn't think we'd get caught. And we wouldn't have, really, except Mr. Pritchard has a camera set up in the lab. Which I don't feel should be legal. Do you? I think there's something there. How is he allowed to just record us without anybody knowing?"

I groan. "Annie, still. Even if you weren't going to get caught . . . what does your mission accomplish?"

"It's a statement," she says, as if she and the Friends of Nature Club are writing a letter or making a speech. Though I guess she's not wrong. From the photos, there is absolutely a statement to be taken away from the bloody art display in the biology lab—the specimen meant for dissection gruesomely laid out in puddles of costume blood as if they've been freshly murdered.

Annie narrows her eyes. "Why should any animal be dissected in a biology class?"

I shrug. "I don't know. You know I never did it. Made me queasy."

"We don't dissect humans to learn about anatomy," she says, barely stopping to take a breath. "It's so effed. I am sorry I got in-school suspension for the next week, but I am *not* sorry to stand up for animals that can't stand up for themselves." Her eyes lower and she flicks her hair over her shoulder. "Even if they're already dead. It's the principle. The big idea."

"Maybe there's something we can do. Maybe you can do ISS next week instead. After the trip."

Annie sighs. "There isn't time before graduation. And, seriously, this is my reduced sentence. If Mrs. Rushmore hadn't stepped in—which, come on, we never dissected any animals in her class! Even though we had to dissect things in *middle school* marine biology, which, honestly, I can't believe we even took in middle school. Such a Florida thing." She nods, realizing she's going on another tangent. "Anyway, if Mrs. Rushmore hadn't stepped in for me, I seriously think I might not be walking at graduation."

Of course, Annie was the only one willing to do the dirty work while the other Friends of Nature all cheered her on from afar, so she's the only one on the recording. And she's not going to rat anybody out—no pun intended, may those little vermin rest in peace.

"Thank God for Mrs. Rushmore," I say slowly, because I know, logically, Annie needs to graduate, and that having this "reduced sentence" is a good thing. Even if my heart is ripped into shreds over her missing New York.

Having a vegan best friend is such a roller coaster.

"This can't be happening." I bury my face into the canvas of my backpack on the table in front of me and groan. "This can't be happening," I say again, this time muffled and sopping with even more devastation. "I can't believe you did this, Annie."

"It's not like I thought it'd go this way. But it's only four days in the grand scheme of things. And then we'll be back together. I'm sure you can visit me in the proverbial slammer."

She opens her backpack and pulls out some of her ridiculously expensive markers, flips her sketchbook to an in-progress portrait, and acts like she hasn't completely turned the entire world upside down. She's acting like her protest, while noble, hasn't resulted in a cataclysmic shift in everything we've ever known.

I jerk up and blink. "Annie, I don't think you understand. I can't go on this trip if you don't go."

"What?" She rolls her eyes and examines two blue markers next to each other, comparing the shades. "Come on, Teddy. You've always dreamed of going to New York."

"Yeah, but not like this."

This is the part where, if this were a musical, I'd have a solo ballad—exaggerated frown, eyebrows that curve like sadness, and a single spotlight. This is the end for me, after all.

Now it's my turn to roll my eyes, though, because of course I'm going. Because I'm going to meet Benji Keaton. "Annie, we were supposed to do this together. Do you realize I now have to stay in a room with Sebastian Hodges?"

Annie shrugs and offers a smile, settling on one of the markers. "You could end up being friends!"

"Sebastian isn't friends with anyone," I counter. "I'm still not even sure why he did tech. Maybe he was being punished or needed extra credit."

"Or maybe he was hoping he'd make friends," Annie says.

I furrow my brow. "Except he didn't talk to anyone."

"So, he's shy." Annie throws her hands up. "I know, I know. It might be a little awkward at first, sure, but *how would you feel?*"

Annie is amazing at considering how other people feel. On the other hand, I have a hard time stopping all my own absurd thoughts and fears and ridiculous feelings from getting in the way. The idea that Sebastian might have wanted to make friends and failed? That didn't even cross my mind.

"Annie, maybe you can talk to Mrs. Rushmore—"

"I can't go, Teddy."

"But we had an entire plan," I say. "Remember? We had the whole thing—our outfits, our BenjiToks, our playlists. We were going to—"

"You had a whole plan." She says it like a reminder. "Teddy, we don't even know *for sure* that Benji is going to be at that after-party. What even are the odds?"

This is the thing about people. Even people we love, like Annie, can sometimes have their minds set to, like, Standard Earth Mode. It's not even reaching for the stars to imagine Benji Keaton may attend an after-party for his own show, but everyone keeps reminding me that I "don't even know for sure." Except I do. I know, in my bones, with every ounce of anything I am made of, that Benji

Keaton is going to be at that after-party, and that I am going to meet him.

I just know it.

"There isn't anything left for me to do," she adds, so resolute it's like a dagger.

I sigh, but the way she's so nonchalant, I perk back up. "Did you do this on purpose?"

She groans. "What?"

"Did you do this because you don't think we're going to meet him, and you thought I was going to be too much?" I feel my cheeks go hot. Sometimes I *can* be too much. But I didn't think this would be one of those times.

"No, of course I didn't. I do want to go, but it's just . . ."

"If you wanted to go, you wouldn't give up so easily," I say. "You didn't give up for the bunnies!"

Annie lifts her palm. "They were rats. And I'm not giving up. I'm just not going to do that thing where we get all excited and then it doesn't work out."

"But it *always* works out," I say.

She shakes her head. "Not this time."

This is a familiar dynamic. Annie pushes back a little—she has some anxieties about logistics, like weather or transportation or hydration, and then I assure her none of those things matter. Obviously. All that matters is whatever the goal is. The rest works out. Rainy forecasts turn sunny, traffic disappears, and we find humans are able to withstand incomprehensible lack of hydration when waiting in line for anything Benji Keaton–related.

It has been a slow and steady metamorphosis beginning in sixth grade, when Annie and I first met. I pushed her out of her comfort zone and the world didn't end.

I've always loved singing and making music, and I knew I could sing well enough. Enough that people constantly commented on it. In sixth grade, my mom paid for me to go to a voice coach. I'd go to the soundproofed little bungalow guesthouse in her backyard, and she'd teach me how to control my voice.

The problem, it seemed, was knowing what to do with my voice. There aren't record labels or producers or mentors in Citrus Harbor, so my voice coach recommended a fun use of my time to hone my skills:

Musical theater.

The summer after seventh grade, I convinced Annie to sign up for camp with me at the local community theater. We ended up spending most of the time fumbling through choreography and hanging out with the counselors, because most of the other campers were in elementary school. We learned to have fun with improv and tons of theater games that I never thought I'd feel comfortable playing in front of a crowd—one full of ten-year-olds or otherwise.

It was in eighth grade that Annie and I made our friendship bracelets.

That's when everything started to really pick up.

In ninth grade, the unthinkable happened. Annie and I decided to audition for the spring musical, the "high school edition" of *Heathers: The Musical*. And I got cast as the male lead, J.D. A *freshman*—the male lead!

That was my intro into the drama club. I expected people to be pissed that a freshman got such a huge role, but it was the opposite. The senior girls, who played the Heathers and Veronica, all treated me like some kind of rock star.

I knew it was the lucky bracelet that was making everything happen. Suddenly, I could do anything. Without it, I probably couldn't have gotten Pugsley in *The Addams Family* sophomore year, or Jack in *Into the Woods* junior year. People called me all sorts of things in the reviews—charismatic and like a human ray of sunshine or even a firework.

Things are going to get a royal shake-up when Annie moves to London after graduation in a couple weeks. She's going to live with her aunt and go to *university* and travel around Europe whenever she can.

Annie Taylor: pre-vet and exploration; London.

Teddy McGuire: undeclared; Citrus Harbor Community College.

I love musical theater, but I just don't see myself on Broadway or doing theater as a career. I'd love to be a musician, but let's just say my brief foray into songwriting was . . . Well, it was brief for a reason.

I need a little more time to figure out what I want to do with my life, which is fine, I'm okay with that, but if a lucky bracelet sounds silly, get this: I don't know what I am going to do without Annie. I know I'm the one with the ideas and the unwavering optimism, but it'll be harder if it's just me. I don't know if I have all of it on my own.

Only now, apparently, I don't even have to wait for graduation to find out.

"I mean, really, the timing here, Annie . . . But it's fine, I have my good luck charm," I say. I glance down at my bracelet. "I'll meet Benji. It'll be amazing. Who knows? Maybe I'll see a live set. Addie Harlow is filming a movie there."

Annie laughs. "Dream big."

"Don't say it like that," I counter. "You never know what could happen in New York. Especially with the lucky bracelet. You know how—"

That's when I notice.

Of all the terrible things that could happen—zombie apocalypse, natural disaster, supernatural disaster—this has got to be the worst possible debacle for the Tuesday afternoon right before the biggest trip of my entire life.

What is she thinking?

"You're not wearing your bracelet."

"Oh?" She holds up her right arm, where her tortoise-shell Apple Watch band is stacked on top of rose quartz beads, a festival bracelet from spring break, and an elastic gold hair tie. "I took it off because I didn't want to get paint on it."

"Very practical," I deadpan. "Annie, no wonder you got in trouble. Hello? *Lucky* bracelet?"

She smiles and pulls out the bracelet from her backpack, dangling the bright blue loop before me. "I have it. Isn't that the rule, anyway, it just has to be on our person?"

"Don't try to *blame* the bracelet."

"Look, Teddy." She sets the bracelet down. "Maybe these are—"

I hold my hands up. "Don't even start." Then I take one giant deep breath before reaching across and grabbing her bracelet. "You know what? I'm going to bring you this bracelet back with Benji's signature on it."

Annie pulls a face. "How is he going to sign it? It's, like, all ratty and some of the braids are loose."

Appalled at such a response, I feel my jaw drop. "It's not *ratty*, Annie. It's weathered. And I don't know, but I'm sure he's signed tons of stuff. Even if it's just his initials here or something." I point to a section of knots that are lighter, and still very much intact.

"Well, I will understand if for any reason you can't."

"I'm going to. You'll see! This is all great. This is all fine. I'm fine."

I was fine until I saw the scrapbook on the floor beside my bed.

The scrapbook with magazine letters cut out to spell "Teddy & Annie Take Manhattan" on the cover. Our heads cut out and pasted onto models, who are cut out and pasted onto photos of New York. Collages of us hanging out with Benji at Ralph's and on Broadway—a dream we've had for years before this whole after-party thing was ever a possibility. This is our thing. This *was* our thing.

Now, staring up at my ceiling, I'm sharing my bed with a half-packed suitcase, slung open to serve as a visual depiction of the tug-of-war going on in my head. Half of me wants to throw everything into my suitcase and start the adventure now, but half of me wants to go over every detail one more time—is there really no way for Annie to come? With every folded shirt I place in it, there is one more piece of me committed to going to New York alone. I can't even start on socks and pajamas. It's too real.

In my earphones, Benji sings of heartbreak, and though he's lamenting about a breakup, I find myself cut by the words as if I, too, were mourning something greater than myself.

Aren't I though? Is it any less painful than a breakup? To have the very foundation I'd come to rely on crumbling beneath me with no warning? With every sorrow-soaked note, I bet if anyone would understand this feeling, it's Benji.

I've never been in love, or had my heart broken, but somehow, I think I understand. Especially now, as he sings about a lost battle.

All of the sails were tattered,
none of the wails even mattered.

Sometimes, when I have to quickly conjure an emotion for a scene, my secret trick is to play Benji lyrics in my mind. Even if I've never been through a breakup, the words make me feel like I have.

I squeeze my eyes shut tight.

The lost best friend trip aside, I'm not entirely comfortable staying in a room with some random guy I don't know for three nights.

I pat around for my phone and bring it up to unlock it, navigating to Instagram.

Finding Sebastian isn't hard, but he's private. I try to squint and figure out what his profile picture is, but it's too small and grainy and I have absolutely no idea what the pixels amount to.

Do I send the request? Is that weird? I mean, it can't be that weird. We're about to be roommates. I should be able to see his profile—make sure he's not an axe murderer in his spare time or something.

I tap to submit the request and instantly wince.

Great, now if he doesn't accept before tomorrow, it's awkward and I seem overeager. Or if he does accept, I guess I'll still seem overeager. What if he doesn't accept at all? What if he denies me? All signs point to awkward—what was I thinking?

I mutter under my breath and pull my earphones out, sitting up and glancing around my room. It's organized chaos. One bulletin board has become a shrine to the drama department—photos, tickets, programs, a masquerade mask, and other random trinkets stuck to the cork with colorful pins. Across my room, another bulletin board is covered with photos with Annie and with my family. There are some academic ribbons—English is the only class I'm any good at—and postcards Annie has sent me from her trips over the years.

My dresser is open, and so are my closet doors, and they taunt me—*come on, Teddy, pack your damn clothes.* Begrudgingly, I pull shirts from hangers and jeans from drawers, folding and stacking until my suitcase is all set.

Above my desk, the framed photo of the New York skyline almost gets a smile from me. This is a dream come true, after all, even if a major wrench has been thrown in the plan.

Footsteps pad against the hallway floors before Mom knocks on my door, nudging it open and leaning against the frame. She peeks into the suitcase. "You're just now packing?"

Mom and I have the same wavy brown hair, though mine stops at my ears and hers is shoulder-length and mostly tied up into a messy bun right now. She's wearing a T-shirt and jeans with white Adidas, though I can tell by her makeup she's gone into the restaurant today. Eye shadow days mean she went in for meetings, and no eye shadow days mean she worked from home. Simple science, really.

She looks only marginally concerned. Obviously, having raised me, my mother has become slightly indifferent to A Day in the Life of Teddy McGuire. It isn't my fault if I become overrun with my emotions. That's biology, not choice. It's also not my fault that the universe has randomly decided to launch its most cruel, targeted, and incomprehensible campaign against me on the day before the biggest trip of my entire life.

"I can't go and share a room with Sebastian Hodges," I say, falling back onto my bed dramatically.

"Teddy." She smiles and shakes her head. "We already paid for this trip, so you are absolutely going. What is with all the dramatics?"

I close my eyes. "Dramatics? I don't know, I guess I'm trying something new."

"Annie is going to be here when you get back," she says, entirely nonchalantly. Which is so like her. "You know you might end up having fun. You occasionally tend to catastrophize—you thought it was the end of the world when you had to do the talent show solo, and look where that got you?"

My eyes snap open.

How could she bring that up? October brought the single most embarrassing moment of my entire life—the moment I metaphorically (though it may as well have been physically) stood at the edge of a cliff and jumped in front of everyone to prove I could fly, only to fall in a bloody, disgusting mess.

My original song was such a flop I think I lost the ability to even register rhymes for a full two weeks.

Tiny echoes of scattered applause while I stood there, vulnerably, lit under a single spotlight.

My first performance that earned no award, no

accolade, no write-up in even the school paper. Maybe my expectations were a little too high, or maybe I just needed to be humbled on an atomic level.

Starring in the spring musical seems to have distracted everyone and made them forget all about my song. Thank God.

"Where did that get me, Mom? Tell me where?"

"Can't you at least muster up some positivity for the fact that you might get to meet Benji?"

There it is. *Might*. I swear, moms have a unique talent for saying just the right thing to replace all the air in the room with carbon monoxide. Or dioxide. Whichever one slowly kills you.

"Why do you always say that?" I groan. "Why do you always have to do that?"

She closes her eyes. "Here we go again."

"It's not fair," I say. "If I told you that I *might* live to see the sun another day, how would you like that? Hmm? If I said you *might* have your dreams come true? It implies the alternative possibility, Mom. Why would you imply the alternative possibility? Haven't I been through enough today?"

"Okay," she sighs, and nods. "Well, I was going to do a nice homemade meal as your big send-off, but this conversation has exhausted me, so I couldn't possibly cook now."

"Mom!"

"Oh, not a fan of the dramatics after all?" She gestures for me to get up.

"What is wrong with Theodore *today*?" Dean joins Mom at my doorframe.

Groaning in disapproval, I shake my head at my older brother, who has just returned for the summer from his second year of college. "I'm only coming out of mourning. For the trip of a lifetime. For everything I've ever dreamed of. And then Mom has the audacity to bring up the *talent show*." I omit her little foray into the world of "might."

Dean nods, thick eyebrows pushing together very seriously. "Right. Well, do you want to go to the club with me? Jared's getting a couple large pizzas and we're all going to hang out at the pool."

I scoff. "Dean! I'm in *mourning*."

Mom raises a brow and turns to Dean. "You all had better be on your best behavior, I know how you and Jared and Tyler can get, and the club is not a frat house—"

"We're going to be on our *best* behavior," Dean says, standing up extra tall. He grins. "Isla and her friends are coming."

To Dean, this is the equivalent of winning the lottery.

"Not *Isla*," I cry. "Dean, you cannot date Eden's sister." I look to Mom expectantly. "*Mom*! Can you even imagine? A joint Christmas with the Blooms? A little half Dean half Isla running around?"

"Would be a cute kid." Dean looks off wistfully. "And they would be athletic *and* dramatic." He knocks Mom's arm. "A Nike model."

Mom sighs. "Dean, please do not antagonize your brother."

"I'm not antagonizing," he says, looking to me now. "Come on, Ted, Isla is hot."

"And that's it." I blink. "She's just Eden but two years older. And that is something to be very, very afraid of."

Next, Dad appears, and I swear, I never realized how wide my doorframe is as they all stand there looking at me like I'm an exhibit at a museum.

"Am I missing the party?" Dad raises a brow. He's wearing a McGuire Grill T-shirt *tucked into* jeans with a belt. I've tried to tell him, but he's beyond help, honestly.

"No," I say. "No party. Dean is going to the club; I'm going to scream into my pillow."

"You can't go to the club, we're doing a nice dinner to send off Ted," Dad says.

Dean throws his hands up. "Come *on*. You guys didn't even do a nice dinner to send me off to college. And I'm, like, across the country."

Mom and Dad both give Dean a look, and I know what it means—*you're not as sensitive as your brother, you don't need the same kind of attention*. But that's only half-true! Because Dean's high school basketball dramatics were almost stage-stealers. He had to be the star of the show, and while he didn't get some over-the-top college send-off, that's because he went out with his friends the night before and was hungover on his last day here. Plus, Dean got many, many nice dinners to celebrate sports-y accomplishments.

"You can definitely go to the club," I offer. "Like I said, I'm in mourning."

"I'll stay for dinner," Dean says, giving half a smile. He turns to Mom and Dad. "But after that, I'm going to the club."

"To fraternize with the enemy," I sing. "If it weren't ruining my life tangentially, I'd say it's romantic."

Dean snaps his fingers together. "Kinda like—what is it? *West Side Story*?"

Mom, Dad, and I all simultaneously tilt our heads.

"Yeah, I don't really think that's—"

"Maybe not."

Dean shrugs. "I'm not really one for the singing and dancing anyway."

Mom and Dad take the opportunity to leave, so Dean sits in my desk chair and swivels a bit before reaching over to drum on the suitcase. I look away, to the wall where I have two posters—the *Versailles* poster, and one I got from Neptune's Theater at the midnight premiere of *This Side of Paradise*.

"Doing stuff by yourself isn't bad, Ted." Dean shrugs. "You may actually like it."

I wince. "But I'm not doing anything by myself. That's not the problem. I'm with someone I don't know. And without Annie."

Dean nods, sitting back and crossing his arms. "Right.

Well, I thought Reggie was the biggest weirdo ever when we moved into our dorms, remember?"

"Reggie *is* the biggest weirdo ever." I blink.

"Yeah, but now we're, like—" He crosses his fingers. "He's awesome. Come on, you like Reggie."

I nod. "He is pretty cool. For someone obsessed with serial killers and scary clown movies."

"And he just started a new podcast," Dean says. "They're hopping on the unsolved cases train—like that show, remember? Selena Gomez and Steve Martin?"

"And Martin Short," I say. "Interesting."

Dean waves his hand in the air. "I don't know. Anyway, the point is, you never know. You have to give people a chance. That kinda is like *West Side Story*, right?"

"Kinda." I can't help but laugh. "I'll give him a chance."

"You guys could end up . . ." He crosses his fingers again and grins before I throw my pillow at him. "And who knows! You might even meet Benji."

I close my eyes and sigh a long, drawn-out, and dramatic sigh that I hope will carry me into morning.

Wednesday

Chapter 3

What Dreams Are Made Of

I'm stuck with the window to my right and, to my left, a woman who's eating peanut butter bites for breakfast, smells of hair spray, and is aggressively jamming questions into Google—*Can a plane run out of gas? Can a plane be too heavy? Odds of a plane attracting lightning?*

She's already done several superstitious little gestures—kissing her fingers and then the top of the cabin, that kind of thing. She needs a lucky bracelet.

And I need caffeine. Dean agreed to drop me off at school this morning, but he and his friends had a little too much fun at the club pool last night, so waking him up at 6:00 a.m. was a whole production and I didn't get my coffee.

This should have been a fun flight, sharing headphones with Annie and taking selfies with her Polaroid. Instead,

I'm sitting here overthinking something incredibly simple: how to switch seats with the person next to Sebastian.

He hasn't accepted my follow request, but I did notice none of the numbers on his profile have changed since last night. No new followers, no new following, and no new posts. Not that I'm, like, purposefully keeping track, because that'd be weird. I just happened to remember.

I debated undoing the request, but it'd be unbearably cringeworthy if he had seen I'd requested and then backed out.

Whatever. What is most important is going to sit with him and giving him the lowdown on our scavenger hunt strategy.

From the intel I've gained, if this year's trip is anything like previous years, the scavenger hunt items are going to vary. Some might be silly and easy, while others are extremely difficult. There will be fun facts about the city, urban myths and legends, red herrings, and a lot of Broadway references.

In theory, I could have researched more, since it's pretty much like the SAT, except more important. But I know it's all going to work out and I'm going to meet Benji. There's no way this opportunity would be so perfect and not work out. That would be sadistic on the universe's part.

I peer over the seat behind me.

There he is.

We haven't even taken off yet and Sebastian is already leaning back with his eyes closed, completely unbothered.

He's wearing black over-ear headphones—which he used to wear around his neck during classes—and a charcoal Manchester Orchestra "Angel of Death" tee.

I have his number from the cast sheet, though I've never personally used it. He's never responded in a group text, and there hasn't been a reason for me to reach out. Until now.

ME:

Hey, can you come try to switch seats with this lady?

I look back to make sure his notifications are on. He opens his eyes and reads the text before glancing up and making eye contact. I raise my brows expectantly and he shifts his focus back to his phone.

SEBASTIAN:

Why do you want me to do that?

ME:

Because we're roommates and scavenger hunt buddies now

SEBASTIAN:

Right, but we're not airplane buddies

Oh my f— Annie was wrong. He is not trying to make friends.

ME:

Can you please just get her to switch seats with you?

SEBASTIAN:

I like my seat though

ME:

But I need to talk to you

He's somehow an even more difficult person than I imagined.

SEBASTIAN:

Oh

SEBASTIAN:

Don't take this the wrong way,
but I like to sleep on flights

So far, many things have been less than fun: my phone wouldn't let me get a virtual boarding pass, and there was, of course, something wrong with the computer so it took forever to get a printed one, and I didn't get to have food court breakfast with everybody else. Then the magnetic security thing didn't work when I walked through it, which held up the queue and resulted in many grumbling random people shooting me evil eye daggers. I finally barely jammed my carry-on overhead, but not after smacking myself in the face with one of the wheels.

Now, Sebastian is seemingly determined to continue the joyous start to the trip.

It's fine. It's all going to be fine; it's all going to work out. In fact, I saw a TikTok that said the more challenges you're presented with, the closer you are to your manifestations coming true. So, like, I'm *super* close.

ME:

Okay, I'll come sit with you

SEBASTIAN:

The guy next to me already popped Ambien

SEBASTIAN:

He's out like a light

ME:

Can't you just please come sit up here

SEBASTIAN:

What even makes you think
she'd switch with me?

I don't know, actually. This was Dean's idea. He said I should try to maneuver a seat switch so I could sit with Sebastian, since Annie's seat was given up to standby.

ME:

She seems nice

She's currently watching a plane disaster movie compilation on YouTube, which is literally the last thing anyone should ever do, but I figure she can do that from any seat.

"Excuse me?"

Locking her phone quickly like a caught teenager, she whips her head over and offers a wide-eyed expression. "Yes?"

"Would you by any chance be open to switching seats with my friend?" I glance down at her phone. "He and I like to sit together on planes . . . because. Well, I know it sounds silly. I don't know if you believe in superstitions, but we have this good luck thing. Yeah, if we're sitting together, everything goes smooth. But if we're not . . ."

She leans in a little, eyes going even wider.

"Well, once he got up to go to the bathroom and we immediately hit turbulence. I mean, thank God he peed fast, because it was a *bumpy* ride. Who knows what would have happened if he had taken a second longer."

Nodding violently, the woman reaches down to grab her purse. "Yes, get him over here. Please."

ME:

She said yes

ME:

Come on

"And make sure he pees before we take off."

The woman stands up and Sebastian appears behind her with his headphones around his neck, hugging his backpack to his chest and scrunching up his brows as she gives him a once-over before shuffling back to his seat.

"What was that about?" He gives me an odd look and checks over his shoulder.

"Nothing," I say. "Thanks for finally coming up here."

Sebastian sits and puts his bag under the seat in front of him. "Well?"

This guy either has no social skills or no interest in trying to come across as polite. I'm guessing it's the latter, but I try to ignore it.

Everything's great.

"Okay." I open an offline Google Doc on my phone. "A few of the past seniors compiled some New York City trivia—a lot of it is common knowledge, but it's sorted by obscurity, so we can hopefully navigate the document fairly quickly."

Sebastian eyes the screen, poking his tongue to his cheek.

"There's also an index of Broadway song titles and some key facts per show." I scroll back up for a while before landing on the first page. "See?"

"Not at all over-the-top." Sebastian nods.

"Look, it's better to be prepared for this kind of thing."

"Oh, right." He snaps his fingers. "This is all for that scavenger hunt or whatever?"

I force a smile. "Right."

"You know, we could just forgo the whole thing. Less stress. Besides, Eden and Briar are going to—"

Locking my phone, I turn to face him full-on. "Sebastian. What are you talking about? We're not going to *forgo* the scavenger hunt."

"I just don't think it seems worth all the hassle," he counters. "It kind of puts a damper on the trip to be all frantically running around trying to figure out clues. I mean, just look at your document—no chill."

No *chill*?

"Okay, look. The winners of the scavenger hunt get to attend the after-party on Friday, and I absolutely have to go to that after-party." I take a breath. "Benji Keaton is going to be there. So, we are absolutely doing the scavenger hunt."

Sebastian blinks. "Oh, Benji Keaton is going to be there?"

I close my eyes. Of course. I should have seen this coming from the guy in the classic rock tee. Cue the anti-pop tirade, I'm sure.

"Sebastian, this is important, okay?"

Opening my eyes, I'm met with a look that is part apathy and part repulsion. "I should have known this was all about you meeting Benji Keaton. Of course. What makes you so sure he's even going to that party? He probably has plenty of other things to do after a show."

"I'm not going to get into this with you."

"I know you're, like, obsessed with him. But he's so . . ."

"I'm not *obsessed*." I shift a little in my seat. "And he's so what?"

"So . . . *manufactured*."

I exhale. "I'm not having this conversation."

"'Banana Milkshake'? Really?"

"That song was tongue-in-cheek about objectification and fame and—" I stop. "Sebastian, look, I'm meeting Benji in New York. Hopefully it won't put too much of a *damper* on your trip, but I don't think you understand how important this is."

He studies me for a moment, thick dark brows furrowed, and brown eyes tightened ever so slightly. I hope for a moment, since this eye contact is so heavy I hesitate to swallow, that he's telepathic.

Sebastian Hodges, we are doing this scavenger hunt.

I take the challenge to study him back.

There are no clues to be found in the aforementioned

band T-shirt, since I'm definitely not sure indie rock is going to factor into the scavenger hunt in any way. He's not wearing any bracelets—no signs of interests or lucky charms. There are no hints of his personality anywhere. If Sebastian were a billboard, it'd only say Your Ad Here! at this point.

Then I notice a book in the side pocket of his backpack, where a water bottle might normally go. It's one of those mass paperback kinds.

"What?" he says, looking from me to the space under the seat before him.

"What are you reading?"

Sebastian cocks a brow. "Orwell."

"Right." I blink. "Which is, like, end of the world stuff, right?"

"Or . . ." He looks around and then shrugs. "Middle of the world we're living in stuff."

"Great," I say, wincing. "That's totally not depressing at all."

Fighting a laugh, Sebastian lifts his shoulders. "Reality is depressing."

"No, it's not."

"Maybe you're not fully acquainted with reality."

"I'm not going to get a lecture on my relationship with reality," I say. *If only because, sure, maybe it is sometimes a dysfunctional one.* "I'm perfectly capable of living in the real world *and* being optimistic. You could try it."

Sebastian smiles. "I'll let you have the half-full glass.

You're the one with the lucky bracelet after all."

Squishing my brows together, I tilt my head. "How do you know about my lucky bracelet?"

"How many times have you held up rehearsal or a performance to make sure you had it?"

"I'm sure not that many," I say.

Sebastian gives me the intense eye contact now. "Not that many? How about *yesterday* at the assembly? On the tech walkies they would say it was *Teddy Standard Time*. Gave us a second to run to the vending machine, mostly."

I scoff. "There's no way that's true. I'm a professional. And I'm prepared."

"And superstitious."

"It's not a superstition," I point out. "It's a truly, undeniably lucky bracelet." Before he can argue with me, I lift a finger. "In fact, that is one of the reasons we have to win this scavenger hunt. I'm getting Benji to sign Annie's bracelet. I have it in my backpack."

Sebastian doesn't say anything to that.

"Well, look, there's almost always a scavenger hunt clue that leads to the Strand." I try to give an encouraging smile, but I'm only met with a blank stare. *Come on, Teddy, this is just improv, only instead of an enthusiastic partner, it's with a brick wall.* "It's a bookstore? A majorly huge bookstore. Eighteen miles of books. You could be totally helpful for that clue."

"I know what the Strand is. Sorry, I just don't think

I'm going to do it," he deadpans, bringing his hands up to his headphones. "Is it okay if I . . . ?" He lifts them off his shoulders and when I don't say anything, he places them over his ears.

I sit back. Flames are burning in my skull and I'm unsure of what exactly it is I'm feeling. The sadness over Annie's absence has dissolved into this frustration. Sebastian "Too Cool for the World" Hodges is *not* going to cost me Benji Keaton.

"Sebastian," I say, leaning over a little and forcing another smile.

He opens one eye and taps his headphones, mouthing: "Can't hear you, sorry."

I slam my head back onto my seat and pop open my AirPods.

This hot, boiling whirl of anxious agitation in my chest is different. It's something I've never even felt toward Eden.

Before we have to put our phones on airplane mode, I text Annie.

ME:

Sebastian is 😴

ME:

This is beyond

ANNIE:

Give him a chance, remember

ME:

He hates Benji Keaton

ME:

And he's reading Orwell like it's a newspaper

Which, whatever, even if it is, I don't need him to condescendingly tell me about the state of the world.

ANNIE:

People can like
different things it's okay

ME:

Loathing, Annie. Unadulterated loathing

ANNIE:

Well as long as we're not
jumping to conclusions

ME:

You not coming on this trip has
singlehandedly ruined my life

ANNIE:

Safe travels! ♥

Chapter 4

All That Jazz

New York City is everything I ever thought it would be.

We take a Mercedes fifteen-passenger sprinter from LaGuardia into the city, and the view of the skyline is even better in real life—Pinterest photos don't do it justice. The dazzling glass windows of the skyscrapers are painted bright blue, and I recognize the glittering Chrysler Building just as my gaze falls upon the Empire State Building next to it. The silhouette is iconic, graced by Meg Ryan and Tom Hanks, King Kong, and Percy Jackson. I swear I feel a jolt of optimism and excitement surge through me when I see it.

If I listen to "Welcome to New York" as we drive into the city, that's between me and God.

After we cross the bridge and take a few turns in Midtown, we're let out at the Midtown Regent Hotel on East

Forty-Second Street. On the sidewalk, we seem to be a major inconvenience as our group gawks at the buildings and snaps photos on our phones. We're brushing shoulders with fast-walking men in suits and women in dresses and designer sneakers who can't seem to get around us quickly enough.

The city smells interesting. Not quite how I'd expected—maybe a little naïvely, I thought every street would smell like a bag of assorted treats from Dylan's Candy Bar. Instead, it smells like a strange amalgamation of gas, steam rising from the potholes, garbage, powdered sugar, and a particularly wet, soggy meat. Still, it is the best smell I've ever come in contact with.

We've been off the van for two minutes. The luggage hasn't even all been unloaded, and Sebastian has already disappeared. I try to pick him out of the busy sidewalk, but I don't see a bored scowl or indie T-shirt anywhere, so I just grab my suitcase and roll it inside, following Mrs. Mackenzie as she power walks toward the front desk.

The inside of the hotel looks way bougier than I expected considering our drama club could afford it. The intricately carved columns and velvet rugs lining the marble flooring are like something out of a glamorous 1920s movie set. Potted palms are paired with dusty-pink crushed velvet sofas that have become workstations and breakfast nooks, and a massive chandelier draped in teardrop diamonds hangs over the center of the lobby.

Eden is already taking selfies and Briar is fawning over her for good measure—we wouldn't want her to have a dip in self-esteem or anything.

While Mrs. Mackenzie talks to the staff, I look around for Sebastian again, but only see his suitcase unattended on one of the bellman's carts. I'm assuming it's his because of the stickers haphazardly thrown across the matte black plastic—random chemical elements, a taco truck logo, and bands I haven't even heard of.

Where the hell have you disappeared to?

Everyone else is with their partner, but here I am, alone with my luggage and an extensively researched list of historic and fascinating tidbits about Manhattan.

After a few moments, Mrs. Mackenzie gathers us all between two of the columns so we're not obstructing as much of the lobby. She's holding a sparkly black binder.

"I am so thrilled for another year of my *famous* scavenger hunt," Mrs. Mackenzie says in her typical singsong fashion. She is always acting. I wonder, even, if she's acting at home with her cat, Grizabella. At the grocery store, does she interlude when she asks for lunch meat from the deli? Does she pirouette when pumping gas? Offer flowery jazz hands when waiting on a bank teller?

Eden stands up extra straight, and her grip tightens on the poor suitcase handle in front of her.

My phone goes off and I expect it to be Annie, but it's only a text from Dean, who is seemingly knee-deep in conspiracy theories about aliens. I figure that can wait and give Mrs. Mackenzie my undivided attention.

"My amazing theater seniors. You've been magical throughout the years, accomplishing so many wonderful things. Putting on so many wonderful shows! You know every step, and every song . . ." She pauses for emphasis, as if any of us would miss a *Hairspray* reference. "But how much do you know about New York City?"

Pause for even more emphasis. Ideally, I think, she's looking for an *ooh* and an *ahh* here, though we're all getting a bit antsy.

"While the prize for this year's scavenger hunt is admittedly better than previous years, I have kept some of the *fan favorites* on our list." She brightens at the thought. Mrs. Mackenzie is the type to love something like a "fan favorite," especially when it comes to any of her brilliant scavenger hunt items.

Opening her binder, she pulls out a stack of papers and relishes in the way we all seem to take a baby step closer—gravitating toward the lists like dogs eyeing bacon—all of us, of course, except my partner.

And I thought there was nobody harder to work with than Eden.

"This is not only a scavenger hunt through New York City," Mrs. Mackenzie says, almost turning solemn as she distributes the lists. "This is a spiritual journey. This is a chance to find yourself, among the bustling streets, tucked within each neighborhood. You can discover so much about yourself . . . if you choose to."

Her eyes land on me and she hands me the last paper.

Of course I'm going to choose to.

Well, if I'm honest, if I discover myself is absolutely secondary to discovering Benji Keaton.

"Now!" Mrs. Mackenzie stuffs the extra papers in the binder and claps it shut before hurrying over to a large canvas tote bag sitting next to our luggage. "As you all know, no doubt, you will each get a Polaroid camera to capture your scavenger hunt adventures. Rules are at the bottom of your lists. Please do not waste the film, it's not free. And try to be careful with the lanyards on the camera, they're not indestructible."

The Polaroid photos are always included in the seniors' photo dumps and TikToks. Wide-toothed grins in Times Square or with the Brooklyn Bridge towering behind them. They always look like the most fun, exciting moments of their lives.

"This is going to be so, so amazing," Eden coos. She and Briar exchange giggles. Of course, what she's doing—declaring how amazing this will be so loudly for everyone—is asserting dominance. She's saying "*this is going to be amazing because I'm going to kick all of your asses at this scavenger hunt.*"

Briar then tilts her head. "I think there's a typo. Ferry . . ."

I glance down at my list when I notice Mrs. Mackenzie sigh deeply.

THE LIST:

**Tickets to AMNH, The Met, and Empire State Building in the PDF!!!*

1. Our Strange Duet—Find a vinyl record with a duet that describes you as a pair
2. Not Your Disney Chef—Catch a subway rat in action
3. Life Finds a Way—Assign each other a dinosaur alter ego
4. Mountain Climber—Find a rock and climb it
5. Underground Concerto—Discover a subway concert
6. Empire State of Mind—Self-explanatory
7. Story of Your Life—Pick a book that represents each other at the Strand
8. We'll Cross That Bridge—Get to it!
9. Ferry Princess—Again, self-explanatory, people
10. As the Romans Do—Mirror the pose of a Roman statue
11. So Well Composed—Show off your best ballet moves in front of the epicenter
12. At the Stroke of Midnight—Visit Grand Central Terminal at midnight
13. Frozen—so SOME OF YOU don't forget this should be fun—Get some ice cream!

"It's not a typo," Eden snaps. Her face falls. "We have to go on the ferry . . ."

"Not great for the hair," Briar says.

Mrs. Mackenzie has had enough, I guess, because she's shaking her head and walking back over to the front desk. The rest of my classmates are chatting with each other, fingers tracing the list as light bulbs go off and smiles warm.

I do another sweep, hoping to find Sebastian leaning up against a column with his hands in his pockets, but there's no sign of him anywhere.

It occurs to me that he might be anywhere. Finding an indie record store or glumly shuffling down Madison Avenue, directionless and listening to some angsty song I've never heard before.

What if he's, like, a runaway?

What if Sebastian's already on a bus heading upstate? What if he's joined a band of pickpockets or petty thieves who run a small but meticulously organized crime ring? He's never struck me as a pickpocket or a henchman, but I'm not sure where else he's disappeared to for so long and immediately upon entering the city. It's like he stepped off the sprinter and decided it was time to make a break for it.

Though his bags are here, at least, so I think I will have the joy and great fortune of seeing him again.

So not a runaway. Then what?

Reading through the scavenger hunt list, I immediately start to visualize a map of Manhattan. I spent hours poring over Google Maps to prepare for this moment, obviously. I bet we could easily knock some of these out this afternoon. Maybe we head uptown and find a rat, do some ballet, then cross the park and take a picture on one of the rocks before going to the Met. Easy, day one down. Then tomorrow we can go downtown, cross the East River, and then work our way back up to Midtown.

We can finish the list by tomorrow evening and have Friday free before we inevitably win the competition and go to meet Benji.

Perfect . . . This plan is perfect.

I tap my foot.

Now, if only we could get started . . .

I tap my foot faster.

Okay, this is just not going to work.

"Mrs. Mackenzie?" I find her leaning against the counter on her phone. "Any chance we could talk really quick?"

She nods. "What is it?"

"I was wondering if we are able to switch partners. Because—"

"No, no." She waves her hands around emphatically. "No, there won't be any changes. There is simply no time."

Sighing, I cock my head. I was expecting this answer. "But, Mrs. Mackenzie, it's just that Sebastian—"

"Teddy." She looks at me very seriously.

"Well, maybe could I just do it on my own?"

"No, Teddy. Both students must be in each Polaroid for them to count. You either do this scavenger hunt with Sebastian Hodges or you don't do it at all."

So resolute. So intense. It's like she's auditioning for a soapy drama, playing a stern, strong-like-iron drama teacher—her mission is to enforce and to inspire. She shall not fail.

I consider a counter remark, but she blinks, looking around.

"Where *is* Sebastian?"

You either do this scavenger hunt with Sebastian Hodges or you don't do it at all.

Well, I'll be damned if Sebastian Hodges is going to cost me Benji.

"He's in the bathroom," I say. "You know he has that dairy thing."

"Oh," she tsks. "Well, you shouldn't be trying to leave your lactose-intolerant roommate during his time of need, Teddy. Honestly."

I nod. "You're right. I'm just too eager to get started, and who knows how long he'll be . . ."

She straightens up. "I think I have enough of the visual, thank you."

Once I leave Mrs. Mackenzie, I'm alone with the Polaroid camera hanging around my neck and the list of items that I can't even begin to make progress on. Impatience threatens to burn me alive from the inside out and a feeling of fear sets in—what if we *don't* complete this list?

Like she can smell that fear, Eden materializes in front of me.

"Teddy." She looks around and forces a puzzled expression. "Where's your *buddy*? Aren't you going to start on the scavenger hunt?"

Avoiding her intense stare, I curse Sebastian in my mind.

"Don't tell me he ditched you?" She smirks. Asserting dominance in the way she does, with one hip popped and disinterested wrists hanging in front of her stomach.

I don't want to give her the satisfaction of showing any affectation, but I know it's written all over my face. "He didn't ditch me."

"I mean the prize this year is unreal. I know Mrs. Mackenzie is friends with the stage manager, but I have no clue how she managed to get two extra invites. And, like, for me, it's not like I care much about meeting *actors*." She rolls her eyes. "But that party is going to be crawling with Broadway big names. People in casting, I'd bet. And I love to network."

It's fine. She's just trying to get to you.

"Look, Teddy, if I were you, I'd just try to have fun. Sometimes we win, and sometimes we don't. And if you want, I'll try to get a video of Benji saying hi to you or something. Is there anything you want me to tell him?"

I lengthen my spine, tired of being intimidated by her. "I'll tell him myself."

Chapter 5

I Can't Do It Alone

Everyone has checked in and left to start exploring the city, including Mrs. Mackenzie, and I have spent at least ten minutes pacing frantically in front of the revolving doors, waiting for Sebastian to show.

There are a few different scenarios I've imagined, and none of them excuse the fact that this guy snuck away from our group. And this is New York City, it's not like he slipped away during Grad Bash and is wandering around the confines of a theme park. He could be anywhere. He could be in *danger.* He could be—

"Mrs. Bloom?"

At my words, the woman before me stops and turns around.

She is basically a forty-something-year-old version of Eden, with evenly spray-tanned skin and roots that are somehow brighter than the rest of her hair. She's wearing a black dress with sneakers and lets the bellman take her suitcases. She wasn't on the plane or in the sprinter, and it seems she just arrived.

"Hi, Teddy," she says, putting on a fake smile.

"Are you chaperoning our trip?"

Mrs. Bloom raises a brow, jutting out her neck a little as if to see if I'm kidding. When she can tell I'm not, she nods slowly. "Yes, Teddy. I am chaperoning the trip."

"Cool . . ." I say. Weird she wasn't there to chaperone the travel portion . . . but it's not like I'm complaining.

The drama club parents come in all varieties. There are the parents who you only ever see at pickup or drop-off, the ones who pretty much only show up to the performances (like mine and Annie's), the ones who are mega-involved, and then there is Eden Bloom's mother.

She is the last person anyone would want chaperoning this trip.

Including Eden.

"Shouldn't you be off working on the scavenger hunt with Sebastian?"

How does she know that?

"I should be," I agree. "Yes, I should be."

I think it's important to be fair in life. That is to say, I don't think I believe in villains. I don't believe in things like revenge. I tend to believe everyone is good, which might be naïve, or it might be that I'm lucky in my dealings with people.

That said, if I did believe in villains, I think Mrs. Bloom would be an animated Disney film witch.

She would live in a sparkling tower that, from the outside, looked to be a glittering palace of chrome and crystal and silver adornments. But the closer you get, the more you notice the edges are all sharp, and there are traps and armed guards and maybe even some little demonic dragon things flying around.

When she stares into my soul, it's as if she could make a curling gesture with those long nails and whisk my soul from my being, leaving me with hollowed cheeks and sunken eyes, doomed to haunt the Midtown Regent for all of eternity.

But, again, not a witch. Just . . . manipulative. After all, this is the woman behind the removal of the most delicious, sugary snacks in the school vending machines.

"Why are you looking at me like that?" she laughs.

"Like what?"

"Like I have something on my face?"

I shake my head quickly. "No, sorry, I just was thinking."

Mrs. Bloom adjusts the strap of the Burberry tote on her shoulder and smiles, this time with some semblance of sincerity but lacking in patience. "You know, if I were you, I'd go on and start the scavenger hunt. All the other groups are out wandering the city."

Duh. That's why Mrs. Mackenzie put up with having her as a chaperone. Because she isn't going to chaperone!

She may be hyper-involved in Eden's life, but it's often at the expense of the rest of us. Any of the other parents might be a little more concerned about the fact that we're all just out freely wandering around the city, even if we are mostly eighteen.

"I'm going to start," I say. "But I'm waiting for Sebastian."

"You must be devastated Annie couldn't come," she says. "But I want you to know that you should enjoy this trip, Teddy. It's not only about winning, after all. You're in the greatest city in the country—even if it's dirtier than I remember."

I quirk a brow, now ready to defend this city I barely know.

"And anyway, who needs an after-party with the seats we've got to *Versailles*?" She claps her hands together. "Make the most of it, don't set yourself up for disappointment, and you will have the best time."

Sebastian appears in my peripheral, pushing the revolving door lazily with his shoulder as he looks down at his phone.

"I've got to freshen up," Mrs. Bloom says, just in time. "Plane rides destroy my complexion—the altitude. Anyway, just remember to have fun."

Not ready to let any of Mrs. Bloom's words sink into my system, I run over and stop Sebastian before he reaches the front desk. I tug at his sleeve, and he scoffs, pulling one of his headphones off.

"What the hell, Sebastian?"

"Hello, Teddy."

"Don't *hello, Teddy* me. You cannot just disappear."

He pokes his tongue in his cheek. "Can't I?"

"No, you—" I inhale. "Sebastian, you're on a school trip. You're not Holden Caulfield, despite your best efforts."

"You would."

"Oh my God." I clear my throat. "Look, we have got to stick together. Okay? I covered for you with Mrs. Mackenzie, even though I had *no* clue where you were. Because I need to win this scavenger hunt, and I need you to help me win said scavenger hunt. We both have to be in the Polaroids for them to count."

I hold up the camera and the list.

Sebastian frowns. "I know this is important to you, but—"

"No, it's important to you, too." I smile tightly. "Look, I mapped out the most efficient way for us to finish most of this scavenger hunt in two days, then we have an improv workshop and our final item Friday morning. So, you can do whatever you want on Friday afternoon. And I won't tell Mrs. Mackenzie about any of your sneaking off. You can go soul search and listen to whatever depressing music you want to while, I don't know, feeling lonely even in the crowded city and questioning the meaning of life."

I can see the gears turning as he grabs the scavenger hunt list and looks over it. "All right, if you cover for me, I'll do it. But I have plans on Friday evening."

"You have plans . . ."

"I have plans."

"No, I heard you, it's just—that's when we're seeing *Versailles*."

"I know, I'm going to miss it. The first act, at least."

"You're going to miss it? You can't just miss *Versailles*. Sebastian. It's *Versailles*."

"Let them eat cake."

"She didn't even say that."

"I know she didn't say that." He rolls his eyes. "Look, I have plans."

I shake my head. This is unacceptable. Even for Sebastian.

"You're going to miss an amazing Broadway show. For what?"

"Plans."

"*What* are your plans?"

"Teddy, look, they're just plans, okay?"

"Fine, I know you and I don't know each other very well," I say. "I mean, we've gone to school together our whole lives, and I think we've spoken more today than we have collectively over twelve years—"

He cocks his head. "We were partners for the shark dissection in eighth grade."

I groan. "Right."

"When you wouldn't touch the shark, and Annie pretended to pass out."

"She wasn't pretending!" I say. I swear dissection has

come up far too much recently. "Anyway, look, I'm acknowledging I don't know you very well, so I get that you don't want to tell me what your big, secret plans are. But I do feel comfortable politely asserting that you have to attend the show, and whatever your plans are will just have to be rescheduled."

He laughs. "Thank you for politely asserting. But I can't reschedule."

"Unbelievable," I say. "You're going to miss *Versailles.*"

"Nobody has ever said *Versailles* this much in one conversation. Not even French historians."

"How do you have plans on Friday evening in New York City anyway?" I ask. "On a school trip?"

Sebastian tilts his head. "Do you get out much?"

"Fine. You have plans," I say, holding my hands up. "Great. You'll just miss *Versailles.* Then we'd better hurry, because we need to cross off four of our items tonight if we're going to stay on track."

"Shouldn't we go check in to the room?"

"Our stuff isn't going anywhere," I say, starting to walk toward the exit. I raise my brows when he stands there, sighing. "Come on, we've got to get moving! You have plans."

Chapter 6

I Think I'm Gonna Like It Here

As Sebastian and I walk up Forty-Second Street, it occurs to me we should find some common ground. How else am I going to survive this trip? My mind is currently going a million miles per hour—I can't stop mentally playing out how each of today's scavenger hunt items should go and I become hyperaware that even though we're walking quickly, people are passing us at an alarming rate.

I attempt to silence my brain and, instead, focus on possible topics of conversation. I come up blank until we reach Fifth Avenue. Standing on the edge of the sidewalk and waiting for the light to change, I notice him studying the New York Public Library.

It's huge and ornate, with columns and arches and two giant stone lions on either side of the stairs.

"Wow."

It's absolutely not the most intelligent thing I've ever said, but it's so hard to *begin* with Sebastian.

"Yeah," he says flatly.

Maybe we can work our way up, syllable by syllable.

"So cool."

He looks from the library to me.

"Do you want to go in?"

I shake my head. "We don't have time. We have to get to the subway station . . ." When I see his lip form the slightest frown—when he nearly emotes—I study the map on my phone. "But we could, like, get closer. We can cross here and then walk down to Fortieth?"

He nods. "Okay."

Somehow, Sebastian's verbal withholding has become contagious. I'm someone who can normally find something to say, but there are just no words forming in my head right now.

I pull out my phone and message Annie.

ME:

SOS I have literally nothing to talk about with Sebastian

Across Fifth, a group of girls come out of Zara and are laughing loudly as one of them holds up a vlogging camera and the others show off their bags.

"I feel like we should not be able to hear them from all the way over here," Sebastian says.

I shrug. "They're just excited. It's New York."

"What does that mean? '*It's New York.*' They're influencers. It's manufactured excitement, Teddy."

I watch the girls for a few more seconds. When the camera gets stuffed into a crossbody, the excitement doesn't just simmer or sizzle, it's completely put out as if instantly drowned.

"Influencers aside, you must know what I mean. You can't tell me you don't feel excited to be here."

He lifts his shoulders. "Yeah, it's cool. I'm not going to skip or click my heels or anything."

We cross the street once the white walk symbol flashes.

"What *would* get Sebastian Hodges to skip or click his heels?"

"Nothing."

"There must be something."

"There isn't."

He continues walking and I want to put my hands around his throat, but I just sigh. "Not even your big, secret plans?"

"Especially not my big, secret plans."

"There isn't anything wrong with wanting to skip and click your heels," I say. "Just so you know. I think it's probably a sign that you're a human with a full range of emotions and expression. In fact, it might be good to find something . . ."

Once we're in front of the library, he tilts his head and marvels up at the statues carved up in the stone façade.

"If there ever is something that makes me want to skip and click my heels, you'll be the first to know, how about that?"

"You like books," I offer, gesturing toward the library.

"Not that much." He exhales and then turns on his heel, starting to walk toward Fortieth Street. "And I guess you don't have to tell me what you like that much?"

Here we go.

"Benji Keaton, musical theater, the buzz of the big city."

I don't know if Sebastian Hodges is innately the most annoying person to exist in New York City right now or if he just wants to be—if he's maybe a better actor than any of us thought, since he was on the tech side of things—but I'm feeling that strong, warm sense of annoyance bubbling up in me again as I catch up with him and we turn the corner toward Sixth Avenue.

"It's not like that's insulting," I point out. "There isn't anything wrong with being excited about things. Having passions and interests is human. It's something most people use to relate to others, even."

"I didn't say I was trying to insult you," Sebastian counters, tilting his head with exaggerated innocence as we walk by Bryant Park. He's agitating me, so I'm not sure I'm fully taking in how the light reflects off the buildings and filters through the trees or how beautiful the architecture is, even in just the marble railings.

"Well," I say. "It was obvious—the way you were saying those things."

“I wasn’t saying them in any specific way,” he says coolly.

That warm, bubbling annoyance is on its way to a broil.

We cross Sixth Avenue and continue to walk along the sidewalk. Though the sounds of the city lean toward cacophonous, the chaos is almost calming as I try not to let Sebastian get to me. Eventually, we reach Broadway, and to my right, I see a glimpse of Times Square. The billboards are so bright, even in the daylight. It doesn’t quite feel real to see it in person.

I snap a photo quickly—my first time seeing Times Square—but keep walking, since I know I’ll get a better one up close later. I just want to remember how cool it was at this very moment.

Once we reach Seventh Avenue, Sebastian looks to me expectantly.

“We need to find these little green globes,” I say. Then I shrug. “I read online you can find subway stations by finding the green globes. So, wherever . . .” I point across Fortieth, toward two spheres on poles at the entrance of the subway—the top half of each globe is green, and the bottom half is clear and lit up with a warm light. “There you go.”

“Nice,” Sebastian says. We make our way down the stairs, descending into the subway.

This is a momentous occasion. Everything is going to feel like that while I’m here, I realize, but this is my first time going on the subway. My first time traveling around the city like a New Yorker. I know there won’t be a magical symphony waiting to play as we cross the turnstiles, but I might imagine one for the sake of it.

I stop at one of the MTA card kiosks, and Sebastian taps me on the shoulder.

"It looks like you can just use Apple Pay."

Frowning, I can see he's right as people thoughtlessly tap their phones to the turnstiles. I turn to the touch screen and shake my head: "I want a MetroCard, though. It's, like, a souvenir. Don't you want one?"

"I mean, I don't really need one if I can tap my phone to get in without all the hassle."

"It's hardly any hassle," I say, tapping through the prompts to get a new card and add twenty dollars to start. "And it's worth it to have the memory."

The yellow paper card pops out and I hold it up for him to see.

"Okay," he sighs, and follows the steps on the screen, taking the card and gesturing toward the turnstiles. "Are you happy? Ready to go?"

The little yellow card feels like a golden ticket, electric between my fingers, so I nod. "Yes, I am."

As it turns out, this subway station is *massive*. I've placed my MetroCard in my wallet, pocketed it, and checked my phone to double-check which line we're supposed to get on. I think we might walk in circles for a few minutes, trying to follow the hanging signs through the bustling crowd, until we finally come up on the red-labeled 1 train going uptown.

"Is this as magical as you always hoped?" Sebastian leans up against one of the metal columns and is standing dangerously close to the yellow line we're *not* supposed to cross.

The subway isn't exactly magical, but it's still cool. Nobody else around us seems to think so, but I'm not going to let that stop me from being excited. I'm not going to let Sebastian's slightly mocking tone bring me down either.

In fact:

"You know, if you want the subway to be magical, it can be."

"Oh, yeah?"

I nod. "What fun is it to go through life just focusing on the bad stuff?"

Sebastian chews on the inside of his cheek for a second. "It's not exactly focusing on the bad stuff, but it's just not trying to make magic out of it. Like, there's really nothing magical about the dried vomit over there"—he points to his left—"or the girl who just broke her high heel"—he points over his shoulder—"or those rats."

When he points down at the track, my eyes go wide and I grin, which causes Sebastian to look at me like I've truly lost it.

"That's so great," I say, fumbling with the Polaroid camera. "Come on, come on!"

I pull him over to the edge of the platform and snap a selfie of us. As the flash goes off, a couple of people give us strange looks, but mostly nobody seems to notice or care about the two teenage boys taking a photo with subway rats.

"Number three on the list," I say, handing Sebastian the photo to put in his backpack. "We had to catch a subway rat in action, and luckily for us, your aversion to positive thinking just got us our first scavenger hunt item."

Chapter 7

Dancing through Life

We get off the subway at Columbus Circle and climb back up to the daylight, one item on our list down, with plenty more to go. The sidewalk is packed with tourists and a zigzagging line for the hot dog stand, and a silver globe is postured above the subway steps.

I'm taken with the view—the way the buildings tower over us and yellow taxis zip around the roundabout, anchored by bright green trees and a tall statue of Christopher Columbus. I snap a few photos as Sebastian takes it all in beside me.

"You know, Benji has a song about falling in and out of love here."

"Here?" Sebastian glances around.

I nod. "It's called 'Full Circle.' There's a metaphor, you know? About how it starts, and it ends, and he looks back and it's done. It fell apart without him even realizing it."

Furrowing his brow, Sebastian watches some of the cars slowing to a stop.

"There's this line that's so good, actually. '*Summer love in the back of the cab, glad for Columbus Circle traffic, but all the trees died and it's cold, and now the story seems so tragic.*' I don't know, it just . . . It says a lot."

"Maybe that's clever," he concedes, voice low.

I blink. "I'm sorry—what was that?"

Sebastian rolls his eyes and clears his throat. "Where are we headed, McGuire?"

Content with hearing Sebastian admit a Benji Keaton song is clever, I decide not to push for him to say it again, though I *really* want to. Instead, I check my phone and spin around, pointing away from Columbus Circle.

"Lincoln Center," I say, starting to head in that direction.

"Maybe send me that song," Sebastian says slowly, before holding up his hands. "I'm only *mildly* curious."

I nod. "There are a lot of songs you'd like, I bet."

He groans.

"You never know," I offer. "He's a lyricist, first and foremost. And the words just . . . It can be something so simple, but it can tell an entire story. I know there are those songs that you hear on the radio and they're, like, high school dance pop songs, I get it. But then there are these songs about things like his grandfather, or his childhood best friend, or how he wishes he could just change one singular moment because then he'd be with the love of his life."

Sebastian doesn't say anything, he just nods slightly, hands in his pockets.

"I don't know. His songwriting is just next-level. The way he feels things and then the way he puts it into words. God, I'd kill to be able to do that—" I catch myself.

"Well, you can write songs." Sebastian quirks a brow.

I shake my head. "Please. It's a pipe dream. Not even a pipe dream. Not even a dream at all."

He pinches his lips together, as if he's trying to think of what to say.

"Benji is just really good at it," I say, as if to assure him he doesn't need to reply at all.

"If you want to write songs, you should."

It's a nice idea, and one I used to desperately cling to alone in my bedroom with notebooks full of words that just didn't click.

"I've accepted the fact that I'm better singing someone else's words," I say with a smile.

As we head up Broadway and the Polaroid camera bounces at the end of the lanyard straps, I am consumed with an overwhelming sense of emptiness that I had pushed away for so long. Thinking about Benji Keaton's lyrics—about what it must feel like to love so deeply your heart aches and a whole city becomes a torturous reminder of a pair of lips—I can't put my finger on the sense of longing in my chest. I don't know if it's for the experience or for the talent or the sense of purpose or for something I can't even recognize yet. Maybe all of the above.

If Annie were here, I'd tell her how I'm feeling. But she's not here, and she hasn't even texted me back. Instead, I'm in New York City with Sebastian Hodges, having emo hours for no apparent reason.

"Anyway," I say, trying to restore a more chipper timbre to my voice. "I hope you're ready to plié and pirouette, Sebastian."

"I am absolutely not ready to do either of those things," he sighs.

I inhale as we turn left, walking in front of the Empire Hotel, and toward—as the list describes it—the epicenter.

"Lincoln Center is an iconic institution," I tell him. "The New York City Ballet is world-renowned."

The property is massive: at the top of the steps, three buildings line the courtyard and its giant fountain. People are lounging on the stairs, eating half-wrapped sandwiches or petting their dogs as they bob their heads to whatever music plays in their earphones. Families take selfies and one girl has her tripod set up, popping her hips left and right to whatever TikTok sound is currently trending.

"I'm not doing ballet moves," Sebastian deadpans. "In front of all these people?"

"You don't seem like you'd care what a bunch of

strangers think," I offer, then I pull a face: "I meant that in a good way."

"I don't care what a bunch of strangers think, I care what *I* think. And I think I would rather listen to an entire Benji Keaton album front-to-back before I did ballet moves in front of a camera at super-busy Lincoln Center in New York City."

There are dark gray blocks that line the top of the steps, maybe sculptures or maybe just benches. I point to them: "We can prop the camera up on one of those, turn on the self-timer, and snap the photo. It'll be over before you know it."

"I'm not flexible," Sebastian grunts as he follows me to one of the blocks.

"You don't have to be flexible," I say. "You're not actually *performing* in the ballet. You just have to literally hold a pose for ten seconds."

I set up the camera and check the viewfinder to make sure it looks okay. I tell Sebastian to take a couple of steps back, and then to the left, but back to the right just a tiny bit, until he's in the right spot, situated beneath the arches and glittering windows of the building behind him, and with a great view of the fountain.

Before I turn the camera on, I raise my brows.

"Okay, what is the easiest ballet pose I can do?" he asks.

I shrug. "You could . . ." I stand up tall, with my arms over my head, touching my fingers together. My heels meet and I bend my knees.

"Absolutely not." Sebastian shakes his head.

"How about you just touch your heels together, turn your feet out . . ." He begrudgingly follows my instructions, and I shrug. "Then just hold your arms out to the side and do, like, a little baby squat."

"A little baby squat?" He groans.

"Just a little bend of the knees," I suggest.

He shuts his eyes. "This is humiliating."

He's doing the right pose, but I don't think Sebastian Hodges is by any means a natural ballerina. I want to laugh, but I know this is my only chance to get this Polaroid, so I hold it in and give him a thumbs-up before starting the timer and running over to join him.

As the timer counts down, I get up on my tiptoes and put my arms straight up in the air.

Sebastian bursts into laughter, and so do I, just as the flash goes off.

"I didn't know you could actually laugh," I say, hurrying over to grab the camera.

He shakes out his arms and composes himself. "You just looked ridiculous."

"I looked like a primo ballerino," I say.

"Did you just make that up?"

"No, it's what the male ballerinas are called," I say. "You've never heard that?"

He looks at me very seriously. "In all of my many long

conversations about ballet, I have yet to come across that term."

"Whatever, it's a real thing. I didn't make it up."

The Polaroid develops as we walk back toward the Empire Hotel. It's actually a good photo. It looks like two old friends sharing a laugh, even, and the smile and crinkle in Sebastian's eyes suit him, though I can't imagine he'd agree.

Chapter 8

Where Did the Rock Go?

We've been wandering through Central Park for about ten minutes, and I don't think I can admit to Sebastian that I'm not entirely sure where we are.

There may be something magical about Central Park. Maybe it's the fact that it's the first week of June, and the weather is perfect, and the vibes are just right, but the sprawling lawns are so lush and emerald green, like something from an enchanted forest. The trees are lively, tall, and exceptionally strong looking. When we reach a road completely overtaken with cyclists, there is more of that New York City energy absolutely bouncing off the hot pavement and making me want to pull an Amy Adams in *Enchanted*. Which I don't do. Obviously.

Still, for as gorgeous as Central Park is, we've somehow managed to miss all the giant rocks I've seen in my research.

I know they're here, and I'm expecting to find them crawling with kids and couples and influencers, but we've been meandering long enough that I'm slightly confused.

The plan was to walk up the park to the Upper West Side, specifically to the American Museum of Natural History, and to find the giant boulders along the way so we can check off number 4, Mountain Climber, obviously. We've passed a few rock formations that are really low to the ground, which I guess we could have used. Now that we're far beyond them, I wish we did. I just thought it'd be better to find a larger boulder. One to jump from or something, since that seems like the right thing to do the first time one climbs a rock in Central Park.

"We're lost," Sebastian says for the sixth time.

I shake my head. "No, we're not."

We come across someone sitting on a bench with a sketchbook, and I decide to distract Sebastian from the fact that I've gotten us lost.

"What do you like to do?" I ask, watching the artist make long, sweeping strokes with the pencil.

Sebastian looks over at me. "What do you mean?"

"Like, I don't know. What are your hobbies?"

"Hobbies?" He looks to the artist as we pass him. "Why are you asking me about my hobbies?"

I tug at the lanyard, which is rubbing against the back of my neck. I'm not sure which part is worse—that it's sweaty or itchy.

"Would it be the worst thing in the world for us to try and . . ."

"Try and . . . ?"

He has this unique ability to make every interaction the emotional equivalent of a tooth extraction.

"To try and be friends?" I offer. "We're stuck together for this trip. We're going to go all around New York City and just stay strangers?"

The corner of his mouth lifts as he looks to me. "You're not a stranger. You're Teddy McGuire. Birthday in December and you make a big deal about it. You love Benji Keaton and Broadway. You're superstitious. You go to the beach during lunch hour a lot. You buy things you see on TikTok, like those water bottles you and Annie were obsessed with."

There is that tooth extraction feeling. Sans Novocain, even.

Lucky me.

"I do not make a big deal about my birthday," I say.

"You do, too. The drama club made you a tribute video like you were winning Artist of the Year or something."

I shrug. "I didn't ask them to. They're just being good friends. And they're theater kids—something over-the-top is sort of to be expected."

Sebastian nods. "I mean, the crew kids are a little more chill."

"Lighting and sound are," I say. I know he's only been

part of the tech crew for his senior year, but surely he's noticed the theatrics are pervasive. "I mean, stage managers are dramatic AF."

"It's a power trip thing," Sebastian agrees. "Gregory was pretty over-the-top."

I nod. "Exactly. And costuming? Props?"

"Okay, fine," Sebastian concedes. "Well, anyway, what about the fact that McGuire Grill is disco-themed every December?"

I smile at the thought. The way the mirror balls go up immediately after Thanksgiving—a variety of sizes, from golf ball to car tire—hanging from the ceiling or stacked around the restaurant in a "bespoke" manner with twinkling lights, as Mom says.

"It's a tradition," I offer. "One my parents started, might I add."

He shrugs. "Okay, but you're not out here objecting."

"Why would I object?" I ask. "Don't you like celebrating your birthday?"

It's immediate.

The sinking feeling in my stomach because I think I just said the wrong thing.

When he doesn't say anything and his eyes briefly lower, I know I've *definitely* said the wrong thing.

"It's just a day," he says. "Everybody has birthdays, so I guess I don't see why it's such a big deal."

His body language and the brief hoarse hook of his

voice say there's more to this, but I'm not going to push it. We come to another fork in the path and I veer left, hoping Sebastian thinks I seem confident about our direction.

"Fine, fine," I say. "So, I'm not a stranger, I guess. But I don't know much about you still."

"You never asked," he says, a teasing smirk contrasting the sincerity.

I nod. "Touché. But to be fair, you never made it seem like you wanted me to. Or anybody to, really."

"Am I supposed to?"

"Yeah, I think that's how people make friends," I say.

He lets out a long, exaggerated breath and throws his hands up. "All right, McGuire. What do you want to know?"

"Literally anything," I say. "I mean, we must have something in common, right? That's probably a good place to start—figuring that out."

When he goes quiet again, I sigh. "And before you say something sarcastic, I know you probably think I'm just some disco-birthday-loving Benji Keaton bubblegum pop airhead or something, but there is more to me than that. Okay?"

This causes another laugh, and this one even brightens his eyes a little. "I was literally just going to say we both like pizza."

"Oh."

"But feel free to continue?"

"Everyone likes pizza," I point out. "So, I feel like that is a *really* surface-level choice. I appreciate the effort, but I think we could find something at least a tiny bit deeper than that."

He shakes his head. "Not everyone likes pizza."

"Not *everyone*," I agree. "But enough people like pizza that it is one hundred percent not some kind of bonding fun fact. Hit me with something else."

Sebastian groans. "We both like *The Phantom of the Opera*."

I stop walking. "Wait, no way. You like *Phantom of the Opera*?"

"I mean, I think *this* is a better example of something *everyone* likes." He stops too, turning to me. "What? What's happening?"

"You like *Phantom of the Opera*," I say. "It's just painting a whole new picture. I'm seeing something entirely different. Sebastian Hodges, curled up in a cozy bedroom—some indie rock posters, of course, only they're paired with antique, brass sconces. You're candlelit and listening to 'The Music of the Night.' Forlorn. Crestfallen. Your bedding is, like, crushed velvet. Scarlet."

He blinks. "You done?"

"One last detail I need filled in: Are there any pets joining you for your Andrew Lloyd Webber jam sesh?"

"I have a fish," he says. "Best I could do. My mom works a lot at the hospital, and I'm at school all day. Not really great for a dog, and I don't want a cat."

"I'm not a cat person either," I say. "What is your fish like? Is it named Christine?"

"No," he says, starting to walk again. "My fish is named Poe."

"For the forlorn, crestfallen poet?"

He rolls his eyes.

"No, I'm kidding, of course," I say. "Edgar Allan Poe is amazing. Obviously."

"Obviously," he agrees. He pulls out his phone to show me a photo. Oh my God, the photo—it's his profile picture on Instagram. I recognize the pixels now. He has a photo of his fish named Poe as his profile photo.

I don't say anything, but I feel like I'm getting such a crash course in Sebastian Hodges right now.

"I don't only like things that are forlorn and crestfallen, anyway," he says.

I nod. "There's not necessarily anything wrong with it if you did. Do you like a lot of poetry, or just Edgar Allan Poe?"

"I like a lot of poetry." It's short, like he's slightly embarrassed to say that out loud.

"I think poetry is amazing," I say. "When you think about it, people putting their hearts into words like that? And the kinds of things Edgar Allan Poe writes. People who would only be memories . . . poets turn them into scripture or something. They live forever."

He studies me. "That is so not very disco ball, bubblegum pop of you."

"I love words," I say. "And, anyway, songs are just poems. Plus, a lot of bubblegum pop is so much more. Slow it down and put it against a piano, and it might make you feel completely differently."

"And all my days are trances," he says. *"And all my nightly dreams are where thy grey eye glances."* We lock eyes. "It's one of my favorites: 'To One in Paradise.'"

"It *is* giving forlorn and crestfallen," I laugh.

He doesn't laugh along with me. "Have you ever felt that way?"

"That my days are trances?" I lift my shoulders. "Sure. I guess sometimes. Yeah."

"Maybe some days that aren't in December," he says, offering a smile that might be forced, but I can't tell.

"Even some days in December."

We keep walking through this emerald scene, past a guy painting caricatures and a woman playing violin, and I don't know what exactly dawned this moment between us. If any of my days are trances, it isn't something I even get into with Annie. It's not something I really expect anybody to understand. I've isolated any meandering thoughts about meaning or monotony to stay between Benji and me, listening to his more poetic ballads.

And now it's between Sebastian and me.

"Sebastian, I think we are getting to know each other."

Before he can respond, I gasp and grab him by the arm. "Look!"

We've finally found some boulders, and just like I'd imagined, they're crawling with kids and couples. Still, they're jumping height, and I think I have to at least try it after we get our photo.

"Self-timer again?" Sebastian scratches the back of his neck.

"Or we can ask someone to take it," I say.

"No way." He shakes his head. "We don't want to bother any of these people enjoying the park."

"What about that girl?" I say, gesturing toward a blonde on a bench in biker shorts and a big T-shirt taking selfies. "She's creating content. It's fine."

"Teddy—"

"What's the worst thing that can happen? She says no?"

His face is red as I approach her. I think she's probably an influencer, based on her slicked-back ponytail, vintage Gucci sunglasses, and matte nude lip.

"Hi," I say, and she turns her head toward me. "Sorry, I just was wondering if you would mind taking a photo for us with this Polaroid camera? We're doing a scavenger hunt, and we're supposed to climb one of these big rocks."

"Oh my gosh, of course. That is so cute." She smiles, taking the camera and popping up. "Okay, just, like, tell me when."

We climb up the rock, and Sebastian is grumbling

under his breath about how he *cannot believe I just asked this girl to take our picture*, but I ignore him and once we get to the top, wave at her.

"Okay," she shouts. "Do something cute!"

"Like what?"

She seems like she'd have good ideas, so we're in safe hands.

"Maybe a cute little kissing moment?"

Sebastian and I exchange glances.

"Oh," he says.

"No, we're not—"

"Yeah, we're not going to—"

She cocks her head, then, pointing from Sebastian to me: "Or put your arm around him."

He shifts uncomfortably and I think we're back to the tooth extraction feeling, only this time he's the one in the proverbial dentist's chair.

"I mean . . ." I start to offer some way out, but he's already putting his arm around me and the girl at the foot of the rock claps. He's taller, and I sort of fit under his arm like a puzzle piece, but that's not something I'm going to mention literally ever. Instead, I just smile and throw my arm up like I'm posing in front of the castle at Disney World.

"Aw, so cute." She holds up the camera. "Okay, ready?"

Once the photo has been taken, we quickly detach and make our way down to grab the camera.

"You guys are so adorable," the girl says.

I thank her and Sebastian is absolutely blushing, giving her a tight-lipped smile and nod as she goes back to her spot on the bench.

We navigate toward Central Park West as the Polaroid develops, and I am astonished at how, yet again, we actually do look like close friends in the photo.

Maybe Sebastian is right—maybe we aren't strangers at all.

Chapter 9

It's Only a Matter of Time

The American Museum of Natural History is larger than I even imagined it would be. We stand across the street from the grand façade with its columns and inscriptions and statues tall above the pedestrians. People sit on the steps and a bunch of kids rush onto a school bus, which tells me we've come at just the right time.

The traffic is busy, and it always is, but it does feel especially claustrophobic right here, zipping along between the crowded park entrance and the massive museum flooded with tourists.

Smoke blows in front of our faces and I spot where it's coming from: a hot dog stand. There are several carts, actually, some with blue-and-yellow umbrellas.

My stomach grumbles.

"We should get New York hot dogs," I say to Sebastian.

"That sounds disgusting," he says.

I shrug. "Maybe, but it seems like a very important part of being in New York. Haven't you seen it in all the movies?"

He shakes his head.

"Well, I can't think of one now, but I'm sure I've seen it. New York hot dogs are famous."

"Famous for making people shit themselves?"

I pull a face. "Come *on*."

"I just would like to spend my time enjoying the museum rather than running to the bathroom."

"Thank you so much for that visual." Then I hear what he said: "Wait, Sebastian Hodges wants to *enjoy* the museum?"

"Oh, dear God, let's get the damn hot dogs."

So, we hop in line at the nearest cart. I would be exaggerating if I said the aroma was appetizing, but we have been rushing around the city and haven't had lunch, so this is going to hit just right, I'm sure of it.

The woman in front of us takes her hot dog and walks away. I've noticed New Yorkers seem used to all the things I'm in awe of. They just walk through the city like they're not living in a fairy tale. We have hot dog carts in Citrus Harbor, sure, but they're by the pier and it's just a different vibe—I can't explain it.

"Hi." I smile, as one does, and the man behind the cart blinks, as one does. "Could we get two New York–style hot dogs?"

He lifts a brow. "New York style?"

"Well, we're visiting."

"You don't say."

Sebastian kicks his toe into the cement and groans quietly.

"But there must be, like, a New York classic, right?"

The man laughs and takes my cash. He works behind the cart and Sebastian tries to give me money, but I tell him it's okay. When I turn back to the guy working the cart, he hands me two aluminum-foil-wrapped hot dogs. I thank him, and then Sebastian and I move to one of the green benches along the stone half wall separating the sidewalk from the park. The trees above rustle as the wind blows.

"Here you are," I say, handing him one of the hot dogs. "Do you like hot dogs?"

"*Now* he asks me." Sebastian accepts the hot dog from me.

"Don't make that face," I say.

He shrugs. "Just imagining the risk here."

"*Nothing real is without risk*," I say.

Sebastian nods knowingly. "Benji?"

"It's all up here." I tap the side of my skull. "All right, let's see. The grand unveiling. A Central Park West hot dog, New York style."

We unwrap the aluminum foil at the same time, and the reveal is genuinely surprising.

"What is this?"

Sebastian snorts. "Looks like onion relish, spicy

mustard, and sauerkraut."

"Sauerkraut . . ."

"Don't like sauerkraut?"

I shake my head. "I don't know, I've never had it."

"You guys don't have it at McGuire's?"

Again, I shake my head. Then I swallow and hold up the hot dog. "Well, I asked for a New York–style hot dog. So here we go."

The first bite is a strange one, but honestly? It's not bad. It's certainly not something I would have ever thought of, but it is a unique mix of sour, spicy, and savory.

As I'm swallowing bite two, a chihuahua pees on the sidewalk a foot away from me. I hold my breath and take another bite, and a malamute pees on the same spot.

The combination of smells going on is less than ideal, but that's New York City charm, I guess.

"It's not bad," I say when I have a couple bites left.

Sebastian has balled up the aluminum foil and wipes his thumb across the corner of his mouth.

"You finished?"

He nods. "I was starving."

As I take another bite, I cover my mouth: "You need to go ahead and admit you loved the New York–style hot dog."

Sebastian rolls his eyes. "Come on, McGuire. It's museum time."

The inside of the museum feels even more massive than it looked. It makes no sense. New York City is a collection of optical illusions.

Mostly, I'm wondering if the dinosaur bones are real. We're standing in the Theodore Roosevelt Memorial, in the rotunda as lines wrap around for tickets, and there are two giant dinosaurs serving as well-mannered centerpieces. They stand out against the ornate barrel-vaulted ceilings and red marble columns, but they're especially different in style from the murals on each wall.

If the bones aren't real, I'm sure that'd be something people would talk about, right? Why would they put them out here, front and center, if they weren't real?

The pristine shape of the architecture in the hall suggests a certain movie was purely fiction, and everything inside the museum doesn't come alive at night. After all, the one dinosaur with the absurdly long neck would absolutely wreck the stone and marble if it started whipping its head and tail around after hours.

"What are you thinking about?"

I turn to Sebastian and gesture toward the dinosaurs. "Do you think those are real?"

He chuckles. "No, they're casts."

I furrow my brow. "How do you know?"

"I just do."

"And I bet you know what kind of dinosaurs they are too, then, hmm?"

He narrows his eyes on me. "The tall one is a *Barosaurus*, and the smaller is an *Allosaurus*."

"You know about *dinosaurs*?" I gasp. "Or are you making that up?"

"Feel free to fact-check me," he says. "We could even bet money on it to add an element of fun."

Ignoring him, I pull up the email from Mrs. Mackenzie that includes the subtly titled attachment: *SENIOR-DRAMA-CLUB-NYC-TRIP-IMPORTANT-DOCUMENTS-FINAL-DONOTDELETE.PDF.* Within its pages are our museum tickets, purchased at group prices and folded into the cost of the trip. I scan my barcode, and Sebastian scans his, and once we're walking into the Akeley Hall of African Mammals, I turn to him.

"You really weren't kidding about wanting to enjoy the museum," I say. "You are a paleontologist."

"I'm not a paleontologist!" Sebastian stifles a laugh.

"Yes, you are."

"Teddy, that would require a degree."

"Okay, right. So, like, you're a dinosaur stan."

"And *you're* ridiculous."

For effect, I gasp again. "Is that where you snuck off to earlier? Are you part of a secret society?" My eyes bug. "A *fan club*?"

"What is the scavenger hunt item here?" He holds his palm out, so I hand him the folded-up list from my pocket. He unfolds it as I examine the elephants in the room.

The hall is two stories, with depictions of African mammals in their natural habitats, but obviously constructed and fabricated, like to-scale dioramas. Again, not the spot I'd want to be in if everything came to life at night.

"Some of these items are inane," Sebastian points out, handing the paper back to me.

I nod. "I love it."

"Do you realize what the prompt is for this museum?"

"Yes."

"Pick out dinosaurs for each other," he says. "What in the absolute—"

"Hi." A voice creeps around the back of my neck, and I turn to find a girl with butterfly clips in her hair, wearing a sunflower-printed top and jeans. "Sorry, I just wanted to tell you I love your socks," she says.

After traveling and a day of wandering around, I can barely remember what I decided to put on this morning, so I glance down and angle my foot to reveal my lightly tie-dyed socks. Their embroidered half sun peeks out above my high-top Vans, and when I look back to the girl and our eyes meet, there's a sort of cosmic alignment.

"Thank you so much."

"I wanted to get them, but they sold out so fast." She reaches into her pocket and pulls out a cluster of keys, revealing the same symbol in an enamel casting. "Got the key chain, though."

"I love it!" I marvel at the sun over the squiggly lines meant to be waves.

She smiles so big it's like I just gave her the biggest compliment ever, and then she offers a tiny wave. "Anyway, that's all. Hope you have a nice day."

"Wait," I say. "If you want a pair, I have an extra. They sent me two and told me to just keep them. I meant to post on TikTok to see if anybody wanted them, but I honestly just totally forgot."

The girl blinks. "Are you serious?"

"Sure!" I pull out my phone and open Instagram, handing it to her. "Follow yourself and send me a message! I'll ship them to you when I get back home."

She types quickly, like the opportunity will disappear if she's not fast enough. "I'll pay you for them of course—"

"No way," I say. "They were included accidentally. So don't worry about it."

"I can't believe you're just going to send them to me." She hands me back my phone. "That's so nice of you."

"It must be fate we found each other," I say with a grin.

She thanks me again, smiles at Sebastian, and then she scurries off.

Sebastian blinks.

"What?" I ask, starting to walk toward the back of the hall.

He scratches the back of his neck. "What was that?"

"What was what?"

"Do people just come up to you and tell you they like your socks all the time? And then you offer to send them an extra pair? Like . . . what?"

I laugh. "They're Benji socks."

"Oh, they're Benji socks . . ." His voice sounds mocking.

"I've never had someone come up to me like that."

Prickling, I say, "Then I guess you need some Benji socks."

"You don't think it's weird at all?"

I shake my head. "Why would it be weird?"

"She's just some random girl, I don't know."

"She was nice."

"She was," he agrees. "It was just so random."

I try to see it from his perspective, but I don't see what's so strange. Annie and I have made so many friends at Benji concerts, and on BenjiTok, and just through cute, quick little moments like that.

"I think it's nice people can find each other like that," I say. "Because we love the same thing. It brings people together."

Sebastian's head bobs. "I guess so. I mean, it is nice you're going to give her the extra pair."

"Next time Benji sells socks, I'll get you a pair, too." I smile. "Okay, let's go, I can't wait to hear all about the Jurassic period from the president of the dinosaur stan club."

Chapter 10

Back in Time

This museum continues to feel like Mary Poppins's bag. Because how in the hell does each hall get bigger and bigger? Do the laws of physics not apply here? (Is that even physics?)

My favorite so far has been the Hall of Biodiversity. It was incredibly immersive and all the animals mounted along the walls looked really cool.

Plus, there were butterflies, and I love butterflies. Even if they remind me of my horrific, cringeworthy song at the talent show, they mostly still are little symbols of hope and possibility.

There's a *giant* whale in the ocean hall, and then the museum just keeps going. Seriously, it never ends. There's even a planetarium.

The Hall of Saurischian Dinosaurs is another massive entry—swarming with people, lined with visuals, and starring majorly dramatic to-scale (I think) dinosaurs.

Seeing Sebastian try to play it cool around a bunch of fossils is the best thing ever.

It's also made me go down a little bit of a rabbit hole in my own mind, though. Because when did Sebastian Hodges go from a dinosaur-loving kid with wide eyes and a smile of missing teeth to a loner with a permanent scowl and a furrowed brow? When did he learn his wonder was to be locked away? Marvel and bewilderment meant to be traded in for apathy and detachment? When did that spark get doused?

I've taken it upon myself, it seems, to reignite it.

Sebastian and I are shoulder to shoulder, looking up at a display that lays out a "Tree of Life" behind panels of glass. Chrome lines link species and draw out the evolution of bone structures. I think.

"The dinosaur age is basically, like, the book. And then there are chapters?"

"The *Age of the Dinosaurs.*" Sebastian nods. "Well, basically during the Mesozoic era, there were the Triassic, Jurassic, and Cretaceous periods."

I clap. "I know those."

"Yeah?" A faint hint of a smile forms on his face as he looks down at me.

"I think we need to establish which period we'd be."

"Which period we'd live in," he corrects. "Okay. Smart thinking."

"What are, like, the defining characteristics? What are the aesthetics?"

He folds his arms and lifts his chin. "The aesthetics?"

"Like, okay, when Benji was in his *Premonitions* era, it was this supernatural high school vibe. Or *Sweet Vicious* was glamorous and all about New York. Or—"

Sebastian pulls a face. "The dinosaurs' eras didn't really have aesthetics."

Trying to mask my disappointment, I hum. "Not even . . . I don't know, different vegetation? Because I could pick based on flowers or something."

I've said something *genius*, I can tell by how Sebastian offers an approving kind of pout. "There were developments throughout the periods. So, we see things like seeds and ferns and more basic trees during the Triassic. And then, of course, the plant life evolved."

"Of course," I say. "Then I guess I want the most evolved period. Because I think there should be flowers."

"So you'll be a dino from the Cretaceous period." He tilts his head. "Do you want to live on land or in the sea? Or both? Do you want to fly?"

"What do you think I would do if I were a dinosaur?" I ask. "I can honestly say I've never considered this, so I'm going to need to lean on the stan club's expertise."

Sebastian looks at me, glances up and down, and turns

back to the display. He then begins walking into the hall, and I follow him down the middle of the aisle. Children, who must be finishing up their last weeks of school, dart around us, and couples seem to be in no short supply, snuggly and cuddly like these fossils are the most romantic thing they could lay their eyes on.

We stop in front of a huge dinosaur—one I recognize, even. The silhouette is iconic, with small arms and a jaw of sharp teeth only a mother could love.

"You." Sebastian points up at the staggering collection of bones.

I laugh way too loud and several people turn to stare.

"Me?" I press my palm to my chest.

Sebastian stares up at the dinosaur, unmoved by my indignance.

"Sebastian, come on."

"You asked for my expertise."

"Then you're admitting you *are* the Dinosaur Stan Club."

He shrugs. "Sure."

That is satisfying, but I am still not sure if I should feel complimented or insulted right now.

"Why would you think I am a *Tyrannosaurus rex*?" I gawk.

"Look at its massive, thick skull," he says, pretending not to hear me. Then he smiles and offers the lightest chuckle before gesturing around the museum. "Just kidding. No other dino would do, Teddy."

A wave of warmth rushes over me, starting in my chest or maybe in my cheeks. Was that a *compliment*?

"I'm not going to expand on this decision," Sebastian finally adds. "But I will just say I am very confident in it."

Studying the curves and ridges of the bones, I imagine myself as a *T. rex* and I have to admit, it does seem pretty great. I obviously don't know much about the Cretaceous period, but I'm fantasizing about running through a tropical landscape, slow-motion with the wind in my hair—or against my . . . *scales*? The fantasy is less appealing the more reptilian I imagine myself.

Still, it'd be fun to have a mighty roar and an imposing gait. It'd be fun to kind of run the show, since I'd be head dino, basically.

"A *Teddysaurus*," I say, entirely too pleased with myself. Though, once it comes out, I pause. "Not sure about it."

"Don't think I love it," Sebastian agrees. "How do we document this one?"

"I guess we take a selfie with each of the dinosaurs?" I ask.

Sebastian seems displeased with this. "That'd be the only item on the list that would require two Polaroids."

I shrug. "It's Mrs. Mackenzie. At least one portion of this was bound to be unlike the others. Let's be real."

We'll figure it out.

Looking around at the hall, it occurs to me there is

so much I don't know about dinosaurs. I mean, really. What were their brains like? How developed were they? I imagine they had personalities and cliques and relationships and enemies. Did they smell terrible? They probably smelled terrible. Are they misunderstood—friendly, hospitable, even? Or were they really vicious like in the movies?

And then I wonder how much anyone really knows about dinosaurs. I know scientists are smart and they have tools and technology to figure out all kinds of stuff that goes way over my head (most of it does, just see my report cards), but how do they *know*? It's not like anyone has gotten in a time machine and spent the day with a dinosaur.

So, then, how am I supposed to figure out what dinosaur Sebastian would be? In a way, their mystery is perfect for this, since he's still such a mystery too, but that doesn't help me narrow it down to one.

I don't think he's a flying dinosaur. I'm not sure why, but there's just a vibe. If I'm remembering anything correctly, Pterodactyls are high-pitched and shrill, which is definitely not Sebastian.

He doesn't strike me as a water dinosaur, either. Like, Sebastian wouldn't have fins. He just wouldn't.

Triceratops have a sort of stubborn sense about them, and it doesn't feel *just right*, but I think I'll keep it in my back pocket in case.

Then I turn around, and directly across from the *T. rex*, there's Sebastian.

Duh.

"You're that one," I say, pointing to the dinosaur with a neck and tail that nearly span the entire hall. "You're totally that one."

He laughs. "The *Apatosaurus*?"

"Sure?" I walk over to check the placard. "Yes. The *Apatosaurus*. It's tall, you're tall . . . There's more to it, I'm trying to figure it out."

Sebastian puts his hands in his pockets, and I fiddle with the Polaroid camera hanging from my neck.

"Maybe it has to do with evolution," I say. "I could see you evolving from this one."

His eyes bug and his jaw drops. "Are you joking?"

"Kind of," I say.

"I mean, you do know humans didn't evolve from dinosaurs?"

I scoff. "Of course."

I mean, that makes logical sense, even if I barely skated through biology class.

"Sad, though," I say. "I wish I evolved from the *T. rex*, it would make things more interesting."

"It's not like we're Pokémon or something, Teddy." He smirks. "And the dinosaurs were gone millions of years before humans showed up."

I figure out if we stand at just the right angle toward the beginning of the hall, we can actually get a single selfie with both of our dinosaurs in the background. No clue how everyone else is doing this one, but we take our Polaroid, and I think I can see the resemblance between us and our dinosaur alter egos.

Checking the time, I realize if we stay here much longer, we'll probably literally only have time at the Met to take our photo with a Roman statue.

There are so many amazing galleries, and I wanted to see the whole Met, but Sebastian is clearly in his element. He's enjoying himself, and it's fun getting to know him a bit better. Plus, a happy Sebastian is great for the scavenger hunt as a whole, so I figure I can compromise some of the Met. It'll be the last thing I'm thinking about when I meet Benji, anyway.

As we walk through the museum, I assure him we have plenty of time.

Sebastian really does know a lot about evolution. And about biology, and geology, and just, like, a lot of stuff in general.

"How did you get into all this?" I ask while Sebastian is examining a fossil. "So. Much. Science."

"My dad is a physicist," he says nonchalantly. Then, it's like he realizes he's told me something personal, because his eyes dart from me back to the fossil. "Do you see the little ridges there?"

I nod, and after a moment: "Are you and your dad—"

"He's not in the picture," Sebastian says. Short. Maybe a little snippy, even.

So, I drop it. "What about the ridges?"

Sebastian explains all kinds of things, like the difference in the halls—the saurischian versus the ornithischian dinosaurs, differentiated by their hips. Who would have thought? The other hall is where we see the *Stegosaurus* and the *Triceratops*.

He teaches me about the way animals with vertebrae went from water to land and then into the skies. I'm a little confused by it all, but in general, he's a good teacher.

I think, though, as we discuss origins and progress and instincts, mine are still to turn life into some dramatic metaphor. Because instead of focusing on the bones hanging from the ceiling, I'm watching Sebastian and wondering if this is going to be a distant memory one day. I wonder if Sebastian and I will share these special New York City moments, only to watch extinction get the better of our friendship before it can even develop.

It's unnecessarily dark, but I can't help but feel like this is so fleeting now. Like I want to make sure to have the best time ever, so even if this does become a memory, it'll be one I want to hold on to.

"There is a *Dino Store*!" I'm looking at the map on my phone, and I say it with as much enthusiasm as anyone has ever had about such a merchandise shop. Sebastian is paying more attention to the saber-toothed cat fossils, so I blink. "Do you get it?"

"Yes, I get it," he laughs. "I'm not going to buy anything, though."

I frown. "Why not? Not even a T-shirt?"

"A T-shirt?" He lifts a brow. "Come on."

"Are you embarrassed?"

"No, I'm not embarrassed."

I roll my eyes. "There's no reason to be embarrassed. Why not show the world you think dinosaurs are cool? I'm sure you could make it look very Urban Outfitters."

He sighs. "Urban Outfitters? Teddy, Teddy, Teddy."

"I'm so not cool enough for you," I say. "But I still think we should go the Dino Store."

Souvenir bag with two AMNH T-shirts in hand—not matching, though I did try my best—we take a cab across Central Park to save time.

The Metropolitan Museum of Art reminds me of the New York Public Library a little bit just by the architecture, but it's even bigger. A magnificent sprawl of full green trees and symmetrical fountains leads to the steps—also massive, though made small compared to the lofty façade of enormous arches and columns. The museum takes up several blocks and backs up to Central Park. There are cabs and food carts lining the sidewalk, and even as the sun begins to set, it's bustling like the museum just opened.

As we make our way closer, a familiar toss of blond hair ties a knot in my stomach. Eden is posing on the steps, having changed into a bright white dress with a light pink beret, as Briar catches her angles. She straightens up when she sees us and I know it's too late to turn around or pretend we haven't locked eyes, so I start up the steps toward her.

"Oh, Teddy!" Eden grins and the pearls around her neck reflect specks of golden sunlight. "And Sebastian. What a dynamic duo. You came to get the Roman statue checked off, hmm?"

The way Eden speaks, you can't help but always feel you're walking into a trap. Her slightly venomous tone pulls you in, against your will, like you've just flown too close to the sun and now you're going to get scorched. It's obvious in the way her smile is so self-satisfied and her brow arches.

"Well, I'd say great minds think alike . . ." She stands up and Briar snaps to attention. "But I guess only one of us planned ahead."

I sigh.

I can tell where this is going. Somewhere horrible, since any bump in the road is derailing the entire itinerary I have so carefully crafted for this scavenger hunt. We can't afford detours or things going wrong, and I immediately worry that any hint of things going awry is going to cause Sebastian to give up on this entirely.

"The Met closed early," she says. "Some charity gala. Not *the* gala, obvs. But yeah. Closed."

"Spotted on the steps of the Met . . ." Briar whispers under her breath with a satisfied smile.

Sebastian shoots her a confused look, and Eden rolls her eyes.

"Anyway, we have what we need." She pulls out her phone. "Come on, Briar. I want to see if Bergdorf's has something sparkly—I need the perfect dress for when I meet Benji."

Chapter 11

The Point of No Return

The Met cannot be closed early. This is the worst luck. This is worse than the worst luck. This is planet-ending, soul-crushing, light-absorbing luck. This is worse than a day that's a trance. We're not going to win this scavenger hunt now, and we're going to hang our heads in shame, watching as Eden and Briar post completely planned "candid" photos with Benji, laughing like they've known each other for years, or focused on an intimate conversation, the subject of which the rest of us can only ever guess.

Well, *I'm* going to hang my head in shame. Because Sebastian is going to be off doing his thing. Gallivanting around the city, meeting God-knows-who and getting into God-knows-what. Immersing in an underground interactive Edgar Allan Poe experience or going to see *The*

Phantom of the Opera. Wait—it closed. So truly, who knows what he will be doing.

"Now everything is screwed." I hate how whiny I sound, but we've made it to the top of the steps and Eden wasn't bluffing: the doors are closed. We're not getting in.

Speaking of crestfallen and forlorn. I sit down on the top step and bury my face in my hands.

"This is what Benji is talking about in 'Wish I Never Knew,'" I say.

Sebastian narrows his eyes. "Do I ask?"

"It's about how the worst thing is knowing what you lost," I groan. "Knowing what slipped through your fingers. A freaking scavenger hunt item that costs you everything."

"It's not slipping through your fingers yet."

"'*Not knowing can't hurt, but watching you pass me by, that still suffocates me in the middle of the night.*'" I look to Sebastian. "This is going to suffocate me in the middle of the night for the rest of my life. The time I almost met Benji Keaton in New York City."

Sebastian grins. "There's the drama I was waiting for." Then he exhales. "Okay, Teddy, maybe we can do something else tonight? And then come back here tomorrow instead?"

"We're going to be downtown," I say. "We aren't going to be able to squeeze something else in tomorrow."

"Then maybe we can just go somewhere else," he suggests. "The list doesn't actually say we have to go to the Met, just that we need a statue."

"Where are there more Roman statues, Sebastian?" I look up at him. "Do you want to wander the city looking for an ancient Roman statue? It's just . . . we're supposed to stay on schedule."

Sebastian scratches his chin. "Could we split up tomorrow?"

"No, we both have to be in the Polaroids. Remember?"

He nods. "Right. Okay, well, Teddy. We'll figure it out. Let's just get up and start Googling?"

I stand up. "Why are you suddenly so into the scavenger hunt?"

"I'm not."

"You are. You want to win, don't you?"

"I absolutely do not care about winning," he says. "Can we just figure out where we're going next?"

With one more sigh, I turn and look at the closed doors. Through the glass, I can see people walking around, who look like security and event coordinators and stressed caterers.

I cannot lose to Eden. What would she *do right now?*

She wouldn't stand here, staring wistfully. She wouldn't wait for this to suffocate her in the middle of the night for the rest of her life.

And I guess it's that thinking that leads me to tug on my lucky bracelet, step forward, and start knocking on the door.

"Teddy—" Sebastian starts toward me, but a woman in a lilac suit and perfectly coiffed brunette curls is already making eye contact. Before I know it, she's unlocking and pushing open one of the doors.

"The museum closed early today," she says.

I consider saying I left something, but what? An umbrella? It hasn't rained all day. An inhaler? Seems like bad karma. It also occurs to me that this woman smells like honey and oranges and her makeup is perfectly done like she has an entire professional team to meticulously place her lashes and line her lips. She doesn't strike me as someone who is going to fall for some improv.

"Is there any chance we could really quickly run inside and take a photo with one of the Roman statues?"

The woman blinks.

"We're doing a scavenger hunt for our school."

"Oh, you're doing a scavenger hunt . . . for your school."

Our entry is seeming less likely by the second.

"We only need to take a quick photo. It's really important. And we'll buy tickets."

She smiles at this. "Oh, wonderful."

I smile back.

We're getting somewhere!

"You'll buy tickets. Well, that changes things. You could come to the gala, even? You are more than welcome to participate in the silent auction, and I'll bet they even play 'Shake It Off' on the dance floor. Just for you."

The sarcasm was not necessary.

Sebastian puts his hand on my shoulder. "Come on, Teddy."

"'Shake It Off' is a fun song," I say just before she closes the door and marches away. Left at the top of the steps with Sebastian, I raise my brows. "It was worth a shot."

"I'm going to find another Roman statue. There must be more Roman statues."

I look out at Fifth Avenue, watching the buses and cyclists and black town cars as they seem to slowly drift away. I've always imagined what it must feel like to take a deep breath and soak in New York City. To be watching Fifth Avenue with reverence. This city has come to life in my mind through so many songs, movies, and television shows, and though it is so much more electric in real life, there is also the possibility of being swept away by the sense of feeling so incredibly small. I hadn't accounted for the fact that a woman in a lilac suit could make me feel so insignificant, and that I'd be standing here realizing nobody else cares about what is life-altering for Annie and me.

"I am kind of dramatic," I admit, sitting on the steps again.

Sebastian nods. "I know."

"So, did you find another Roman statue, or should I find some comfort in a warm and fuzzy Edgar Allan Poe verse?"

He sits next to me. "There's a statue of Athena in Queens."

"I feel like Mrs. Mackenzie will kill us if we go to Queens," I say.

"I feel like you might be right." He turns his phone over

between his fingers. "Well . . . let's take a look at the list."

I pull it out of my pocket, and as I unfold it, the paper is caught, snatched from my fingers by a gust of wind and fluttering toward one of the fountains. I immediately leap up to follow it, and I almost tumble down the stairs, which realistically would be the logical next step in this shit spiral, but I steady myself, giving the paper just enough time to fly away again.

The paper catches the eye of a girl in a sequined champagne dress with multiple canvas tote bags weighing down both of her arms. She catches our list, teetering a bit before glancing from it to me and waving it in the air proudly.

"Thank you, thank you, thank you." I hurry over to her, and once she's handed it over, I hold the paper to my chest and sigh. "Lifesaver."

"No problem." She adjusts the bags on her forearms, revealing deep-set red marks.

"Do you need some help?" I offer.

She inhales, pausing. "I would normally say no, but these actually are *killing* me. If you don't mind?"

"Of course." I fold the paper quickly and stuff it in my back pocket, holding out my hands to take some of the totes from her. They're impossibly heavy and I don't know how she's made it any considerable distance with so many of them draped on her arms.

Sebastian appears beside me, taking a few of the bags from her. He gestures for more, but she assures him she has it from there.

She starts up the steps and I look back warily to Sebastian, who just offers a smile and a shrug.

"Are these for the gala?"

"Yep." She looks back to us. "Raffle prizes or something. I'm just an intern."

"Not *just* an intern," I offer.

"Just an intern," she confirms. "Trust me. I fetch tanning drops and pick chickpeas out of salads."

That doesn't sound entirely fun, and this is clearly another not-so-fun task. Still, I try to remain positive. "No small parts."

"Sure," she laughs.

The girl heads to a different door than I knocked on, and she pulls it open. It's just open. Accessible. Just like that. I hadn't even considered it. Which might be for the best, since opening it and proceeding in would have probably been trespassing or something. But now, we're being invited in, so this is totally legal and totally better.

The woman in the lilac suit seems to be long gone, but I'm distracted by the lobby. A majestic and capacious room, with arches and domes towering above marble floors and a wraparound second-level balcony, it feels even bigger inside than it looks on the outside, just like the Museum of Natural History.

"This way," the girl says, leading us to the right. We pass what must be some kind of information center, which anchors the room and is currently being transformed with flowers and layered, multi-height brass candleholders and elegant cream tapered candlesticks. "They're having the event in the American Wing for some reason. I think people like the façade or something."

We follow her up the most massive stairwell, like it belongs in a European castle, which is also being decorated by crew in black T-shirts and pants.

"I guess they want to do this whole thing. Walking up and then through the Medieval stuff before seeing the American Wing all decorated with the lights and the high-tops and everything. I guess it's, like, an experience."

Sebastian gawks. "How much does all of this even cost?"

"Oh my God." The girl barks a laugh. "It's ungodly. I mean, the amount of money put into throwing these charity events . . . I guess they earn enough in donations and through the silent auction to justify it. But these galas are major."

"Bet your boy Benji will be here," Sebastian says to me.

The girl looks back, continuing to guide us along. "Benji Keaton? Yeah right. Though there are a lot of influential producers and entertainment moguls or whatever coming tonight. I don't think there are any A-list celebs though. Or if there are, my boss hasn't told me. And, anyway, they probably are looking forward to being incognito."

"Incognito?" I ask.

She nods. "It's a masquerade. For no reason at all except to add even *more* drama."

"Right up your alley," Sebastian says, knocking his shoulder against mine in an uncharacteristically friendly display.

I can tell we're coming up on the main event space by the bright pink lights and the bass thudding against the marble floors as Lizzo's voice becomes clearer with every step.

"You guys can take some free food or something for helping me," she says. "I really appreciate this. I think I would have collapsed on the stairs."

Looking around, I realize there isn't anything innately glamorous about collapsing, fetching tanning drops, or picking out chickpeas, but surely there is something about . . . *this*. Surely a moment like this doesn't go unnoticed.

"Do you like your internship?"

The girl makes a humming noise. "Do I like it . . . ? Sure. No. Yeah, I guess. Well . . . I don't know. Entertainment is, like, nepotism and narcissism and never feeling like you're doing enough. And I guess that's not the best environment for things like mental health. But, you know, big opportunities and all that."

"It sounds like a real treat," Sebastian says, effortlessly tapping into a tone that is more asshole than apathetic.

I shoot him a look. "I'm sure it'll pay off."

The girl stops walking. "We basically have to decide if we are willing to sell our souls for a bright future."

"And you're going to?" Sebastian asks.

She shrugs one shoulder. "Ideally no. But I'm a college student trying to survive in New York City. My parents aren't wealthy, I don't have a rich boyfriend. It's not like I have the luxury of being too picky."

"What do you want to do?" I've never seen Sebastian so curious.

"I want to work in costume design," she says. "But it's competitive. And this is the kind of internship that opens doors. It's the kind of internship where you meet people." Then she looks from Sebastian to me. "What about you guys? What do you want to do? What are your names, anyway? I'm Carrie."

"I'm Teddy," I say, since she currently has her eyes locked on mine. "And I have no idea what I want to do."

Sebastian raises a brow. "He's going to be a famous pop star, probably."

My cheeks burn and my chest lights up—starts buzzing like Sebastian's playing Operation and he's just dragging the metal against the borders on purpose. I can't tell what this searing feeling actually is. It's some blend of surprise and embarrassment and the near-violent urge to deny.

"I am *not*," I say, hating how I involuntarily add a laugh that sounds much too nervous. "Why would you say that?"

Sebastian ignores me and offers the ghost of a smile, ever so slight, to Carrie. "And I'm Sebastian. I'm hoping to be a geneticist."

"You are?" Again, involuntary.

"Geneticist," Carrie says, mouthing it over and over like it's a foreign word she's never heard. "Are you getting a degree in, like, genetics?"

"Molecular biology," he says. "I just accepted a spot at MIT in the fall."

"You *did*?" I don't mean to sound shocked, but I am.

Carrie smiles. "You two are funny. Are you . . . ?"

She gestures her hand between us.

"No," I say immediately. More involuntary nervous laughter. "Why do people keep asking that?"

Sebastian quirks a brow.

"There you are, thank God."

We're stopped before the American Wing, before the grand reveal, which I nearly stand on my tiptoes to catch a peek of. A girl in a scarlet floor-length dress rushes over, the fabric pooled around her feet and snaking from side to side like an ocean current as she shimmies toward us.

"Who are your friends?" Scarlet Gown asks, giving us a wave. "Carrie is always adopting strays." Then she winces. "Not that you're strays."

"And Ruby is always putting her foot in her mouth," Carrie teases, offering us an apologetic smile. "They're just two kind citizens who offered to help with these absolute death traps. Teddy and Sebastian."

"How generous," she says.

I nod. "We're here for a school trip. We do this scavenger hunt for our drama club, and we came to the Met to get a picture, but it was closed early, obviously, and then Carrie saved us when the list almost flew away, and here we are."

"Where are we offloading these?"

"We'll pass them along to Harper and Viv," says a

voice from behind Scarlet Gown. It's a guy, and when he appears, wearing a fancy black suit with a satin bowtie and holding up a black masquerade mask, he offers a friendly smile. He runs his hand through his hair—a dark brown tangle of curls that suits him and helps his formal vibe feel just the right amount of effortless.

It takes a second, because he's the last person I'm expecting to see here, but the second he drops the mask, I gasp: *I know this guy!* He was in the drama club, a year older than me, and he wrote some plays.

"Harry Kensington?"

"Teddy McGuire!" He rushes over and envelops me in a hug. "No way. Are you here for the senior trip?"

"Yeah, there's a scavenger hunt item at the Met," I say. It's a warm feeling, to unexpectedly run into someone from home. "What are you doing here?"

Harry gestures back toward the American Wing. "I have this part-time job as a personal assistant for a producer who splits his time between LA and New York, and he's one of the honorees tonight."

"Personal assistants get to go to things like this?" Sebastian looks impressed.

Ruby smirks. "When your boss is batshit and needs emotional support."

"Ruby." Harry's eyes widen. "He's not entirely batshit. He's just going through a divorce. And his guru is on a wellness retreat, or she'd be here instead."

"A guru." I nod. "This all sounds very Hollywood."

"Totally," Harry says. "All of us have to wear these crystal bracelets to protect the energy. But he won't even need me tonight. Lloyd is totally preoccupied with this set designer who is coming tonight. They went to a spin class together this morning and then to some super bougie herbal tea brewery or something after. He won't even notice if I'm here."

There's a tinge of annoyance, and I watch Harry shut his eyes and inhale.

"Sorry, it's fine. I'm excited to be here."

Carrie scrunches her nose. "How convincing."

"I'm sure it'll be fun," I offer.

Harry smiles. "Yeah, totally. It's just that my boyfriend has this really big dinner tonight—he's trying to score a major internship—and I wanted to be there for him. This kind of thing happens all the time, so . . ."

"So, it's frustrating your boss keeps you around without any regard for what's important to you or happening in your life?" Sebastian tilts his head.

"Kind of." Harry laughs. "But it's okay. It'll be fine."

"Or your relationship will suffer like Lloyd's did," Ruby counters, dodging a pointed glare from Carrie. "I'm just saying. This is, like, the third thing you've missed."

I frown. "I wish there was something we could do to help."

"Thanks," Harry chuckles. "But unless you can think of some way to be two places at once . . ."

"Or if there were two of you," Carrie hums.

Ruby, Carrie, and Harry exchange looks.

"Oh my God." Ruby's mouth turns into a sharp smile. "Yes, yes, yes. I'm living for this. Keeping it interesting for once."

"Sorry, living for what?" I ask.

Harry raises a brow. "No way, it wouldn't work."

"It would too," Carrie says. "You *just* said Lloyd is going to be preoccupied. Anyway, he doesn't need *you*, he just needs *someone*."

"Oh, no way," Sebastian says, holding his hands up.

How is everyone having an entire conversation without me? What the hell is happening?

"And this would be so *fun*," Ruby pleads. "You guys have the same eyes and face shape."

I bite my lip, realizing their grand idea. "Uh . . ."

"I mean, it could go horribly wrong . . ." Harry says, looking off down the hallway, biting at his knuckle before looking to me. "Teddy, what do you say to a little fun New York adventure?"

"I don't know . . ."

"Look, it's only for an hour or two. I just want to lend emotional support during his dinner and then I'm free while they have their business talk." Harry shrugs. "You can have some good food, get your scavenger hunt item checked off, and by the time they get to any of the important stuff for the night, I'll be back."

"I don't think anyone will believe I'm you," I offer.

He studies me. "Sure they will. It's a masquerade. That's

what makes this absolutely bonkers plan so perfect! We'll ruffle your hair a little, and you'll be set."

"What about me?" Sebastian asks.

"Right," I say, trying to process all of the potential outcomes here before I commit to anything. I tug on my bracelet, and I can hear Annie now: *Just do it! It sounds like a scene in a movie!* But it also sounds like it could get all kinds of screwed up.

"Of course." Harry nods. "You and your . . ."

"Sebastian," I blurt.

"Right, you and your Sebastian." He fights a laugh and turns to Sebastian. "Well, you're already in, so you can just act like you're supposed to be here." He looks him up and down. "You might be a little tall, but you can wear my backup suit . . ."

"You have a backup suit?" Sebastian blinks.

"You never know when you'll need another suit," he says. "Clearly."

Chapter 12

Chip on My Shoulder

The plan is simple. Keep my mask on, wave from afar if I see Lloyd, who I've received a thorough mini seminar on, and if he gets too close, pretend to be on a very important phone call before disappearing briefly. Allegedly, he'll be way too stuck on the set designer to even look for Harry/me, so it should be smooth sailing.

The plan might be simple, but the whirring feeling in my chest is anything but.

Nothing about this is even remotely normal. It doesn't really feel like it's happening on the same plane of reality as the rest of my life. Last week, I was helping to wait tables at my parents' restaurant and sipping gas station ICEEs with Annie. Last week, the biggest event I could fathom was our upcoming graduation ceremony, which takes place at a medium-sized amphitheater at the beach.

Now, I'm in a suit and black masquerade mask in the Metropolitan Museum of Art with Sebastian, who looks alarmingly dashing in a suit that fits him just right, as if by some New York magic. I still have the Polaroid camera around my neck, and I'm hoping nobody notices how out of place it is or asks for a photo, since we only have a limited amount of film.

The night is happening in slow motion. Beneath the courtyard's skylight, it's an evening under the stars, with impossibly gorgeous, masked figures sipping bubbling champagne from crystal flutes, glowing beneath the strings of sparkling lights. It's cinematic and glamorous and a violinist is playing trending instrumentals with a little added bass.

"You look stressed," Sebastian says as we get to an unclaimed high-top that's elegantly dressed in a black linen cloth and warmly lit by votives.

"I'm impersonating someone. And I feel very out of place here," I say, setting the camera on the table. "Overall, yes, it's kind of stressful."

He scoffs. "*You* feel out of place? You think I'm in my element? At least you fit in."

"I don't fit in any more than you do."

"You do, too. Disco ball birthday party, McGuire."

"What does that even mean?"

"You just fit in. Here. In a place like this."

Sebastian seems to think he knows an awful lot about me. I want to take it as a compliment, but there's not really a single fiber of my being that feels like I have anything in common with these guests.

"Why did you say that back there?"

Sebastian pouts. "Which thing?"

"About me being a famous pop star?"

A waiter walks by with a tray of hors d'oeuvres, and Sebastian grabs a napkin and a couple of fancy-looking tiny snacks, thanking him. I don't take any, but I do raise my brows, waiting for his answer.

"Did that upset you?"

"No, it didn't *upset* me. I just don't understand why you would say that."

Smoothing his hair with his free hand before shoving one of the hors d'oeuvres into his mouth, Sebastian looks off. Once he's finished, he goes to eat another, but I stop him.

"Hello?"

"Hmm?" He cocks his head.

"We were having a conversation," I sigh. How is one human being so impossible? So predictable, yet, in fleeting moments, far from expectations.

"I know, but I'm also hungry. We haven't had dinner." He eats his little green hors d'oeuvre and sets the napkin on the table, rubbing his hands together. "All right. You were asking why I said you're going to be a famous pop star?"

I nod. "What would possess you? It's so . . ."

"Well, I just don't see you seriously pursuing Broadway—you've never expressed interest in it like Eden. Not that you couldn't, it just doesn't seem like your goal. But I do think you love music. And you have the personality to be a pop star, I guess. You don't think you will be?"

"I certainly do not, Sebastian."

His lip curls. "Sorry, I think I missed the part where saying you would be a famous pop star was an insult."

"It isn't an insult."

"But you're offended by it?"

"I'm not *offended*."

"You're bothered."

"I'm not bothered, Sebastian." I groan and drum my palms on the table. "I . . . did used to think I wanted to be a *musician*. But I can't."

This causes his smile to drop immediately.

"You could absolutely be a musician." He says it sternly. "Give me one reason why not."

"I don't have anything to say." I shrug. "There's *the* reason. What draws me to Benji, creatively, is how he tells stories. How he makes art. It's not necessarily the pop star part, but what he does with his voice and his talents. He's a songwriter before a pop star, and songwriters tell stories. They express things. Connect with people. They're creative. They create."

Clearly not willing to let this go, Sebastian shakes his head. "You express tons of things. You connect with people. And you actually are creative, so I'm confused."

"I play characters, though. Sing other people's songs. And I'm good with that. Songwriters like Benji create art, I just present it."

"Well, what's stopping you from creating it?" He looks around. "Want a drink?"

"Like, alcohol?"

"If you want?"

"We're on a school trip," I whisper. "Mrs. Mackenzie would flip."

He smiles at one of the waiters with a tray of champagne, accepting two flutes. Handing me one, he clinks our glasses together. "And she wouldn't flip if she knew we basically snuck into a black-tie masquerade gala?"

"Fair," I say, taking a careful sip. I take advantage of the distraction to change the subject. "You're going to MIT?"

"That's the plan." He says it quickly, not interested in elaborating. Or redirecting. "What's stopping you from creating art?"

"I don't have anything to say," I repeat. "Look at any great songwriters. Their songs are about their lives. About people and feelings and you can't just make up that kind of stuff. It has to come from a real place to mean something. I don't have any salt and pepper shakers."

"Salt and pepper shakers?"

"They were a gift."

"Salt and pepper shakers . . ."

"Benji has a song about the salt and pepper shakers he can't get rid of. And it's obviously a lot more than that. But I don't have anything given to me by someone who broke my heart or whatever."

He nods. "So, you don't have salt and pepper shakers. I'm sure there's some story you can tell."

"But there isn't." I pause, noticing a slight tinge of embarrassment over the admission that's coming next. Because maybe there's something wrong with me—maybe it's my fault somehow. "I've never been in love. Never had my heart broken."

"Careful saying that," he says. "I know you believe in jinxes, and I would enjoy being a stranger to heartbreak for as long as you can."

He swallows.

"Was that sincere advice?" I hold my hand to my heart and take a sip of champagne. "What happened?"

"I just know heartbreak," he says. "Old friend. We go way back."

"Be serious." I set the flute down on the table. "I didn't know you dated anyone?"

"Junior year up until this fall. He went to another school."

For someone who's typically monotone unless sarcastic, this is a new tone. Solemn. Remembering, I think, in real time. I watch his eyes darken as he purses his lips.

"But it's fine. I mean, I'm fine."

"I'm sorry," I offer. If anything, I can tell he's not fine. "I haven't ever been through it, but I've imagined it a lot. Is that weird? And not, like, yearning for sadness or anything. It's not that I'm desperate to have my heart broken, but somehow, I swear music can actually make us feel things we've never experienced. And I know listening to songs about it isn't even remotely close to what you went through, but I can only imagine it wasn't easy."

Sebastian nods slowly. "I think it's the worst and the best thing. It hurts and it feels insurmountable, sure. But we grow and learn from the hard shit. It's just how life works. No point in trying to get around it or avoid it. Best to just put our heads down and make our way through."

"Maybe *you* could write a song," I say.

"I don't know about that."

"Sounds like you could." I bite my lip. "Sounds like you've got salt and pepper shakers."

Sebastian furrows his brow. "Can't your magical lucky bracelet help with the songwriting?"

"No," I say. "It doesn't just, like, give talents. I already was good at singing and acting before I had the bracelet, so it just helped me do well. But songwriting . . . Not so much."

This troubles him, and he brings his finger to his lips, which form a frown. "Who exactly makes the rules here?

For how the magic and the luck work?"

"Well, I guess in this case, me." The rules are based on years of observation, but he clearly is a nonbeliever.

Sebastian scoffs. "You can't just make up rules and then say they can't change."

I narrow my eyes. "Well, Sebastian, who makes the rules of science?"

"People who do a lot of research," he says. "And the rules of science *constantly* change with new information."

I offer a tight-lipped smile. "I know science is real and how it works, I just was trying to prove a point."

A text comes through and I straighten up. "Harry says Lloyd is running late, so we can get the scavenger hunt photo now if we're quick."

"Okay." He nods, standing tall and looking me in the eye. "Tell me something that makes you sad."

"What?"

"Anything. Well, except for Benji Keaton songs. Something from your life. What makes you want to cry just thinking about it?"

The answer comes to me instantly, but I hesitate, because I don't want to cry in the freaking Met wearing Harry's suit.

"Let's just go find the Roman statues," I suggest. "Before Lloyd gets here."

He shifts. "I saw that."

"What now?"

"I saw your face. You thought of something."

"Sebastian, you cannot just ask someone what makes them want to cry," I say. I down the rest of the champagne and leave the flute and Sebastian at the high-top, heading toward a glass door with the Polaroid camera in hand. I'm not sure where the hell I am or where the Roman statues are, but I'll find them eventually.

As I make my way back into the central Medieval area, with the giant choir screen and religious statues, I hear footsteps catching up behind me.

"I wasn't trying to upset you," Sebastian huffs.

I keep walking, and I wave it off. "I'm not upset."

"You seem upset," he says, running just to stop beside me. I indulge him, pausing and turning to face him. "But can you tell me what it was?"

I'm not a stranger to being sad, and I know most of the time when I am, it's because I'm being melodramatic. I'm romanticizing something or finding a flaw or problem where there isn't one. My life isn't that hard, and overall, I should just be a happy kid. So, I try to be. Usually, people would say a masquerade gala in New York City is not the optimal time to trigger feelings of melancholy for the sake of conversation.

"This isn't the place for a conversation about sadness," I offer.

Sebastian lowers his eyes. "We're alone, in a quiet hall of Medieval sculptures."

"But we're at a gala," I argue. "And if I talk about it,

I'm going to get upset. Now, even thinking about it, I am starting to feel sad."

And I am. Because when I think about this, I don't think I am being melodramatic Teddy. I don't think I'm conjuring up grief for the sake of a part or because things have gotten boring. This isn't the same thing as listening to a Benji song alone in my room or overlooking the ocean.

Sebastian implores me, with his brows and the way his eyes soften, to go on.

"My whole entire life is going to change," I sigh. The bridge of my nose is tingling, and my chest is beginning to feel like there's an elephant on top of it. I fight mist forming over my eyes. "When we graduate, Annie is going to move to London."

Frowning, Sebastian nods. "Right."

"We talk about how it'll be fun, and exciting to share our new lives with each other over FaceTime." I swallow. "But it won't be like that. She really will have a new, fun, and thrilling life. She'll be going on adventures and meeting people who show her new corners of the world. She'll be five hours ahead, and we'll talk a lot in the beginning, I'm sure. But then one day we'll realize we haven't talked in a while. Or she will, probably, because I'll be painfully aware of it. And at that point, our friendship will be different. Everything will be different."

That hangs between us in this room. There's a gravity to what I've said. A gravity I haven't even fully accepted or said out loud before. But it's true—how could it not be?

Annie's moving to London, and she's going to grow, and travel, and learn about herself. And I'll be back in Citrus Harbor. Like always.

"I can't handle the thought of Annie and I growing apart," I say. "So, when you ask what makes me want to cry—that's it."

Sebastian nods. "I'm not going to stand here and offer some niceties. I'm not going to say you're wrong or that everything is going to stay the same, but I also don't believe it's going to be as bad as you think."

Now that the conversation is happening, I'm fully suffocated by the feeling of losing Annie. Because that's what this is. That's what this feels like.

"You guys are so close; she's not just going to forget about you because she moves away and makes new friends."

"You don't have to do this," I say, pushing my knuckle up against my eye when a tear nearly rolls out. "It's fine. I know it probably sounds nuts, anyway. I tend to be dramatic."

Rolling his eyes and then offering a smile, Sebastian folds his arms. "I don't think you're being dramatic." He brightens. "For once."

I sniffle and laugh. "Well, thanks."

"Anyway, I asked you that because I think that is your story."

"My best friend moving to London?"

He shakes his head. "Your friendship."

"I don't think I'm following. How is that a story?"

Sebastian starts walking, and when I follow, he keeps his eyes locked ahead. "Maybe you don't have salt and pepper shakers, Teddy. But you've got other things. Friendship bracelets."

Chapter 13

Lost!

Sebastian and I find ourselves in another empty hall, only this seems to be exactly the right place. It all feels very European—with one wall made up of white marble stone and arches, while the opposing wall is an entire building's façade, almost like this is an extension of an old building beneath a glass ceiling bridging the connection. Which it likely is, the more I look at it. I do remember reading that there have been different iterations and additions to the Met when I was researching.

"When in Rome," Sebastian says dryly, scanning the various statues.

"How do we know which ones are Greek or Roman?"

"No idea."

My mind has temporarily wandered from the scavenger hunt, which I can't quite believe, but I can't stop thinking about what Sebastian said. Is there really a story I can tell about my friendship with Annie? I've tried to write poems and songs about things I haven't gone through like love and heartbreak, but those have been failures. Regurgitated phrases and mirrored lyricism lacking authenticity and emotion.

But what if I wrote about a subject that meant something to me?

"Oh, this one." Sebastian rushes over to a statue. "Nope. French. Damn it. These all look Roman to me."

In the middle of the room, there's a statue of Perseus holding Medusa's head. "Isn't that Roman?"

Sebastian shakes his head. "No, it's Greek. Percy Jackson?"

I nod, walking over to it. "But it says the artist is Italian. So . . ."

"Hmm."

"Will Mrs. Mackenzie really disqualify us? We're not going to be art majors. How are we supposed to know all these things?"

I pull out my phone and look up the artist. "Antonio Canova . . ." I say mindlessly. "Perseus . . ." I do some skimming and then shrug. "I think it was sculpted in Rome."

Sebastian nods. "Let's take a selfie with Perseus and Medusa, then."

"We should probably try to cover his . . ."

"Penis?" Sebastian quirks a brow.

"Yeah."

"You can say it," he says.

"Will you just get in front of the statue?"

Sebastian walks over and looks at me expectantly.

"We're supposed to mirror the pose," I say. "You can be Medusa."

"Why can't you be Medusa?"

"You're taller, and Perseus has his arm stretched above him to hold up Medusa's head. It just makes sense."

This is amusing to him, I guess, because his mouth forms the tiniest smile. "Okay, let's do it."

Posing like the victorious Perseus, I grab a fistful of his hair and can't even hide my laugh when he gives me a pointed look.

"Easy, McGuire."

"Say '*oh no, I just got my head chopped off!*'"

Holding out the camera as far as I can, I get us into a strategic angle and take a photo of us with the statue. As the picture comes out, I take it between my fingers and wave it around triumphantly. "We're making progress, Sebastian."

"That much closer to meeting Benji."

"That much closer."

We are fully on schedule. Which means meeting Benji is actually a very real possibility still. Of course it is, because I know I will be handing Annie a signed bracelet when I get back to Citrus Harbor. But this means I need to figure out what I'm even going to say to Benji.

"What if I make a total fool of myself?" I blurt out.

Sebastian is a few yards away, looking at another sculpture. "I don't think you will. Unless you're a fainter."

"I'm not going to faint," I say. "At least, I don't have a history of fainting. What if I cry or something? I don't want to cry."

With his hands together behind his back, Sebastian studies one of the statues. "If you think you're about to cry, just think of something funny."

"But what if it's, like, one of those moments where all of my thoughts fly out of my brain and all I can think about is the fact that I'm in the presence of Benji Keaton and I just cry?"

"Or faint," Sebastian adds. "We can't rule it out completely."

"Not helping," I say.

He keeps walking farther, the echoes of his footsteps getting quieter as he moves toward another sculpture. "Do you have anything that helps calm you down?"

"Kind of. I don't know if anything will work in this situation, though."

There's a lump forming in my throat, and it's not because I might faint or cry or find myself speechless in front of Benji. It's because now, I hear the things I said about Annie leaving. My mistake was admitting them out loud. Now I feel that sense of loss. I feel the reminder that our bracelet might one day be a memory in a box. Her friends in London might not think it's cool, and though Annie's not one to care much about what others think, maybe they'll get her something more stylish and her Benji-signed bracelet will go in her nightstand drawer.

I swallow the lump and try to avoid the way it almost makes me feel lifeless, even in New York City at the Met in this fancy suit, to walk toward a life where Annie and I aren't attached at the hip. It isn't imaginary. It's inevitable.

This is all Sebastian's fault, really. This sinking, viscous sadness in my chest. If he didn't ask me that question to try to *inspire* me or whatever. Maybe I would just be enjoying this night with all its extraordinary circumstances.

"What's *your* thing?" I ask, desperate to shift the focus from me entirely.

He looks back. "What do you mean?"

"What makes you want to cry just thinking about it?" I clarify.

"I don't want to—there isn't anything that makes me want to cry."

There's a sharpness to his delivery that's more pointed than I've ever heard him, even at his most sarcastic.

"Oh, come on. You made me tell you mine."

His jaw flexes as he looks up at the sculpture in front of him. It's a woman, chained to a rock, reaching up. To be saved, maybe?

"Nothing makes me want to cry."

I laugh, and I don't know what exactly is happening right now, but it's bringing back that irritating, prickling sensation—like it's burning beneath my skin. Why can he push and prod and poke, but when I ask him the same question, he's irritable and standoffish?

It's thanks to him I'm hyper focused on the Annie thing. It's thanks to him I'm forced to face the fact that I don't have anything to say and can't write songs, which I'd come to terms with and buried a long time ago. He gets to blow up my emotional state like it's no big deal—and for what, I have literally no clue—but he can't bother to answer.

"It doesn't make you cool," I say.

He chuckles, then lifts his shoulders and turns to face me. "I'm not trying to be cool."

"Graduation?" I offer. "Or a sad movie?"

Silence. He's back to mysterious Sebastian. Back to withholding.

"A particular work of Edgar Allan Poe . . ."

Why can't he just share something? Why does he expect me to, but then he's exempt?

He can dish it, but he can't take it, and his silence is irritating me more and more. It's also a stark reminder of the purposeful fog surrounding his secret plans. The agitation leaps up my throat.

"Or is it what you mentioned earlier?"

This gets his attention. "What?"

"Is it your ex?"

As soon as I say it, I realize there's not going to be any satisfying response from him now. My annoyance with him isn't going to be resolved by me picking back, and I might have just gone a step too far, bringing up something I know nothing about.

"It's not my ex," he says, his voice low and gruff. "Why are you being like this?"

"Me?" I scoff. "I was just asking you the same question you asked me."

He finally turns back to face me, and his eyes are somehow darker. "And I gave you the answer."

"You gave me *an* answer," I counter. "You're a terrible liar."

"Am I?" He takes a few steps toward me. "Well, this might be really shocking to you, but we can't all live in a fantasy world."

All this progress we'd made, so swiftly thrown away.

For a split second, everything goes blurry. Annoyance is engulfed by rage, but it only lasts a moment before it's extinguished, doused by a sense of sadness. A sense of hurt. Just a few moments ago, we were laughing like friends, but now he's putting me down and there is no familiarity in his eyes, only coldness.

"I thought for a second there we were getting along," I say, my voice coming out a little too shattered for my liking. If only I could employ my acting skills right now. If only I could act like my feelings aren't hurt.

"I think, clearly, trying to force a friendship here is a mistake."

I shake my head. "What is happening right now? Is this all seriously because I asked—"

"Let's just not do this. Okay? I'm doing the scavenger hunt, right? I agreed to do this. And we got our last picture for the night, so we're done." He stalks off toward the Medieval hall.

"Sebastian, stop."

"I'm going," he says over his shoulder, not slowing down.

I cannot believe this.

"What am I supposed to do?"

"Go pretend to be Harry and drink champagne and have fun and then when you're done living your NYC fairy-tale adventure moment, take a cab down Fifth to the hotel. Maybe Harry will invite you to an after-party with disco balls and A-listers."

"You're just going to leave me alone?"

"You need cab money?"

"No, I don't need cab money." He keeps walking, winding between marble statues, and my thoughts and my heart are racing. "Sebastian, please, just wait. I don't even know why we're fighting right now, and I'd like to—"

He stops, turns on his heel. "We're not fighting."

"We are, aren't we?"

"No, we're not. We're just not pretending anymore."

Chapter 14

No Good Deed

I wander around for a moment before sinking down to sit against one of the cold marble walls in an empty corridor like I'm in an early 2000s music video.

It's not like Sebastian owes me anything at all, not even kindness or sensitivity, but the way he left just has me feeling like I mean absolutely nothing to him. The way he said we were pretending, when I was so sure that we were getting more real. How could all of that have been an act?

Maybe everyone is right about my head being up in the clouds.

Sebastian's left Harry's extra tux in the closet, and the Polaroid photo of us burns in my pocket.

Plus, now, dejected and indulging in a melodramatic moment, I'm left with the painful thoughts about Annie moving away. I'd never been able to fully avoid it before, but now it's been brought to the surface and it's not going away anytime soon.

A melodramatic moment during a black-tie gala at the Met was not on my New York bingo card, but maybe it should have been. This is somehow unsurprising and shocking all at once.

I open the Notes app in my phone, fingers hovering over the keys.

With no clear direction of where it's going, I type out a few simple words, and then I backspace, and then I type a few more, and then I delete it all.

Why don't I have anything to say?

Sighing, I figure that's a place to begin, so I start again:

Words don't come easily,

Not like people leaving

Too dark. Too depressing. I just don't want that to be my thing.

Why, then, am I only coming up with lines in moments like this? Why can't I come up with something sparkly and fun?

I don't want to feel sorry for myself. Even if there's an aching in my core, and my entire being feels heavy, I don't want to feel sorry for myself.

I manage to get up and dust myself off, metaphorically and literally, and remind myself I'm here to play pretend. I need to be Harry—be happy, living in New York City with a cute boyfriend and fun friends. I'm living my best life.

Only I'm so not. I'm tortured by the echoes of Sebastian

leaving and the reality of Annie going away for university. Those pits in my stomach don't go away no matter how big I smile at strangers as I pull my masquerade mask back on and reenter the hall.

My energy is depleting with all the overthinking, but I look around and I'm reminded this might be a once-in-a-lifetime thing. Maybe I'll end up at more masquerade events, but will they have giant chandeliers lying around, installed as art pieces with masks and tinsel strung about their brass finishes? Will they be *this* swanky? Couture gowns with hand beading that reflects light like mermaid tails?

A waiter offers me a glass of champagne, which I refuse politely. I'm here alone, after all, and I need to be present and aware of everything happening. I need to keep an eye out for Lloyd, and then keep a healthy distance. I need to keep everything in order.

And then I need to navigate back to the hotel on my own. Harry will help, I'm sure, or at least one of his friends will. I'd forgotten about them, actually, and I look around for allies in this crowded room that smells like expensive, woody perfumes.

I spot the champagne and scarlet dresses at one of the high-tops and hurry over to Carrie and Ruby. They're watching the crowd with a diligence, like hawks eyeing prey.

"Hey, *Harry*." Ruby smirks.

Carrie laughs and turns to me. "How's it going?"

"Oh, it's going great," I say. "Really awesome."

Ruby looks around. "Where's your date?"

"Not my date," I correct. "And he left."

Carrie and Ruby exchange glances.

"It's not like that," I say. Suddenly I wish I'd come up with something clever to say instead, but now it's out there. "He's not really into the whole black-tie gala thing."

Carrie nods. "Right."

"Seen Lloyd yet?" Ruby asks. "I'm curious if this is actually going to work."

My jaw falls open. "What do you mean you're *curious*? I thought you said this was a brilliant plan! Foolproof, even?"

"In theory!" Ruby shrugs. "In theory . . ."

"There he is." Carrie points toward the far corner of the room, past the golden statue of an archer.

My heart threatens to beat out of my chest when I see him. Certainly the man from the photos Harry showed me—an intimidating, surgically modified jawline and thick brows visible even behind his red mask. His black hair is slicked back, and while I can't see the salt and pepper from here, I can see the distinct stripes of gray above his ears.

I struggle to draw in breath when he looks over and spots me, too.

This is the moment.

Standing up tall, I am suffocated by the weight of this incredibly impulsive decision. My chest is constricted, like a boa wraps around me and squeezes as tight and viciously as possible, purposefully trying to pop my lungs.

What even happens when he comes over here and realizes I'm not Harry? Because how believable can I be, really? I'm a good actor, but I don't sound like Harry, and I'm a little shorter. We don't have the exact same mannerisms. There are a hundred tells, I'm sure, including some I can't even think of.

Will he escort me out? Fire Harry?

What have we done?

I want to puke. I want to run away, and given the way the night has been going, I just want to go cry somewhere. Now, locking eyes with Lloyd across the courtyard, I suddenly *do* want to feel sorry for myself because for all my optimism and for all my lucky bracelet can do, I fear Harry and I have set ourselves up for failure here.

Instinctively, the thought of my lucky bracelet causes me to tug at the string hanging out from the shirt and suit sleeve.

Lloyd nods my way.

And then, just before he starts to walk toward me, he's intercepted.

I pause, breath held, to see if he redirects back to me, but he doesn't. Instead, he laughs and walks off with a couple of model-tall women in sleek black dresses and feathered masks.

"Oh my God," I exhale.

Carrie and Ruby are unaffected, paying attention to their phones.

The nerves don't have anywhere to go, though, and there's no release of sweet relief. Instead, they are starting to pour into layers of tears on the bottoms of my eyes.

"Are you okay?" Ruby asks, glancing up and cocking her head.

I sniffle, nodding quickly and hoping against all odds I will be able to keep it together for once. Tonight is just a little bit too heavy though, what with the talk of Annie leaving and whatever that was with Sebastian, and it's not something that's going away no matter how hard I will it to.

Instead, it swells.

"Oh . . ." Carrie says slowly.

In an attempt to get far, far away from here now that Lloyd has seen me, I step backward, desperate to escape before the tears start to fall.

At the same time, it's slow motion and it's too quick to avoid—the tip of Harry's dress shoe, just a little too long, catches on the flooding tablecloth and I stumble back, grasping at the air for anything to catch my fall. A man behind me catches me by my elbow and I am able to steady myself, but not before my shoulder knocks into a woman in a white gown and crimson wine splashes from her glass all over the ivory fabric.

I gasp, and so does everyone around us, and now the tears are just going to do their thing.

"I'm so sorry!"

My hands wave around in a weak attempt to do literally

anything, but she's rushing away and her husband, the guy who'd caught me, is running after her.

I'm left standing there, with Ruby and Carrie covering their mouths, and a small crowd around us watching me like a carnival act.

That's my cue, I think, to exit stage right. I hurry away and I don't even know where to at this point, but I find myself once again sitting on the ground with my back against the marble wall.

I tear off the mask and cry for a minute or two, now a mix of so many emotions I can't possibly name them—shame and embarrassment rearing their ugly heads to act as the headliners—and I debate calling Annie. But I don't want to get into the fact that half the reason I'm so upset is because I'm looping scenarios in my mind obsessively as if I'm already grieving our friendship.

"There he is."

Ruby and Carrie are escorting Harry over, and they leave him with me after making sure I'm okay. I assure them I am—*perfectly fine, just overdramatic and out of my league.*

Harry sinks down next to me.

"You're back early?"

"Only by a few minutes," he says. "Had a feeling I should get back sooner than later."

"I don't think Lloyd realized it was me," I offer, wiping at my cheeks with the back of my hand.

Harry offers a small smile. "What's wrong? Ruby and

Carrie said there was an incident with wine?"

"Oh no," I say, now looking at Harry and putting it together. "Everyone's going to think *you* knocked into that woman."

He waves his hand. "Pfft. I've done way worse. Don't worry about it."

I laugh. "I'm really sorry."

"Honestly, don't give it another thought," he says. Then he sighs, running his hand through his hair. "This was an exceptionally questionable idea, even by my standards. *I'm* sorry. I shouldn't have asked you to do this."

I shake my head. "No, you were right, it was a fun New York adventure."

Harry lifts a brow. "Seems like you're having plenty of fun." He glances around. "Where's Sebastian?"

My voice squeaks when I try to talk, and my cheeks go hot.

"Oh." Harry nods.

"He just had to go."

Harry's quiet for a moment. Then he sighs and links his hands together. "Are you guys going to be okay?"

Now I'm quiet. Because I don't know the answer to that, and I didn't realize just how much I cared about us being okay. I knew my feelings were hurt, but I was removed from the fact that I was starting to like the friendship that we were starting. And I don't think I believe it was pretending.

"I think I am just too much," I say finally. "You know?

Do you ever feel like you're too much and you just can't get anything right?"

Harry laughs. "You're talking to the king of being too much and not getting anything right, Teddy. But you have to give yourself some grace and know it'll be okay. And anyway, who decides what 'too much' is?"

"I just never know when to quit," I say. "I push too far or something. I should have let it go."

Of course, Harry doesn't know what I'm talking about, so I walk him through the basics. Annie not coming on the trip, having Sebastian as my partner, the ways I'm starting to get to know him, and all of the Benji in between.

"I love Benji," Harry says. He beams. "My best friend, Hailey, and I slept in a parking garage once to see him."

"As you should," I laugh, thankful for the levity.

Harry knocks his knee against mine. "I don't think you're too much, Teddy. I think, probably, you and Sebastian had a long day. Probably, you're both a little tired, hungry, maybe a little moody?"

I laugh again.

"And I think you and Annie are going to be perfectly fine," he adds. "I cried when I left Citrus Harbor and Hailey stayed in Florida. And it is different now. But we're totally still best friends. It's normal—part of life, even—especially after graduation. But it'll be okay. I think this is all just . . ."

"Dramatic?"

He lifts his shoulders. "Maybe a little. But as someone

who is also dramatic, I would say you should just focus on moving forward. You guys have a full day tomorrow, and then Friday too."

"If Sebastian will even do the rest of the scavenger hunt with me," I say.

Harry purses his lips. "I'm sure he will. And, also, if I may give you some advice about that whole song thing? Writer to writer?"

"Please."

"When I feel like you're feeling . . ." He offers a look, a softness in his gaze, that tells me he really does understand. "It always helps to write it out. Maybe the words won't be perfect, but there's something helpful about channeling into your creativity."

I run my fingers over the braided threads of my bracelet. "It's not like I've never tried that. I even performed for the talent show . . . and my song was humiliating. The metaphor was so juvenile, like I was an elementary schoolkid." I groan, and when I can tell he's waiting for details, I grit my teeth. "I wrote about feeling like a butterfly onstage. I want to cringe just thinking about it."

In theory, it was a nice idea. Meaningful, even. My grandma always said I was like a butterfly, and she still says it every time she sees me perform. It felt so deep in the privacy of my room. But out loud? Not so great if you don't have the wordsmithing talents of Benji Keaton.

Harry shrugs. "It sounds like there's something there."

I shake my head. "And then, when I do finally get

inspiration to write again, it's depressing."

"Well, not all songs are happy."

"Just look at Benji's career, though," I say. "He started out with the *Seventeen Summers* album, and that's what made everyone love him. And he only got into more emotional, deeper music later on."

Harry tilts his head. "But you're not Benji."

"Of course I'm not," I say. "I just don't want to only write sad songs. I don't even have reasons to be sad. I want to write happy, upbeat things. And I want to inspire people."

"You don't have to deny your feelings, Teddy."

"I'm not," I say.

"Well, I think you should write whatever comes to you, and worry about the rest after. You never know what might inspire people. But maybe easier said than done. What do I know?"

"You know plenty. Thanks, Harry."

He grins. "Anytime. Especially for a fellow Citrus Harbor thespian. I mean, what are the odds?"

"Fated."

"Totally. Though I think I do need to change into my suit and go back to the gala. Will you be okay?"

I stand up and grab Harry's hand to help him up, too. "I'll be great."

"Yeah, I know you will."

Chapter 15

Something Bad

The pep talk worked temporary wonders, but when I get back to the hotel lobby, I swear I've never felt more excited to just lie in bed and listen to sad music and get all of this out of my system.

Eden is sitting on one of the velvet couches near the front desk, dolled up in a blue striped dress.

"What's wrong with you?" she asks, tone dry and uninterested.

I might have cried a little in the back of the cab, watching all the lights and happy people on Fifth Avenue. I don't know how things went south so quickly, but it feels absolutely horrible. And somehow, even after talking with Harry, fighting with Sebastian has sucked all the magic out of New York City for the evening. The cinematic nature of a nighttime cab ride after a magical gala, with the Empire State Building slowly coming into view, or the glamour of the hotel and the sounds of the city outside the window—all reduced to background static as I tried to figure out where things went so horribly wrong.

Confrontation is not my favorite thing. Honestly, sometimes even playing a role where there is too much confrontation gives me anxiety, but this isn't just a part.

The last person I want to confide in is Eden.

"Nothing," I say, forcing a smile even though I know she can clearly tell I've been crying. "Just a rough night."

"Can't be any worse than mine." She blows out a breath and rolls her eyes.

I pause. I'm not sure what's happening here. Eden isn't one to open up about a rough night or console someone in a hotel lobby just because.

"What happened?" I tread lightly.

"My mother ditched me at dinner for some old college friends. They're going to a club."

I genuinely don't mean to, but I can't help but laugh. "Your mom is going to a club?"

"She is going to a club."

"You couldn't get in?"

"I didn't get an invite. She said I needed my beauty rest."

I frown. "Where's Briar?"

"She went to a dessert function with Maribel and Tiffany. A *dessert function*. Whatever the hell that is. Mrs. Mackenzie organized it. Ugh, I don't know why they want to treat this like an actual school trip. I mean, hello, we're eighteen."

"Well, I'm sorry you're by yourself," I say. "But, look, you're in New York! The city that never sleeps. You could go have fun. Maybe go to the dessert social. Eat an ice cream sundae and just, I don't know, dance around or find something entertaining."

Always easier to give advice than to actually follow it.

"Do you want to go together?" Her eyes widen.

"Oh, um," I stammer.

"I'm kidding," she cackles. "I'd sooner die." She raises her brows. "Where is Sebastian?"

"He's . . ." I shift my weight onto one foot.

Eden studies me for longer than normal. But soon enough she gives up waiting for me to answer and stands up. "My mother says not to worry about you and Sebastian for the scavenger hunt. She really wants me to meet with Marcos Britton—that casting director? Actually, I think she believes Mrs. Mackenzie is going to magically conjure up a third ticket to the after-party for her. That, or she's going to take Briar's when we win."

I wince. *When.*

"I don't know, it'd be nice if you and Sebastian could pull it together." Eden claps her hands and purses her lips. "Competition makes things fun, Teddy." Then she exhales and takes a step toward the elevator. "Well, I'm going to do my skin-care routine before Briar crawls back in an ice cream coma." Then she lifts a brow. "I wonder if the continental breakfast has a yogurt bar . . ."

Eden doesn't wait for me to respond, just walks away, and I'm not quite sure what just happened.

When I talk to the front desk to get my key, the receptionist tells me they've brought our luggage to our room, along with a delivery. He only tells me it was a floral arrangement, and I thank him.

I finally head upstairs, and of course, Sebastian isn't here, though his bag has already claimed the full-sized bed closer to the door. I'm sure there isn't any way he would have known I wanted the bed near the window. Probably just lucky that he threw his bag on the first bed he got to. The bracelet is still working in some small, inexplicable ways, even if Sebastian's vibe is throwing off the trip. It can only do so much, I suppose.

There is a clear vase of flowers on the desk, as promised. They're deep shades of red and bright yellows, mostly, with thin green stems and leaves.

It has Annie written all over it—gifts are her love language—but when I open the tiny little card stuck in a wire holder, I realize these aren't for me.

Welcome to the city, Seb!!—Blake

I quickly stick the note back into the holder and stand there for a moment, blank. It's like I just read something I shouldn't have.

Of *course.* Sebastian was sneaking off to meet someone.

Someone named Blake.

Someone named Blake who sends flowers.

I don't know why he wouldn't just tell me, but it all seems out of bounds now. I guess he really is over his ex.

Maybe he's with Blake right now.

Shaking off the thought, I'm truly not sure I've ever been more thrilled to take off my shoes and get in a hot shower. Once I'm all refreshed, I put on an old drama club T-shirt and long, plaid pajamas, even though I know I'm going to be sweating in my sleep. I'm sharing a room with Sebastian, so I've adopted a policy of modesty. I can't imagine he's going to waltz around in only his boxers or anything, though the guy is full of surprises.

Lying on my bed, I pop in my AirPods and go to Face-Time Annie. It's honestly not that late, even though it feels like it's past midnight, and it's a Wednesday, so she should be around.

But it keeps ringing and ringing until it says she's unavailable.

The good news is, I'm not the dramatic type. I wouldn't, say, have a bad night and feel like the world is collapsing around me because a FaceTime didn't go through. I wouldn't sense the city swallowing itself in an apocalyptic nightmare, consuming us all until we're burning in the earth's crust. I wouldn't jump to conclusions about how this is truly it—*this* is the beginning of the end and this is when it all changes.

"Why are you making that face?"

Dean *did* answer my FaceTime, and I throw my head back on the pillow.

"Do you believe in curses? Could I be cursed?"

Dean is sitting at his desk, with wet hair, wearing a UCLA hoodie, and I can tell he has propped his phone up against the giant candle Mom ordered him from Nordstrom because she wanted his room to smell less like a locker room. He turns away, typing on his laptop.

"What happened?"

"Start spreading the news," I say softly, trying to steady my voice.

He furrows his brow. "Huh?"

"It's a song," I groan. "About New York. I was being ironic. Never mind. It's just all going so terribly. Sebastian hates me and thinks I live in delusion, and Eden was being weirdly . . . *friendly*? Almost? I have no story to tell, just dramatic emotions that Harry says may inspire someone, though realistically, I'm just a big baby. But the worst thing is that Annie is moving on and she's going to put our bracelet in her nightstand drawer!"

Dean clears his throat. "Teddy, buddy, you're spiraling."

"No shit, Dean!"

"Where is Sebastian?" He gets close to the screen, like he's going to be able to see more of the room if he does. I can't help but laugh, and I hold the phone out, showing him more of the space.

"He's disappeared again," I sigh. "It's his thing. Disappearing. Brooding."

Dean frowns. "Too bad you can't brood together."

"I don't brood," I say. "I immerse. And only when

nothing else seems to work. Besides, you know it's healthy to feel your feelings?"

"Okay, well, of course it's okay to be sad. And feel your feelings and all that stuff. But you're in New York, and this trip is a big deal, so how do we get you out of this spiral?"

The thing about Dean is that he likes to fix things. Which, depending on the situation, is good and bad. In many ways, I fear, I am unfixable. But this situation might actually benefit from some of Dean's more practical advice.

I sit up. "All I need to do is make Sebastian like me, win the scavenger hunt, figure out what I'm going to say to Benji when I meet him, maybe try to write a song . . . and find a way to move to London."

Ignoring the last bit, Dean shifts in his chair. "Wait, wait, wait. Write a song?"

"I know." I suck my teeth. "Do you think it's dumb?"

"No, I don't think it's dumb at all. I just thought you were done with it."

"I was done with it," I say. "I may still be done with it. I don't know, Dean. Sebastian made this comment about how I could be a famous pop star and he said I do have a story to tell, and I am talented and then—"

Dean holds up a hand. "Going to stop you there. That doesn't sound like something you say to someone you hate."

"Well, Sebastian is a confusing guy."

I wonder where he is right now. I hope he's safe, keeping

an eye out for cars and not going anywhere dangerous. Even if we had this fight that he says wasn't a fight, and even if I have knots in my stomach about how awkward it's going to be when he walks through the door, I still want him to walk through the door.

"You need to do your breathing exercises," Dean offers. "It doesn't sound like anything is going too bad up there."

"Well, we went to this black-tie gala, and it was a masquerade, and I was pretending to be Harry Kensington, who also went to Citrus—it's a strange coincidence, I know. But things were going well until they weren't, and we got into a fight, and he left, and I'm here alone just thinking about . . . everything. I also knocked into this woman and got red wine all over her white gown. As Harry."

Dean winces. "That actually sounds pretty bad. Okay, well, I have a lot of questions but . . . what if this is a good time to try writing a song?"

"Maybe it is," I say. "Or maybe Sebastian is just wrong. How well does he even know me? You've read my stuff; you know it's all shit."

"It's not shit," Dean says. "You just need to start. That's always the first step. Start. And, you know, you mentioned not knowing what to say to Benji? Maybe you ask him for some advice."

I laugh. "I can't just ask Benji Keaton for advice."

"Why not?"

Taking into consideration that, if achievable, getting advice from Benji would be the best thing to ever happen to me, I wonder why this never occurred to me. Maybe because the idea of writing songs was dead to me up until a few hours ago.

"For now, why don't you just start writing some of your feelings? Then get some rest. And in the morning, try to smooth things out with Sebastian. I don't know what the fight was about but based on the other stuff . . . it doesn't sound like he hates you."

After Dean and I hang up, I am very confused.

Surely, he's wrong? Maybe Sebastian doesn't *hate* me, but things are not going well.

I look at the flowers, and I imagine Sebastian walking hand in hand with some cool New York City guy named Blake. He's probably telling him all about me. They might be laughing about me wanting to meet Benji.

Still, I can't seem to work out how today went. I roll over to grab the Polaroids from the pocket of my shorts on the floor. Looking at our smiles, I realize there might be some truth in Dean's assessment. I'll apologize to Sebastian, since I obviously hit a nerve and got lost in the moment, and hopefully we can start over.

Shifting my focus to an empty Note, I take Dean's advice and do my breathing exercises. Close my eyes, in through the nose, out through the mouth. When I've done a few and open my eyes, I'm horrified to find a brilliant song hasn't magically appeared on the phone in my hand, written in gold cursive letters like the contract Ariel signed for Ursula.

I stare at the blinking cursor, my fingers hovering over the keyboard.

Harry's advice was smart: write what I'm feeling and then figure it out. Except now, after such a long day with Sebastian, and then the heart-to-heart with Harry, plus the weird conversation with Eden, and now more advice from Dean, my own emotions have become far off and inaccessible. Everyone else's words are echoing in my mind, too loud for me to have any of my own.

How do I describe whatever I'm feeling right now if I'm not even sure what that is?

Here I am, desperate to pull some semblance of a sonnet—a couplet, even, just to prove to myself I'm capable of accessing the English language, of expressing a thought or a feeling apart from the couple of random lines I jotted down at the Met.

But I've got nothing.

So, I decide to put on Benji's *Sunset* album and maybe let a few final tears hit my pillow until it looks like a Rorschach because this is the only time I'm giving myself to wallow.

A text from Dean comes through:

> **DEAN:**
>
> You got this, Teddy! Hope you have the best time! You deserve it! You don't need anyone else to have the time of YOUR life, you've always been my cool independent younger brother who does all the crazy things people just talk about doing. I love you ♥

I feel warm reading the text, and I realize Dean is right. I grasp at the spark of inspiration.

When I wake up, it'll be a new day in New York City, and there is much to see and so much to accomplish. When I wake up, I'm going to channel Tracy freaking Turnblad greeting the Baltimore morning air.

I brush my teeth and lie there, with the covers up to my neck, praying for a poem and anxiously watching the door. I'm not sure if I'm going to pretend to be asleep or try to make up once he gets back, but I don't get the chance to decide before my eyes fall closed.

Thursday

Chapter 16

Good Morning, Baltimore

New York City sure is beautiful.

The perfect bright green of the trees lining the picturesque brownstones, the brilliant blue and cloudless sky, the vibrant yellow of the taxicabs. It's idyllic, the way I can only smell artisanal coffee and freshly baked croissants. I think I can even hear Henry Mancini playing through an open window as somebody happily hums along.

One of the cabs stops along the sidewalk, and when the door slowly opens and a leg stretches out to find the sidewalk, all the air leaves my lungs. It's not just any tall brunette guy climbing out of the cab, wearing light wash jeans and an oversized hoodie, hiding beneath large gold sunglasses and clutching a lilac journal.

It's Benji. And the warmth rushing right to my cheeks

is met not with a look of anxiety or an immediate retreat, but with a smile.

Angel choirs sing, flowers bloom, beams of sunlight paint the street, and when I step forward and open my mouth to speak, a loud banging noise behind me catches my attention, and then my eyes snap open.

Of course, that was a dream sequence.

"So sorry."

Sebastian pulls his headphones off and leaves them around his neck. He's standing next to his bed wearing a black band tee—the National—and loose jeans, going through his suitcase as steam clears from the bathroom. The sun is shining through the two layers of gauzy cream curtains, making a rainbow on the bathroom door's full-length mirror.

"I was trying to be quiet. Though you're, like, a ridiculously heavy sleeper."

Clearing my throat and rubbing my eyes, I sit up. I'm imagining my hair is going in a thousand directions, I have drool on my chin, and my eyes are crusted shut. It's the most appealing I'll ever be.

Music is still coming out of Sebastian's headphones and he hurries over to grab his phone from the desk, pausing it.

"Look, Teddy, I'm sorry about last night."

I perk up. *Am I still dreaming?*

"You are?"

He nods, sitting on the edge of his bed and folding his

hands together. "I really shouldn't have left you there. And I'm sorry for what I said, too. I just . . . your question really struck a chord. And I will admit, though it might be hard to believe, I am not the best at handling my emotions."

Teddy McGuire. Did you have a full-on existential meltdown last night for no good reason?

Me? Never.

Like he senses the wheels turning: "But if we could leave it at that?"

"Yeah," I say. "I'm sorry for pushing. I got upset and just took it out on you."

"We're good, then." Sebastian stands up, going back around to the other side of the bed and taking his headphones off from around his neck. He points to the flowers. "Can we also just pretend those aren't here?"

I open my mouth to speak, but I know there's no use. There's no reason to ask about Blake since it's clear Sebastian doesn't want to talk about it.

I nod.

"What's on the agenda for today?" he asks.

I sit up and grab the list from the bedside table, trying to remember the plan. "First one is so up your alley. Bookstore."

Sebastian smiles. "Nice. Okay, good start."

I check my phone next.

DEAN:

I thought it would cheer you up to know mom and her book club ladies took gummies

and it's 9 at night on a Wednesday and
they're all laying in the backyard on beach
towels looking for planets in the sky

DEAN:

Daphne Martin asked me if I was
going to play in the Super Bowl

DEAN:

I didn't have it in me to remind
her I play basketball

ANNIE:

SORRY I was at a movie

ANNIE:

are you already asleep omg

ANNIE:

tell me everything in the morning ily

I add laughing reactions to Dean's texts and then respond to Annie.

ME:

last night was so chaotic

ME:

i don't even know where to begin bestie

ME:

we're about to start on today's list, but i'll
text you once I'm back, we can facetime

I stand up and tap my finger to my chin as I look through my suitcase. I go for a cream T-shirt with a sun painted across the chest in hues of bright and burnt gold.

Paired with a pair of light blue drawstring shorts that hit at the thigh and a pair of high-top white Vans, the sun gives me a sense of confidence. I'm manifesting. I'll show Benji one of the Polaroids, of me wearing this T-shirt. It'll happen.

"What were you listening to?" I gesture toward Sebastian's headphones.

I think he considers if he is going to tell me, but only for a moment. "A song called 'Fuel on the Fire.' By Bear's Den." Then: "It's good."

I nod. I want to ask him to play it out loud, but I think, somehow, sharing music seems like a very personal thing for Sebastian. So, I play it safe.

"We're both wearing artist T-shirts," I say as I tie my shoelaces.

He cocks his head. "Let me guess."

"From his Solar Flares collection," I say proudly. I sit up and show off the shirt. "He donated proceeds to a few mental health organizations."

Sebastian nods approvingly. "Well then. Go Benji."

Once we're on the street, I take a moment to pause and soak up this feeling.

New. York. Freaking. City.

Will it ever get old? How could it? I watch the way people disregard the little things—the vibrance of the traffic lights, the buzzing in the warm June air, the literal twinkling spots where the rising sun bounces off the buildings. I swear the sidewalk beneath our feet pulses. The entire city is alive, and I just want to remember every single thing about it. I guess channeling the Tracy Turnblad vibe isn't so hard.

"Coffee?" Sebastian asks.

"Coffee."

My Maps app has become my best friend. It looks like we need to take the subway from Grand Central Station, and as excited as I am to see it, we're going at midnight for the scavenger hunt, and I want that to be a truly magical moment. So, I find the next subway station we can take.

"We can walk down to Thirty-Third," I say. "And then get on . . . a green train. The 6. We can take the 6 from Thirty-Third Street to Fourteenth Street and then we just have a quick walk."

Sebastian nods. "Sounds good. I'm sure we'll stumble upon coffee before Thirty-Third Street?"

"It's, like, nine blocks. Surely?"

Along with pure admiration and wonderment, there's something else that reverberates inside me. A central pounding in my chest collects limited city air in tight breaths, and it's a restricted kind of feeling—*anxiety*. Today has to go better than last night did. So far, so good. But I wouldn't have guessed the night could turn so terribly so quickly; I just need to keep my eye on the prize.

We walk along the Park Avenue sidewalk, and I can see why this street is so famous. It's wide and vibrant, with its own brand of upbeat morning energy. Suits and pencil skirts, designer tennis shoes and tote bags. People push along the pavement with purpose.

When we finally find a Starbucks, I'm alarmed at the amount of cups sitting at the mobile order counter. New Yorkers are nothing if not efficient—ruthlessly efficient. When one person grabs their cup and sprints out the door, another takes its place, only to be swiped up in seconds. Rinse and repeat.

Sebastian and I stand in the line, which is alarmingly short, next to the few others who didn't order ahead for their .04 second coffee pit stop.

"Vanilla sweet cream cold brew?" He doesn't look at me, just keeps scanning the menu and pokes his tongue in his cheek.

I tilt my head. "How do you know that?"

Now he looks at me. "You always get the same thing."

"But how do you even—"

"Literally every rehearsal, in the drama club group chat when someone asks for Starbucks orders, you say the same thing."

Huh.

"Well, I just . . . do you remember everyone's order?"

He stiffens up. "Yeah."

"What's Eden's?"

"Black iced coffee with two pumps of sugar-free vanilla." He winces. "I remember hers because it sounds so horrible."

"Really horrible," I agree. "Okay, what about Annie's?"

Sebastian pauses, and then studies me. "I can't remember."

I find it strange Sebastian remembers my Starbucks order. It isn't anything extraordinary. He's never gone out to get drinks for the drama club, only occasionally asked for a tea or something. I think. I can't remember, honestly. Which is why I find it so hard to wrap my mind around his eidetic memory regarding the group text. How could someone's brain have space for such tiny, extraneous details with no relevance to their life?

"Iced toasted vanilla oat milk shaken espresso."

He nods quickly. "That's right."

"She's vegan, so it has to be oat milk."

I can tell a shade of embarrassment has rushed to his face, starting at his neck and warming to his cheeks, so I don't push any further.

"What are you going to get?"

Shrugging, Sebastian crosses his arms. "Not sure. Coffee."

"Right."

I don't really mean to, but I catch a particularly pleasant glimpse of Sebastian's biceps. They're not huge, but they're nice to look at, nonetheless. His skin looks soft and there's the slight outline of a vein running down the widest part of his arm as his knuckle pushes up against it.

His eye catches mine, and it takes a moment but his lip curls up into a devilish grin.

Oh, no, no, no. I am not about to go there with Sebastian. He must be nuts.

And, anyway, he has a Blake.

"You know," I say, "crossing your arms is, like, saying you're closed off. Body language."

"Body language?"

"Yes, body language. Actors know these things," I offer, blinking a little too quickly and trying to make a believable case for why I was looking at his arms for a moment too long.

Sebastian laughs. "Maybe I want to be closed off."

"Maybe you do." I nod. "I guess that's fine. I just thought you should know. In case you were unintentionally—"

The barista calls us up, and I'm beyond grateful for the interruption. Sebastian orders my vanilla sweet cream cold brew for me and then he orders an iced cinnamon dolce latte, which I find entirely surprising. He does specify that he doesn't want whipped cream, which isn't surprising, but manages to throw me off again by maintaining that he would like "the little cinnamon sprinkle" still.

I try to pay for myself, but Sebastian is insistent he's got it. I have no idea why he'd do that.

When we stand off to the side, far out of the way of the conveyor belt of people zipping through like the Flash, I watch him chew on the inside of his cheek and rock on his heels.

"What does your body language say?" he asks, giving me a once-over.

I'm in a resting state I had to practice, just like I am following blocking directions. Open chest, shoulders back, just a little, and chin up.

"Oh, well, I guess it says I'm confident." I bark an ungodly laugh before I cover my mouth, instantly self-conscious but thankful nobody in New York seems to give a shit about anybody else around them. "Sorry, it's just ironic."

"Why is that funny?"

I roll my eyes. "I'm not sure how confident I *actually* am."

"You're not crossing your arms, at least," he says, then he seems to reflect. "I think you are pretty confident."

"Maybe it's acting," I admit. "And the funniest part is, I don't think I ever really have said that out loud, and I don't know why I am right now. It's just—you threw me off, asking that, and then when I heard the answer, I swear it felt like a character I was playing, reciting a line or something. Doesn't that sound nuts?"

"It doesn't sound nuts, it just sounds like you've spent a long time worried about how other people perceive you."

I nod. "That's an understatement. But come on, you're telling me you're not worried about how other people perceive you?"

Sebastian shakes his head. "Not any more than I should."

"What's that supposed to mean?"

"It means I don't worry too much beyond trying not to be offensive or something. How people perceive me is none of my business."

That's rich.

"If that's true, I'd love to experience what it's like to be you. Even just for one day."

"No, you wouldn't. You should be glad to be you."

It's impossible not to hear the serious tone in his voice.

"This is becoming a very deep conversation to have before coffee."

Sebastian agrees, and as if cued by my comment, his name is called, and we grab our drinks off the counter. Little cinnamon sprinkle and all.

We take the subway downtown, standing on either side of a pole, and Sebastian sips his latte. My cold brew is perfect, and this train is a little louder and a little more wobbly than the one we took yesterday. If any of these New Yorkers—some sleeping, some reading, but all completely stoic and unimpressed—could read my mind, they'd think I'm some small-town Florida boy, starry-eyed and naïve, yet to be jaded by the big city. And they'd be absolutely right.

The Fourteenth Street station is ginormous. Literally, I think there could be an entire scavenger hunt just for this station. When we climb the stairs up to street level, I'm taken by how we can be in the same city, under the exact same sky and just a mile away, and it can feel like a whole new experience. Union Square is bustling, with a park in the center, all bright green trees, old men playing chess and couples on benches, and dozens of people spilling in and out of the various subway entrances.

"Are you just so excited for the bookstore?" It's silly, but I suddenly want to elicit a giddy reaction from Sebastian. "Eighteen miles of books. Called the king of indie bookstores by the *Times*. I'd bet you could just get lost."

Nothing but a slight nod and a little twitch of his eyes as he looks over at me. "What are you up to?"

"I'm not up to anything!"

"Right. Is there some weird catch here?"

"No, I just thought—Sebastian, would it kill you to be excited about something?"

"Now wouldn't be the opportune time to find out, would it? Then you might not meet Benji."

I inhale the fresh summer air as we pass a flower stall, bursting with bright blooming magenta peonies, stems of emerald, and blue hydrangeas.

"Well, I'm excited."

Truly, I'm not *that* excited for the books. For an iconic New York staple, sure, but my comment about getting lost has led me to worry ever so slightly. How exactly do eighteen miles of books get stuffed into a store anyway? And in New York City, no less? Though, I guess in some strange way, if it's going to happen anywhere, it'd be here.

"What's the prompt again?" Sebastian asks as we cross the street.

"We have to pick out books that describe us."

His eyes get smaller. "That's impossible."

"This is going to be a piece of cake," I say.

Soon, we stand across the street from the Strand Bookstore. It's immediately obvious, just from the exterior, why it's iconic. It looks like a landmark, even. A movie set. With pops of crimson—the wraparound awning, the book carts lining the sidewalk, and the giant flags waving in the wind. I'm still not sure how exactly they've fit eighteen whole miles of books inside, but I guess that's what we're about to find out.

Chapter 17

Hundreds of Stories

Sebastian doesn't have to give me a giddy verbal reaction to the inside of the Strand—his eyes do it for him. I've never seen them light up like this, though I guess I've only really been looking at them for a little over twenty-four hours now. I'm not sure if he is more excited about the books than he was for the dinosaurs, or if he's starting to feel more comfortable with me. Either way, his excitement is clear as he bounds forward with a little extra pep in his step, through the entryway, and past the initial tables of new titles and bestsellers.

The store is huge, with a large section of merch tucked beneath the staircase and extending toward the registers, which are already busy, even though the store just opened. There are long stretches of books along the walls and in carefully curated stacks on various tables. At the back of the store, past more displays, there are even more shelves with so many books it seems like an optical illusion.

"What book describes Sebastian Hodges?" I ask as he stops to look at a table of repackaged classics.

He holds up a book and pulls a face. "Not a terribly redesigned Hemingway. Honestly, it's astounding anyone even thinks they have the right to put this cover on this book. One of the greatest writers, a literary legend, reduced to some—what? Post-modern vector art with a quirky font?"

"Tell me how you really feel," I say. Though from what I do know about Ernest Hemingway, I don't think he's wrong.

Sebastian sighs, setting the book down. "Okay, I honestly have no clue what book to choose. There are too many options." He keeps walking before turning back. "What are you going to pick?"

I shrug. "I don't know. Is it too on the nose to pick something from Benji's Book Club?"

He considers it. "I think you could get a little deeper."

"Fine. What about something about Icarus?"

"Icarus?" He pulls a face. "Why would you choose something about Icarus? You don't want that to describe you, I don't think."

Laughing, I shake my head and follow him around a corner. "No, because Icarus is one of Benji's things." I point to the sun on my shirt. "You didn't know that?"

Sebastian stops at a table of historical fiction and picks

up a random book before turning his nose up. He sets it down and exchanges it for another, scanning the summary on the back. "You know, now that you mention it, I do know that one song . . ."

One of his most famous songs. "Icarus Complex." Which happens to also be the name of the album it served as lead single for.

"It was a meaningful moment for him," I say, wondering if Sebastian really cares. "A super-famous critic compared him to Icarus. Said he was going to burn too bright and lose it all."

Sebastian considers this before giving me a strange look. "Why would he care what one critic said?"

"It wasn't just the one critic. People picked apart his relationships, his songwriting, his style. He couldn't ever do anything right. It hurts my feelings if one person comments something about my performance in the musical on the school Instagram account. I can't even imagine what it must feel like to have the world rip you apart like you're not a human being."

He forms a fist and turns his knuckles over on the table. "You get upset over Instagram comments?"

I laugh. "Of course. Nobody wants to read that someone doesn't like them."

"Well, they're not saying they don't like *you*, surely."

This is true. Nobody has ever commented saying they don't like me. But they've mentioned if I ever stumbled over a line or the one time the music skipped during

Heathers and I accidentally broke character for a split second. They've mentioned how I had an empty stare when I was supposed to be in love with Veronica. They laughed at my costume for *Into the Woods*.

"It feels like they are, I guess."

Maybe that's what Sebastian means about not caring more than necessary.

"You always do a great job in the plays," he says. "It's not worth worrying about someone commenting on social media. Promise."

"You only spent one year doing tech," I say. "But thanks."

"I still saw the other musicals. I'm cultured, come on."

I laugh at this, though for some reason I find it hard to believe he's seen the others. It occurs to me this might have been something he did with his ex, and I'm not sure why that causes a strange jolt in my chest.

Sebastian nods, setting the book down and studying my shirt. "Well, I guess I think that's kind of clever, then. Using the critic's words like that. And I guess we all know who won out there."

"Definitely Benji. That album and tour were huge. And then, when he went through a bad breakup, he had the *Sunrise* and *Sunset* albums. He's always used a lot of sun imagery and metaphors in general, but those three albums were all heavy on them."

This piques Sebastian's interest. "Two albums for one breakup?"

"Now you sound like one of the critics," I say.

Quickly shaking his head, he turns back to the books. "Not judging. There just must have been a lot of material."

"There was a lot of material," I say. "That's for sure."

"Isn't it weird to think even someone like Benji Keaton gets his heart broken?" Sebastian frowns. "Nobody is safe. Nothing shields you from that. No amount of money or fame."

"We're all just people," I say.

This is something I've thought about a lot. How funny is it that we treat these famous artists like they're less than human, but consume the products of their deeply felt experiences for our own benefit? People put their heart and soul into something—a song, a film, a book—and we look at them and ask for more and tell them to shut up at the same time. I think Benji must have a really good therapist or something, to take all of the criticism he gets and still find a way to pour his feelings into his music and performances.

Sebastian nods. "Depressing."

"I don't know, maybe it's nice. We get to feel things through Benji's music. I might not be able to relate to the breakup lyrics explicitly, but if I'm sad, or if it's just a totally shit day, there's something to be said for not feeling alone."

"There's that glass half-full." He brightens a little. "Okay, but can I challenge you—I don't think there's anything wrong with wanting to pick a book related to Benji, because he's important to you. But what if you pick one that's just about . . ."

"Me?"

He lifts his chin, as if testing the waters. Curious what my response might be.

"I don't even know where to begin. What book describes me . . . ?"

I glance over to another table, and there's not any title that stands out to me. I think I might be best at looking outside myself to be told who I am. Right now, as the titles all blur together and the covers blend into abstract artwork, I know I'll have to look inward for an answer.

"There must be something wrong with me," I say. "I just don't know myself at all."

Sebastian shakes his head. "Nobody knows themselves. Even if they think they do, they only know what they think they know."

I laugh. "Well said."

He doesn't laugh with me, though. "I mean it, Teddy. How many people eat something for lunch because some article told them it's good for them? Or worse, that it's cool? How many people listen to music because they want to fit in with their friends? How many people buy clothes they don't even like because some girl on TikTok said to? And how many people, if given the chance, could actually start at square one and live authentically, just the way they want without anyone's input?"

He isn't wrong, but it's all a little deep.

"Anyway, all I'm saying is, there's nothing wrong with you. Maybe you're ahead since you know you want to find yourself. You're not pretending to be self-actualized at eighteen."

"Are you sure I can't just pick something to do with Benji?" I sigh.

Sebastian picks up another book. "You can pick whatever you want."

"But you're going to judge me if I can't come up with something better. Something that's just me."

He flips through the book. "I'm not going to judge you. But even if I did, it doesn't matter."

Sebastian's whole existential, bigger-than-reality philosophical bit doesn't quite hold up when applied to real life. Because of course it matters if he judges me. Of course it does. I'm not sure why, but it does.

I'm not going to be able to come up with anything meaningful, thinking so hard and feeling so much pressure.

All right, Teddy. Who are you?

I like my family, my friends, musical theater, music in general, the beach, and . . .

And?

I barely have my phone out of my pocket before Sebastian turns to me.

"Are you about to text Annie and ask *her* which book describes you?"

A lump catches in my throat. "No, of course not." I

quickly hit Instagram, showing him the screen. "I was checking social media."

Of course, he's caught me, but my defense has led to me viewing Eden's story.

She's taken a selfie with the wide-angle setting, of her, her mom, and Briar in workout gear and a bright white locker room. **More than half the scavenger hunt down and squeezed in a SoulCycle this morning xo**

"We have to pick our books!" I nearly *squeal*, my voice gets so high with panic. "Look, Eden is blowing through the list. She even fit in a workout."

Sebastian takes my phone and studies her story. "Or she's bluffing to freak you out."

"If she is, it's working. Come on, let's pick our books and go."

"But this is supposed to be the most fun one," Sebastian says, with a little hint of a whine. "We haven't even gone upstairs. Or downstairs. We haven't even browsed."

Prompting him to follow me, I turn around and head down the stairs. We look around and I gesture for him to lead the way. He blows through sections filled with scientific books, psychology essays, and random mathematics books with *titles* that fly way over my head.

How is it an eighteen-year-old can't pick a book that describes him?

Sebastian is enthralled by the very existence of this bookstore. He's taking in every square foot, it seems, probably stopping to inhale each waft when someone shuts an old dusty leather-bound or plastic-wrapped nonfiction title. He is entertained by books without even reading them, which is something I certainly cannot relate to.

I guess I should have read more. I guess I still can, but it doesn't help me right now to plan for some future bookworm version of Teddy McGuire.

Who are you?

We head back upstairs, and I pull the list out of my pocket, unfolding it.

"Oh my *God*," I groan.

Sebastian lifts a brow and frowns. "What?"

"I misread it. We're supposed to pick books that represent *each other*." Shutting my eyes tight, it dawns on me: "Oh, you mean to tell me I've had this entire existential crisis over *who I am* for nothing?"

He only laughs. "Maybe not for nothing. Thought starters are good. What are you going to pick for me?"

I look over at one of the tables and pick up the Hemingway he ripped apart earlier.

"No, I refusc to take a photo with that."

On the same table, with a few other titles, there's one that stands out, and I hand it to him. He rolls his eyes.

"*The Stranger*?"

"I feel like there's still so much to learn about you." I say it like a joke, but I find it rings true.

He nods and then focuses on a table across the room before bolting and returning with a green and gilded book. Of course he's chosen a children's book for me. I could throw it at him when he hands it to me, but I study the cover, with the shining gold accents and typography.

The Annotated Wizard of Oz.

Dorothy and Toto sit in the O, while the Lion, Scarecrow, and Tin Man appear in gold-bordered rectangles, like doors, on the side of the book. It's heavy, a special edition, I think.

"Judy Garland is a literal legend," I say, leading with my defense. Then I look to him. "Why did you pick this? Are you saying I'm brainless? I need courage? I know I have a heart, if anything it's too—"

He laughs. "I was just going to say you're not in Citrus Harbor, anymore."

I raise a brow. "Oh."

Then he points to the scavenger hunt list, which is poking out from under the book in my palms. "You've got your own sort of yellow brick road, too."

The weight of the book extends from my hands, up to my chest like vines growing too quickly and starting to suffocate me. I don't know what has just happened, because I swear a millisecond ago, I was just fine.

But it's like right here, in this moment, I realize I am graduating high school.

Why am I hit with these earth-shattering realizations with Sebastian? I'm just trying to complete this damn scavenger hunt.

"Are you okay?"

I look down at the book and feel a sense of something

I don't know how to identify. It's not only nostalgia, not only appreciation for the last four years and how it's all led up to this moment in New York City, but it's that feeling of loss for the fact that it's all over.

The Wizard of Oz does mean something to me. Many things to me, actually, and apart from the time I've spent listening to the MGM Studio Orchestra just to daydream, it reminds me of when I really started on the yellow brick road.

"I sang 'Over the Rainbow' for my first ever audition," I say. "And I can't believe how that feels like only a few hours ago, and a million years ago at the same time."

I avoid looking at Sebastian. It probably makes no sense why that small tidbit would make me sad. There's so much more to it. More gained and lost and learned. So, I avoid looking at him because I don't know if right now I'm in the mood for some sarcastic comment or joke, but he doesn't say anything at all.

Instead, most surprisingly, he only says: "I get it."

I've been barreling through high school at the speed of light, focusing on the fun times with Annie and the drama club, desperate to put an end to early mornings and pop quizzes and tedious homework that I bet the teachers don't even want to grade.

Graduation has been this light at the end of the tunnel. It's been this finish line.

But my yellow brick road hasn't even been leading to graduation, I realize. It's been leading to *this*. To New

York. This is the Emerald City. And I'm no longer on the yellow brick road. I'm here. And when this is over, graduation is the nail in the coffin. It's all over for good. No more drama club, no more looking forward to the senior trip, no more random fun times with Annie. Everything changes.

Going to community college undeclared with no direction or idea of my future has never sounded so scary or depressing as it does now that I might want something else.

I shake my head. "It's fine," I say. "I just hadn't thought about that in forever. And it literally hit me like a ton of bricks."

He nods, smiling a little. "Like I said, you're not in Citrus Harbor anymore, Teddy."

In a short time, New York City has stolen my heart completely, and I realize Citrus Harbor might not be where I end up if I click my heels three times.

Chapter 18

Apex Predator

Sebastian does a bit more browsing. I'm actively trying not to tap my foot with the knowledge that Eden is somewhere in the city waltzing through the scavenger hunt list and having the time of her life, so smug and sure she's going to be snapping a photo with Benji tomorrow night.

He doesn't buy anything, though I insist he should. There's no use trying to argue with him, but I'm sure he might regret not having a souvenir to remember this giant bookstore and the wonderment that befell him in the stacks.

We leave, having taken our Polaroid with *The Stranger* and *The Wizard of Oz*, and head back up toward the Union Square station. It's toasty, and I wonder if Sebastian is hot wearing jeans. If he is, he doesn't complain or mention it, just keeps walking, facing forward and focusing on the way the buildings rise over the trees in the park.

I stop to take a photo as we cross Broadway. The image is perfect—bright green foliage, vibrant taxicabs lined up at the edge of the white painted crosswalk, and the Empire State Building standing tall against the deep blue, cloudless sky.

And then there's another photo, as I switch to the wide-angle option, and Sebastian is crossing, midstep and looking over at the Empire State Building. And another: he looks to me with a slight smile.

"Oh no," he says. "Delete, delete."

"No!" I lock my phone and put it in my pocket.

He groans but doesn't seem to actually care much. "Teddy, can we agree to actually have lunch today? Real lunch?"

"Are you already hungry?"

"No, just maybe after a couple more scavenger hunt items."

Making our way back to the subway, I watch Sebastian's profile. My book choice wasn't entirely fair. He isn't wholly a stranger anymore, but maybe it was a play of some kind. If I put that word out there, he'd feel compelled to share something with me. To let me in a little bit, or to reveal more about his life. I don't even know what questions to ask to truly get to know him, to form a friendship with him.

Of course, if it was a play, he outmaneuvered me. Sebastian isn't compelled by things like that. So, what *is* he compelled by? What gets someone like Sebastian on a drama club trip to New York when he doesn't even truly socialize with the drama club?

Surely he isn't literally only on this trip for Blake?

He isn't wholly a stranger, but he isn't yet more than an acquaintance. I'm not sure what it says about me, but that gray area is unsettling.

Descending into the subway, this time at a different intersection, I decide to try for progress. "I want to hear more about the genetics stuff."

Sebastian thinks this is hilarious, judging by the way he almost cackles, throwing back his head and pulling the yellow card from his wallet to swipe through the turnstile. "*The genetics stuff*? Sure. Like what?" Then, dryly, but with a slight smirk, he adds: "I'm an open book."

I don't know what reaction I expected, but it should have been that one.

Wrestling with my own wallet—my Metro card is stuck between my ID and debit card, reluctant to slip free—I finally swipe through and join him on the other side.

Before I can think of a question or topic to start off our exploration of his soul's depths, there's a rapid, tinny clanging of cymbals. Immediately, an entire accompaniment of hollow drums and an electric guitar fill the echo chamber of tiled surfaces in the subway. I don't know where it's coming from, but an entire concert has just begun.

Watching my face light up, Sebastian raises his brows. "Buskers."

"Yes!" I grin. "This is perfect, we haven't found one yet. And it's on the list. Underground Concerto! We're catching up, Sebastian, we're catching up. Okay, let's go find the band and snap another Polaroid."

It isn't too hard to find them, actually. They're right up one of the ramps and to the left, set up against one of the walls. On one side of them, steps lead down into the Uptown NQRW, and on the other, the Downtown.

"This is actually seriously cool," I say.

As we approach them and I grab the camera hanging around my neck, Sebastian holds his arm out to stop me before he grabs a few dollars from his wallet, tossing them into the black velvet hat filled with bills and coins. The musicians nod and then he gives me a look of approval.

We take the photo, and I swear Sebastian's smile is getting bigger in every photo. As it develops, I notice the musicians are grinning, too, and one of them is holding up a peace sign. I thank them, and I'm thinking this is pretty idyllic in terms of encountering friendly buskers to take a selfie with like a total tourist, but I'm immediately brought back to earth. I turn around and find a less-than-friendly face heading toward the exit.

"How cute." Eden pouts, her peach, glossed lips feigning

the existence of any emotion other than contempt.

She and Briar are both wearing chunky white sneakers, but while Briar's lanky, self-tanned legs are accentuated by biker shorts under an oversized T-shirt, Eden is wearing a black leather skirt and baby pink ribbed tank. A thick gold chain with interlocking Cs hangs from her neck and it's honestly a little annoying how they just look like ridiculously cool New York girls.

It's clear, by the way Eden is looking at me right now, that she's not going to acknowledge our little chat last night. Now, with Briar and Sebastian present, we're back to the ruthless competition.

"Are you guys, like, following us?" Eden's lips part to reveal her bright white smile. "It's a big city, Teddy. We've conveniently bumped into you twice now."

This is true. And very weird. Sebastian and I haven't posted to social media, so there's no way anybody would know where we are. And we haven't run into any of our other classmates or Mrs. Mackenzie. Only Eden.

Then it hits me.

"Well, we mapped out an efficient way to knock out the list."

Eden swallows, her smile fading as she realizes what I'm saying.

We're both gunning to win this thing. Which means we both figured out the quickest way to make it up and down New York City. That's why we ran into them at the Met.

And why we're running into them now. Only, at the Met, they'd beat us. Now, they're one step behind us. Guess Sebastian was right, and I guess that SoulCycle class wasn't the best use of their time.

Eden's brows turn down, arching with annoyance.

I take a step closer.

I'm not fully confident. I'm not entirely sure I'm going to beat Eden, as much as I want to believe it'll happen. But in this moment, knowing she's thrown off her game and I might—even if just for this moment—be a step ahead, I'm emboldened.

"Well, I'd say great minds . . ."

And then I walk past her, and I just assume Sebastian is following because I don't turn back until I've rounded a corner.

"That was so good, wasn't it?" I say, adrenaline pumping through me like electricity. "I mean, that was a for real one-liner moment. Not scripted or anything. Right? That was kind of awesome."

Sebastian looks at me like I'm one of the impressive old books at the Strand, with big eyes and a smile of disbelief. "That was very badass, Teddy. Bravo."

"I mean, you know, for me. It's, like, whoa."

He laughs, squeezing my arm. "Don't downplay it. Badass."

"So, you were right. She was bluffing."

"And she seems to regret that right about now."

"Which means we need to stay on our game and keep up a good pace," I say as we find the subway heading downtown. "She's going to kick it into overdrive now. I wouldn't be surprised if she finds some way to booby-trap the city."

He nods. "And suddenly Eden Bloom is a supervillain in the MCU."

"We both know it would only take an A-lister on the poster and she'd be in."

"Oh, for sure."

Chapter 19

There! Right There!

Corlears Hook is our destination, to catch the ferry, but I think I misjudged how close it was to the "nearest" subway station.

It's fine, though, because we've walked for a bit, and have found ourselves between the Brooklyn and Manhattan bridges, overlooking the water and strolling along the sidewalk. As passing boats leave a wake, the salty water splashes up and seagulls hop around, pecking at scraps of bait the fishermen have dropped. The sun beats down on us and it feels like summer.

We might have lost some time, except it says it would have been a nineteen-minute walk last time I checked. I've been walking at my normal pace, with Sebastian keeping up, so it will only take ten.

"Strolling" is slightly misrepresenting the pace, but we

are making our way.

Though we do stop for just a moment, to put our forearms on the railing and look out at Brooklyn.

"I love it here," I say.

Sebastian nods. "I know."

"You still don't think it's magical?"

The Brooklyn Bridge is iconic, and I knew it would be cool to see it in person, but we've stumbled upon a spot where the view is beyond incredible. It's a boardwalk area, lining a modern building with grass that almost looks fake, and people sit along steps and people kick their legs off swings that face the water.

From here, the Manhattan Bridge, which we just walked under, is closest, and behind it the Brooklyn Bridge is visible in near-perfect composition, like this spot was just made to be photographed and framed, with the downtown Manhattan skyline perfectly stacked on the right, and Brooklyn buildings glittering in the daylight on the left. The sounds of the gulls, the dancing sun on the East River—it's no wonder people fall in love with this city.

"I'm just not going to describe a city as *magical*," he says with an obnoxious grin.

"Okay, so safe to say, you might be thinking it's magical, but you're just not going to say it out loud."

He rolls his eyes and leans over, his shoulder pressing into mine. I think he realizes how comfortable of a gesture it is at the same time as I do, because he pulls back, though he acts like it was nothing, maintaining his smile.

"I think it's nice here."

It might be the best I'm going to get, and somehow it's enough.

"Do you like movies?"

The question genuinely catches him off guard.

"What do you mean?"

"Do you like movies?" I repeat. "I don't know how else to—"

"Well, yeah." He scrunches up his face. "Of course I like movies. Doesn't everybody like movies?"

Nodding, I glance out at the water. "I'm just trying to think of some questions. To get to know you better."

"Right. So I'm not *The Stranger*," he offers. "Okay, well, I like a lot of movies. You're sure this is your angle?"

I sigh emphatically. "It's not an *angle*. I'm just trying to learn more about you, Sebastian. Maybe a better question would be why you think it has to be an angle. Why you have such a hard time just making a friend."

Sebastian considers this very seriously before shaking his head. "No, now you went too far to the other end of the spectrum. I think we can do a little better than movies, but a little less than psychological analysis."

"Fine, do you have a suggestion?"

"I love fall."

This feels like a trap, but it also feels like he might be making an effort, so I consider my response carefully. "I wish we had real fall in Florida."

I think I've said the right thing, because his eyes soften

and he smiles a little, looking out at the bridges.

"Me too."

He hasn't said much, but somehow, it's like we just reached an understanding. It's like we're back, talking about Edgar Allan Poe, like he's volunteering a part of him that's clearly deeper than just favoring one season over the others.

"I have a dream of, like . . ." His cheeks flush, but he goes on: "Rhode Island, maybe? Real seasons. I just want to wear a scratchy sweater, and there are leaves on the ground, and I have hot apple cider, an old book."

That sounds poetic, honestly, and I'm imagining it as if I were there.

"Have you ever been?"

"No," he says. "I mean, I toured MIT when the leaves were changing. But I didn't do any of the coastal New England stuff. Hopefully one day. I think it would just be nice to experience. Just to feel something different."

I understand what he means. I've dreamt of a million different lives. I've let myself imagine what it'd be like to call so many places home, or even just to visit. Just to smell the air. Croissants and sugar in Paris. Earl Grey and jam in London. Wildflowers and the Pacific in Los Angeles.

"Benji has a whole album called *New England*," I say. "But it's not like his pop stuff—not like 'Banana Milkshake' or *Icarus* or anything."

Sebastian glances over at me. "Always trying to sell me on Benji."

"Well, this one is pretty, but it's very sad." I wiggle my nose and squint as the sun bounces off a boat's window.

His jaw tightens. "How sad?"

"Sad. You know, he's singing about memories. Lost love. That kind of stuff. He has this line that they use on a lot of merch from that album—*Nowhere is as haunted as New England*."

"That doesn't sound sad at all," he laughs. "Sounds like he loves it there."

"Oh, had the *best* time," I agree.

Snapping his fingers together, he points at me, standing straight. "That one song—'Clam Chowder.' From that album?"

"Yeah, exactly," I say. "You know that song?"

Sebastian leans against the railing again. "Yeah, I like it. Who knew an autumn breeze and clam chowder could be gut wrenching?" He drums his fingers on the metal. "*Drowning in a dirty martini, fallen, struck down, misfired malice, this bar was once our town*."

I gasp. "You are a Benji Keaton fan."

He laughs, waving me off. "No, I just like that song. It's a good song."

"All this time, you're making fun of me and acting like Benji is for middle school girls or something, but you have some of his lyrics in your back pocket."

Sebastian takes this as his cue to push off the railing and start walking away. "Come on, we'd better get on the ferry before Eden."

"Wait," I say, following him, but now *he's* setting the pace and I know he's going fast on purpose. "Sebastian, wait, are you a Benji Keaton fan?"

The way he groans and slows down a bit so I can catch up, I think this might be erring dangerously on the side of risky if I'm going off last night. I don't want to push him and upset him again, but this is *Benji* we're talking about.

"I'm not a Benji fan," he says. "Really. I'm not."

"Well, why are you being so weird about it?"

He shoots me a look. "I'm not being weird."

We walk and we walk, and I stay quiet. There's clearly something going on. Why would he be ashamed to be a Benji Keaton fan? And with me, of all people?

Eventually, we arrive at Corlears Hook, and we go through the process of downloading the app to buy ferry tickets. We purchase our tickets, and we board the boat when it arrives, all without any additional mention of Benji.

Climbing the stairs up to the deck, I watch Sebastian carefully. Have I upset him? I can't imagine why this is a big deal at all, but I'd rather not get into a fight.

A group of kids who look about fifteen are sitting in some of the chairs, eating chips and drinking sodas. I wonder if they're skipping school, since it's a Thursday morning, but I realize if it were me, and I lived in New York City and Annie wanted to get on the ferry for fun on a weekday, I'd probably be down without much need for persuading.

Across from the kids playing hooky, a girl with a long blond braid leans her head on her boyfriend's shoulder. I catch Sebastian glancing at them before he decides to sit on a bench by the stairs.

I watch the frothy wake behind the boat before turning to face the bridges. We head toward Brooklyn, and as the Manhattan Bridge gets closer, as the skyline swells, my ability to keep my big mouth shut shrinks.

"So, what is it? You just happened to click on that one song because you want to go to New England?"

Sebastian slumps over, burying his face in his hands. "Teddy, come on."

"I'm just confused. This is something we have in common."

He exhales. "It isn't."

"Are you embarrassed to like Benji Keaton songs? Because you know I, of all people, wouldn't think you're any less cool or anything."

This makes him laugh. "I don't want to be cool, Teddy. I just want to drop Benji Keaton. He writes some good lyrics. He has some catchy hooks and bridges. But I'm not going to wear one of his T-shirts or watch his documentary."

Oh my God, he totally likes multiple Benji songs.

"Okay, top five Benji songs." I don't mean to sound so eager, but this is major. I wouldn't have expected this, given Sebastian's dismissal of Benji. I'm so curious what his Spotify looks like now. "Go."

"No," he says.

"Top *three*?" I offer. A little compromise never hurt anyone.

Sebastian glares at me. "Teddy."

"Fine. But." I don't know why he's being so cagey about this. It's not a big deal at all. If I liked something he liked, I'd tell him about it. "At the very least, if you like Benji's lyrics so much, what's your favorite one?"

He looks right at the skyline. "I'm not going to—"

"I'll leave you alone about it if you tell me. I just think it's really interesting to—"

"I used to love sunsets, now I'm by myself on our beach."

He says it almost automatically. His eyes are still set, narrowed on the buildings beyond the bridges, and his mouth is curved downward, his jaw squared and then he sighs, turning away from me.

It tells me everything I need to know. There are memes and TikTok trends about how heartbroken someone must be if their favorite Benji song comes from *Sunset*. And if he's listening to "Sunset" and "Clam Chowder," I can only imagine he's listened to "Harrowing" or even "Full Circle," which I'd mentioned when we saw Columbus Circle for the first time.

And the reason Sebastian doesn't want to talk about Benji Keaton or his discography is painstakingly clear as well. And it occurs to me he's right, in at least one way: this isn't something we have in common, after all.

"I'm sorry."

It's not the most intelligent or thoughtful apology, but it's only because I'm surprised. By my ability to senselessly push him, again, because I can't empathize with what he's going through. I'm surprised how often I've been wrong about Sebastian, and how I can entirely understand why all the talk of Benji is, at the very least, sobering considering his foray into the discography.

He doesn't say anything, and I wonder if he's upset again. He can't storm off like he did at the Met. Not yet anyway. I hope he's not planning to once the ferry docks in Brooklyn.

"I really am sorry." I wince, like the pain is inflicted on me and not him, but he doesn't see that, thankfully. "I got overly excited about you listening to Benji. I only want to try and get to know you. I want to try and be friends, and I thought this was going to be some magic common ground."

Sebastian finally looks at me. Unexpectedly, he smiles. "You really do just think there's a magical solution to everything, don't you?"

"Of course I do," I laugh. "There has to be. Otherwise, life would be horrible and depressing and pointless."

He makes a face, as if to say *maybe it is.*

"You know, you don't actually lose anything by believing in things like luck and magic."

I live my life for luck, really. I live my life as if luck is a currency, and I hold on so tight to any shred of it I can because without it, I don't know what I'd be able to afford.

Sebastian isn't inclined to believe me, I can tell, but

he doesn't argue. He doesn't make fun of the idea or my staunch belief in things that are easy to dismiss.

Instead, he does something else entirely unexpected. He opens up.

"I listened to a few of Benji's songs a lot after my breakup," he says. "And I still have the playlist—the breakup playlist—hidden in a folder on my Spotify. I need to delete it. I don't like listening to those songs. I don't like thinking about them."

I frown. "I understand. I mean, I don't. Of course. But I'm sorry for making you talk about it. We don't have to."

He shrugs. "It's okay, I'm not upset about it anymore. Really. I just don't want to relive it. Breakups are about as fun as you might expect."

"Benji cries when he sings 'Sunset,'" I offer. "He does it on the piano sometimes, and even in a stadium, it gets silent."

Sebastian nods. He recognizes this is my way of getting as close to understanding as I'm able to.

"Do you miss your ex?" I ask softly.

"I do not." Sebastian laughs, and the next thing I know, we're both laughing. We're both throwing our heads back, even, eyes dry from the wind and the sun's glare. I don't know what exactly is funny about it, except that his answer is so quick and so immediate, and maybe his laughter is contagious. Maybe he should laugh like this more.

"It's really just the songs," he says, once we've collected ourselves. "I don't know. You just don't want to go back to that place. Being all sad and whatever."

Again, I get it, but not fully.

"But I don't miss him. He cheated on me. A few times, I think. And there were other things." He pulls a face. "I'm just trying to say . . . I guess . . . Not all love inspires great art. You just find refuge in it, instead."

I love Benji. I know all his songs by heart. I've seen him in concert. I have his merch. I've made TikToks to his songs with Annie. I'm here, in New York, to see him on Broadway and meet him.

And yet, for the first time in my life, I feel disconnected from Benji. It's so hard to figure out this feeling, but Sebastian actually connects with the lyrics. Sebastian gets what he's saying when he sings of lost love and heartache. I can't relate.

Questioning my connection to Benji and his music is surprisingly existential.

Luckily, I think Sebastian might sense the dramatics brewing in my mind, because he knocks one of his knuckles against the Polaroid in my lap.

"Don't we need to take a photo on the ferry?"

"Oh my God, yes, we do. Thank God you remembered."

Get it together, Teddy. You can't go having existential crises now—you're so close to finishing the scavenger hunt.

We take a selfie, and Sebastian even throws up bunny ears behind me, squinting as the sun paints us golden.

Chapter 20

Now or Never

The ferry drops us off at a landing right next to the Brooklyn Bridge.

"You promised lunch," Sebastian says as soon as we step off.

I pull out my phone and look at what's around. We need something quick, because I can only imagine Eden is trying to recalculate and reroute to optimize their course.

"There's a Shake Shack," I offer. "Do you like burgers?"

"Of course I like burgers."

"And then, once we're full and sluggish, we walk across the Brooklyn Bridge," I say. "Is it weird that I am *super* excited to walk across the Brooklyn Bridge?"

Sebastian chuckles. "I think I'd be concerned if you weren't."

"It seems like such a rite of passage, you know? I mean

it's the *Brooklyn Bridge.*"

"Maybe say 'Brooklyn Bridge' one more time."

"Brooklyn Bridge." I grin and we walk over to Shake Shack, which is only a few minutes away, and takes up the first floor of an older brick building. It's really busy, which makes sense, since it's just past noon.

I get a few texts while we're waiting in line.

ANNIE:

how are things going?

ANNIE:

i'm choosing to believe radio silence is a good thing and you're not having anymore chaotic breakdown moments

ANNIE:

in school suspension is literally the biggest joke

ANNIE:

mrs. v doesn't care what we do, she puts on movies and just like goes on walks and shit. honestly, i could have put a cardboard cutout of me and snuck on the new york trip

ANNIE:

anyway, hopefully you're having a reasonable amount of fun without me!!

I am both amused and disappointed. I'd almost forgotten, while actually getting along with Sebastian, that this was supposed to be a best friend trip. Right now, in this Shake Shack line, I should be listening to Annie go on about the limited vegan options. She should be wearing her Benji shirt beside me. We would have shared AirPods and listened to "The Best Part" on the ferry. We'd be posting selfies on Instagram, and maybe we'd have made a TikTok to one of Benji's New York songs. Maybe we'd have gotten his attention, even.

I feel a little guilty for having these thoughts, which I find strange. Sebastian wouldn't mind, but I start to question if I'd change things. He's still a mystery, and I want to keep getting to know him.

"Something wrong?"

Sebastian isn't looking at my phone, but at me. It's a small thing to notice, but I like the way he doesn't try to look at my texts, like so many other kids would.

"No, just Annie texting from in-school suspension."

"How's she doing?"

I laugh. "She says it's a joke."

"I had it once," Sebastian says. When he sees my reaction, he shakes his head. "Nothing exciting. I just skipped too many AP Government classes. And, not to brag, but I had an A. So obviously it wasn't detrimental if I didn't listen to O'Grady talk at us on half speed."

"You took AP Government?"

"Sure." He shifts his focus to the menu on the wall. "It wasn't bad."

"It sounds horrifying."

I respond to Annie while we wait, letting her know things are going well and we'll still FaceTime tonight. I imagine Sebastian is going to disappear again, though I do need to make sure he's back in time for us to be at Grand Central when the clock strikes midnight for a Polaroid.

"Is she super bummed to miss out on New York?" Sebastian asks.

I put my phone in my pocket. Strangely, I realize the answer isn't the one I'm expecting—or want. "I don't think she is *super* bummed."

The thing is, if it were anyone else, I might write off an unfazed façade as just that—brushing off disappointment and sadness to keep up appearances. But it's Annie. And I know Annie. She doesn't want to be stuck in Citrus—and doing in-school suspension, no less—when she could be here, but I don't think she seems half as sad as I might like her to.

I've seen Annie sad, and this isn't it. Shouldn't she be, though? Shouldn't she be devastated that our last hurrah has been taken away from us?

It suddenly hurts my feelings just a little to know she's not more upset.

"Have you started writing any lyrics?"

Here we go again.

"I don't know if I'm going to."

We get to the counter, and we each order the same thing: a ShackBurger combo. Only Sebastian adds bacon to his, and he also gets cheese fries, insisting we have to at least try them. I try the Fifty/Fifty, which is half lemonade and half iced tea, while Sebastian goes for straight lemonade.

Sitting at a table by the window, Sebastian rests his forearms on the table and leans forward. "I think you could write a song, Teddy."

"I think you could."

"Don't try and deflect," he says. "Anyway, I told you, I'm not torn up."

"I'm not torn up either," I insist. But it's pointless to say this when just last night I completely spilled my guts about how torn up I am. "Well, not enough to write a song about it."

He doesn't press again until we have our food. After I've taken a giant bite of my burger, and we've both agreed that these are the best cheeseburgers we've ever had in our entire lives, he taps his chin, almost mischievously.

"Could we try an exercise?"

I shake my head. "I don't like exercise."

"This is, like, character work."

"Oh?" I set my burger down and grab one of his cheese fries, incredibly glad he thought to order them. "Now you're, like, a director?"

"I've just been trying to figure this out," he says.

"Go on," I say.

Sebastian picks up a fry and waves it around, thinking. "Maybe if you think of it as a role, you can commit to diving deep."

"It's not that I can't dive deep," I say. "There isn't

anything to dive into. That's the problem. Things happen to people. Life happens, and love happens, and then you put your feelings into art. Right? But things don't happen to me. And I don't really want to complain . . ."

I knock on the wooden table.

"I thought we decided you could write a song about your friendship?"

Though there's a particular vulnerability in the things I've already shared with Sebastian, there's another depth to admitting I couldn't even begin when I tried.

"Feels so Disney movie," I say. "I'm eighteen years old, and the best thing I can write about is that I'm sad my best friend is moving away?"

Sebastian eats another fry. "People write songs about all kinds of things, Teddy."

"People write songs about love," I insist.

"They write about whatever is important to them. Their hometowns, their grandparents, their feelings of inadequacy."

Sitting in this Shake Shack in DUMBO, across from Sebastian, I'm not sure I could even write about my feelings of inadequacy. I don't know how to actually describe them, except for the fact that they make the restaurant get bigger, and me feel smaller, wanting to sink into my seat.

"Why do you care so much about me writing a song?" I pick up my drink, but I don't take a sip. I just hold it, waiting for his response.

He bites his lip, looks off, out the window, and then

back to me. "I don't know."

It's a simple answer, and not at all what I expected.

"Well, then, it's all good. We can just let it go. I don't know how this all started anyway."

He frowns. "I think you could do it, but I'm not going to force you to see that."

"Maybe one day when—"

"You can't live life on 'maybe one day,' Teddy."

I don't intend to live my life that way, but I don't argue because I realize I just might end up doing it anyway.

"What is your favorite part of New York?" I ask, desperate to change the subject. "So far?"

Unlike me, Sebastian isn't going to push when it's so painfully clear the conversation has expired. I could learn a thing or two.

"The architecture," he says plainly. "What's yours?"

"The way I feel." Sebastian looks intrigued, so I go on. "My expectations for this city were sky-high, and somehow, it's lived up completely. Even though we've only been here for no time at all. We haven't even done that much, in the grand scheme of things, but there's something about this place."

He smirks. "Makes my answer feel pretty dumb."

"No, the architecture is totally my second answer," I offer with a smile.

We finish our burgers and fries, and I think we're starting to talk more and more like friends. I find Sebastian still thinks before he responds to things—something Annie and I both are pretty bad about *not* doing enough—but I take it less as a sign of mistrust or caution. It's just who he is.

"Let's go cross the Brooklyn Bridge," Sebastian says as we head outside.

We get to the bridge, and we walk up some stone steps and along the pavement as bicycles and other pedestrians head toward the city. I notice, though, maybe a bit too late, that there are a lot more people heading the opposite way, back to Brooklyn. A lot of them are groaning, complaining even. It's when we reach the yellow line to cross onto the wooden pedestrian walkway of the bridge that I see why.

This absolutely cannot be happening.

Pedestrian Walkway Closed for Filming!

Chapter 21

Razzle Dazzle

I glance up at the giant Brooklyn Bridge ahead of us. The gothic arches are massive, and the sheer size of the suspension bridge is another one of those things that can't be fully comprehended from photos alone. An American flag waves at the top of the tower, right in the center.

Right down the middle of the bridge is the pedestrian walkway. We should already be making our way through, and I can't help but worry Eden might have already crossed or is planning to cross later, once this is all cleared away, and that she's using this time to check something else off. Even if she wasn't, we'd be so behind if we had to come back to cross later tonight or tomorrow. It's so far from Midtown and there aren't any other items we could check off down here to make it worth it.

Sebastian is mumbling something, but then he clears

his throat as I start walking toward the blockades. A few other people are lining them, maybe trying to sneak a peek, but security guards or tech of some sort are asking them to leave.

"Uh, Teddy? What are you doing?"

"I'm just seeing what our options are."

I don't have to turn back to know he's looking at me like I'm nuts.

"We don't have any *options*," he says. "What are you going to do?"

"I have no clue," I admit.

The thing is, we just have to make this work. I'm not even channeling anybody else or asking *what would Annie do?* I only know there has got to be some way to get onto this bridge.

"Come back here," he says, grabbing my arm. Again, with the unusually comfortable gesture. Surprised, I follow him back a few steps and stand off to the side as the cluster of pedestrians bump shoulders. "We can't just go up to the set."

Looking around, I know he's right. Obviously two random kids can't just wander onto an active, closed set. But we also aren't really even *on* the bridge yet, so there's no way we're going to be able to cross this off.

"We could get the photo with the bridge in the background," Sebastian says.

"No way, we have to walk across, remember? It's a rite of—"

"Hey, sorry, we got caught in all these fucking people—" A girl with her hair in space buns settles in next to us. Her eyes go wide. "Oh, God. I'm so sorry. You look just like one of the other extras we were with the other day."

"No worries," I say. It's like the universe just dropped this gift in my lap. In *our* laps, I think, giving Sebastian an overly confident smile. Three quick tugs at the strings of my lucky bracelet and I straighten up. "We were trying to find the other extras. It's so crowded up here."

The girl nods. "A whole mess. Okay, come on. We'll go find Alessandra."

Sebastian's eyes bug as we follow the girl and her friend up to the barricades.

"Are you with Greyson?" I come up with a random name, but say it like he's somebody really important.

"No way," she laughs. "I found this through a random group, but usually I book through my agent at Atomic."

Thank you, lucky bracelet.

"I was with Atomic," I say—this is just improv now. "But my agent left. Small world!"

The girl frowns. "You should have gotten a referral. I'm with Monique—she's amazing."

"Maybe I'll look into going back," I say.

Sebastian's glare is burning a hole in the back of my skull, but this is just how it's done.

"Honestly, I took this one because you know with big names the craft services is bomb. And they actually let us take advantage of it," she says.

One of the security guards says something, and she flashes him her phone. The four of us are let past all the other onlookers.

We're on a set. Holy shit, we are on a movie set. With big names, *did she say?*

"Speaking of, I'm going to grab a croissant." She looks around. "See you guys in a few."

I clear my throat, hoping for some more fake confidence. "Oh, hey, when is, um—like, when are we—"

"Call time was forty-five minutes ago," she laughs. "So we'll probably be shooting in fifteen. You know how these things go."

"*Totally.*" I force a laugh, but it's not entirely fake. I do know how these things go. At the high school theater level, at least.

Once it's just me and Sebastian, standing next to a couple of large black Pelican suitcases on the side of the Brooklyn Bridge pedestrian walkway, he gawks.

"This is *absurd,*" he says. "You just—we're trespassing."

"Since when are you all obsessed with the rules?"

"With the *law,*" he points out. "I mean . . . we're eighteen, so I think we could go to jail."

I shake my head. "Nope. We were invited onto set. Voluntarily brought on."

"You think that would hold up?"

"Of course it would." I frown, and tapping into my masterful acting skills, I let my voice shift up nearly an entire octave, offering big doe eyes: "*We didn't mean to, I swear.*"

He laughs. "All right, then. Now what? We take the Polaroid and then just apologize? 'Sorry, we got lost'?"

I look around the set. A few of the classic black director's chairs are lining one side of the walkway, next to a few displays that are currently switched off, and a huge black camera hanging from a mechanical arm. Cords snake around the ground, and there are neon orange and pink markers—pieces of tape stuck to various planks, some crossing each other to form an X.

This is surreal. And who are the big names, I wonder?

There is one woman who is absolutely too fabulous to not be an actress—wearing a vibrant canary sundress and black flip-flops, she's hunched over a table flipping through a binder. Her hair is fiery, perfectly wavy, and magically unfazed by the wind at the top of the bridge.

Wait a minute.

She stands up tall, grabbing a cup of coffee and when she turns around, I almost faint. Anyone in the world would recognize her. With that oval face, those deep red lips, with the iconic cupid's bow, and her striking emerald eyes.

"It's Addie Harlow."

"Holy shit."

Addie Harlow isn't just an actress. She's a *movie star.* She's ethereal—she's larger than life, and her presence instantly makes this entire bridge feel smaller, but not in an intimidating or suffocating way—it's like you're lucky to be so incredibly close to her.

She catches us looking and offers a teeny, tiny smile. I wonder if it's just natural for her. I wonder if she's rehearsed that smile, when people are gawking at her, the way her lip curls up and she bats her lashes quickly before turning away. She gives the smallest acknowledgment of our presence, but she doesn't give anything more than that. Polite niceties. It's more than a lot of big stars would give extras, I'd bet.

Back to focusing on the binder, a couple of assistant-types scurry over to her, consumed in their phones.

I look at Sebastian. "I cannot believe we are on an Addie Harlow film set right now."

"I am honestly terrified."

"No, this is amazing. Don't you see? New York City really *is* magical, Sebastian. We're going to be in an Addie Harlow movie."

He swallows, as if this is occurring to him now. "Maybe. We *might* be in an Addie Harlow movie."

"Well, nobody will know it's us unless we point ourselves out," I say, nodding. "We'll just be blurred in the background, I'm sure, but it'll be really cool. I'm choosing to believe we'll make the final cut. How exciting."

Sebastian doesn't say anything, he just blinks slowly, staring at Addie Harlow.

"This is an amazing sign," I say. "I think it means things are going up from here." Then: "Oh my God. Eden is going to lose her *mind*. And Annie is going to *flip*! I manifested this, Sebastian. I said this would happen. It's fate. It's magic." I take a quick, covert photo. It's grainy and barely catches Addie Harlow's side profile, but it's clearly her.

ME:

omg omg omg omg we are going to be in an addie harlow movie

I send through the photo.

ME:

i truly can't believe this is happening

ME:

it's addie harlow

I imagine she'll walk over to us, and she'll find us adorable. She'll say it's obvious we're not New Yorkers, but in a funny and cute way, and she'll ask us if we want to take a photo to share with the rest of the drama club. She'll insist we're less blurred than the rest of the extras, and she'll ask us if we want to have a coffee with her. Maybe a glass of wine—she won't tell. She's cool. And she's all *Hollywood.* There are hardly any rules she has to follow.

When I call her Addie Harlow, she'll say: "Oh, please, just Addie is fine!"

And we'll laugh and she'll marvel at the fact that it doesn't take long at all for us to feel like old friends.

"It's so nice to be treated just like everybody else," she'll say, a gleam in her eye.

We'll get on so swimmingly, she'll invite us to her hotel. She's probably staying at the Pierre, in a suite that overlooks Central Park. We'll sit on tufted couches, and then we'll end up laughing, fully clothed in the empty bathtub with champagne flutes, celebrating what a happy coincidence it was that we all met. Even Sebastian will be overjoyed, with no commentary to offer about how superfluous the grandeur is.

After room service comes and we have decadent mousse, shortcake, and petit fours, we'll flip through the TV and watch TikToks and gossip about all of her past costars. Somehow, Benji will come up, and I'll act shy when Sebastian says I'm a huge fan.

"Oh my gosh, let's invite him over!" Addie will say, and then the night will take a turn for the even more unimaginable.

All because of this scavenger hunt, we'll be dancing in the largest suite at a luxurious hotel with two of the biggest stars, and Sebastian will have no choice but to admit New York City is pure magic.

Our lives will never be the same.

"Teddy," Sebastian says, nudging me.

I snap to and realize my fantasy scenario has just become alarmingly distant, now that Addie Harlow has moved a few yards away and is preoccupied with a hair and makeup team, touching her up as crew members set up giant round silver disks and booms.

"They called for extras," he says, hushed and nodding toward a small crowd farther down on the bridge. "This is our last chance—we can just get the photo and get out while we're ahead."

"No way. We have to do this."

One of the crew members gives us a sideways glance when we join the group. He's wearing a burgundy flat-billed cap, black-rimmed glasses, and has a dark mustache with no other facial hair.

"Who are you two?"

Chapter 22

When He Sees Me

I pull a face when Mustache asks who we are—as if he should certainly recognize us. In fact, in accordance with this skit I'm doing, I'm very thrown off by his question, since we go way, way back. "What do you mean?"

He looks as if he might be trying to recall whether we are actually extras.

"We're with Monique," I say, like I'm helping him connect puzzle pieces he already has. "From Atomic?"

"Oh," he says, nodding quickly. "Right, okay."

I hold back showing any sign of the relief washing over me.

The group is interesting. Everybody is paired up with a buddy, and most people are coordinating outfits, so Sebastian and I do stand out a little. We are decidedly not on the outfit coordination stage of our newfound friendship or whatever this is, but we'll just play it off. We're both wearing musician shirts, at the very least.

I glance over my shoulder. We are supposed to be crossing this bridge. We have to cross the bridge. We can't come to New York City and walk some of the bridge, but not the entire thing. That is completely missing the point.

While it might not be the most opportune time, Mustache seems generally congenial.

"Just curious, when we wrap, would we be able to walk over to Manhattan?"

Mustache squints, turning to face the city. "Uh, yeah?"

"Okay. Cool." I nod. "Just making sure."

He doesn't say anything else for a minute, but he does study me like I'm ever so slightly suspicious, though he can't quite place why. He checks his phone and then claps to get everyone's attention.

"We'll just have a standard walk-on, walk-off," Mustache says. "You're enjoying the gorgeous day; you couldn't be happier. This is the best day of your whole entire fuckin' lives. Literally nothing has ever made you light up with more joy and excitement than this moment on the Brooklyn Bridge. But it needs to feel natural, too. Don't give me some caricature shit."

I look at Sebastian, and he doesn't look concerned, but he's got to be thinking the same thing as me.

We might be a little out of our league.

"All right, everyone, let's go. It's time to convince me

you're a happy couple!"

I've played my fair share of parts. I've taken on roles that are entirely different from me. Let's face it, I'm no Troy Bolton or J.D., and I'm certainly not a Pugsley. But that's what makes acting fun—being someone different. Playing pretend.

Embodying a happy couple with Sebastian in the background of an Addie Harlow movie? I only wish extras got Oscar noms.

We stand close together, and I have a feeling we're not exactly giving off swoon-worthy couple energy, but I am also not exactly sure how we'd go about doing that. With another actor playing opposite, I'd be able to make this work, surely, but it's Sebastian.

I mean, it's *Sebastian.*

Sebastian is handsome enough. If I were a scholar, studying the male form or something, he's objectively and empirically handsome enough. His nose is long and sharp. He has thick, but well-proportioned and spaced eyebrows. Brown eyes. A squared jaw. Full lips. Fluffy brown hair, pushed back, with curls dancing in the wind. Overall, an effortless quality to his good looks.

Especially, I think, when the sunlight glows from behind his profile—lashes gold, his brows drawn a little tighter as he squints just a bit, and his mouth turned into a slight pout, Sebastian looks—

I catch myself.

What the hell are you doing?

I know I'm not admiring Sebastian in the warm glow of the sunlight.

Surely this is just me getting into character. I'm not admiring, I'm only *appreciating*.

But he's picturesque. This is a scene from its own movie. This is its own album cover. Sebastian with his ridiculously handsome and squared profile, the worn fabric of his T-shirt revealing the top of his collarbone, set against the gothic arches of the Brooklyn Bridge with the flag waving in the wind, the sky a clear blue, and the downtown Manhattan skyline stacked like it was put there just for this moment.

I snap a Polaroid.

"Hey, dude." Mustache throws his hands up. "None of that."

Sebastian gives me a very confused look.

"Just thought it was good lighting," I offer, entirely to Mustache, ignoring Sebastian's surprised eyes. "Sorry."

I'm not sure what came over me, but I am struck by the sight of Sebastian on this summer day in the city. It feels like I'm living in a song.

I don't wait to look at the Polaroid, I just shove it in my pocket, and he rolls his eyes, thinking I'm making fun of him or something, I'm sure.

"Get cozy," Mustache says, gesturing toward two girls. One is wearing overalls, and one is wearing a skirt and crop top. They hold hands, and their body language makes me question if they might be an actual couple—they're comfortable, naturally close and well acquainted.

Addie Harlow is cued, and the clapboard signals us all to start walking. She'll be in focus, of course, and we'll all just casually stroll around her.

She places her phone to her ear, clutching her chest with her other hand before she cries out: "Oh, please don't do this, we're in love!"

Apart from the fact that my heart was maybe beating a little faster because of *Sebastian*, I'm a little bit distracted by the glamour of everything happening. So, I almost bump into one of the other happy couples.

"Cut!"

Mustache is getting his ass handed to him by someone else who looks very important behind one of the screens, and then he heads over to us as we all set back in our places. I'm taking cues from the other extras, and so is Sebastian.

"All right, we look like a bunch of zoo animals let loose on the bridge. We've got too many people gawking at Addie, and we're not giving happy couples enjoying the gorgeous day. The fuck?" He points at Sebastian and me. "You two look like you're on a first date."

He raises his brows expectantly, and Sebastian takes my hand.

I inhale sharply, but I don't want him to notice. We're actors. He's clearly taking the role more seriously than I am, which is never a good thing in terms of sharing a stage. We need to meet each other's energy. I need to *act*.

So I inch closer, our arms practically enmeshing.

"Uh-huh." Mustache looks at the group. "Guys, we've been over this. She's getting her heart broken, and all around—as her heart literally is fucking shred into tiny pieces—she's seeing all these happy couples. Happy. Couples! It's ironic. It's symbolic. It has to be slightly exaggerated to make the point, but it can't be too over-the-top. Give me a little more this next take, people. Please."

Sebastian keeps his eyes focused, straight ahead, and squeezes my hand a little.

As Mustache walks back to join the crew and Addie resets, I begin to notice what it feels like to hold hands with Sebastian. I begin to notice how it feels like the buzzing of power lines in summer, starting in the center of our palms. I begin to notice how it travels, in jolts at first, up my wrist and how my breathing steadies but my heart races.

And once I've noticed all of these things, I wonder if Sebastian is noticing them, too. I wonder if this is electric for him, too. I wonder if he's only acting, or if he's maybe paying attention to my heartbeat against his fingers.

"Oh, please don't do this, we're in love!"

Addie's voice breaks, her heart is being shred into tiny pieces, just like Mustache said, and the happy couples revel in summer romance all around her. One older woman even blows bubbles with a small yellow wand, which I'm assuming is a prop she's been provided, since nobody reacts. It's a nauseating display of love, and as we walk, Sebastian flashes me a convincing, if not nearly too debonair, smile. The sun complements him, painting his lips ruby and highlighting his cheeks and the tip of his nose like he's born for this.

"CUT."

That one doesn't sound good at all. Much quicker, snippier.

After some deliberation, Mustache returns.

"We need more." He looks at Sebastian and me, very pointedly. "Can you guys turn it up a few notches?"

If Sebastian can feel my heartbeat, he can tell that it's at a nearly inhuman pace now. So fast it might even be worrisome.

A few notches?

Mustache takes a few steps back and lifts a shoulder, running his thumb and index finger over his chin as he studies the group as a whole. "Maybe we need some kissing."

Nobody moves.

"Come on, you all act like you've never seen lovey-dovey couples before. I want you to make me sick. Disgust me, make me puke with how cute and adorable and garishly in love you are. This isn't that difficult. Make Addie *feel* the devastation of loss as she sees your joy."

That's bleak.

"KISSING."

Everyone resets.

"Oh, please don't do this, we're in love!"

Sebastian is leading this time, as we walk closer to Addie, his hand firm in mine. My heart skips when he quits walking and looks down at me.

Our eyes meet.

In my periphery, I can tell Addie has turned to face us, with her profile facing the camera.

It feels like all eyes are on us, but that doesn't stop me from getting lost in the amber specks of Sebastian's. They're simultaneously familiar and brand-new. His lips are parted just a little, bright cherry red, and when he swallows, his Adam's apple bobs against his throat.

He squeezes my hand a little tighter. His eyes lower. To my mouth.

The space between us has become fuzzy, like TV static. Like the space between two magnets, desperate to be closed.

"Cut!"

Sebastian drops my hand, jerking away.

"That's it. Amazing. We got it!"

"Good job," Sebastian says, entirely nonchalant.

I nod, taking a breath and a step back. "You too. You should have been *on* stage, not doing tech!"

He laughs. "I'm not half the actor you are."

That was all it was, after all. Acting. Of course it was. It's not like I actually thought it was anything else, surely. I was just fully in character. Fully invested in the story we were telling.

Addie smiles at me again, only this time she doesn't

seem to do it out of necessity. She doesn't smile and then, without missing a beat, look away. She just nods ever so slightly, like maybe she was fully invested in the story we were telling too.

And that's how I top this once-in-a-lifetime experience. By getting a Polaroid selfie with Sebastian and Addie Harlow on the Brooklyn Bridge before we walk right across to Manhattan.

Chapter 23

Freeze Your Brain

"We're literally going to be in an Addie Harlow movie," I say, bounding down the sidewalk with the bridge towering behind us. "And we have a selfie with her. We have a selfie with Addie Harlow."

Sebastian can't hide the fact that even he is awestruck. "I'm not going to lie. That was ballsy. You just went right up to her and asked her."

"I don't know what came over me."

Of course, that's not true at all. The magic of being in New York City came over me. The realization that I was in a once-in-a-lifetime situation, pretending to be an extra with Sebastian—or, I guess, not even pretending—on the set of an Addie Harlow movie.

Maybe our rom-com montage wasn't going to happen

at the Pierre, but I could still have something to remember this by.

And then there was also, perhaps, the need to quickly detach from the performance Sebastian and I had just put on. I was entirely too caught up in the hand-holding and the near-kissing and the *appreciating* Sebastian, and I had to move away from that immediately.

"What's up next?" Sebastian asks once we're standing in front of the gigantic Municipal Building.

"A vinyl store," I say. "For Our Strange Duet."

He gasps dramatically. "You told me the book one would be my favorite."

I nod. "Well, I was trying to motivate you!"

"A vinyl store," he repeats. "Oh, this is going to be good."

Bringing up Maps on my phone, I wag my finger. "Don't get too excited. I don't think this is going to be our easiest prompt."

He scoffs. "What is it? Find a vinyl that describes each other?"

"Find a vinyl with a duet that describes us. So easy!" I say, pausing for comedic effect. When he doesn't laugh, I shrug. "I'm sure there will be something."

"*Something.*" Sebastian nods.

Only, we both are silent on the entire walk down into the subway. When we push through the turnstiles and stand behind the yellow line waiting for the train, we don't speak. As we board and sit down, and as the train stops and starts, stops and starts, we're both entirely quiet. It's only when we get out at a stop called Astor Place that Sebastian finally sucks his teeth and sighs.

"I know a lot of songs," he says.

"I know you do."

"And you know a lot of songs," he adds.

"True."

"And between the two of us?"

"Definitely not a song that describes . . ." I pause. "Us."

I don't pause because it's strange that there isn't a song. I pause because it's strange that there is, decidedly, some form of an *us* between Sebastian and me now. Whatever the hell that may be—some seedling of a friendship, with the New York City magic acting like an organic fertilizer—it's there.

We come up to street level and my steps slow. It's like every single time I get out at a new subway stop, I'm enamored. Like New York smacks me in the face again, as if to say *you didn't think there wasn't more magic left?*

Dean FaceTimes me, and at first I think I should tell him I'm busy, but I figure he might like to see the city, so I answer.

"Hi," I say, holding my phone with one hand and shielding my eyes from the sun with the other. "What's up?"

Sitting on his bed, Dean is tossing a baseball up in the air and catching it repeatedly. He always does this, which drives my mom up a wall. We'll have family movie night, and Dean will have a ball to toss. Mostly it's fine, but since he's knocked out two lamps, an expensive CB2 statue on the coffee table, and struck out on a glass of red wine and an espresso at the same time? Mom is basically always watching him out of the corner of her eye.

"Just checking in on you," he says. "Seeing how you are after your mental breakdown."

I almost snap my neck looking over to see if Sebastian heard.

He did.

"I didn't have a mental breakdown," I say, laughing way too excessively. "Did you have one of the book club gummies?"

"Are you having *another* mental breakdown?" He raises a brow.

"I'm good," I say. I pan over to show him Sebastian. "Dean, this is Sebastian. Sebastian, this is my older brother, Dean. He hallucinates."

Dean grins and waves. "Hi, Sebastian!"

As outgoing as ever.

Sebastian, surprisingly, lights up a little—more than he normally would, anyway—and waves slightly. "Hi."

I bring the phone back to focus only on my face. "What are you doing today?"

Then I switch to the back camera and show him the city as we head down East Eighth Street.

"Oooh, look at that." He sets the ball on his chest as

he lies back on his pillow. "Looks awesome. Ummm. Not too much. Probably go down to the beach. Maybe get a sandwich."

I blink. "Sounds like you have a big day ahead of you."

"There are a lot of options for sandwiches," he sighs. "Anyway, I'll let you go, but just, you know . . ." He makes a face, clearly wanting me to interpret it as: *try not to have another mental breakdown*. "Have fun. Bye, Sebastian!"

"Bye," Sebastian says, peering over to look at Dean, even though Dean's still got the skyline view.

When I hang up, I wait for it. Sebastian doesn't miss a beat.

"Mental breakdown?"

"I was just processing."

"When was this?"

"Last night," I say. "But it's all good. I was just. Processing."

He nods. "You said that."

Desperate to change the subject, I point across the street at a bright pink storefront.

"What?" Sebastian asks. He looks at me like I'm nuts. "What?"

"Number thirteen on the list," I say. "She wants us to *have fun*. Eat ice cream. We should knock it out while we're here. Since there's an ice cream store right there."

The store is called the Wonderland, and there is a line of about four or five people standing outside who all appear to be Sebastian's favorite—fashion influencers. There are *so* many influencers walking around this city.

"Well, we could get ice cream anywhere," he says. "There's a line over there."

"But that probably means it's special!" I argue. I aim for an upbeat inflection: "Don't you want to see what they're lining up for?"

He eyes the line. "Not really?"

"Don't be grumpy," I say.

"I'm not being grumpy," he deadpans. "Waiting in line is going to help Eden get ahead of us."

Clever play, Sebastian. But one of the girls has already been let inside, so I shake my head.

"Come on, it can't possibly take that long."

It's also not lost on me how he said Eden would get ahead of *us*. He's totally invested.

The sign doesn't make a ton of sense to me until we're closer and I can see inside.

Sebastian is going to love this.

"It's, like, a magic-themed ice cream shop," I say. "Oh my God. Look. You get a tarot card with every cone or cup."

He lets out a long, breathy sigh. "Why am I not surprised we've ended up here?"

"We were *brought* here," I say. "Clearly."

"I am a man of science," Sebastian reminds me.

The line doesn't move for approximately ten minutes. During this time, I narrowly avoid Sebastian's gaze. I pretend I don't notice him rocking back and forth on the balls of his feet, and I pretend I can't hear when he grunts or groans and huffs or mutters something under his breath about how long it takes to make a cup of magical ice cream.

You can't rush magic.

When the line finally does move, two girls are let in, but we still have three ahead of us.

"This ice cream had better give me the ability to fly," Sebastian says.

I turn around and make a face. "You're joking. *That* would be the power you'd want?"

"Don't judge me," he says. "Anyway, I just said the first thing that came to mind."

"I'd choose mind reading," I say turning back to face the line. One of the girls gets let in as a couple leaves.

Sebastian doesn't say anything for a minute. "I think you'd have Chaos Magic."

I whip around. "Any comparison to Wanda is the greatest compliment."

He turns up one brow. "But would you use your powers for good?"

"Obviously," I say. "I'd make sure you and Poe had a great life as NPCs in my little conjured-up town."

"You would be so ridiculously good at conjuring up a fantasy reality," Sebastian laughs.

The girls in front of us give us looks like we are out of our minds.

They would *not* be welcome in my fantasy town.

Maybe Wanda was on to something, though. I mean, the way she went about it was very questionable—though she did have literally everything taken from her—but I could think of several reasons to conjure up a new reality.

If I could make anything, I'd maybe want to live in a reality where Annie doesn't move away. One where Dean doesn't go to college for months at a time. One where I can write songs, and not feel like some undeclared, directionless loser. And I guess if it was a reality from my imagination, Benji and I could have fireside chats about songwriting and artistry. That might be a plus.

Unfortunately, even my delusions have limits. And anyway, it didn't turn out so great for Wanda.

"You watched *WandaVision*," I say. "I did clock it earlier in the subway when you mentioned the MCU. But I didn't take you for a stan."

Sebastian looks amused. "You know there is, like, an in-between. You don't have to be a stan if you like things."

"I just like messing with you. Though I do think you might be a dinosaur stan. You know more than most people off the top of their heads."

"It's our turn." He points toward the door. "Besides, literally everyone likes *WandaVision*."

"Did you cry?" I walk up to the door but turn back when he doesn't respond. "You so did."

The inside of the store looks like a grenade of glitter and pink went off, splattering the walls with unicorn-aesthetics. There are also disco balls everywhere—maybe not as many as McGuire Grill for my birthday month, but I appreciate the effort.

"Welcome to Wonderland!"

The girl behind the counter is dressed in a sparkly silver top, with a pink name tag on her chest. I can't read it from here, since she's moving around and there are rainbows and disco ball reflections bouncing around everywhere.

"Is it named after, like, Alice? Or Taylor Swift?" I mean to ask it sort of quietly to Sebastian, but clearly I'm louder than I mean to be when the girl behind the counter answers.

"The Wonderland is a realm of its own," she says with a too-big smile.

Kind of giving a cult vibe, but it's really cute, at least.

It's tiny, and most people are waiting in line—to order, or for the back wall clearly designed to be a photo opp as it showcases a neon sign and tarot cards hanging from the ceiling on beaded strings. Lining the wall opposite the counter, there are three white café tables with two chairs each. It's almost as if they don't want people to sit and eat, the way they're so tiny and squished together.

The counter displays an assortment of colorful ice creams to choose from, all with names like Karmic Caramel, Ascended Apple Pie, or Empress Espresso.

Once we're actually in the line, I notice the girl's name tag reads *Melody.*

"Is it your first time here?"

"In New York or Wonderland?"

She lifts her shoulders, exaggerated like she's playing a princess at Disneyland. "Either!"

"Both, actually."

Sebastian is eyeing her, I think trying to determine if she's a trained actress or not.

"Well, we have plenty of options—many are gluten-free and vegan—and we also add a little bit of magic to every cup, plus a tarot card to offer some guidance."

Guidance . . . I glance around at everyone taking photos of their ice cream with the miniature tarot cards sticking out on plastic holders.

I'm in no position to turn down guidance. This really was fated.

Of course, there's the tiny little fact that I don't like ice cream.

We're up to order, and I think it's best if I just ignore that detail.

It's not that I absolutely detest ice cream, and I think it might be one of my weirder traits because I haven't ever met anyone else who hates it. Even Annie is obsessed with her vegan ice cream. It's just not something I ever *want*. I'm never like "oh, ice cream sounds so good right now."

And honestly? This ice cream is so aesthetic—all pastels, and little decorative flowers, and perfect missing chunks where it's been scooped as if even *this* is meant to be photographed—and it's still doing nothing for me.

Anyway, I order a scoop of Psychic PB&J. Can't go wrong with PB&J.

The scoop is miniature, and the little wooden spoon they stick in the ice cream looks like it's meant for a Barbie doll, not a human.

Sebastian stares at the display, and I don't know what to expect. Maybe he'll go for something chocolatey, or maybe something totally out of left field like the bubblegum-pink swirl with (hopefully edible) glitter dust all over it.

"I'm good," he says to the guy with the scoop, and then turns to me. "You got yours?"

"What? We both have to get ice cream."

"I don't like ice cream," he admits. "So, I'm okay. Can't we just take the Polaroid with yours?"

I consider this. "I don't know. I don't think so. You don't like ice cream?"

"No, I don't."

"I don't like ice cream either," I say, feeling seen for my strange affliction for the first time in my whole life. "I've never met anyone else who doesn't like ice cream."

Sebastian huffs. "Too cold."

"Exactly!"

The staff are all looking at us now, and it's very clear we have offended them by expressing our dislike for the very heart and soul of the Wonderland.

"I think you still should just get one," I say. "And we can suffer through it together. For the scavenger hunt. It'll be fun."

"You have the strangest ideas of fun."

The guy with the scoop lifts a brow. "What flavor would

you like to suffer through? We have a line."

Sebastian knows he won't win here, so his mouth forms a tight line and his shoulders fall. "Could I please have the . . ." He gives me a sideways glance. "The Mystical Maple?"

I pull a face because of how strongly I dislike maple, which the employee definitely sees as another strike against us.

By the time we're ready to pay, I think we've alienated ourselves from the entirety of the staff. A girl with pink hair sets my tiny little cup on the scale, and then she gives me the fakest smile I've ever seen before she turns the iPad toward me and I see the price.

"Eighteen dollars?" I gawk. I sound like a boomer—but I'm astounded. "Sorry, I just didn't expect that little scoop of ice cream to be eighteen dollars."

Sebastian raises a brow. "Uh, I don't think I really need mine then."

"Yeah," I say awkwardly. "We don't even like ice cream."

The girl smiles harder. "We heard. But we've already scooped your ice cream. I'll give you guys our first-timer's coupon—we love to provide a little extra magic whenever we can."

"How generous," Sebastian mumbles.

And that is how Sebastian and I end up each paying $15.30 for a single, miniscule scoop of ice cream that we do not want with a tiny little tarot card stuck onto a holder.

We rush out quickly, each free of the desire to spend

more time in Wonderland.

"My ice cream looks . . ."

"Why is everything *miniature*?" Sebastian asks angrily. "Teddy, Wonderland was a mistake."

"It might not have been," I say. "Maybe we'll get some valuable insights about our future or ourselves or something."

As we walk along the sidewalk toward the record store, he asks, "You mean from a card some NYU student randomly stuck into our ice cream for a cool fifteen dollars?"

"That's exactly what I mean," I say. "Didn't you read the signs? They're intuitive readings. We get the card that is meant for us."

"How do you believe in everything?"

"Don't you believe in anything?"

He pulls his card out of the holder and laughs. "The Wheel of Fortune. How fortuitous."

I type the card into Google and lift my brows. "Well, Sebastian, you're going to hate this. Guess what your card says? Trust in the universe. Trust destiny, and fate. And have a little faith."

Sebastian nods. "I'd bet plenty of tarot cards mean that."

I shrug. "I'm not sure, but I think yours is on the nose. It's not bad to have some faith."

"It can lead to disappointment," he says.

"Or inspiration! Faith inspires us to take chances," I say.

"Which can also lead to disappointment."

I huff and look at my card.

The Magician.

"Ooh, I like mine." I look it up, though I want to come up with my own meaning that I am, like, some totally badass wizard. "It says I manifest. I'm basically magical—I make my goals a reality."

This amuses Sebastian. "They could clearly tell you're into that kinda stuff."

"You have to admit our cards are pretty perfect for us. I manifested Addie Harlow. You just said I'd be Wanda."

"The cards happen to fit us," he admits. "But it could be any number of coincidences."

"You're not taking your card's advice to heart," I say. "Why are you *so* against it? What if magic is real? Then what?"

Sebastian takes a bite of his ice cream and makes a sour face. "If magic is real, then a lot of scientists are going to be out of jobs."

"Why can't science and magic exist at the same time?" I pause. "I mean, they do. So . . ."

He laughs. "Teddy, I don't think you're going to change my mind on this. I told you, I am a man of science."

In this city of constant magic, I wonder how he can't see it. How he can't feel it coursing through the streets.

"Why did you do drama club?" I ask. "Was it purely because you like *Phantom of the Opera*? I mean, you like genetics and evolution and dinosaurs. Why would you do theater?"

Sebastian pockets his tarot card. "I did *tech*."

"But with the drama club," I say. "Not robotics or . . . science . . . club?"

"I am in multiple societies," he specifies. "But I like theater."

"Really? You like theater?"

"You are almost insufferably relentless."

"Almost." I smile.

He shrugs. "I like theater, and I also knew there was a New York trip."

"So you were playing the long game," I say. "You joined last spring, so that's over a year of planning. And all this to mastermind your way to New York because . . . ?"

Sebastian takes a deep breath. "Why did you join drama club?"

Knowing he's not going to budge, I take a bite of my ice cream and now I am the one making a sour face. How can people charge so much for something that isn't even good?

I pause to think about how to answer, because drama club has become my whole world. At least, for the last few years. And somehow, now that it's shifting from the other side of the windshield to the rearview mirror, I am aware of the fact that I've been driving way too fast.

"I just wanted to sing," I say. "I did a theater camp and loved it, and I auditioned for a show, and it just all . . . clicked."

He smiles, tossing the rest of his ice cream in a trash can as we walk. "It definitely all clicked."

"I didn't even want to do musical theater," I say. "Believe it or not, I was disappointed when I pitched moving to Nashville at thirteen and my parents said no."

This elicits a laugh, but I'm very serious.

"Anyway, I love the drama club. And if I didn't do drama club, I might not have gotten into Broadway. I wouldn't know the magic of *Wicked*. The talents of Taylor Louderman, Chris McCarrell, Elizabeth Teeter, Angie Schworer. Just to name a few."

"I'm sure the list goes on," Sebastian says.

"Oh, it does." I suffer through a little bit more of the ice cream. "I'm sure you're glad you joined the drama club, too. Even if you only did it for this trip."

Even if you only did it for Blake . . .

Sebastian nods, looking at me with doe eyes that make my heart skip a beat: "Yeah, I am really glad I did."

Chapter 24

Thank You for the Music

We walk in silence the rest of the way, past a couple of kids on scooters, someone selling roses, a gaggle of fluffy dogs, and overstuffed wire trash cans.

After a few blocks, we turn left. The sidewalk is lined with blue Citi Bikes, and it seems like we've stumbled upon a small little old European town randomly plopped in New York.

We get to the vinyl store, and I decide not to tell Sebastian I found it on TikTok. I can only imagine he'd think that is the peak of Basic Teddy.

It's called Right Round Vinyl, and from what I've seen online, it's amazing.

A bell chimes when we enter, and a guy with a huge beard and small, round tortoise-framed glasses waves to us from behind the counter, though he's totally engrossed in a book splayed open before him.

The store is eclectic but organized. With colorful, imported rugs layered on the wide-planked wood floors and bright posters on the walls—big names, like Paul McCartney, Janis Joplin, Jimi Hendrix.

We browse through a few records, and I realize this is going to be impossible.

Even though I tend to be somewhat self-deprecating and dramatic, I do hate to find myself faced with anything truly impossible. But, alas, we're standing here, two guys who are hardly friends, and we're tasked with defining the dynamic in a painfully particular way.

Naturally, I gravitate toward the pop albums, and there is an entire white cardboard box decorated with gold stars and sun stickers. Mismatched letters, cut from magazines or elsewhere, messily spell out *Benji Keaton!* And I immediately recognize the bright yellow bleed at the top of *Sunrise*.

I've got all these records on vinyl, but it's still fun to place my finger on top of them and tick through, examining each like it's the first time I've seen it.

Icarus Complex is first, which makes sense because it's his newest. Inspired by Bernard Picart's painting, the cover shows a cropped image of a shirtless Benji, with wings strapped to his arms, falling with his eyes closed. There are drifting feathers and clouds and it's all warm, bleeding and burning hues. The image is beautiful but painful at the same time.

Then there's *New England*, a 30 mm shot of Benji. It's one of the most iconic, I think. One people re-create all the time. Hanging his head on a bench, surrounded by fallen orange and red leaves, with a brown paper bag beside him—a bottle of wine on its side, with the top visible and a waterfall of crimson splashing against the sidewalk. It was controversial at the time, funnily enough, because he was just starting to actually act like an adult after catering to an audience of young fans for so long. This edition has a round maroon sticker in the top right corner, with white text, the same font as the album title: *2 Bonus Tracks: "Red Line" & "Sweatah Weatha."*

Behind that—and out of order—is *Harrowing*, which is just a close-up of Benji's face in black-and-white. Simple. Eyes that scream. A mouth full of poems about heartbreak.

Sunrise and *Sunset* follow, and I instinctively move *Harrowing* to be after them. I can't help but correct it. The progression feels important. From black-and-white heartbreak to a bleeding sun painting an ocean and Benji in a hoodie with sand on his knees, to a purple-and-pink sky behind palm trees and the blurry Santa Monica Pier as Benji walks away from the camera.

Sebastian creeps up behind me, and I only know he's there because he blocks a sliver of the sunlight that was reflecting off the plastic-wrapped records.

"I'm imagining this is the part where I get an oral history."

It hangs there between us for a second.

Are we, two mature, eighteen-year-old guys, going to laugh at the fact that he just said *oral*? I bite my lip, because it's not funny or awkward or *anything*. It's a word. I'm an adult now, technically.

"No, I won't bore you."

I flick to what's after *Harrowing* and pull out *Sweet Vicious*.

"Except this is the album with the Columbus Circle song," I offer. I hold up the record, which features Benji in his brighter pop days—Ray-Bans and a white T-shirt with rolled-up shirtsleeves—as he leans over the railing on the Staten Island Ferry, the downtown New York skyline taking up the rest of the album cover in the background.

"Right, this is the 'Banana Milkshake' album," Sebastian laughs. "And that one song about dancing through Central Park."

"It's *supposed* to be funny," I groan, putting it back.

After that one—I continue to re-sort them—there's *Premonitions*, from 2013. Benji is standing in the road, caught in headlights with tall pine trees fading behind him.

"Moody," Sebastian says, and nods. "I haven't heard a single song from this album, I don't think."

"Not 'Fever Dream'?" I can't even fathom someone not knowing 'Fever Dream.' Actually, I can't fathom someone not knowing so many songs on this album. "*Premonitions* was, like, dark pop. I guess he was going through some stuff."

Behind it, there's his debut album, *Seventeen Summers*.

It's kind of wild to think of how far he's come.

The cover is so vibrant. A rainbow beach umbrella and a bright blue sky in the background as seventeen-year-old Benji eats bubblegum-pink ice cream and laughs with a group of girls in saturated swimsuits. It's all very family-friendly, which he commented on recently, the way he's wearing a T-shirt at the beach and the girls are wearing one-pieces, and the one brunette in a bikini is also wearing an ivory cover-up.

"This is the one with 'Sunkissed.'" Sebastian nods. "Dear God. That song."

Objectively, I get it. "Sunkissed" has basically become associated with shopping at Claire's and middle school dances. But it was his first hit. It's *the* song: no matter who you are or where you are, if you hear those opening instrumentals, you know it.

"This album surprised everyone," I say. Sebastian looks intrigued, so I shrug, looking back to the cover. "It broke so many records. They suspended him as an opener on a huge tour and gave him his own almost immediately. That was the first time Annie and I saw him. We had to beg my mom to take us to Miami, and Dean tagged along, it was a whole thing. This was the album that told the world who Benji Keaton was."

Sebastian stares at it. "Imagine that."

"Imagine everyone thinking they know you from this."

I don't mean it in a negative way, obviously. It's an

amazing album. The songs hold up, if you ask me, even if they're mega-manufactured pop tunes that play at malls and grocery stores. The tour was incredible. The music videos were all fun—shot at the beach, on a boardwalk, in a cozy café, or at a carnival—and the merch was ridiculous. We're talking Benji dolls, Valentines for the entire class, bobbleheads, blankets, ornaments, lunch boxes, *tape dispensers*. If there was a product, they put Benji on it.

And yet, looking at Benji now, I wonder if it was ever him at all.

"Did he write the songs on this album?"

"He did," I say. "But they collaborated with all these *major* producers. In his documentary he talked about how they distorted his vision. They wanted to change his words, even. I guess, clearly, there were some things that got changed around."

I tilt my head.

"He got his foot in the door," Sebastian offers. "I'm sure he's happy with it all."

I shrug, pushing all the albums back so *Icarus Complex* is on display again.

"I see what you're doing."

"I'm just *saying*," he offers. "You have to have your 'Sunkissed' before you get your 'Icarus.'"

"Did you find anything yet?" I ignore his comment because I don't even have a 'Sunkissed.' I don't have anything for my own *Seventeen Summers*. And, anyway, Benji got started at fifteen and was famous by sixteen, with his first full album dropping at seventeen.

I'm eighteen with no leads. No ideas, even. So it'll be years before I'd even get anywhere.

I'm behind.

Or, rather, I would be behind. If this were something I'm actually considering. And, I remind myself, before Sebastian started with all these wild ideas, it was not something I was actually considering.

"I'm stumped," he says.

We go through some old rock records, but there aren't any duets. Nothing that makes any sense, at least.

Sebastian lingers on one, though. It's got a baby with wings on the cover, and I scan to the top: *Van Halen*.

"Rare or something?" I ask.

He stands up straight and shakes his head, continuing to flick through the albums.

Okay, Teddy. Let's show some restraint, shall we? No need to push. I think we've done that enough.

Jaw clenched, I nod quietly. I'm not going to bother him to tell me why he paused and stared at that record for so long. It's fine. It might be about his ex, in which case I absolutely do not want to dive into that again. Or maybe it has something to do with Blake, the mysterious New Yorker he won't say anything about.

He moves on, toward jazz.

But why was he looking at it like that? What did that record mean to him?

I don't know anything about Van Halen. Literally

nothing. Not a single song, not a single member's name. I wonder if Sebastian would consider that blasphemous.

Why are you so nosy, Teddy?

An interesting question, indeed.

Why do you need to know every detail?

Annie once told me I need a lot of information so I feel like I have a sense of control. Actually, she has told me that many times.

My inner monologue is decidedly getting too deep.

"I know you're trying not to ask," Sebastian sighs, resting his palms on the table in the middle of the store where the country vinyl records are in white boxes, sorted in alphabetical order.

Shaking my head, I take a few steps toward him. "Nope, it's not my business."

"It's my dad's favorite," he says. "Happy?"

"Your dad?"

I don't know too much about Sebastian's family, I realize, except that he mentioned his mom works at the hospital and his dad isn't part of his life.

He doesn't say anything, and I'm wondering if that was it. That's what he concedes. Transactionally, even, to ensure I don't ask more.

But then he pokes his tongue in his cheek. "I shouldn't even care what his favorite album is."

Then there's a change in his entire demeanor.

So quickly, like an actor on a stage, his expression is giving everything away. Only he's not an actor, and he's not on a stage. He's standing in front of me in this record store, with eyes that have slightly turned down—glassy and dimmed as if exhausted and devastated at the same time. His lips form a pout, and he shrinks into himself completely, but only for a moment, as if he senses this and goes to correct.

"We don't have to talk about it," I say.

And this causes him to lift his chin, for his eyes to meet mine, and his mouth turns up just the teensiest bit.

"He has a whole new family," Sebastian says. "Which sounds so cliché. Because it is. But yeah, like I said before—out of the picture."

"I'm sorry," I say.

He brushes it off, turning back to the records. I'm sure he's trained himself to play it off. Taught himself to act like it's no big deal.

But I can't imagine if my family broke up. There are lots of things that elicit dramatic reactions, but that would be the straw that broke the musically talented camel's back.

"I know that can't be easy," I offer. "For what it's worth, he's missing out."

Sebastian laughs. He laughs loud, and it almost comes out like a bark. The employee at the front looks up at us before turning his attention back to his book.

"What's so funny?"

"You don't have to say that."

"I'm not saying it because I have to say it. I just think it's true."

He raises a brow, skeptical, before thumbing through some country albums. "Oh, really?"

"Sure. You're super smart. You're insightful. Passionate about the things you like, which is cool. You are caring and supportive, even though I know me saying that makes you want to cringe, probably."

As I say these things, I know it's crossing an imaginary line for me. Admiring his looks on the bridge was one thing, but now, admitting out loud that he has qualities and characteristics I like—it's somewhere we have not yet ventured.

Sebastian pretends not to notice. "You're probably giving me too much credit."

"I think you're a good person, Sebastian." I frown. "I'm sorry if your dad doesn't realize what he's missing out on."

Our eyes meet again.

"Thanks."

And I might melt, just a little, because this moment feels . . . warm. And delicate and brand-new and like it's supposed to be happening. Without realizing it, I think I've started to see the boy in the vinyl store in a completely different light.

"Oh!" He lights up, pulling a record out of the box he's been browsing through. "I've got it."

Sebastian holds up a black record, with worn corners and a tear down one of the sides. But I think I might get butterflies—what has he picked to describe us?

"I love Johnny and June," I say, trying not to gush.

He grins. "Me too."

Okay, then he must feel something *here, too. I mean, Johnny and June?*

Maybe I was wrong about Blake. Maybe he's just a friend!

He flips the record over. "And . . . yep, here it is."

"Which one?"

I've never had any inkling of a romantic moment. One that belongs to me, and not a character I'm playing. So, even though I know this is only a small little step—that it'll probably be a hint that he sees me too—I make a mental note to remember. The way we've slowly gotten to know each other bit by bit, and the way he looked in the sun under the arches of the Brooklyn Bridge. The way he looked at me when he realized I saw him. The way he looks now, even.

"It's kind of perfect," he says with a tiny laugh. "'It Ain't Me, Babe.'"

My heart and my stomach both plummet—gravity increases exponentially, and I'm crashing through the earth's core.

"Oh?" I squeak.

"It's funny," he says. "Get it? Like . . ."

"No, I get it." I nod, and I force a laugh, only this time I make sure I'm really acting. I make sure he can't tell it's forced or fake or hiding some strange disappointment.

What was I even thinking? Sebastian?

He looks at me expectantly. "Well, come on, let's take our selfie."

So, we stand together, and he holds the album up between us as I snap the photo.

My stomach is in knots, and I don't even know how I'm feeling let down over something I made up entirely in my own mind. And from what? There seems to be a disconnect, since my recognizing his attractiveness on the bridge was entirely one-sided. So what if he thinks I'm talented? So what if he thinks I could be famous or something? That doesn't mean he thinks I'm cute or wants to describe our relationship with a romantic duet.

And they say imagination is the true sign of genius. As if.

I want to disappear. I want to get sucked into a black hole. This is so embarrassing.

Sebastian tilts his head once he's put the record back, and he looks at the Polaroid.

"Your eyes are closed."

"No, they're not."

But, as the film slowly develops, I realize he's right. Well, half-right. One of my eyes is closed.

"Want to retake it?" He goes to reach for the record, but I wave him off.

"It's fine. I don't want to waste any film."

He examines it. "Your smile is sort of off, too—"

"Okay, well, anything else you want to point out?"

"No, I didn't mean to—I just thought . . . !"

I know he means well. He's only trying to save me from a horribly embarrassing photo, which I would normally appreciate. Because normally, I'd rather not look like I just jerked awake for a photo, mid-nightmare, but in this instance, I'd rather just leave this scavenger hunt item far, far behind.

"It's funny," I claim.

And he doesn't say it, but his face does: *You're not laughing . . .*

"It's hilarious," I insist. "Look at me. I look like half my face got numbed at the dentist. It's a fantastic look for me. Let's go."

When we start to head out, the employee looks up at us, offering a frown and willowy eyebrows like a human embodiment of Eeyore. "You guys aren't going to buy that?"

I shake my head.

"Okay," he says slowly, going back to his book. "Come back and see us again soon."

The door chimes as we leave and my cheeks are warm, my heart all jittery, and my palms a little sweaty. I want to hide, but I'm stuck with Sebastian until he decides to disappear again. It only takes an awkward moment—one that makes you want to hide under the covers far from society—to make you realize just how little space you have from someone.

Chapter 25

Hopelessly Devoted to You

Not to be dramatic, but this is one of those moments where I think maybe I'm just not as good at real life as other people.

Or maybe I just do it wrong somehow?

My parents have always said this about me when things don't go as planned: "*You throw out the baby with the bathwater.*" It's a horrible, and somewhat violent, metaphor, and I know it's true, but I don't think I can help it. I have big reactions and feelings and sometimes the tiniest thing can make me completely spiral. It's not like I *want* to throw out the baby.

As we walk along the sidewalk toward Washington Square Park, I'm overwhelmed. Embarrassed. It's worse than rejection, what happened in the vinyl store, because it's more pathetic—it was all in my own head. He wasn't even thinking any of the things I was. And it's all like a storm inside me that Sebastian can't know about because then the embarrassment would be enough to make me explode.

And I know *this* is the baby and the bathwater, this is one of those moments, when my parents would tell me I'm being dramatic, but I'm humiliated and the fact that I have to keep it all to myself only makes it worse. I don't even know why I'm blowing this so far out of proportion, because nothing has changed—we're still just Teddy and Sebastian, the same two guys we have been. But *I* know there was a switch in my mind, and that's enough to make me want to crawl in a hole.

"You seem . . ." Sebastian considers his words carefully. "Off."

I shake my head. "No, I'm good!"

"Right."

We walk into Washington Square Park, a small plaza of trees and grass surrounding a fountain and a huge white marble arch that looks sort of like that one in Paris. There are birds chirping in the trees, moms with strollers and shirtless runners whisking past us. People sit around the misting fountain, laughing or talking on the phone or scrolling mindlessly. Police officers stand around the arch as we walk under it. And though it's a beautiful park, as we leave, I start to notice more people have mouths that are turned down. More people look tired, apathetic.

"I'm calling bullshit," Sebastian says, once we've stopped at the corner of West Eighth and Fifth.

"What now?" I instantly regret how much attitude accompanies the question.

"*That!*" He points at me like we're playing Clue and he just solved the mystery. "I can tell something is wrong. You're not navigating us toward anything, first. You're frowning a lot. And we just walked through Washington Square Park, past the iconic arch, and you didn't mention one thing about the New York City magic. You didn't even take a single photo."

Come on, Teddy, you're a better actor than this.

But I've been found out. I've given myself away. And the last thing I'm going to do is say, "Oh, I thought we were having a semi-romantic moment earlier, but it was all imagined and I'm mortified and can hardly look at you or stomach the thought of my humiliation."

"I can't stop thinking about the song," I say.

I'm not entirely sure why I say it. Partially, maybe, because it always seems like Sebastian wants to talk about me writing songs. More, of course, because literally anything sounds better than the truth out loud.

He drops his shoulders. "Oh, that's it?"

"I know, it's stupid," I say. "I just . . . wish I had an idea."

"No need to get down about it," he offers. "You know, something will come to you eventually. It will."

I lean in to cement this as my reason for moping: "I know you wanted me to write about what makes me sad, but I want to write happy songs. I want to write uplifting songs."

"Fair," he says. "But, like, why?"

"I don't know fully," I say. "I just do. But I need something better than—"

I stop myself, because Sebastian didn't work tech for the talent show, so there's absolutely no reason to tell him about my embarrassing butterfly song.

"I don't know, I'm sure you're right. Something will come to me eventually."

He studies me but doesn't respond.

He isn't wrong about me not navigating us, either. I'm not entirely sure what we're doing, walking aimlessly. Still, we keep wandering, since I'm not in any rush to get anywhere. Our next scavenger hunt item today isn't until midnight, when we take our photo at Grand Central. Then just one left for tomorrow—and all of this will be over. It doesn't exactly cheer me up.

Sebastian seems unimpressed with our stroll up Fifth Avenue.

"Where are we headed?"

I shrug. "We don't have time to squeeze in the Empire State Building and get ready for our dinner."

"What dinner?"

Thankfully, this makes me laugh, which feels nice and fills the space that has become like fuzzy static in my chest. "You didn't read anything for this trip, did you?"

"I read most of it," he says. "I at least skimmed everything once."

“We have a drama club dinner,” I say. “Tonight, at six.”

He groans. “We’ll see.”

“What do you mean? It’s not optional.”

“Look, for now, how about we work on cheering you up?”

Again, I’m grateful for a laugh.

Sebastian rolls his eyes. “Fine. Forget it.”

“No.” I hold up my hands. “No, sorry. Okay. How are we going to do that, exactly?”

“There’s only one way.” He smirks. “Obviously.”

Back in our hotel room, I stare at myself in the bathroom mirror while Sebastian is browsing the menu for room service that we certainly cannot afford. My phone buzzes.

ANNIE:

honestly, it really isn’t that embarrassing

ANNIE:

he has no idea, and it could have been sooooo much worse

ANNIE:

maybe just try to have fun for the rest of the trip, i’m sure you’re beating eden still

“What even happens if we order something?” he shouts. “Does Mrs. Mackenzie end up paying for it?”

I laugh. “We’d probably get in huge trouble.”

“It’s not written anywhere,” he says. “I don’t see any rules around room service.”

“I think it’s just kind of unspoken—students on a class

trip shouldn't order a thirty-dollar burger or twenty-dollar side of French fries."

"Yeah," he sighs. "I guess that does sound like a kind of generally agreed-upon type of thing." Then, after a few beats: "What are you doing in there?"

"Vitamin C treatment," I say, eyeing the untouched skin-care products in my palm-leaf-printed Dopp bag. "The city air. You know."

Sebastian laughs. "No, I do not know. Backstage versus onstage, I guess."

I furrow my brow at that, looking right into my own eyes. I feel like I am always on freaking stage.

I text Annie back.

ME:

my brain does not accept this 'it could have been so much worse'

ME:

but I'll try

ANNIE:

good

ANNIE:

i'm ditching suspension to go to a movie with becca lol

ME:

omg

ME:

if you get caught you won't be able to graduate

ANNIE:

won't get caught

ANNIE:

have fun, k? you're in new york

Setting my phone down, I decide to run the hot water. Once there's steam coming from the sink, I splash it all over my face, and then pat one of the plush white towels against my skin. I put some moisturizer on my palm, pumping some Vitamin C serum in and slathering it all over my face. I don't even know what any of this does, it's just become part of my routine ever since one of the older girls suggested it when I was in *Into the Woods.*

"You want your face to be, like, bright and happy."

That's what she'd said.

I don't know that my skin is any brighter or happier, but I'll admit it does give me some sense of control. Maybe false, sure, but I *feel* like I'm doing something good for my face.

I swear, this trip I've noticed more about my feelings than I have in my whole life. Things I can't help but feel. Things I want to feel. Ways I control my feelings. Feelings that don't seem to have words to describe them.

I feel moderately stressed about Annie getting caught and not being able to graduate. I feel happiness—that she's having fun with Becca, at least—and some level of stabilization around my embarrassment—*he has no idea, and it could have been sooooo much worse*—and a little jolt of energy at the reminder: *you're in New York.*

At least my skin feels good.

"When you say you're doing a Vitamin C treatment," Sebastian calls, "are you growing a citrus tree in there or something?"

"You know, some people like privacy when they're in the bathroom," I say, sliding open the door and folding my arms.

He's sitting in the office chair next to the desk, and he raises a brow and nods. "Oh, you needed *privacy* in the bathroom."

"No, I didn't," I splutter.

"It's okay." He tries to hide the hint of a smirk forming across his face. "Whatever you were doing in there—"

I roll my eyes. "Do you not see this bright and happy glow?"

"You do look brighter," he says. "Very nice, McGuire. Maybe I need some."

I shake my head. "Your skin is fine."

"Come on." He stands up, tossing the room service menu on the desk. "Can't I get a little spa treatment, too?"

I gesture toward the bathroom. "Your side of the sink is a disaster, so it's not exactly a relaxing spa experience."

"It's not a *disaster,*" he says, walking past me. "Deodorant, toothpaste, brush, floss. Am I not supposed to have bathroom products in the bathroom? Because if that's the case, I am so, deeply sorry for—"

"You are such a smartass," I say, joining him in front

of the mirror. I dig through my Dopp bag and pull out a matte, frosted glass jar.

Sebastian tilts his head. "Kate Kensington. Isn't her stuff, like, *very* expensive?"

"I only have it because she's in my mom's book club and she gives them little gift bags all the time." I unscrew the top. "It's Harry's mom. You know, Harry? From—"

"I know who she is," he says. "Are we about to do face masks?"

I shrug, and he walks out of the bathroom.

Classic Sebastian.

Only, not at all. He opens the closet door and grabs the two fluffy white robes hanging on the gold pole.

"You're kidding," I say.

"I'm not kidding," he deadpans. "This is a luxurious experience. We're supposed to be cheering you up. You've derailed my room service plan, so it's spa time. You can't be cheered up until you're in a fancy hotel robe." He turns back and grabs the packages of slippers from the closet, too. "And these."

I can't help but laugh. The very idea of putting these on with him is comical. He cannot be serious.

"You're not going to put that on," I say. "I cannot believe you are even suggesting this."

"Why wouldn't I?"

"I don't know." I look for the words, but all I have is: "It just doesn't seem like something you'd do."

"Funny how you can call me *The Stranger* and, at the same time, assume you know everything about me already." He narrows his eyes. "Anyway, that's where you're wrong. If I'm in a fancy hotel doing a fancy face mask, I'm putting on a fancy robe."

Chapter 26

A Million Dreams

The next thing I know, Sebastian and I are sitting on our beds, ankles crossed with our robes and slippers on. His face is a ridiculous bright green. I wanted to use a Summer Fridays Jet Lag Mask that goes on clear, but he stopped me as soon as he realized, so both of our faces are painted bright pistachio.

"The next step is the most important," Sebastian says.

He grabs the remote and navigates to Netflix. And, as he's been known to do recently, he surprises me. The cursor lands on *Charming the Sun: Benji Keaton*.

"We don't have to watch this," I say.

"I'm actually curious, not going to lie." He nods. "And anyway, this is part of my Cheer Up Teddy plan."

I don't let on how much *that* cheers me up.

A lot of times in the last few months, if I felt lonely,

when Dean was away at UCLA and Annie was with the Friends of Nature Club, I'd put this on. And, judging by the way I know the entire beginning montage by heart, I was lonely more than I realized.

After the opening titles and credits, it cuts to Benji standing on the rocks at a beach, looking out at the water. He turns back and laughs. "Sometimes it helps to just try and turn it all off—to come and, I don't know, think."

He exhales and points out to the ocean. "I wrote 'Sunset' about this exact beach. And, you know, when you're writing songs, you find the words everywhere. Places that used to be sacred become . . ." You can tell he's always careful about choosing his words. He pauses. "Battlegrounds. Graveyards. Memories. You know? This is one of those places."

There's something serious in his eyes. Something I haven't ever felt. But he smiles. "Makes for a hell of a song, right?"

And then it cuts to him performing "Sunset" at Madison Square Garden.

I look over to Sebastian, who is watching with such focus. I already know this song is one he knows. His favorite lyric is from this song. And I don't imagine it's particularly fun to hear, considering the memories he must associate with it.

But he doesn't get teary or even frown. He just watches. The clip is short—there are longer snippets further in the documentary, other songs from studio sessions and concerts—but it's enough to tug at your heartstrings. It's enough to show you Benji still has a hard time performing it.

I wonder if maybe now when Sebastian hears the song, he'll think of this moment together in the hotel room instead of the heartbreak he associated with it before.

Maybe that's a stretch, or maybe it's too optimistic, but I'd like that for him.

"People want something different all the time, so I don't try to anticipate what people want anymore." Benji is sitting in a hotel room now, with the ocean and palm trees in the window behind him. "They wanted fun, so I gave them fun, but then they wanted more—*deeper*—so I did that but it 'wasn't me' anymore. They said they didn't know what to expect. So I just don't try to be what anyone expects."

We get a montage. Benji when he was a kid, and then in the middle school and high school drama club. Then he's performing at an outdoor amphitheater, more palm trees. Then we're in the *Seventeen Summers* era—morning shows, tour, a guest spot in a Disney Channel show. Then *Premonitions*. It's darker, a little edgier, but still clean-cut and preppy, even. As we move through the eras, we see the evolution. We *feel* it. We get behind-the-scenes footage of Benji in *This Side of Paradise*. He's supposed to be in the 1920s, wearing a Princeton sweater, and he's laughing with his costars and toasting everyone with champagne.

His voice-over rolls. "People are either going to love it or they're going to hate it."

And then we see him smiling, big, in 1920s New York City.

"And at some point, it's none of my business."

Sebastian points to me, pausing the documentary. "Did you hear that?"

I nod. "Yeah."

I've heard it dozens of times by now. And I love it for Benji. He should be able to separate himself from people's opinions. He deserves that. He's worked hard. He's proven himself. He's made a name for himself. Why should he let anybody tell him who he is or if something he does is any good?

"That's what you need—I don't know, you need it *tattooed*. Or put that on a Post-it!"

I roll my eyes.

"You must have watched this so many times by now," he says. "You never . . . That part never resonated with you?"

Shaking my head, I blink. "No, because I'm not Benji. I'm an eighteen-year-old kid from Citrus Harbor, Florida, who does school plays."

"And writes amazing songs, I'm sure." Sebastian lifts his brows as if to goad me on. "Oh, come on, Teddy. It's not that complicated. You're paralyzed by the fear of it being good or bad—of it being wrong or right. But if you just did it. If you just wrote something, whether you thought people would like it or not, you never know what would happen."

I shrug. "Maybe. Okay? Maybe you're onto something.

But you paused just before he gets his Oscar!"

He presses play.

There are some magazine covers. Shots from the movie premiere. Some footage of Benji and his friends winding down after. It transitions, and the hotel room is empty now. It's just Benji and his best friend, Sadie.

"That was [beep] magic." Sadie swirls ice around in her cup. "You were so good. Do you feel good?"

Benji nods, and then the mood shifts a little. The camera is a little shakier, and there are some long pauses. It then becomes obvious Benji is holding back tears, and he shrugs. His voice is quiet, and they've added subtitles to the scene.

"It's not . . . Seeing it, you know, the final cut. It's hard when you know you could have done things so much better. And you pick apart every little thing. You just know it could be better."

Sadie moves to sit next to him, and the camera is a little shakier as it moves away. She comforts him.

And then we cut to more clips. Entertainment news, talk shows, and podcasts.

"Benji Keaton nominated for an Academy Award for his performance in *This Side of Paradise*."

"Nobody's really expecting him to, you know, I mean—it's nice and all!"

"Oh, his fans are going to lose their minds."

Then it's Benji, in a custom Christian Dior suit, like the 2020 Resort line, but in a silky champagne. His hair slicked back, and a camp collar satin button-down with an art deco print to echo the marketing for *This Side of Paradise*. Camera bulbs flash and he smiles, one hand in his pocket, playing it cool.

"And the Oscar goes to . . ."

It's a moment nobody really expected, I think.

"Benji Keaton!"

And some of the faces are so unapologetically surprised. Others are forced—accepting or faking tolerance for the sake of saving face on television.

He takes to the stage and accepts his award.

"I can't believe this," he says. "I'm just really grateful to be here at all."

And then, as the screen fades to black-and-white, and in slow motion, Benji silently goes through his speech, more voice-overs:

"Are we going to pretend these award shows have any meaning? I mean this is, like, some kid. A pop star. His first acting credit, and he's getting *Best Actor in a Leading Role*?"

"I honestly thought it might be a joke. Publicity stunt? I was waiting for them to go: sorry, there was a mistake."

"It's a little embarrassing for the Academy, I think. There must be some nepotism we don't know about."

Benji's now in New York, in the back of a car, wearing a hoodie and sunglasses.

"I don't know, I do try to remind myself . . . it's none of my business. Right? I said that. It's none of my business if people like it or don't like it. If they like or don't like me." He sniffs, and his Adam's apple bobs. He's still trying to act composed. "It's a whole new world. A whole different ball game. A whole different crowd to adjust to."

Then an article flashes across the screen.

Vanity Fair. A piece by Paul Scott.

Benji Keaton, from Sunkissed to Sunburned: the Icarus Complex

Sebastian nods. "There it is."

I sigh. "There it is."

Sometimes, I think about that title. *From Sunkissed to Sunburned.* I think about what it must have felt like for Benji to read that for the first time.

When I played Pugsley in *The Addams Family*, I overheard one of the sound girls say we were *so* lucky Vanessa carried the show as Wednesday. It wasn't a direct dig, but I remember taking it so personally. Every time we did "Pulled," I was self-conscious. It wasn't my song, but I just stood there behind her, watching her and wondering if everybody wished it was just a Vanessa concert instead of a musical with the rest of us desperately trying to keep up with her.

It didn't help that I had to hold my arms up like I was chained up to be tortured.

Anyway, if one little comment—not even about me—made me feel that way? How do celebrities deal with people throwing out opinions and criticisms like they're not even humans?

"Earlier I told Sadie I can't believe I have to do this tour when it feels like nobody wants to hear anything from me," Benji says. "And you know what she said? She said I *get* to do this tour."

He smiles.

And then it cuts to Benji in his dressing room, and he's on FaceTime with a producer.

"I know, it's totally nuts, but I want the album to come out before I start the show in New York."

"You don't have time to sleep. With the *New England* tour, then rehearsals."

Sebastian pauses it again. "How in the hell does he do all of this?"

"I have no clue," I say. "Sometimes I'm too tired to put the Nutella back in the kitchen when I have a late-night snack."

He snorts. "Benji is . . . cooler than I expected."

"You love Benji," I sing. "It's fine, it's okay to love Benji."

Rolling his eyes, Sebastian scoots over to the edge of his bed. "I think it's time to wash these face masks off."

I nod. "Yes, but first we absolutely have to take a Polaroid."

"For our eyes only," he says. "In the name of cheering you up."

I try to remind myself that Sebastian only wants to cheer me up because that's what friends do. And so we take a silly selfie with the Polaroid.

Once we've washed our faces and we're both sitting

back on our beds, Sebastian checks his phone.

"So, do you think you can cover for me for this dinner?"

I sigh. "Can't you just come? We have to go to Grand Central tonight, too."

He looks off, as if calculating. "We do?"

"Yes, we have to be there *at* midnight and get a photo. There's a clock we can stand in front of."

Sebastian sighs. "Well, I'll be there at midnight. But I just . . . Can't you tell Mrs. Mackenzie I have an upset stomach or something?"

"Where are you sneaking off to?"

He frowns. "Please, Teddy?"

I'm sitting there, in my hotel bed, wearing this ridiculously cozy white robe. He's sitting in his, and the look on his face is the same one an actor puts on before they go out onstage.

Knowing it's an uphill battle, I throw my hands up. "Okay."

"Thank you," he says. "We'll finish the documentary and then get ready."

I nod. "That sounds good."

"And then, when you're done with dinner, go explore. See more of the city. *Do* something. Don't sit in the room."

My immediate reaction is one of annoyance, and I cross my arms like a kid. "I wasn't planning on just sitting in the room."

I was maybe planning on just sitting in the room.

"Good. You might just find some inspiration."

I remember even *attempting* to feel inspired last night. "What is it with you and me writing songs? Honestly, you have no reason to believe I have even the slightest talent, and—"

Sebastian holds up a hand. "We both know you do. And we both know you *want* to write a song, Teddy. So just try. And then I'll text you, and we'll meet up."

We watch the rest of Benji's documentary. Sebastian enjoys it thoroughly, and he even gushes a little about some of the *artistry* of it all. And, though I would be the first to say all the same things, I am so damn shocked to hear them coming out of his mouth.

After the documentary, we listen to some of Benji's songs. Mostly from *Premonitions* and *New England*, but a couple from *Sunrise* and *Sunset*. Sebastian even reads the lyrics to *Icarus Complex* as we listen, pausing to point things out from the documentary.

Something about this feels vulnerable. Like I've shared my inner depths with him, even though they're not mine at all. They're Benji's.

Still, it's unnerving, a little, when Sebastian turns to me during "Battle at the Shore," one of the songs from *Sunset*, and has the lyrics pulled up. "The internet says this is one of his most iconic bridges."

And the bridge is one I really love. It's the words, sure. But there's something about the beat, the bass, the gruff quality to his voice as he surrenders. It's scratchy, and vulnerable, and it's not a side to Benji we get very often, even in his sad songs.

"No troops, no peace treaty,
just tears, just two lovers bleeding.
You were armed, and I was not,
it was just too late, gave it all we got.
The lines were drawn in summer sands,
the red had stained both of our hands.
Your bloodshot eyes, the setting sun,
called it love, but nobody won."

He sounds broken. He sounds damaged. And Sebastian looks at me like we're sharing this moment, now. We're reveling in the way Benji can just rip your heart open.

"Maybe you just need to explore more metaphors," Sebastian offers, getting up and walking over to where he's placed his suitcase next to the bed. "Like how Benji compares this to a battle. Or like how, in *Premonitions*, even, there was this archetype thing—the jock becoming a monster under a full moon."

The only metaphors that come to mind are ones Benji's already used.

Sebastian raises his index finger. "Oh, or what about getting into some sensory details? Like on *Sunset*: *The devil is in every detail—sand grains, wine stains, lost lenses, pretenses, the sky's pastel in heartbreak hell."*

"God, you're a Benji stan," I say.

"I just think there are a lot of options for how you can approach this." He scrolls on his phone and a different song from *Sunset* plays in the background.

The lyrics are so Benji—they're so personal: *In quicksand, on burning pavement, in a riptide, thought you would save me.*

And I'm here, in this moment, once again feeling like I have nothing to say.

There are questions I want to ask. Tons of them, especially as I look at the flowers from Blake next to the TV.

Who? What? When? Where? Why? Are you in love, and I am a fool?

Today has been such a whirlwind, and it's not even over. Honestly, I want to just nap.

"I'm going to shower," Sebastian says, heading to the bathroom. He stops, first, and turns to look at me. "Maybe just less thinking, more feeling."

Right . . .

As I sit there and go over everything that's just unfolded—really, everything that has happened over the last forty-eight hours—I may know Sebastian a bit more, but I'm also more confused than ever.

Chapter 27

Summer Nights

With the Citrus Harbor High Drama Club, it's never just a casual bite.

It's always dinner and a show.

Clyde and Yasmine are doing magic tricks at one end of the table, and Eden is showing off a new lilac designer bag to the other end. We showed up seven minutes late to our reservation, and we were told there was a very strict *five*-minute grace period, which we'd missed. Mrs. Mackenzie launched into a monologue, and at some point, overwhelmed by either our drama teacher's speech or the congestion of theater kids in the reception area, the hostess decided to seat us.

The restaurant itself is trendy, with light blue velvet booths, exposed bulbs, and gold hardware everywhere.

The bar is marble and walnut, with a shiny turquoise backsplash. There are palm plants in corners and string lights dipping over the tables.

The menu is nice. French and American. There are plenty of options. I could find something to be excited about, I'm sure, but I am mostly preoccupied, covering for Sebastian with Mrs. Mackenzie, worrying about what he's up to, and thinking about him and Blake.

It's probably silly, and it's not like I should be forming any kind of attachment, since it's been hardly any time at all. Still, I'm imagining all kinds of things that bring up all kinds of feelings—ones I'm not familiar with.

I'm picturing a billion ways their night is playing out. Sebastian and Blake wandering the cobblestone streets of Chelsea or Brooklyn, or having more fun at one of the museums. It's not like the museums are *our thing*, but my mind is quick to remind me they could become theirs. I feel like Sebastian has shared things with me, but maybe that isn't actually as special as I'm chalking it up to be because maybe he's sharing those things with Blake too.

Maybe—in fact, likely—he's shared much more with Blake. Glances and touches and feelings.

I'm not the reason Sebastian is in New York, after all. I'm who he's stuck with. Who he obliges with details and conversations and occasional jokes. Blake is the reason he's here. The one he wants to spend his time with.

I sigh and take a sip of my water, glancing around to find nobody is paying any attention to me at all.

Eden brags about only needing two more items until she finishes the scavenger hunt, but she won't tell any of us which they are. I know well enough not to trust she's going to be *too* predictable when it comes to a competition. So, today when we found out we'd mapped the same order, she definitely threw a wrench in things somehow, some way.

I could go down the rabbit hole right now, worrying about Eden beating us to the finish, but we're tied, which is good enough for now. My thoughts return to Sebastian like there's only so far out of his orbit they can travel before they're yanked back.

Mrs. Mackenzie does a small speech, but it's uneventful. She gives speeches *all* the time, and they are always grandiose and metaphorical and quasi-inspirational. I nod along with everyone else, and then we go around and talk about how much we love New York so far. We're all so excited to see *Versailles* tomorrow evening, and she, for the millionth time, feigns regret to not be able to bring us all along to the after-party.

"It is such a private evening, you understand. I tried my best."

When she says it, I think about the speech she just gave. How she talks about loving us all so much. How she claims we're like her children, really.

And now just showing us her enormous, fluffy cat Grizabella napping on the sofa from her kitty cam.

After appetizers, dinner, dessert, and a round of

cappuccinos, we're set loose upon the city.

I say I'm going to go check on Sebastian, but really, I just start walking. And for a bit, I'm not paying any attention to anything at all. I'm in my own head, in some kind of dream world. For a split second, I consider trying to find Sebastian, but I realize it'd be nearly impossible in a city this big. And maybe I don't *want* to see Sebastian with Blake on a romantic date or whatever it is they're doing.

I pop in my earphones and decide to listen to *Sweet Vicious,* since it's Benji's New York album. The opener, "Eye Contact," is this delicate, piano-driven song. It's soft and synthy, and it makes everything feel more magical.

Chelsea is lively.

It's alive.

It's breathing and sparkling—sequined and colorful patterned gowns in windows; lanky girls in disco ball dresses and platform heels, pastels and long legs heading toward dinner or drinks or both. And there's something enchanting about the old cobblestone street, like there should be some kind of glow between each stone. Fireflies, even.

I don't have to romanticize it, but I do.

I stop and stand on the sidewalk and watch a group of college kids as they huddle around to light a cigarette, and for a moment I feel so much confliction. Why do I feel jealous of people I don't even know? Doing something I don't even do?

When they throw their heads back laughing, two of

them with their arms linked, I realize *that's* why. I'm all alone, and they're not.

Benji sings in my ears, and my mind is flooded with imagery. Butterflies and twisting vines on fire escapes. Kisses on the forehead in Central Park, love in the air at Sheep Meadow. Bedsheets spun from gold by Aphrodite.

It's jarring to know this same song is about the love Benji had in mind when he wrote "Full Circle." It's sad to think how short-lived it was. It's maddening, to imagine two people going from magic to chaos to memories. It's hard to imagine how often it's happened to Benji, when I think about how many of his albums show that progression.

People go from being pillars in our lives to just stories. Will that be Annie and me? Will that be Sebastian and me, too? Will this entire New York trip just be a faint memory one day?

Alone with Benji's words, I head up toward the High Line. It's a park that stretches above the streets on, if I remember correctly, an old railroad. I've only seen photos of it in the daylight, the bright green shrubbery, cherry blossom trees, and flowers lining the paths while crowds walk and chat on the benches. I climb the stairs and find it is still cool at night.

I walk for a few minutes, until I'm under what I believe is the Whitney Museum. I rest my elbows on the metal railing and look out over the street.

I've gone through a few songs by now, and while Benji's

relationship deteriorates, I try to pay attention to the way he writes—how he tells his story.

Said you'd never felt this way before.
Eastside, candlelight, long night, a crying fight.
Said I deserved so much more.
Guess it's not our New York anymore.

God. I just don't have anything like this in me. And I don't know, I wasn't so painfully aware—until Sebastian started this whole songwriting thing back up—that my life is just not very interesting. And now it's plaguing me.

Pulling up Pinterest, I start to type *Benji* and click on the first suggestion: *Benji Keaton Lyrics Aesthetic*

There are dozens of fan-made graphics. Handwritten lines with scribbles and doodles. Collages. Contemporary fonts scattered across night skies and shorelines.

From *Premonitions*, a popular lyric: *Wolves with bloody teeth, blamed me when I'd bleed.*

Or from *New England*, heavily used as breakup captions: *My favorite eyes became the cruelest, I miss your laugh, but not enough to go back.*

And of course, there are so many from *Icarus Complex*. I think a lot of fans cling to that album as some beacon of truth. It's the most honest Benji has ever been about everything in his life, including fame and his career. From the title track, I study part of the bridge like there might be an answer I've been searching for.

Of course I aimed for the sun,
what was left for someone so desperate?
What game do you play when you've already won?
They pray the fall is as impressive.

Looking through these fan graphics, I notice there are a lot of things that differentiate the lyrics from each other. Who they're about. The metaphors. The general feeling of the album that trickled into each one—or maybe it was the opposite, and the feelings of each song made the feeling of the album.

Regardless, what makes them different doesn't matter, because there's one thing that makes them the same:

They're all so *Benji*. Somehow, words become his. Phrases are strung together in a way that I just know was by his pen. And maybe not everyone would think that reading some of them, but to me, I can't just hear him in them—I feel him.

And that's what is missing in anything I write. A feeling.

Maybe Harry's right, but I can't shake this idea that I should look at Benji's progression as a road map. Not only that, but I want to share a positive message. I would want my image, as a songwriter and artist, to be happy.

Right?

Once I've seen enough on Pinterest, I go to the Notes app.

What am I feeling right now?

The city below is both calm and excitable. I feel the

same. I am worried about Sebastian, confused about why I'm suddenly finding him cute and feeling disappointed that he doesn't seem to think the same about me. I'm morbidly curious about Blake. About what makes him worth missing *Versailles* over. I'm stressed over this scavenger hunt and trying to stay ahead of Eden—or hoping we're ahead, at least—and I get butterflies when I even think about the fact that, in twenty-four hours, I could be meeting Benji. I'm overwhelmed by the fact that I might really want to give songwriting a try but can't seem to get it right.

And yet, I feel at peace. It's the melody in my ears—a new song now, about chasing dreams in the city—and it's where I am.

It always comes back to how magical this place is. Despite everything, it's pure magic.

"Excuse me?"

I jerk away instinctively, because it's dark and I'm alone, but the pale girl with a black bob to my right doesn't look at all threatening or ill-intended.

"I think you dropped this," she says, handing me a Polaroid.

"Oh my God," I say, taking out an AirPod. "Thank you so much."

It's the one from today, Sebastian on the bridge. I was nervous to leave it in the room, not because I think he'd go snooping, but just in case. I don't know, maybe he'd go looking for one of the pictures because he liked them or maybe housekeeping would come at a weird time.

It just felt safest in my pocket.

And it clearly was not.

"He's cute," the girl says. She's wearing a cream floral midi dress with a denim jacket over her shoulders like she just couldn't be bothered to put her arms in the sleeves. It looks so cool.

I put the Polaroid in my pocket. "I can't believe I almost lost that."

I realize I'd be upset to lose this picture, and I wonder what exactly that means.

"Who is he?" She narrows her eyes. "Don't tell me it's some weird voyeuristic—"

"No," I say, laughing and waving my hands frantically. "He's just my classmate."

The girl nods, leaning up against the railing next to me and glancing over. "Having a Lizzy McAlpine moment?"

I shake my head. "A Benji Keaton moment."

"Interesting." She kicks the toes of her Doc Martens into the ground. "Is your classmate the reason you're having a Benji Keaton moment? Sorry, I'm nosy. I'm hiding, actually, from an absolutely miserable date. Just waiting for my friends, and now I'm intrigued by this Polaroid you're carrying around of your classmate."

Biting my lip, I stifle a laugh. It hits me: I don't know this girl. She doesn't know me. We're in a huge city, and what I say here won't ever reach anyone else.

"I might have a crush on him," I say. "I think?"

"You think?"

"I haven't really had a crush before." I realize I must sound *so* small-town to her. But she doesn't look like she's judging. "I mean, I've had crushes, I guess. But in a larger sense. Like an actor, or a guy in another grade, or a random barista or something. This is the first one where I really know him."

Then, I correct: "Sort of know him. But it would never happen."

"I'm Lucy." She quirks a brow. "Do you want to come to drinks with my friends and me?"

"I can't," I say. "I'm only eighteen."

"So?"

Chapter 28

The Name of the Game

I'm at drinks with three random New York City college girls.

Only, here's the thing. It's more than just drinks, it's trivia.

Which I am terrible at.

They insisted I try one of these cocktails with tequila and I'm not sure if there is no alcohol in it or if it just tastes good. I've had very limited experience with tequila—I once tried a shot with Annie at a Halloween party and proceeded to throw up in a bush when my stomach immediately lurched like I'd swallowed gasoline—so this is very new to me. It's also new to me how easy it was for Lucy to order two drinks at the bar and plop the glass in front of me like it's no big deal.

The bar is themed as a glamorous speakeasy with giant

martini glasses and feathers everywhere, the lighting low but hued in turquoise and pink. We're standing around a high-top, four drinks on gold-rimmed cocktail napkins and the flame of a tiny votive dancing in the center.

Lucy and her friends don't seem too concerned that a strange underage boy has joined them tonight, and each girl nurses her drink, eyes darting around as if on the prowl.

Claudette met us first. She has an afro with balayage coloring and is wearing bright, sparkly gold eye shadow, a trendy pink slip dress, and a cream quilted Chanel bag on a chain over her shoulder. She ordered a Manhattan, and when she offered to let me taste it, I could tell by the smell I would have repeated the Halloween party, so I politely declined.

Piper joined shortly after, a blur of apologies and excuses related to traffic and her cat and the sole of one of her shoes and her boss. She's wearing a tight black dress under a jean jacket. No makeup, a super-messy bun, and scuffed Adidas Superstars. She orders an espresso martini and acts like it quenches her thirst when she takes her first sip.

"Teddy has his first crush," Lucy blurts. Claudette and Piper both react visibly—eyes widening, whipping to face me like fish who just sensed food at the top of their bowl.

Claudette rests her chin on her palm. "First crush?"

"That's so sweet," Piper gushes.

I shake my head. I want to take a sip of this cocktail,

but at some random moments it does have a taste slightly reminiscent of gasoline, which isn't exactly the best feeling going down.

"Not sweet?" Piper's finger traces the base of her martini glass.

"It's maybe not even a crush," I say. "More just like this guy who I have known forever, but not really *known*. But I can't have a crush on him, because . . . Well, there are plenty of reasons. Namely his *Blake*."

"His *Blake*?" Claudette asks.

"I think he's seeing someone."

"You *think*?" Lucy squeals. "So, there's a chance he's not?"

"Did you guys hook up?" Piper asks.

Claudette frowns. I can already tell what she's thinking: *You can't just fall in love after a hookup, sweetie.*

I do know some rules of dating, even if I haven't had to apply them.

"Definitely not," I say.

Lucy winces, her cocktail straw between her teeth. "We got a *definitely not*."

"But you want to hook up with him?" Claudette clarifies. "What does he look like?"

"Show them the photo," Lucy says.

"Well, he's handsome." I place the Polaroid on the table and they gawk and *ahh*. "Let's start there. He's an attractive guy. Tall, with nice eyes, and dark, fluffy hair. He has an adorable smile, when he smiles. Which he does a lot more now."

The girls all have various brands of confused looks on their faces.

"No, he smiles a regular amount. Well. Anyway, I don't know if it's a crush or just realizing he's cute. Because it's not a big deal to think a guy is cute. Right? It doesn't have to mean anything. We think lots of people are cute."

"He *is* cute," Piper says.

Claudette bats her lashes. "Do you get nervous around him?"

"Do you find yourself wanting something to happen?" Piper asks. "Like, if he's too close, do you wish he'd just kiss you?"

I swallow. "Well."

"You're in love," Lucy squeals.

"Don't worry, you're not in love," Claudette disagrees.

Piper sips her beige foamy martini. "Are you going to ask this guy out?"

"Absolutely not," I say.

The atmosphere in the bar shifts as two girls get up to start hosting trivia. I think there are three camps of people when it comes to trivia. People like Sebastian, probably, who are geniuses and pull out random facts you had no clue they knew. They love trivia, because they're good at it. Then there are the people who can genuinely just have a laugh with it; they're not competitive and they don't feel dumb if they don't know something. Third, where I've found myself, there are people who feel like a spotlight is being pointed at them to expose just how dumb they really are.

"The cash prize is a hundred dollars tonight," Claudette says. "Better than when it was fifty dollars."

"If we win, we all get a solid twenty-five dollars," Lucy says to me. "What's the other prize?"

Piper squints at the table. "Signed *Playbill*."

"They always do those," Lucy says, pulling a face.

Claudette squints now. "Oh, that one is kind of cool, though. It's from closing night of *Phantom* last spring."

My palms go flat on the table, and I whip around to find the *Playbill* on the table. *"What?"*

"Oh, we have a superfan." Piper smiles.

"How are you guys so chill about that? How is everyone so chill about that? I mean, that must be really rare and valuable."

Claudette shrugs. "I'm not majorly into *Phantom of the Opera*."

"Me either," Lucy admits. "And it's cool, sure, but . . . I don't know, they've had cooler prizes."

"We have to win that *Playbill*," I say.

"Well then, Teddy, I hope you're good at trivia."

I study the girls before pushing my drink away from me a couple inches. "You know what? I'm sure, between the four of us, we have a breadth of knowledge. What do you guys all do?"

"We go to Parsons," Piper says. "I work freelance at an indie press. We publish contemporary voices."

"I intern with a PR firm." Claudette offers a put-on smile. "We send rich influencers products they don't need."

Lucy nods. "And I work at a bar, but I'm trying to do some freelance writing."

"Wow," I say. "That's so cool. You all have so much going on."

Claudette sighs wistfully. "Packaging and tracking packages of luxury skin-care products. It's a tough job, but somebody has got to do it."

"Claudette has the most glamorous internship of anyone in our class," Piper says, waving her off.

Nodding, Claudette gives in. "Yeah, I guess that's true."

"Do you just love living in New York?"

They all enthusiastically bob their heads up and down.

"It's so horrible, and so amazing," Lucy says.

I roll my eyes. "No way it's horrible."

"New York City will literally rip your throat out and stomp on it and then feed it back to you," Claudette says coolly.

"But I wouldn't have a throat to swallow it with . . ."

She nods. "Exactly."

"And it's still worth it." Lucy grins. "Even when it breaks your heart. Or gives you really, really fucking bad blisters."

"Speaking of heartbreak, give us the details of this date," Piper says, turning her focus to Lucy.

She sags. "It was so, so horrible. Multiple red flags. I think I actually had already ignored a few from our conversation on Tinder, but damn. He brought them all to dinner. And then, he was talking about how his father bought him a loft, and I think it was meant to lead to an invitation . . ."

"Okay, bad date," I say. "But it's kinda cool, you guys are, like, living *Sex and the City*."

"Totally." Lucy nods. "But with much worse apartments and the guys aren't as hot."

"New York City dating is honestly one of the worst things to ever happen to me," Claudette says to me, and the other girls laugh, nodding almost violently in agreement.

"Yeah, so if you found one . . ." Piper lifts her drink as if to toast me.

"To Teddy's crush," Claudette sings, lifting her drink.

Lucy follows. "To Teddy's crush."

"It's so not a crush," I say, lifting my drink. We all clink glasses and I take a sip of my motor oil, wincing a little as it incinerates my esophagus.

The women onstage begin to announce the rules—we'll pick a team name and once they ask a question, we'll write our answer down and send a runner to put the paper in the bowl. Simple. Easy! All we need are brains.

"We have four categories," the hostess with a fishtail braid says into the mic. I brace myself. "First up—Presidents! Then we have Irish Literature. Third, Major League Baseball . . ."

I pull a face.

I don't know anything about any of those! I mean, I could answer some questions about Michelle Obama, but that's about it. Irish Literature? Major League Baseball?

"Final category is Sailing."

Well, I am officially useless here. Damn it. I really wanted to get that *Playbill* for Sebastian.

"God, I swear we've done those before," Claudette says. She looks to me expectantly. "All right, we've got this. Right? You ready?"

"Maybe I'll just watch." I frown. "Not feeling so confident after all. Don't want to be the reason you guys lose the cash prize."

Claudette leans in. "You don't have to do anything you don't want to do, but you *are* in New York City, and we'll be fine with or without the prize money. So, if you wanted to just have fun and make some wild guesses—it wouldn't hurt. Maybe you'll get your *Playbill*."

My fingers find my lucky bracelet and I tug on the string.

"Sorry, guys!" The host taps the mic. "My mistake. Those categories were from last week. Tonight, we have . . . First Ladies, Broadway, Pop Music, and Dinosaurs!"

I glance down at my bracelet as if it just performed a magic spell. "Yes!"

The girls look to me.

"Do you know a lot about dinosaurs or something?" Claudette asks.

Nodding, I take a sip of my drink and ignore the burn. "I do, actually! All those categories speak to my soul."

Thank you, lucky bracelet.

"Amazing," Lucy says. "Guess it really was meant to be that we ran into each other."

"Fate," I say with a smile.

My lucky bracelet and the universe have blessed me with a game of trivia practically designed for Teddy McGuire.

"Team name?" Claudette raises a brow.

"Teddy and the City." Lucy nods, pointing from me to the three of them.

"She's the writer," Piper laughs.

We breeze through the questions—so many from each category I lose count—and the girls fill in any I'm not one hundred percent on. Not only are we in the lead the entire time, we're also the first to submit our answers after each question. There is only one other group who is nearly tied with us, and the other tables are resigned, I think, by the time we get to the end.

"All right, final question for the night: list, in order, the three periods of the Mesozoic era."

I nearly jump up and down I'm so excited.

This night is wild. I never thought I'd run into some girl and make new friends, and then submit a piece of paper with dinosaur knowledge I didn't even know forty-eight hours ago to win a freaking signed *Phantom of the Opera Playbill*.

How, apart from luck and fate and magic, do you explain a night like this?

Chapter 29

Last Midnight

It's fifteen minutes until midnight, and Sebastian hasn't even texted me back.

What the hell could he possibly be doing?

This is absolutely reason to worry, I think. What if Blake has kidnapped him?

Or worse. I shudder when I imagine what he could be willingly doing with Blake right now.

I FaceTime Annie, but she doesn't answer. Then I try Dean, and he also doesn't answer.

My heart is racing, and so is my mind. What am I supposed to do?

Standing in the middle of Grand Central, next to the information booth, right under the golden four-faced clock, I am panicking.

This isn't how any of this is supposed to go. We were

supposed to walk through those heavy doors on Forty-Second for the first time together. Once we passed the subway entrance and whatever else I walked by, we'd be *ooh*ing and *aah*ing, absolutely stunned by the architecture and magnificence. We'd be shocked, because of course we knew it was big, but there's just no way to anticipate the scale of the main concourse until you're standing there, feeling so tiny in the bustling crowd. We'd take photos, videos, sweeping the bright aqua celestial ceiling.

Instead, I barely blinked twice when I got here. I'm only now trying to take everything in.

Eden's on the other side of the information booth, and two other pairs from drama club are circling like vultures ready to pounce on prey—Billy and Gregory are pretty competitive, though they've already admitted they're horribly behind, and Maribel and Tiffany are only here to make TikToks with Eden and Briar, though they're holding their Polaroid cameras too.

My foot is tapping involuntarily.

I'm genuinely concerned. There's no explanation for where Sebastian is. Unless he really was lying, and he *is* a hit man and he lost the plot.

"Sorry, sorry, sorry."

Sebastian's Vans slap against the marble floor as he runs toward me, face red with a sweaty upper lip.

"Phone died."

It's like seeing a ghost. I pick my jaw up off the ground quickly, but what's more surprising than the fact that he's here just before the stroke of midnight is the way he is wearing the biggest smile ever.

"I got you something."

I furrow my brow, suspicious, but he reaches into his pockets and pulls out two small shiny figurines. One is the Statue of Liberty's head, and the other is the Empire State Building. It takes a second, but then I notice they're salt and pepper shakers.

"I saw them, and I knew I had to get them for you."

I nod slowly. "Wow."

He looks at me like I'm nuts. "You—remember? Like Benji's? You said you didn't have salt and pepper shakers, and now you do." Then, when I'm still nodding, he sucks his teeth. "Is that stupid?"

"No," I say quickly, taking them from him. "No, it's not stupid. It's just—Benji's salt and pepper shakers are a sad metaphor, you know? He can't get rid of them, even though he should. Even though they remind him of someone who hurt him. And, uh, he did get rid of them in the end."

Sebastian lifts his shoulders. "Well, yours are different. These will remind you of New York City. Your salt and pepper shakers will remind you of all that magic you see everywhere. And I wouldn't ever . . . Well, you'll be able to keep yours."

"Thank you." My cheeks go hot, then I quirk a brow. "You were nearly late."

"But I wasn't." He grins. "Sorry, though. My phone died."

I shake my head.

"How was your night? How was dinner? Anything exciting?"

"I snuck into a bar," I say. "With this girl Lucy and her friends. They're fashion students. We did trivia—we also sang Stevie Nicks on karaoke to celebrate winning said trivia—and they followed me on Instagram."

"Teddy McGuire, look at you go."

I nod, and then, speaking of winning, I realize I still have the *Playbill* tucked under my arm. I juggle the salt and pepper shakers in one hand and grab the *Playbill* with the other. "I actually got you something too. It's from closing night."

When I hold it out for him, Sebastian's eyes melt into an expression he hadn't yet shown me. "What . . . ?"

"It was the prize," I say, trying to be nonchalant. "For trivia."

"You're giving this to me?" He inhales sharply and marvels at it.

I laugh, but it's getting me a little choked up, seeing how surprised he is. "Yeah, I won it for you."

"You won it for me?"

"Yes, Sebastian." I nudge it toward him until he accepts it.

He blinks, turning over the booklet in his hands and flipping through the pages. "This is *so* cool, Teddy."

"I know, right? The girls I was with didn't seem to realize just how cool."

Sebastian smiles. "Well, I do."

The clock strikes twelve, and like he knows exactly what it means, Sebastian scoots next to me and looks at the Polaroid camera hanging on my neck. We take our selfie, and then we stand there as Eden and Briar give us once-overs and stomp away. Maribel and Tiffany follow like lemmings, and Billy and Gregory wave to us, say good-night, and head back to the Forty-Second Street entrance.

"I hope you don't hate the salt and pepper shakers," Sebastian says after a moment. "I can't return them. And I honestly don't even remember what gift shop I got them from. But I just thought they were kind of cool and, like, kitschy. You can be honest: Hate them?"

"I promise I don't," I say.

Just hoping these don't wind up a sad metaphor like Benji's, I think. I don't say it, of course, but I find myself slipping deeper into this troublesome crush I've developed now that he's gotten me a thoughtful gift for no reason at all.

But he has a Blake, Teddy. He has a Blake! Who he was probably just with all night. Get ahold of yourself!

"I can't believe you won this for me," Sebastian says after a minute. "Seriously, thank you."

"Of course," I say. "Thank the lucky bracelet for giving me the only four categories I could have possibly had any knowledge about."

He shakes his head. "Well it was *your* brain." Then, after

looking around: "Okay, Grand Central is a *lot*."

"It is a lot," I agree.

We stand there for a couple of minutes. The Polaroid we just took has developed, aired out as I pinch the bottom border between my thumb and index finger, the Statue of Liberty saltshaker balancing on my palm as my pinkie keeps it steady.

The salt and pepper shakers are heavy. Not literally—they're impossibly light, and I wonder if wrapping them in socks and T-shirts will protect them in my luggage—but metaphorically speaking, I am so pointedly aware that they are gifts from Sebastian, who I've recently realized is very cute, and alarmingly sweet, and who decidedly sees me as a friend.

My mind is a vacuum, or like one of those wormholes in space where things go in one end and pop out the other just to repeat the cycle.

(I don't know how wormholes work, obviously.)

All I do know is that my thoughts about Sebastian are confusing, cyclical, and spinning around in my mind like dogs chasing their tails.

Blithely unaware, Sebastian glances down at the salt and pepper shakers and grins at me before we head back to the hotel.

We settle in effortlessly, like we have shared a room for a while now. I place the Polaroid on the desk and add our photo with the clock to the thick stack of scavenger hunt pictures. The photo of Sebastian on the bridge stays in my pocket for now.

As Sebastian heads into the bathroom, I put on the TV and sit on the edge of my bed. Ironically, HBO is showing an Addie Harlow movie. I can't believe we are going to be in the background of her new film.

That is a song lyric, I think.

Something like . . .

The shot on the bridge is ours forever,

the cutest boy, the perfect weather.

I put it in my Notes app, just so I don't forget it, but then I roll my eyes. *At myself.* What am I even doing?

As I'm trying to reel myself in, I notice a piece of paper crumpled up on the desk.

It's a class ticket from the Visitor Center at Columbia University. Sitting in on a class isn't my idea of a date, but it makes sense it'd be Sebastian's. Only cemented by the fact that, crumpled up next to it, there's a receipt from a restaurant that has two of everything.

My heart sinks. I am an idiot. I just wrote a little poem about this guy and he was on some intellectual date with a Columbia guy. The more I piece together about Blake, the more I realize it's silly of me to even think Sebastian would consider me more than a friend if he was single. He's going for some older guy who is smart and lives in New York and attends one of the best colleges in the country.

Compared to Blake, I'm a total loser. My claim to fame

is, what? High school theater credits and some mentions in the local newspaper? I'm planning to stay in our small Florida town to go to community college and I haven't declared a major. Which there isn't anything wrong with, and I'm not embarrassed or ashamed, but I'm not on par with Blake. I'm not on par with the ambitious, genius type of guy Sebastian clearly is into.

I stare at the poem. Blake would probably not be happy that I just wrote this about Sebastian.

Yet here I am, pining after a guy who two days ago I hardly knew.

"What's on the agenda for tomorrow?" Sebastian shouts.

My heart pops like a balloon that just got too friendly with a needle.

Because the way the closet door is propped open, the full-length mirror shows Sebastian as he crosses his arms and grabs at the hem of his shirt, pulling it over his head. His biceps seem bigger as he shakes the shirt out and folds it on the counter, his chest broad and more defined than I've ever noticed. I'm not trying to stare, but I just had no idea he was going to look like *that* under his tee.

"Teddy?"

I clear my throat and lock my phone, turning my attention back to the TV screen, back to Addie as she struts down a street in Italy in a disguise.

God, I wish I was in a disguise.

"What?"

"What are we doing tomorrow, again?"

I nod. "Breakfast as a group. Then improv class. And then our last item! You and I are going up to the top of the Empire State Building. Then you're doing your . . ."

Meeting up with Blake, probably.

"Right," he says. "Is the improv class—"

"It is *not* optional," I say. "Very much mandatory. Please don't tell me you want to skip that too, because I am already nervous about the entire thing."

He turns on the sink, and I glance over at the mirror, watching as he runs his hands under the water, and then I quickly look back to the TV. Addie has escaped Rome, and she's in the arms of her lover, on the Riviera. I sigh without meaning to. It's all so romantic and cinematic.

"You're not nervous," he says, once he's flicked the water off. "You're great at improv."

"Not in New York City with, like, a legit Actors Studio or whatever." I groan. "Annie was supposed to be my partner for— Not that . . . I don't mean you're . . ."

Sebastian laughs. "I get it. I'm not an actor. Well, I'll go anyway. If it helps your nerves."

I throw myself back and exhale, a long, relieved sigh. "Yes. Thank God."

"Okay."

"Okay," I say. "So, we do the improv class, and then we run for our lives and get our Polaroid before Eden gets hers, and then we're done. Then I'll cover for you and your Friday evening plans."

Sebastian doesn't say anything for a minute.

Head in the clouds, for just a moment, I wonder if he's contemplating those plans. I wonder if he's thinking he might want to spend Friday evening with me instead.

Then he breaks the silence: "That mask did wonders for my skin."

Friday

Chapter 30

Funny Honey

"This is not your mother's improv workshop."

The CHHS Drama Club has been arranged in two rows of folding chairs. There are two additional rows of aspiring actors behind us, and the space in front of us is the makeshift stage. We're in a ballet studio on the sixth floor of a West Forty-Second Street high-rise. Right by a Target, a pizza place, and a Dave & Buster's.

Two men stand before us, both wearing black T-shirts and pants. They are both probably in their fifties—one, who is taller, has embraced his gray hair and wears silver wired glasses, while the other has turned to a fairly obvious brown box dye.

"I'm Bronson Yardley," the gray-haired man says. "And most of you probably already know me, but if you don't, I am a retired Broadway actor." It's silent. "I teach now, to share my gifts with the world."

"And I'm Dash Pendleton." The other man beams. "I'm also a retired actor. You guys probably saw me on a few daytime soaps. I've been on some competitive reality TV, too."

"And *The Drew Barrymore Show*," Bronson offers.

Dash nods.

"You're here because you're actors," Bronson says, opening his arms wide. "You want to hone your art. And the only way to do it is to . . ." He forms fists with his hands. "Break down barriers."

Sebastian glances over at me. He has his arms folded over his somewhat faded black Volcom T-shirt. The first thing he asked me when we got here is if he's going to have to dance, and I can tell he has his own anxieties about this whole thing.

"So, for today's first exercise," Bronson huffs, taking a few steps away from us and turning to face the wall of mirrors behind him. He seems to be actively struggling to avoid eye contact with us in the reflection. "We really want to come out of our shells."

"Shells are not productive for good acting," Dash says to us with his hand up to his mouth like he's whispering.

Bronson closes his eyes and drops his head. He rolls his neck, and then goes still.

The room is silent.

And then he's unleashing a bloodcurdling scream, his head shaking as he brings his hands up and claws at his own cheeks.

Dash smiles at us, very nonchalant, as the scream ascends into dangerous decibel territory.

Once Bronson is done with his earsplitting wail, he opens his eyes and smiles at himself in the mirror. Then, he turns on his heel and, facing us again, holds his arms out wide.

"What did you think?"

We all glance around the room as if wondering if any of us have even the slightest clue what in the actual fuck is happening. Eden and Briar are stifling laughs, and Sebastian looks horrified.

Mrs. Mackenzie almost looks *bored*, like she's not at all surprised.

"So raw," Dash says, clapping his hands together and stepping forward. Then, he's unleashing his own low, bellowing roar. His doesn't last as long, thankfully, but I still have a brief ringing in my ear. It's like he flips a switch, and he's just standing there, smiling blissfully like he didn't just try to break the sound barrier and shatter the floor-to-ceiling windows.

"All right, your turn now."

We sit in silence until Mrs. Mackenzie, ever the dramatist, howls.

Immediately, everyone joins in. Screaming, and cawing, and violently yelping.

And then it ends.

Sebastian and I are both sitting there, vocal cords unspoiled and eyes wide.

"You didn't do it." Dash gestures between us. He tilts his head and screws up his mouth, pinching it to one side. "Come on, this exercise is helpful in breaking down those barriers."

"It's really not optional," Bronson sighs.

Sebastian laughs into his hand before he opens his mouth and a weak croak comes out, like a baby dinosaur or something.

Dash winces. "That's . . . *something*."

"I'm not much of a screamer," Sebastian says.

Everyone laughs, and he goes red.

"I only meant—" He groans. "My barriers are broken down."

"Mine too," I say.

Bronson blinks a few times. He ponders something for a moment before his lips part into an oversatisfied grin.

"Oh, boys." He rushes over and gestures for us to stand up. "In that case, you can lead our first round of improvisation."

Dash claps, skipping around in a circle like he's hyping up a team. "Four rules. Who knows 'em?"

Eden's hand shoots up.

"You're up!"

"We can only say 'yes,'" Eden starts, beaming. "But not just 'yes.' It has to be 'yes, and.' Like, adding on and stuff. And then we have to make statements, not ask questions. And the last rule is: No mistakes. Make it work."

Dash winks. "Okay, great job. I think that is what the

kids are calling a *slay*."

Bronson looks at us. "You got that?"

Sebastian and I are now standing in front of everybody, and I'm not sure which group is making me more nervous; the random actors we don't know, or the two rows of people we do.

I realize Sebastian is probably mortified, but he just stands there, looking for me to take the lead.

"Got it."

Bronson's smile gets even bigger. "Good. Good. Okay, let's see. Hmm. Are you two . . . ? Together?"

Sebastian and I both make faces. I don't know exactly what his says, but mine, instinctively is one of faux disgust, like *US? No way!*

Dash puts his hands on his hips. "What's wrong with that?"

"Oh, are you . . ." Bronson's voice drops a register. "Straight?"

He says it like it'd be a terrifying revelation.

"No, we're not straight," Sebastian says.

"We're just not boyfriends," I say, perhaps too defensively. "We're friends?"

Eden giggles. "You're *friends*?"

Mrs. Bloom laughs, too.

"Yes," I say. "We're friends."

"I think it might be a good prompt . . ." Bronson wobbles a little as he stares off, coming up with an idea. "It's such a compelling dynamic, especially for the two of you.

Handsome, young. A little awkward. And there's something there—a spark—maybe."

"Don't drop a match," Dash chortles.

A spark?

I sigh, turning to Sebastian. "I guess we're doing this again."

"Again?" Dash quirks a brow.

"We just had to act like boyfriends yesterday," I say. "We were extras. Long story."

Bronson brightens. "Wonderful. Extra work is so valuable. They're like building blocks. Like . . . like a foundation for an actor."

"*You* were extras?" Mrs. Bloom has a look of distaste on her face, her arms folded over her chest and her legs crossed. "In what, exactly?"

"An Addie Harlow movie," I say.

Everyone starts whispering, especially the two rows behind the drama club. Mrs. Mackenzie looks surprised, but beyond that I can't tell how she feels about this. Have we done something wrong? Something right?

Mrs. Bloom cackles. Tosses her head back and *cackles* like a witch. "I'm sorry," she says, clearing her throat and fixing her hair. "Sorry, it's just—are you joking? I mean, Teddy, I know you have quite the imagination, but . . ." Her lower lips drop into a pout, like she's talking to a child she feels sorry for. "Do you really expect us to believe you were an extra in an Addie Harlow movie yesterday?"

"We were," I say, my voice going a little too high. "We

have a Polaroid with her. It's in the hotel room. We took a selfie, and afterward, she said we 'really sold it.'"

Mrs. Bloom and Briar exchange obnoxious giggles, and the rest of the drama club awkwardly look down at the ground to pretend this isn't happening. Eden, especially, seems like she is embarrassed of her own mother.

"I can't wait to see your selfie with Addie Harlow," Briar says with a smile. "It's just too bad you don't have it with you. Since, for all we know, you could Photoshop it and print it." She turns to Eden and pretends to be excited to share a fun fact: "Did you know you can do that? There are ways to get your iPhone photos printed as Polaroids, even."

Eden ignores her, inhaling sharply.

"It's not Photoshopped," I say. I look to Sebastian for assistance, but he just shrugs. "We were on set, and we talked to her."

Mrs. Bloom nods. "We believe you." She looks around, smirking. "Everyone believes you."

Bronson shifts uncomfortably. "All right, maybe—let's just do the exercise."

"Maybe you're not boyfriends," Dash says, tapping his chin. "Maybe you're estranged."

"Oh, I don't know . . ." Bronson shifts his weight to one side, then snaps his fingers together. "I've got it. Let's do a scene where you're *husbands*. Oh, and you're going to rescue a dog."

Dash steps toward us. "I think we should place them somewhere weird."

"Weird." Bronson bobs his head from side to side. "Like Coney Island?"

"No, like a gym locker room." Dash eyes us to gauge reactions. I don't give one, because I know he'll feel satisfied to know my insides are congealing at the thought, but Sebastian gives him the gratification of pulling a face.

"I *love* it," Bronson says. "In *Malibu*!"

"Think the kids would say that is '*giving*.'" Dash nods.

"Okay, boys. You're at a gym locker room in Malibu."

"And you're dolls," Dash adds.

"And you're locked in."

"And you're hungry."

"And you think there might be a wild animal in the locker room somewhere."

Sebastian and I are both laughing at this point, but everyone else in the room has completely straight faces. Dash and Bronson hurry to sit in our empty seats in the front row.

"Whenever you're ready," Dash says, tapping at his wrist and smiling. Then he stands back up. "Oh! We almost forgot the best part. The group will vote for the best improv partners at the end of the workshop, and the winners will get an amazing prize."

"An *amazing* prize," Bronson echoes.

The way they're keeping it a secret, it sounds like the amazing prize is an I Heart NY T-shirt from a Times Square gift shop. Though that could be sort of fun—just extra enough—now that I think about it.

I take a deep breath and look around. I conjure up a locker room.

"I wish we had some food."

"Yes, and a key," Sebastian says, nodding and putting his hands on his hips.

"Yes, and a weapon. I think there's something in here with us."

Sebastian scratches the back of his head, pointing to my left. "Could you use that as a weapon?"

I reach down and grab an invisible baseball bat. "Good thing the baseball players left this behind. Yes, I can use this as a weapon, and I can try to bust down the door, too."

"Yes, and you can knock me out, so I don't have to do this exercise anymore."

He grins, self-satisfied, and it's kind of funny, but nobody in the audience is as amused as I am.

"You were doing pretty good," Bronson says slowly.

Dash frowns. "'Were' is past tense here."

"It usually is," Sebastian says. He shakes his head and scans the room before turning to me.

Dash shrugs. "Okay, let's do another prompt. Maybe you guys can't play funny."

"We can play funny," I say. I'm half protesting because of my pride—I can play funny—and half because I am nervous of the alternative. I'm not going to do a romance scene with Sebastian in front of everyone. I'm playing a dangerous game, finding him so cute and feeling weird feelings I've never felt before when he has a Blake and we're going to end up being strangers again after this trip.

The thought stings.

Good God, does my brain ever just stop?

Bronson confers with Dash. "Do we want sad?" He pauses, then he's struck with an idea. "Oh, or we could do violence."

I lock eyes with Mrs. Mackenzie and try to plead with her: *Please get us out of this.*

But she quirks a brow and smirks as if to say "this is great for you!"

"I think you were right, something romantic with these two," Dash says.

"Please, no." Sebastian says it so quickly it's almost gut-wrenching.

I mean, I was thinking the same thing, but God. Am I that repellent?

"Yeah, I mean, Teddy and Eden had more romantic chemistry in *High School Musical*," Briar cackles. Eden shoots her a look.

"How do we feel about pirates?" Bronson taps his chin.

Dash says, "No, I'm just wanting you two to really step outside the box. I think we could unlock true art here."

Why us?

"I say we send him to war," Bronson says.

Dash nods dutifully. "Seems our only option."

"Devastating," Bronson whispers, all breathy with narrowed eyes.

"To perish in a fight to the death, a la *The Hunger Games*, even." Dash points to Sebastian. "You are downtrodden."

He straightens up. "Oh, fantastic."

"You're downtrodden, too," Dash says to me. "But you have been spared. Of the draft or the drawing or whatever." Then he looks to Sebastian. "You're going to head into a battle you know you won't win."

"My favorite kind," Sebastian says.

"Your loved ones are all terribly sad," Bronson adds. "They'll never see you again."

"The tallest boy in the village," Dash wisps. "Off to the slaughter."

Jesus.

"I'm not that tall," Sebastian says.

"You're tall," I say.

Dash claps his hands together. "All right, the scene is set. It's the night before he leaves, and you have to say goodbye. You live in dystopia. But there's a twist—you have to find out his big secret before he goes or else."

Sebastian looks between Dash and Bronson. "What *is* my big secret?"

"It's improv," Bronson says, with a sort of sad look, like it's almost pitiful how much he has to explain to Sebastian. "But your goal for the scene is to make sure he doesn't find out."

"All right, let's just do this," Mrs. Bloom chimes in. "Some other pairs need to go before the workshop ends."

Mrs. Mackenzie is doing her best to keep her mouth

shut when Mrs. Bloom speaks, I can tell by the way her forehead creases a little.

"If it helps, the prize is actually pretty good," Dash says. "Best scene partners get a backstage tour to *Versailles*!"

I blink. "What?"

"Told you, it's amazing," Bronson says.

"Like, *backstage*?" I ask. "Backstage, backstage?"

"Yes, it's behind the stage," Dash says.

Oh my God. This changes everything. I don't even have time to consider how, exactly, but going backstage to *Versailles* and meeting Benji twice would be amazing. Then he'd remember me, even, by the time the after-party rolled around.

I tug on my lucky bracelet.

"And scene," Bronson says. He looks at Sebastian like a lost toddler, smiling gently. "That means *go*."

Sebastian lowers his eyes to meet mine. He understands. We're playing to win.

Now I'm *acting*.

We are in a deserted dystopia, and the stakes are high—higher than going backstage at *Versailles* and meeting Benji, if one can even imagine such a thing.

"Please, you can't go."

Sebastian is acting too, it seems. His expression is stone, but it came on in an instant—a character he slipped into.

"It isn't up to me," he says. "But you'll be okay here without me."

I frown. "Yes. And I'll take care of your sister. Though, before you go, I need to know . . ."

He shakes his head. "You know I can't tell you. It's a secret for a reason. You know how *they* are."

"Yeah," I say. "And that means I know how important this is."

"Yes," he agrees. "But our time is running out. I have to go. So we should say goodbye."

When he delivers the line, it's so convincing, and so real, I get swept up in it for a moment. I don't need Benji lyrics to help me conjure emotions, these are coming up all on their own. Because I have thought about the fact that this is all just one episode, one chapter—Sebastian and I have this New York adventure and that's it. I've accepted that. But the added layer of actually saying the word is something I hadn't considered. The transactional, formal act of leaving this blip of a trip in hindsight.

I'm not sure how this happened in such a short amount of time, but becoming strangers again feels like a suffocating idea.

Sebastian looks expectant, waiting for me to respond, and the room is silent.

"I don't want to say goodbye."

It's all I can manage. And I'm half acting, but I'm half consumed by the memories of this trip playing in my mind. I'm half consumed by the idea of those memories one day becoming distant, blurrier. I'm now fully consumed by the understanding that while we weren't pretending, we haven't been living in reality. Not one that is going to continue, anyway.

Another expectant look from Sebastian reminds me I'm not playing the part I'm meant to. And I can't lose the prize, but I also know improv is about responding and making the scene feel real—as much feeling and as little thinking as possible.

"Maybe it doesn't have to be this way," I say.

Sebastian takes the smallest step toward me. "Yes, it does. I can't tell you what you want to know."

What I really want to know is what's going on here. Surely this is something? My imagination gets the best of me more often than not, but this isn't some rose-colored daydream—there *is* something between us.

But there's something between him and Blake, too.

There are too many questions, and no answers.

I just need to know what is going on.

"Right, and if you can't tell me . . ." I glance around, and I don't see the audience, but the tall trees around the clearing we're standing in. "We could run away or something."

Sebastian's eyes flit to the side, like he's checking to see if I've broken the rules. "Uh—yes, we could. They might—" I've thrown him, and he stammers. "They might find us."

"Maybe," I say. "But then we don't have to say goodbye. And then maybe we both win."

"Saying goodbye isn't always a bad thing," he offers. "And anyway, we don't know that it's goodbye. It might be 'see you later.'"

"Yes, and . . ." I swallow. "It might really be 'goodbye.'"

I look up at him, at this guy I've so quickly gotten used to having by my side.

I look up at the guy who's gruff and cynical to the world, but who got me New York City salt and pepper shakers. The guy who just wants a cozy fall in New England. Who knows more about dinosaurs than anyone I've ever met. I look up at him and realize how lucky I am to know him better than anyone in this room.

I look up at him and wish there was a way he could have autumn leaves and stay by my side at the same time.

"Great job." Dash claps, and I am startled back to the present.

I sniffle quickly, collecting myself. "We didn't finish the scene?"

Sebastian looks from me to him.

Bronson and Dash stand, walking over to join us at the front of the room.

"It was nice and all," Dash says. "You played serious, for sure, which is so great."

"Really great." Bronson nods slowly and puts his hands on our shoulders, frowning like we're two abandoned kittens in a box on the side of the road. "Really just . . . Well, I love the effort. You get a gold star for effort, boys."

The crowd all laugh, and Sebastian and I go sit down.

"Wait," I say, snapping out of it. "Wait. We can do another one. We can do it better. I really would like another chance, because meeting Benji—"

Dash laughs. "Oh, nobody's meeting anybody. This backstage tour is tomorrow morning. At six a.m."

Everyone groans, and I suddenly feel a lot better about probably losing, so I slump in my seat while they call up Eden and Briar, who seem disinterested at best, though Mrs. Bloom is perched on the edge of her seat ready for Primetime Emmy–level, symbiotic partner acting.

All right, Teddy. Get it together. We've got to finish the scavenger hunt after this, and then it's going to be the best night of your life. You can deal with the Sebastian stuff later.

Right. Totally. I am amazing at dealing with my feelings.

I gulp, and Sebastian turns to me in his seat, voice low: "Are you okay?"

"Yes, I am amazing," I whisper back. "I thought we did a good job, for what it's worth."

He sits up a bit straighter. "Yeah, me too."

It's not goodbye yet, the trip isn't over.

"Empire State Building after this," I whisper. "Last one."

Sebastian smiles. "Hopefully Mrs. Bloom doesn't mind losing."

I fight a laugh. "You mean Eden?"

He shakes his head.

The joke, paired with his confidence in our winning, reignites a fire.

Dash is wrong. I *am* meeting Benji Keaton, and my fate will be sealed in the next two hours.

Chapter 31

Ready, Set, Not Yet

Once the workshop ends, the class disperses, set off on a race to finish the scavenger hunt. Sebastian and I run down Forty-Second Street, across the avenues, up to the hotel, to get the Polaroid camera. I let Sebastian grab the other Polaroids, so once we snap our last item, we can be the first to text the group photo evidence that we've completed the list.

Once we're headed downtown on Fifth, and I can see the side of the Empire State Building sparkling in the sunlight, I realize this is all *really* going to happen.

Tonight will be the night I meet Benji Keaton. June 7 would have to be a national holiday. Even if it is in Gemini season.

"Those improv instructors are crocks." Sebastian rolls his eyes. "I mean, first we're dolls in a locker room? Then we're in a dystopia? What the hell?"

He's been going on about this improv workshop since we left the hotel room with the camera.

"You may not believe me, but it could have been worse." I nod when he looks aghast. "Once, at theater camp, we were all supposed to be pigs rolling in the mud. You don't realize quite how humiliating that is until you're oinking and convulsing onstage in front of a full audience."

He laughs. "Fine, it could have been worse."

We're in lockstep on the sidewalk, and it's not lost on me how, on the plane, I thought the only solution to Sebastian's indifference was that I'd have to invent mind control technology to get him to participate in this scavenger hunt. Now, he's as invested as me.

"And have you noticed how many times people seem to think we're boyfriends or something?"

It's the last thing I'm expecting him to say, so I laugh big and loud and nod. "I know right?"

He glances over, but immediately faces forward again, nodding. "Ridiculous."

Right. Ridiculous. Because Sebastian has something else going on. Sebastian has Blake. And Blake is probably cool and smart, and he probably likes all the same poems as Sebastian. I bet Blake wears cologne that smells like leather or an old jazz club, and he drinks black coffee, and he has a cool tattoo in Latin. Blake is probably this perfect, philosophical poster guy for everything Sebastian wants.

And, anyway, if he didn't have Blake, that wouldn't even mean he'd like *me.* Which would make sense, since I know what I see in him, but I can't imagine what he'd see in me. I'm a dramatic, sensitive daydreamer. This very internal dialogue is the kind of thing he'd find silly and useless, even. So, I guess the stem of the ridiculousness is less important than the overall truth that it is, in fact, utterly ridiculous. To him.

Okay, Teddy, slight spiral happening.

I just can't take it anymore. I can't take the way I'm already prone to imagine things, and the uncertainty here keeps drawing me in like quicksand every single time the thought enters my mind.

I draw in a breath. "But that does remind me. I just am curious, is all . . . I know I agreed to not ask about the flowers, but are you seeing someone? Here? In New York?"

Sebastian looks at me sideways. "Huh?"

"Do you have, like, a New York City boyfriend or something?"

Sebastian's eyes go wide. "What? No. Obviously I don't. How would I— What?"

"I don't know, maybe you met someone on a Dinosaur Reddit forum," I say. He hangs his head. "I'm just saying. You've got some super-secret agenda for the drama club's New York trip. And you got those flowers. And I happened to see your receipt, from when you went to Columbia last night, and you were clearly with someone."

He rubs his right thumb against his left palm, gentle at

first, back and forth, but then he starts to dig—like he's trying to force the skin to peel off.

"If you have a dinosaur forum boyfriend, I won't judge," I say.

Sometimes I get the overwhelming urge to make people feel safer. Probably because I know what it feels like when you want to jump out of your own skin. So, seeing him anxious, I sympathize.

"Or however you might have met," I say.

"This just got all weird." He looks up at me. "Didn't it?"

"No, it's fine. Just tell me what is going on or I'm going to assume you're a hit man and you were meeting with whoever hired you." Levity is sometimes helpful, so I gasp. "Wait, you're not a hit man hired to take *me* out, are you? Only now we've become friends, and you're feeling guilty. You're not sure if you can do it. You're contemplating the two paths ahead of you. You could give up the mission and confront the big, bad boss, knowing you'll have to fight the henchman *and* him and you could end up dead. Does the fear of God set in? Does their creepy hideout become a slaughterhouse for a reformed vigilante? Or . . . you could wipe a single tear from your cheek as you apologize to me and—"

Sebastian coughs a laugh. "What is it like up in there?" He gestures toward my head.

"It's amusing and terrifying," I say. "All right, go."

He nods. "I went to a lecture. There's a physicist who is doing a summer lecture series, and I sort of snuck in."

I laugh. "Right."

"Honestly!"

"Who is this physicist?" I scoff.

"My dad."

My heart sinks.

Sebastian shrugs and lets out a long breath. One that feels as if it's been locked up for too long, escaping narrowly from a crypt to evaporate like dust between us.

"I went to coffee with my stepsister, Blake, after," he admits.

In the quiet, I'm overcome with a blur of emotions. *Stepsister. Step. Sister.* Relief, confusion, as my imagined Blake dissolves into mist, and then . . . urgency, maybe? Because if Blake isn't who I thought, does that mean there's a chance?

"Blake is the one who sent the flowers," he says. "She's a biochem student at Columbia—we have a lot in common, actually, namely a dislike for my father. But, yeah, I chickened out of talking to my dad. Like I told you—I hadn't seen him in person in years. But tonight, he's doing a major talk about his new research on nuclear energy, and I'm planning to go . . ."

"Your Friday evening plans," I confirm.

"Right, my Friday evening plans."

Solace washes over me on one hand, because Blake is not who I thought Blake was at all. But on the other hand, this doesn't feel like a celebratory story.

"I'm confused. Why did you chicken out?"

"I need him to pay for MIT," he says. "I mean, he's got the money. He's one of the most famous physicists in the country for his research on clean, sustainable resources. But he's too busy to meet with me—busy with guest lecturing, or research, or with his family."

The way he says, "his family," my heart breaks. Because shouldn't that be Sebastian?

"But I want to . . ." He avoids eye contact and frowns. "I want to just go up to him and ask him, face-to-face. I haven't ever asked him for anything, you know? But he's spotty over email and barely returns any of my texts, and I've tried to write it but I just can't ever seem to, so I just thought if I can ask in person, maybe it'll work. If he won't pay for it, I can't go to MIT in the fall."

There are no words. I have no idea what to say to that. I can't even begin to imagine how I'd feel if my dad treated me like that.

"Would your mom ask so you don't have to?"

It comes out a little too boldly. I don't think I should feel any other way about a situation like this, except I don't want to offend Sebastian.

Luckily, he doesn't seem bothered. He only shakes his head. "I can't ask her to do that. I sort of told her he agreed . . . She thinks he invited me to the talk."

"Got it," I say. "Obviously it's a complicated situation."

He gives a small, appreciative smile.

"Will you be okay?" I wince at how it sounds. "Seeing him in person, I mean?"

"It seems pretty safe; it's on the Upper West Side." But he knows that isn't what I mean, so he lowers his eyes. "You think I'm going to be overcome with emotions?"

I shrug.

"I don't really get overcome with emotions." He does this laugh that, for a tech guy, comes across as entirely rehearsed. "I don't know. I'm here. I'm in New York. This was the plan. Has always been the plan. Why I joined tech crew. Now it's time for me to man up and ask him. My future depends on it."

"I'm sorry your relationship with your dad is like that," I say as we pause to wait for a walk signal.

He rubs his fingers together before spreading them wide, showing flushed palms, indicating there's nothing to grasp—nothing to hold on to, just thin air.

"People can have screwed-up families and still be happy, I think." Then he tilts his head, creates an apologetic curve with his brow. "That's not, like, a jab. I just mean . . . people who have both parents and siblings . . . it's hard to explain. Have you ever played Trivial Pursuit?"

I nod. I've only played with my family, and I bomb most of the categories, but occasionally I hit in the Entertainment or Art and Literature.

"People are kind of like those little Trivial Pursuit pies. You know? With the six slots, perfectly sized for the wedges to fit into. And people who have all the wedges, they don't think anything of it. It's complete. Not missing anything. But when you don't have your dad, it's like suddenly you're missing a wedge. Or maybe two. Maybe even three."

Sebastian just shrugs and steps out into the crosswalk, a subtle smirk on his face.

"But it just is what it is. You get used to it. You're missing the wedges. It's fine. It's not like I'm going to get them back."

"You might," I say, suddenly feeling a need to lift Sebastian up from the hopelessness. "You never know. Maybe you could even find other things. Different wedges."

He nods quietly.

"I'll cover for you at dinner and at the show," I say.

Sebastian's mouth forms a line. "Teddy, don't look at me like that."

"Like what?" I throw up my hands.

"Like I'm a wounded puppy."

"I'm not looking at you like you're a wounded puppy."

"The most wounded you've ever seen," he insists. "Malnourished and hit by a car, now out in the rain with big, sad eyes."

I scoff. "That is such an unnecessary visual. And I am not looking at you like that at all. I just . . . I'm sorry that you have to go through this with your dad. That's all."

"I have other wedges," he says. "I'm not a wounded puppy."

"I know."

"Okay, good."

"I'm not wounded," he says. "Really, Teddy. I'm not. I'm . . . angry."

Does he really think those two things are completely separate?

"Can we have a nice rest of the day?" Sebastian asks, forcing a giant grin. "Please?"

I nod. "Of course."

When we get to Thirty-Fourth Street, I steady myself.

Here, at the northeast corner of Fifth Avenue, where east meets west, and dreams meet reality, I feel like I have finally arrived. And it's funny, because I thought this feeling would come from seeing Broadway for the first time—and maybe it will, outside *Versailles*—but this feels like I'm *here*. This building, so iconic and resonant and riddled with history, is New York City.

I marvel at it. It's an art deco masterpiece of stacked limestone and granite rectangles, scored with perfect vertical lines of windows and metal. As the Empire State Building rises and gets narrower, it reaches into the clouds and reminds us all we're in the greatest city on earth.

And there's a giant Starbucks at the base of it all. What else would you expect?

I take photos, and so does Sebastian. This is a surreal moment. We're about to go inside and see what I can only imagine is a magnificent lobby, and then we'll go up in the elevator and we'll walk out and see everything from a brand-new perspective. Really, it'll be a life-changing moment.

"Sebastian," I exhale, taking it all in. "I can't believe we're here."

"Yeah. Me either."

We head inside—none of our classmates in sight—and it is as mesmerizing as I hoped. It's like being whisked away into the 1930s. Apart from all of the people with iPhones and AirPods and all of the denim.

Did they have denim in the 1930s?

It reminds me of *This Side of Paradise*, actually. Everything is shining gold. There's an incredible depiction of the building on the far back wall with sunbeams fanned out around it. There's an information desk beneath it, and next to that, in a glass case, is a model of the building.

I'm not sure I knew we were going to walk through a museum. It's a nice surprise. Except for the fact that we fly through it. I think Sebastian and I are both eager to see the city from the eighty-sixth floor observatory.

Still, there is another—more massive, at nearly two stories—model of the Empire State Building between two sets of stairs. There are blueprints and sketches, and facts and videos from the 1920s when it was being built. There are little viewfinders that show what it was like in the city back then, and I think it's wonderful how it might be different, but the magic is still there.

There are photos showing the progression from the opening of the building to now. There are electrical displays for the old elevators, and simulators that are reminiscent of the Tower of Terror and make my knees go slightly weak.

Two giant King Kong hands have crashed through two

"windows" in one room, and there's a room of celebrities who have visited. Mariah Carey in her bright pink and purple, Taylor Swift, Zac and Zendaya. And, of course, Benji. He's standing next to one of the viewfinders, during his *Sweet Vicious* era, wearing a silky floral shirt that blows in the wind.

"There's your boy," Sebastian says as we walk by.

And then, once we're done breezing through the museum, we head to the elevators and step inside. It's more of the art deco style—gray marble, lined with black marble, and an Empire State Building on the back wall. Gold gears and stripes on the floor.

We take the elevator up to the eighty-sixth floor, and I have no idea my life really is about to change forever.

Chapter 32

Defying Gravity

The open-air observatory is spectacular, just like all the reviews said.

It wraps around the entire floor and offers views of *everything*. I've never felt so big, and I've never felt so small. It's windy and cool and surprisingly not horribly crowded. I snap a few photos of the east side, including the Chrysler Building and the river, sending them to the family group chat, and then to Annie.

I do sort of have Jell-O legs, which I knew would happen. When I take the photos, I take a big step toward the edge, ensuring none of the metal bars make it into the shot, and then I quickly leap back as if I'm going to fly right over if I don't.

Sebastian takes notice, and he laughs into his fist, but doesn't say anything.

"We're really high up," I say, putting my phone in my pocket.

"Not as high as we could be," he says, pointing up to the top of the building behind me. "Hundred and second floor."

I nod. "Because we're not out of our minds."

Adding an extra sixteen floors? I'm good. This is perfect. I'm just scared shitless enough.

Sebastian frowns. "You're so stressed out right now."

Without my permission, a terrible and obnoxious laugh occurs. "I am not."

He rocks back on his heels. "Okay, look, I'm going to do you a favor and help you out."

"What do you mean?"

"Close your eyes," he says. When I don't, and my brow crinkles, he smiles. "Really. Come on, just do it?"

With my back almost up against the wall behind me, I close my eyes.

"Imagine you're backstage. No, you know what? Imagine this. You just left Neptune's after seeing a movie set in New York. And it was the coolest movie ever, and the city was so bright and colorful and you spent the whole movie wishing you were there. And now, you're in your bedroom. You're on your bed, sitting there thinking how awesome it would be to see all of that in person. You're imagining it. The hot dog stands and the bustling crowds and tall buildings and honking cabs."

I do what he says. I imagine all of it.

"But you're only in your room. On your bed, in Citrus Harbor. And that's a dream that's far away. Where you are, it's quiet. It's calm. It's nothing like the big dream you have in your mind."

My room isn't quite in grayscale, but it's void of the vibrance I was just imagining.

"It's a little bit of a sinking feeling, right? Realizing how far away that dream is?"

I nod.

"But open your eyes," he says. And when I do, he's grinning so wide, and he gestures for me to join him at the ledge next to the viewfinder. "You're here, Teddy."

That sinking feeling flips on its head when I look out at the city. When I take in the blue, cloudless sky and the expanse of buildings in every direction, my legs aren't Jell-O and I'm not afraid. I know he's right. *I'm here.*

"*We're* here," I say.

He nods. "Yeah, we are."

We look out for a few minutes, and I almost catch myself laughing. We've been through so much in the span of two days. This city is full of surprises, just like Sebastian.

We turn around and Sebastian takes the Polaroid camera, and he holds it up, and his finger presses the shutter. The city is behind us, a sea of tiny rectangles, and my smile couldn't be bigger.

"There's the last one," he says, putting the lanyard around his neck for the first time. "We did it."

I look at the photo as it develops.

"We're going to meet Benji," I say slowly. "We really are going to meet Benji."

Sebastian smiles, looking at me like I'm . . . Well, I can't exactly tell what he's looking at me like. His eyes are gentle, and his demeanor is softer than usual. I want to look away, but I'm caught up in how cute he is, just like I was on the bridge.

He bites his lip a little as he turns away.

"What now?" he asks.

I shrug, and we walk around the deck, to look south. Downtown is sprawling, and One World Trade steals the show, so tall and blue and prominent.

"You want to get lunch?" he asks, leaning up against one of the viewfinders. "I'm hungry."

I nod. "Yeah, that sounds good. We just have to make sure we text a photo of all of our Polaroids to the group thread. Before Eden does."

He bobs his head up and down. "Of course. Did you bring all of them?"

"No, I asked you to, remember?"

"You did not." His lip lifts like he's going to laugh—like he thinks I'm pranking him—but when I don't smile, he just blinks. "I didn't hear you."

"It's fine," I say. "We got a head start, so if we head back to the hotel now—"

Sebastian looks out at the city. "Well, yeah. We can, but maybe let's just walk the full observation deck. We've only seen two sides."

"Okay," I say, and I start walking.

"Slow down," he says, reaching for my arm. "Come on, Teddy, slow down and enjoy the moment. You're in New York City, on top of the Empire State Building."

"I know I am," I say. "But we have to get all of our Polaroids together and take a photo of them, or all of it is for nothing."

He shakes his head at this. "That's a little much, Teddy. Come on. It's not all for *nothing* if you don't win the scavenger hunt."

"Wha-What is it for then?" I stammer.

As if hurt, he takes a tiny step back. He goes to speak and then closes his mouth, looking from side to side, and I can tell he's wrestling with what to say.

"The scavenger hunt is—"

"The scavenger hunt isn't everything," he says. "I'm not saying we can't win, I just think you're missing . . ."

I take a step forward. "What am I missing?"

He holds his arms out wide turning toward the ledge. "Look around, Teddy! This is it. This is an experience. This is a moment. This is life. Right here, right now. You're living your life. You say you don't have stories to tell? You do. You just don't see them. You don't realize when they're right in front of you."

"What are you talking about?"

"*This* is your inspiration," he says. "This is the magic. For your songs and—"

I groan. "Sebastian, what is with you and the songs? I

mean, really? Why are you so obsessed with me writing songs? You and I don't ever speak, for years, and then suddenly, we're on this trip and you have this entire *thing*—you say I'm going to be a star, and write music, and I just . . . I don't understand where any of this is even coming from!"

He looks like he wants to pull his hair out, and he takes a step toward me now.

"You really don't get it, do you?"

I shake my head. "No, and let me guess, you're going to say something sarcastic now?"

He presses his tongue to the inside of his cheek and laughs. "You're unbelievable."

For a moment, I wonder if this is the part where he disappears again.

But he only takes another step closer, so there's just a foot left between us.

"You know why I want you to slow down and take in the inspiration? You know why I want you to write songs or just to, I don't know, embrace the fact that you even can?"

With a lump in my throat, I shake my head again.

"Because, Teddy." His cheeks flash red. "Because I think you're captivating and talented and I think I'm lucky to even know you! I think you're gonna be somebody. You *are* somebody!"

I blink.

"Do you know how I felt when I found out we were rooming together?"

I'm so shocked by all of this, I just stand there.

"I was kind of stoked." He laughs, like he knows I'm surprised to hear him admit such a thing. "I was nervous—definitely mostly nervous—because I knew you didn't want to room with me and you had all these big plans for your trip and I was this, like, dark cloud over all of them. And I didn't know how to even attempt to be your friend. Didn't know if it'd be worth trying, or if I'd just ruin your trip even more. But honestly, I was glad to have a roommate, and that it was going to be you."

"I don't know what to say," I admit. "I mean . . . that's all nice, but I'm not—"

"I know you think so much about what you're not," he says. "I'm here to tell you, from the outside looking in, it's a completely different story."

I want to disagree. I want to say something, anything, but I'm too stunned.

"I act," I say finally. "I play parts. So, the Teddy you think you know is—"

"The Teddy I know?" His eyes widen. "The Teddy I know made a streamlined and efficient itinerary and navigated the subway around the entire city. The Teddy I know asked that random girl to take our picture, and snuck us into a gala, and onto a film set. The Teddy I know marched right up to Addie Harlow like it was no big deal. That wasn't a part. That wasn't acting. That was *you*."

Was that me?

"And the Teddy I know . . ." Sebastian exhales, looking off at the city before turning back to me. "The Teddy I know is . . . *a butterfly spot-lit in spring, with rainbow prisms for wings.*"

I swallow. "That— Those lyrics were— You were at the talent show? You *remember* that?"

Sebastian nods. "I remember."

"This whole time?" It comes out as a whisper. "You never hated me . . ."

"Hated you?" He keeps his eyes locked on mine and takes the tiniest step forward. "I definitely never hated you."

"Did you . . ." The space between us is so small. "Like me?"

"I think I did." He inches closer.

"And, um . . . What about now?"

And then he kisses me.

Sebastian takes my face in his hands, and he kisses me.

His lips press against mine and time doesn't slow down or speed up—it ceases to exist. I close my eyes and melt into the kiss. My heart swells and as his mouth moves slightly against mine, I realize there are no metaphors or lyrics for this. It's beyond symbolism or poetry.

It just comes naturally with Sebastian. I don't need blocking or stage directions. My hands find his waist, and the Polaroid presses against my chest when I pull him a little bit closer, but I don't want to stop. I don't want this to ever end.

And after a moment, the words do start to form. I'd say it's like standing in a neon glow, or the breeze as the subway rushes past. It's a kiss in the castle of an enchanted city, with a mystical and mysterious boy, and finding he's not so much a mystery as an answer.

When we break apart, Sebastian pulls the Polaroid off and kisses me again, this time holding his arm out and snapping a photo. I might be smiling into the kiss once I realize what he's doing, and I might be constantly surprised by this boy.

"For your scrapbook," he says.

I raise a brow. "I don't have a scrapbook."

"You totally have a New York scrapbook."

Nodding, I figure he can know he's right.

"I wasn't expecting this," I say. "I didn't realize you liked me, too."

"Too?" He grins.

"I don't just kiss my friends like that," I offer.

"Thank goodness."

We kiss again, and then we take in the views for a little bit longer. I don't know what exactly we are, or what exactly it even is I'm feeling, but I know it's good.

Of course, as if the universe also loves a good metaphor, as the elevator descends and I check my phone, things come crashing down.

"Oh shit. No, no, no."

Sebastian squeezes my shoulder. "What is it?"

"Eden and Briar finished the scavenger hunt," I say, panic rising before a sense of defeat creeps in. "We lost."

Chapter 33

Come to Your Senses

It's as if the Empire State Building elevator becomes the Tower of Terror. I could be free-falling for all I know, plummeting to my untimely and unfair demise.

For as fast as we went up, we are crashing even faster.

"Look, Eden texted the group," I say, showing Sebastian the thread.

She's attached a photo, all her Polaroids laid perfectly in a grid on a pink Hermès scarf. Brutally extra, and brutally Eden, until the bitter end.

"Oh, no." Sebastian sounds so wounded, it actually breaks my heart even more.

"Well."

There's a blur to the world that doesn't normally exist—a haze, and a sense of total detachment from everything around me.

We lost.

I keep repeating it in my head as we walk out of the building and the humid summer heat envelops us on the sidewalk.

After all of that, we lost.

I lock my phone and slide it into my pocket, looking at a poster of New York sights stuck on a pedicab. Among the iconic buildings, there's Lady Liberty. She is everything I wish I could be right now—strong, resilient, and made of copper, free of a beating and battered heart.

My mind has wandered to so many fantasies lately. Well, not only lately. But these past three days, I've conjured up a new emotion. I've crafted the feeling of meeting Benji, and I've found that fantasy to be the most comforting thing ever. A light at the end of the tunnel. A miracle that was *right there*.

But it's never going to be real now. And it's still *right there*, but it's always going to be just inches too far for my fingers to grasp.

"Are you okay?" Sebastian asks. He runs his hand over my back, and it feels new and comforting and I lean into his side, nodding. "No, you're not."

"I am," I say with a long, exaggerated sigh. "I don't think it has *fully* hit me yet."

"I'm really sorry," he says. "You're right, I should have grabbed the Polaroids."

"No, I should have grabbed them. But anyway, it doesn't matter."

"It does matter," he insists. "I feel like I let you down, and this is my fault."

"No, you didn't and it's not." Frowning, I blink away tears. "Guess it just wasn't meant to be."

"Don't cry," he says.

"I'm not." I turn away. "It's just . . . allergies."

He squeezes my shoulder for the second time today. "Teddy, it's going to be okay." Then, he looks in my eyes. "I really hate seeing you cry."

I nod and wipe away the tears. "Sorry."

He laughs now, shaking his head. "You don't have to be sorry. I didn't mean it like that."

Realizing how silly it was, I laugh, too. "I just really let myself believe. I truly believed we had it."

Sebastian pulls me in for a hug and I rest my head on his chest.

The problem with living in fantasies? The problem with believing in magic?

When reality sets in, and it's not as enchanting as you'd hoped, it hurts that much more.

I should have stayed on earth. Maybe I knew this would happen deep down. I even said as much—the moment I found out Annie wasn't coming: this trip was cursed. Why did I think I could pull off something like this without her?

"I really wanted to get that bracelet signed for Annie."

"She'll understand," Sebastian says.

"She will, but I just . . . It was supposed to be this super-special thing. And, you know, I figured if I got the bracelet signed, she'd *never* get rid of that. So, she'd never forget me."

Sebastian laughs quietly. "I don't think you have to worry about that."

He kisses me, and it's sweet and soft and sincere. I wonder if this is going to be a thing now, because it turns out having a cute boy to comfort and kiss you when you're having a dramatic moment? I mean, talk about a scene-stealer.

Sebastian frowns. "Look, I hate to do this when you're upset, but I'm supposed to go meet Blake in a little bit. And it's uptown, so we should . . . Well, I really don't want to leave you when you're—"

"Let's go," I say, patting him on the arm. I'm not going to make this difficult for him. "We can get to the hotel in fifteen minutes."

He raises a brow. "You have gotten really good at navigating New York."

"I have, haven't I?"

Then he does something new.

He takes my hand, his palm against mine as our fingers interlock. I never realized how badly I wanted or needed Sebastian's hand in mine, but now I want him to take my hand everywhere—each busy street or quiet room.

As we walk up Fifth Avenue, holding hands with Sebastian is as effortless as breathing. When I look down at our hands, I catch the blue of my bracelet.

Sebastian needs this bracelet. My mission is over, and

his is just beginning. But part of me just can't give it up. What if there's some lucky twist? Some way to meet Benji at the stage door, still? *Something* I haven't thought of.

I'm not sure why, but a small pang of guilt comes with keeping the bracelet secure on my own wrist. I want to give it to him, and I want him to have all the good luck, but I'm afraid of what I might miss out on if I take it off.

Sebastian stops walking, squeezes my hand. "Are you sure you're okay?"

"Yeah, totally."

"I mean, I know this was a *huge* deal for you. Your whole trip—"

"It's okay," I say. "You came here for something too. Don't worry about me. I'll just have to meet Benji another time."

"You just never give up," Sebastian says with a bright smile.

"Of course not," I agree, mirroring his grin. "In the grand scheme of things, this is just a tiny setback."

I am alone and the world is a dark, miserable place.

Of course I had to pretend everything was fine for Sebastian. He couldn't be distracted by any of this.

But what I was doing is called *acting*.

Now, alone in our hotel room with the curtains drawn and the lights turned off and sad Benji playing, the show is over.

It's such a strange feeling to make home something outside of yourself, and to be so close to feeling like you're there . . . but then find there's no going home at all.

Eden doesn't even want to meet Benji. She wants to network. And it isn't even that I think what I want is more important than what she wants, necessarily, but is it really *that* important for her to network *here*? Will she be so deprived of opportunities as a ruthless, naturally pretty, petite blond actress with an unbelievable belt and well-connected—not to mention obscenely wealthy—parents? Why does *this* have to be her networking opportunity? Why couldn't she have networked during the whole trip?

On top of everything, I'm worrying about Sebastian. He's probably going through a million different emotions. This is so far outside anything I've ever comforted someone for, and I know he doesn't *expect* anything from me, and a couple of days ago, I didn't even know about his dad at all, but I already feel like I'm going to let him down somehow.

Not only that, but the butterflies in my chest from our kiss? They've transformed. They're grasshoppers. But, like, the mean scary ones from *A Bug's Life*. Their big, sharp wings are tearing at my flesh.

Because what now?

I don't know what to do with a cute boy who likes me. I have absolutely no experience with this outside of seeing it on TV or in movies or through the filter of Benji's lyrics. And the kiss is usually the happily-ever-after moment. They kiss, they ride off in a car that floats over the carnival like in *Grease* . . . Or they kiss, it fades to black.

What am I supposed to do with that? I have no blueprint. And we're about to graduate. Maybe he just wanted to kiss me and check it off and then he's going to do his geneticist stuff and find someone else who's better with things he likes—beakers, Bunsen burners, and formaldehyde. I don't even *know* what geneticists like. I don't even know what they do.

I stare up at the ceiling. Tears are falling down my temples. Why am I so bad at everything? I'm even bad at keeping perspective. At not being dramatic.

Sitting up, wiping at my face, I try to get it together at least a *little*, pausing the music before FaceTiming Dean.

When he answers, he pulls a face.

"Again?"

"You don't understand, this time it's legit."

Dean is at the basketball court by the ocean, settled in a little park surrounded by palm trees. I can see his friends Foster and Tommy in the background, and he motions to tell them he'll be right back.

"What happened?"

He's sweaty and wearing a sweatshirt with the sleeves cut off. I've never understood why he wears this, especially during the summer in Florida.

I tell him everything, and as I do, I feel the gravity of having done all these scavenger hunt items only to lose. I feel the permanence of it. I feel the inadequacy that's creeping in around being there for Sebastian.

"You know I love you, but I think for once, you have to just pull yourself up out of this." He lifts his brows when I make a face. "It's okay to be sad. You didn't win the scavenger hunt. I get it. That sucks. It's okay to be upset. But you had a kick-ass time. Met a movie star. You got a boyfriend"—my eyes go wide, and he holds up his hand—"or you got, like, whatever Sebastian is. You got your first kiss on top of the Empire State Building, which is like a movie or something."

I sigh. He's right.

"You're looking at all the stuff going wrong, instead of all the stuff that's gone right." He tilts his head. "And trust me, Annie will be okay without an autograph."

My dramatization of the world has finally, officially failed me. Here I am, in my room, miserable when I'm about to go see Benji on Broadway. And at some point tonight, I'll have a cute boy to hold hands with and kiss.

"I'm so glad you're my brother and not someone who is equally dramatic," I say.

He nods. "God, me too." Then he scratches the back of his neck. "You know what would help with all of this?"

"What?"

"Do some of your journaling."

"I didn't bring my journal," I say. "I didn't think I was going to have journaling time on my New York trip."

Dean sighs. "Well, don't hotels have those little notepads? Just journal on that. Get your feelings out."

There is a notepad on the desk. I don't see a pen, but I'm sure there's one somewhere in this damn room.

"Fine, I'll journal."

"And what else are you going to do?"

"I'm going to accept my fate with Benji, and I'm going to focus on the good stuff going on. I'm going to get dressed for the show, and I'm going to just have a good last night here."

Dean nods. "Good. No more drama or shenanigans. Maybe for the rest of the trip, just to be safe."

"No more drama or shenanigans," I say.

Before he ends the FaceTime, Dean snaps his fingers together. "Oh, Teddy?"

"Yeah?"

"I told you he didn't hate you." He grins.

When we hang up, I pull myself together. I put on a happy playlist that starts with Taylor Swift's "New Romantics." I shower and, looking in the mirror, realize Sebastian was right—that mask *did* do wonders.

As I undo the buttons of my shirt and wait for the iron to heat up, I decide it's time to take Dean's advice and get some journaling done. I love journaling, even though sometimes it makes me spiral even more when I see all my thoughts on a page, but looking at the tiny notepad on the desk I wonder if all my feelings will even fit.

I go looking for a pen, in my backpack and in the drawers of the desk and nightstand. I move some of my crap—my side of the room is, at this point, organized chaos at best—and the Polaroid of Sebastian on the bridge falls onto the bed.

Picking it up, I study the photo. He looks so handsome, and my heart gets all jittery and beats quick just looking at him. It's special, I think, that I'll have this memory of when I first saw him that way. A boy turned gold.

I set it on the desk, not as embarrassed for him to see it now that we've moved on to kissing and saying we like each other. It's cute next to the other photos from the scavenger hunt. It looks almost artistic in comparison to the rest. The colors, the composition.

I really did get so lucky, didn't I? Even if the Benji thing didn't work out.

Speaking of luck. I grab my bracelet and slide it over my wrist. Honestly, I should have given it to Sebastian. It's not like I need any additional good luck at the moment—the cards have all been laid out, and I am focusing on the positive, not the negative.

But then my phone goes off on the bed, just as I tighten the bracelet.

I squint to make out the text preview.

ANNIE:

ugh, I'm sorry she won ☹ kinda shocked you're not going to just sneak in lol

I gasp, nearly knocking over the ironing board and hot iron as I lunge for my phone.

Opening the text, I blink, my heart beating so fast I think it might sprout legs and sprint out of my chest, and I glance down at my lucky bracelet.

See, I knew I still needed you.

ME:

Annie, you're a genius

ANNIE:

i was very clearly joking

ANNIE:

there was an lol

ME:

No you're right, I have to find a way to get into that party

ME:

bc the universe wouldn't bring me THIS close and want me to give up

ANNIE:

does the universe usually encourage ppl to break and enter???

ME:

the universe is bigger than human rules, Annie!!

For a moment, I think back to what Dean just said.

No more drama or shenanigans.

Trying to come up with a scheme to still meet Benji—since it would probably require sneaking into a very exclusive party—seems like it might, maybe qualify as drama and/or shenanigans. Or at least something that might lead to one or both.

I finish getting dressed, slip Annie's bracelet securely in my pocket, ready for a signature, and consider everything carefully before giving myself a nod of approval in the mirror.

The problem is that drama and shenanigans have sort of become my specialty.

Chapter 34

Memory

The world is now a sparkling marquee, ready for my name.

Sebastian hasn't texted or called, and I don't want to bother him when he's preparing to see his dad, but I *have* come up with a brilliant plan.

Go to dinner, go to the show, go to the after-party, meet Benji.

It's pretty foolproof, if I do say so myself.

Sure, there are some loose ends, but what plan is ever *completely* fleshed out?

As we all meet in the lobby, I deflect when anyone asks where Sebastian is—*oh, he's coming, slight wardrobe malfunction.* I'm once again worrying about him, though this time at least I know the right storyline, so my imagination runs in the correct direction.

For a bit, I felt torn about whether I could talk to Annie about Sebastian's errand. She's my best friend, and we tell each other everything, but this doesn't feel like my thing to share. So, I decided I have to keep it to myself.

I'll keep it inside.

But, unfortunately, I'm awful at keeping things inside, and the longer it festers, the more I have to actively remind myself it's not even truly *my* pain. I'm imagining Sebastian's and picturing him sitting through that talk and then having to find his dad after and muster up the courage to ask him for something so major.

"Teddy." Mrs. Mackenzie wags a finger around. "Where is Mr. Hodges?"

"He said he's going to meet us there." She opens her mouth, but I exaggerate a frown. "The lactose."

Mrs. Bloom is picking Eden's outfit apart, and we all pretend not to hear, but it's hard not to feel sorry for the girl. I give her a consolatory smile when her mom has turned her back, but she doesn't seem to notice.

"I told her it'd be humid," Mrs. Bloom says, laughing to Briar as she pats down some frizz on the top of Eden's head.

I am more and more on the fence about revisiting my whole "nobody is a villain" rule. All the signs are there. She's absorbed in her phone, and so I pull Eden aside.

"Congrats on the scavenger hunt."

She raises a brow, suspicious. "Thank you?"

"Really," I say. "It was a lot. And you won, fair and

square. So, congratulations."

"Thanks," she says, warming up just the tiniest bit. "I think my mother would have disowned me if I lost, anyway. Thank God"—she pitches her voice lower—"she's going to dinner with her friends from the other night. So, I get a break. Until the show, at least." She offers a slight frown. "If Benji is there tonight, I'll ask for a video or something."

"He'll totally be there," I say. Then I look around to make sure nobody is listening. "I am currently trying to figure out how I can sneak in. I've seen people dress up like waiters a lot in movies—think that would work?"

Eden laughs. "Teddy McGuire, you are out of your mind."

"But just out of my mind enough for it to work, right?"

She considers this. "If anyone can do it, it's probably you. Can't Sebastian help?"

I go to speak, but Mrs. Bloom is snapping for us to follow the line out of the lobby.

"If you see me in a waiter outfit tonight, don't blow my cover," I whisper.

We're having dinner at an impossibly fancy restaurant. I'm not sure of the financials here, but I probably would have figured a big group of high school drama club seniors would be better suited at the Olive Garden. We're in a private dining room with expensive-looking gold-framed paintings, walls of paned mirrors, and over-the-top-unique lighting fixtures. This place has white linen tablecloths and napkins that feel way too luxurious. Looking at the prices on the menu, the math isn't adding up.

It's French, since we're going to *Versailles*—that part makes sense—but how is this being paid for with our trip budget?

As the bread is brought out, however, the owner of the restaurant comes in and kisses Mrs. Mackenzie's hand. We learn, through her coy batted lashes and devilish smile, that they were in the same friend group when she was in *Chicago*.

"I didn't know you were in *Chicago*?" I blurt, once he's gone.

Mrs. Mackenzie lifts one shoulder, reaching for her glass of white wine. "There is a lot you all don't know about me."

Eden purses her lips. "Like?"

"A lady never reveals her secrets," Mrs. Mackenzie says.

We all laugh, but I find myself wondering who Mrs. Mackenzie even *is*. To me, she's always been the eccentric drama teacher. It's reductive, I realize. It's confining her to a two-dimensional role. The first thing we're supposed to do with characters is give them a life—a backstory. Mrs. Mackenzie has an entire life and backstory that I've never bothered to ask about.

"Were you in any other shows?" I ask.

Mrs. Mackenzie nods. "I was." Then she sits up a little straighter. "You know, it's funny, this conversation always happens at this exact moment. Every year, on the senior trip, just before we go to the show. No matter what restaurant, or what musical. This is always when it happens."

We're all intrigued now, and she can tell. She smiles.

"I started on the West End, because I had a boyfriend at the time who got a job with a bank in London. And I loved him, so I went with him, even though I'd just started auditioning for parts on Broadway. I was chorus in a couple of shows, and by our third year, we broke up, and I got a call that I'd been cast in a supporting role in *Les Mis*." She sighs. "But I got the call a week after I'd moved back to New York."

Eden's jaw dropped. "You didn't go back?"

"Moving across the ocean twice by twenty-two was already way too expensive," she says. "I couldn't if I wanted to. And that was, oh, maybe 1991. I was heartbroken, alone in the city, not getting parts. I tried everything. Auditioned for everything. And I made friends with everyone. A friend of a friend was writing this musical, and I wanted to be in it so badly, but I'd just booked my first Broadway role. You won't believe that musical he was writing went on to be one of the biggest, most important rock musicals, I don't know, *ever*?"

I shake my head. "You're not saying . . ."

Mrs. Mackenzie takes a bigger swig of her wine. "Oh, I am."

"You were *friends* with Jonathan Larson?"

Another sip of wine, waving her hand. "So, I missed out on *Rent* to be in *Cats*. I was in their ear, though, I had a plan—I wanted to play Grizabella. I wanted to sing 'Memory' more than anything."

She smiles, as if thinking fondly of this period.

"But then, my new boyfriend at the time decided he wanted to move to Los Angeles. And I must have been so, so *stupidly* in love. Because I went. And when we broke up five months later, I was working at a diner in Santa Monica. So, I used every penny to move back to the city, and I lived on a girlfriend's couch for a couple months while I got a job as a secretary."

There's a gleam in her eye.

"Then, this was sort of the best. I did a little run on *Footloose* in the chorus. From there, met a girl who got me a supporting part in *King Arthur's Mage.* I got two solos in that show. I was over the moon. It was finally happening. And one night after a show, at a party on the Upper East Side, I met Frank."

"Frank," Briar says, almost humming.

Mrs. Mackenzie laughs. "Well, Frank was . . . different. Different from the other guys who cared about themselves. He *loved* me in the show. Knew I was going to be a star. And he wanted to be mayor of New York. I mean, you would have voted for him. He was charismatic, and he was just . . . Made you feel like the only person in the room. So, we dated for six months, got married, and his friend from boarding school married this casting director. We'd always have dinner parties, and it was like I was in a movie. I actually got a line in a review for my performance in *King Arthur's Mage*, which was a huge deal. Everything was going so well."

She frowns. "I took a break because I got pregnant, but I had a miscarriage. And all my girlfriends at the time told me it's really common, so I should just rest and relax and come back once things were settled."

The table is silent. Only Édith Piaf's voice over the speakers, with the strings and wind instruments behind it.

"But it didn't settle. It happened again." She exhales. "And Frank wanted kids. No matter anything, he wanted kids. He was a politician. He cared about things like . . . if we had kids on our Christmas card. If he looked All-American. I'd never considered those types of things. I wanted kids so I could love them, and he wanted kids so he could take photos with them."

Even Eden looks somber now.

"Anyway, we decide we're going to see a doctor. We're going to figure it out, because we love each other. And after the third miscarriage, I decided I was going to act again, and that friend—do you remember, I mentioned him? The casting director? Gets me an audition for Roxie Hart. And I . . ." She grins. "I got the part. I beat out all those other women. Women who had played leading roles. I *did it*."

Only it's clear she's not thrilled. This isn't necessarily a happy ending.

"Long story short, during rehearsals, I miscarried. Again. I didn't even know I was pregnant. By then, it'd put such a strain on our marriage. I think Frank blamed me? And he thought maybe if I hadn't been doing these strenuous rehearsals . . . And who knows. Then the doctor says I won't be able to have kids. Ever. And things just got messy. Divorce. I wasn't well enough to play the part, as much as I wanted to. And I didn't have anywhere to live, anyway. All my single friends were married by then . . . Life was just too complicated. I moved home to Citrus Harbor."

The silence at the table stretches taut.

"So, yes. I was in *Chicago*. Or, really, I was *almost* in *Chicago*. That's my life. A lot of *almosts*. But you kids . . ." She sets her wineglass down and smiles. "I get to watch you all go out and do these amazing things. I get to see them on the Instagram. And hear about them when you come to visit. All the *almosts* end up being worth it. I wouldn't trade being a high school drama teacher for anything, believe it or not."

After a few moments, she looks around and raises her brows.

"I made the whole thing up," she says, and when we all start gasping, she shakes her head, laughing riotously. "No, I didn't. It's all true, but you all are just looking at me like I told you a sad story. I didn't. So, let's order, because the owner of this restaurant has had a crush on me for over twenty years, and he's going to give us at least half off."

I order the most delicious roast chicken I've ever had in my entire life. It comes with fancy green beans, and potatoes that are sliced thin and covered with cheese. Everything tastes buttery and perfect.

But nothing feels perfect.

Mrs. Mackenzie's life lesson about *almosts* stings.

My lucky bracelet is burning against my skin.

What am I doing? How long am I going to live with my head in the clouds? Eden is going to meet Benji tonight, because she won fair and square. I should be on the subway right now, on my way to hand Sebastian this bracelet. He's the one who could use some good luck and magic from the universe. He's the one whose fate is up in the air—the one who doesn't have to live with an *almost*—when mine has been sealed.

As everyone eats, I stand abruptly, and Mrs. Mackenzie gives me an odd look.

"I have to go check on Sebastian," I say, trying to word it very carefully.

I offer a faint smile, one that's a little hesitant, because not only will I be missing the show, I'll be officially giving up on meeting Benji. But that was a dream, and if my lucky bracelet can help Sebastian, I'm going to give it to him.

I hurry out to the sidewalk and start typing on my Maps app.

"Teddy!" Mrs. Mackenzie has followed me out, and I'm expecting her to scold me, but she just stares at me.

"I know it probably seems nuts, but Sebastian needs me. And this isn't, like, me giving up on my dream for a guy." I sigh. "It's not. I just know that I don't know much, but it's about *almosts* like you said."

Mrs. Mackenzie nods. "I know."

"You do?"

"Yes." Mrs. Mackenzie just pops her hip. "I know all of you kids like the back of my hand. I know your every move before you do. Which is why I know, in precisely five seconds, Sebastian Hodges is going to be running toward us."

Like clockwork, with his Vans slapping against the sidewalk, Sebastian is red-faced and sprinting.

"I'm here! I'm here!"

Nodding with a satisfied smirk, Mrs. Mackenzie claps her hands together. "And scene."

Chapter 35

Drama Queen

"What happened?" I ask once Mrs. Mackenzie has gone back inside. "I was about to come after you. Shouldn't you be getting ready for the talk to start?"

Sebastian shakes his head. "You know, I didn't really want to hear the guy talk."

"What? Sebastian, what are you talking about?"

He chews on the inside of his cheek, but then he grins.

"What?" I ask.

"I was so nervous to ask him," he says. "So nervous. I couldn't even go talk to him after the lecture on Wednesday night. Blake was trying to hype me up, and I just kept thinking he would say no, anyway, so why am I even going to ask?"

"But, Sebastian, you came all this way to—"

"And then I thought of you," he says.

I think the city goes still.

"I thought about how you never let anything stop you. Even if other people might try, or if the odds seem stacked against you." He smiles. "I mean, there's a reason I picked the *T. rex* for you. You are a force, Teddy."

Flushed, I don't know what to say.

"So, I figured if you could go after whatever you want, so could I." Sebastian grins, standing up tall. "I decided I wasn't going to wait until after the show, and I walked in and told the security guard I was his son, and they eventually got him. Then I told him what I needed. Right there in the hallway, as he had half a face of concealer applied."

"Wow. What did he— What happened?"

His entire face lights up. "Guess who's going to MIT?"

I pull him in for a hug, instinctively, and he wraps his arms around me like it's always been our dynamic, and like we were meant to hold each other.

"Oh my God, Sebastian. I'm so happy for you."

"I really don't know if I would have gone through with it if it weren't for you," he says. When we break from the hug, he glances down. "I've gone through life accepting a lot of things. Expecting to be told no. Being okay with it. Not really taking risks if I thought it might lead to rejection. And you've really just shown me that there's so much more than that."

That merits a kiss, and I'm on my tiptoes with one hand on his cheek and one on his shoulder, pressing my mouth to his.

"You were going to miss the show for me?" he asks.

"I must be possessed," I say.

He grins. "I can't believe you were going to miss the show for me."

"I just wanted to make sure you had a good luck charm." I hold up my wrist, gesturing toward the bracelet.

Then, Sebastian looks around before shrugging. "Looks like the confidence boost you gave me was all I needed."

I squeeze his hand.

"And, also, I don't mean you completed me or something." He winces. "Oh, God. That came out so wrong. I just meant—it isn't like we kissed, and I was like 'oh, now my life's problems are all solved' or something. The wedges are, like, my mom, and my friends, and my hobbies, and college. Am I just completely killing the romantic vibe right now? I'm mostly trying to make sure this doesn't seem like some weird, super-heavy weight I'm putting on you because we're two complete pies and—"

"We are two complete pies," I agree, trying not to laugh. "Don't worry, I completely understand what you're saying."

"But it is true: knowing I had you waiting for me . . . It made it so much easier."

I kiss him again, and then we head back inside to finish dinner with the rest of the drama club.

Times Square at night is beyond anything I ever imagined. It's like the entire universe is here. The lights are dazzling, with screens flashing every color at maximum saturation and brightness. Those yellow cabs I love so much are even more vibrant here, and the glow of blurred headlights fits in perfectly.

I think right now I love it, and I'm mesmerized by it, but by the second or third time I come here I will likely avoid this place whenever possible. The crowd is next-level, and the meat and weird wet steam smells are worse here than they have been anywhere else.

No offense, New York, I love you, but Times Square is a little hit or miss.

It's easy to see why they call this the city that never sleeps, though. There's an energy here that feels like it'll never go away, no matter how late it gets.

My heartbeat quickens three times before we even get to the theater.

Once, when Sebastian grabs my hand, interlocking his fingers with mine.

A second time, when we hang back behind the group, and he kisses me.

And a third, when we're a couple blocks away and I see the first giant *Versailles* sign.

We're stopped at a corner now, shoulder to shoulder with other tourists. It's loud, music, honking, bikers screaming, people talking.

Caught up in the wonderment and Sebastian's smile, I realize this night is already everything. I'll be okay not coming up with some wild scheme to get into the after-party—even if I totally could have pulled it off—in fact, I'll be better than okay.

"Anyway," Sebastian says. "You want to know the actual plot twist?"

"What?"

"I realized I actually am *really* excited to see Benji in *Versailles*."

Laughing, I bump my shoulder against his. "Shut up, are you mocking—"

"No, really! I think you've made a Benji fan out of me."

"Amazing," I say, grinning.

He rubs his thumb against my palm. "I'm sorry you aren't going to meet him."

I laugh. "I actually was considering trying to sneak into the party." Before he can say anything, I shake my head. "But I think . . . I think seeing Benji in *Versailles*, with you, is enough."

And then Sebastian's eyes crinkle as he grins.

That's enough to stop me in my tracks, but it's just in time, because we're here.

I don't even have a moment to take in what Sebastian's just said, because the bright bulbs and flashing marquee are giving me sensory overload. The theater is big, ornate, and has a classic and important, stately vibe to it, like the Met or the library. There's a huge crowd outside the doors, scanning their tickets and all chattering excitedly.

We're all here to see *Versailles*. Many here to see Benji.

I think I might break the bones in Sebastian's hand I'm squeezing so tight.

Everything about my first Broadway experience is a dream come true.

I can't believe it's all even real. Or that I've made it here.

The rich gold-dusted and marble lobby that looks like it's out of eighteenth-century France. There are massive oil paintings of Belle Bramble and Benji as Marie Antoinette and King Louis, respectively, hung in thick baroque frames. Ushers dressed like French guards stand next to the doors, handing out *Playbills* and helping people find their seats.

There are two massive lines leading to the merchandise stands. Mannequins wear pale blue T-shirts and pink sweatshirts with phrases like "*Bisous, Bisous*—Marie" and "Who does she think she is?" from two of the show's biggest songs. There's one from Benji's big Act One finale, "Loveless." There's also a mug that says "the Dauphine's just delicious" and a giant plush stack of gold macarons.

The macarons don't stop there. A Ladurée cart is set up in one corner of the lobby, selling pastries and treats. A full bar, with a neon sign reading "*débauche*," takes up an entire wall.

Gold chandeliers hang from the ceiling, illuminating the crown molding. Brass sconces are decorated with thin baby-blue ribbons tied into loose bows. Instrumentals from the show boom through the entire lobby, violins and light synths and bass.

"We're here," I say, and it's almost breathless.

Sebastian looks to me, and there's a gleam in his eye. "We are."

The entire drama club takes a selfie after we've gotten cotton candy and popcorn and decadent dessert-like drinks, and then we get one of the ushers to take a Polaroid of us all. I guess Mrs. Mackenzie brought one of the cameras with her.

Inside the theater is even more magical than the lobby. Stars and sparkles line the walkways, and the seats are all powder-blue velvet. Everything is themed to mimic the Hall of Mirrors in the actual Palace of Versailles. Vast artificial windows line the right side of the theater, and equally vast mirrors line the left. The ceilings are vaulted, adorned with paintings, and gilded statues along the perimeter hold up candlesticks, ornamented with crystal droplets and simulated flames.

A massive crystal chandelier is projected onto a screen that covers the stage, and written in bright, shimmering gold script across it: *There are many people at Versailles today.*

"Courtiers, find your seats, *s'il-vous-plaît.*" The announcer's voice is deep, echoing throughout the theater and revving up the whispers of anticipation among the crowd.

Sebastian is holding my hand, and I'm flipping through my first ever Broadway *Playbill* next to Eden, who's taking selfies with Briar, and then the lights dim.

A single note strikes, and the crowd goes silent.

It's starting.

"Dear Dauphine" starts. The ensemble dances to the instrumentals, miming whispers. Parisian gossips become royal court members outside Versailles with masterful visual effects. And then, everything stops.

Everyone loses it when Belle Bramble appears on a balcony, lit by a single spotlight as the fifteen-year-old Marie Antoinette.

And I know what this means.

The song progresses, and we follow her down a long hallway.

My heart is racing until she opens the door, and there he is. Facing away from her, talking to a man at a huge wooden desk.

Cheers and roars and screams erupt.

It's Benji.

I almost can't believe, even though I know I am here, that I am in the audience seeing Benji in *Versailles*.

Sebastian reaches over and squeezes my knee with his free hand, grinning like he's just won a prize.

The show is as amazing as I'd hoped it would be. I've tried so, so hard not to listen to too many of the songs. I've tried not to watch too many clips or even to see too many pictures, and I mostly did a good job. I think at least 80 percent of the show is new to me, and I am so glad.

At intermission, Sebastian gushes about how amazing it is, and Eden *touches his arm* across me as they discuss the logistics of the royal ball dance number.

Belle is fun as the antihero Marie Antoinette, who plays the part of victim toward the third act as she attempts to learn politics and repair the reputation of the crown. Her court sings and dances to upbeat pop songs about luxury and excess.

Benji as Louis XVI is breathtaking. He's infuriating as an incompetent and indecisive king, but he brings a level of heartbreaking vulnerability to his songs. He sings a solo ballad, when he isn't able to produce an heir and is out hunting, about feeling like a failure. It's haunting and so decidedly Benji I find myself almost crying.

When the curtain drops, and the show is over, it hits me. The king's head has rolled, and mine is left spinning—this is the end of the line. In my fantasies, there was always more. There was the after-party, and the life-altering moment Benji Keaton and I locked eyes.

But this is it.

Outside the theater, we stand on the curb.

"I just really thought we'd be meeting Benji tonight," I say. I hold up my wrist and stare at the blue bracelet dangling there. "First time it's ever truly failed me."

"Teddy, you know you did all of that stuff on this trip?" Sebastian has a hand on my waist, and he looks into my eyes. "*You*. I know you want to give credit to your bracelet, but you didn't ever need luck. You made everything happen."

"I did?"

He nods. "You did."

If this is true, Galinda really was right about not even realizing when we've crossed bridges.

"I don't know," I say. "Things might have gone way worse if I didn't have the bracelet."

"What if you just tested it out," he offers. "Not wearing it? I mean, what do you have to lose?"

Somewhat begrudgingly, I slide the bracelet off and hand it to him. He pockets it and nods.

"It's all you," he says. "Just watch."

"Teddy McGuire."

Eden stomps up to us, her pink platform heels appearing in my periphery first.

I glance up, and she exhales. When she does, she releases her façade. For a moment, her mask comes off. Her typically arched brow softens. Her smirk relaxes. Behind the perfectly toned blond roots, glossed lips, and pink cheeks, it's the Eden I haven't seen since we were in elementary school.

"Hearing Mrs. Mackenzie talk about all of that stuff at dinner . . ." She shrugs. "You and I have had this little thing, you know? This sort of back-and-forth thing. I guess it hit me that this was our last one. And I know I can be pretty competitive." She rolls her eyes when I pull a face. "So can you, believe it or not."

"I guess you're not wrong."

"I weirdly think of you as, like, a friend." She says it

quickly, like if she spits it out once, and I hear it, she can pretend it didn't happen. "We've spent, like, every afternoon together for four years. And we've done after-parties and pre-show dinners. And I think . . ." She groans. "God, I can't believe I'm going to say this, but I think I am going to miss you when we graduate."

My cheeks go hot. This was definitely not on my New York City bingo card.

"And when Mrs. Mackenzie was talking about us going to do amazing things and coming back." Eden smiles. "I'm going to be rooting for you. Since it's not like we're going after the same parts."

I open my mouth, but she holds up her hand.

"I know you say you're not going to try Broadway, but you're not going to be able to just turn off your talents. You can't just, like, dull your shine."

"My shine?"

She rolls her eyes, laughing. "I want us to catch up when we're both back in Citrus Harbor. Maybe reunite on a carpet one day. So, this is my peace treaty. I only really cared about winning, and I know how much it means to you."

Sebastian and I exchange surprised glances.

"Eden . . . what are you talking about?"

She brightens. "I figured out a way to make amends with you, and piss off my mother at the same time, and I can't pass it up."

I close the space between us, pulling her in for a hug.

And she hugs me back. It's the surprised, kind of

awkward hands on my back that say it all. She doesn't normally hug because she doesn't get hugged. So I hug her a little tighter.

"I'm not doing Broadway, though," I say, once we've broken apart. "I *might* try to write songs."

"Okay, well if we're both up for a Grammy . . ." She shoots me a death glare before laughing. "It's been an honor to duet with you, Teddy McGuire."

"You too, Eden."

"Now go say hi to Benji for me."

Chapter 36

The Wizard and I

When I was a little kid, I was obsessed with Santa Claus. I would stay up as long as I could on the web tracker, and I would wait, staring out my window for a glimpse of his sleigh. My mom gave Dean and me kids' sleep gummies and, I now realize, had us playing in the yard all day on Christmas Eve so we always fell asleep at a reasonable hour. Still, every year I wondered, in those final moments as my eyes got heavier, what it'd actually be like if I met him.

How could he ever live up? He's this magical man in the North Pole, with elves and reindeer and unlimited presents that are neatly wrapped. How could he have time for me? Because young Teddy would have gone Diane Sawyer on Santa's ass—the number of questions I would have had.

Of course, I found out everything that made Santa so special was really thanks to my parents. The "reindeer markings" on the driveway, the handwritten notes from the elves, the half-eaten cookies, and the overflow of gifts.

Now, in this Tribeca penthouse, I am reflecting.

What if this is Santa 2.0? What if the magic of Benji is him being . . . mythical? What if Sebastian choosing *The Wizard of* Oz was meaningful in more ways than one? I'm suddenly nervous this is Oz, and we're about to draw back the curtain to find out the truth about the wizard.

Of course, there is one tiny thing: it's not even confirmed Benji will be here. I don't believe everyone was right all along—that Benji won't even come—but the longer I stand here and he hasn't shown, the more nervous I get.

In a plot twist absolutely nobody saw coming, I am a bundle of nerves.

"Maybe, like, a deep breath?" Sebastian suggests.

He and I are standing next to the grand piano, which is occupied by a pianist in a chunky black turtleneck sweater and silk skirt. She plays the most beautiful melody, and if I weren't about to throw up, I'd really be enjoying it.

The whole loft is making my head spin. It's absolutely absurd how big it is, for starters, and it looks like it's the set of a prestige drama, not somebody's home. The furniture is all mismatched and expensive wood, galvanized metals, furs, and trendy bouclé. The floor-to-ceiling windows lead out to a terrace, which overlooks the Hudson River and Jersey City. Most of the party is enjoying the outdoor space, though here I am, trying not to look as rattled as I am.

"It's just . . . Maybe my entire life has been leading up to this moment," I say. "And I still don't even know what I'm going to say."

Sebastian shrugs. "It'll come to you."

"You think so?"

"Yeah, definitely."

I feel like I'm going to explode. At the same time, I wish I could freeze this moment to calm down and figure out what to say, but I also wish this would speed up because I've waited for this moment forever.

"Teddy, I have somebody I want you to meet!"

Mrs. Mackenzie's voice is like ice. Like an ice cube against the back of my neck. No, more like an ice bath I've been submerged in with absolutely no warning. Oxygen-sucking, blood-flow-constricting, brain-freezing ice.

I can tell by Sebastian's face.

This is happening.

My heart is about to pound right through my chest or leap out of my throat.

I can't tell if I do so quickly or slowly, but I muster up the willpower to turn my torso and then my legs and the next thing I know, I am facing Mrs. Mackenzie, who has brought over Benji Keaton.

"Oh my God."

I only mean to think it, but it comes out as a long sort of whisper as I exhale.

Benji fucking Keaton is standing two feet away from me. He's here, really, in the flesh.

His lips are turned up into a smile, and I am going to pass out.

As if all the abstract light fixtures in this penthouse were designed and positioned just to perfectly align for Benji, he glows, adding his own light to the warm ambiance. His dark curly hair is effortlessly messy, his olive skin is spot-free, and he's wearing a cream satin shirt with rolled sleeves, tucked into wide black trousers. His hazel eyes flicker and his sharp jaw flexes when he holds his hand out, and a gold bracelet slides down his wrist.

I stare at his hand for a moment before remembering this is a gesture humans make to each other upon meeting, and I rush to shake it.

"Nice to meet you, Teddy."

He shakes Sebastian's hand next, and they agree it's nice to meet each other, so simply and nonchalantly as if no skill or practice is required at all.

"I'm sorry," I say, blinking. "I knew I wouldn't know what to say when I met you."

Oh my God. Really?

Mrs. Mackenzie waves off to someone in the foyer and disappears.

Left there with Benji and Sebastian, my mind is completely blank.

"The show was incredible," Sebastian says. "It was my first Broadway musical, and it was so awesome."

Benji brightens. "So glad to hear that."

Sebastian nudges me.

"I loved it," I say.

Benji isn't intimidating from an energetic standpoint. He's warm, inviting, and he smells like earthy myrrh and vanilla—his signature Jo Malone. It isn't overpowering, either, it just sort of wafts around in a friendly and respectful kind of way. Everything about his presence is calming and graceful and yet here I am, completely screwing it up.

"Your drama teacher says you were the lead this spring," he says to me. "Did I hear it was Troy Bolton?"

I nod.

"*High School Musical* came out when I was in elementary school, so it's very nostalgic," he offers.

He's disarming me. He's as nice as all the interviewers and fan accounts have said.

"I'm going to let you guys chat," Sebastian says, squeezing my shoulder in that way he does, and starting to take a step away.

"You don't have to—"

"No, you guys talk! You should really talk. About . . . *things*." He grins at Benji, again, so easy, and so pleasantly surprising given the Sebastian I sat next to on the plane. "So awesome meeting you."

And then there were two.

"Is he your . . . ?"

I laugh. "Oh, no. Well, yes? Maybe? I don't know. We just kissed for the first time today." I cringe. "Slight overshare."

"I don't mind," Benji laughs. "Okay, well a little soon to define the relationship. He seems to really like you."

A little nervous laughter rises in my throat. "What do you mean? How can you tell?"

"You can always tell," he says, a very serious look on his face. "It's in the eyes."

I wonder how long it's been in his eyes. I wonder if anyone else saw it.

Then, Benji tilts his head. "What?"

"Hmm? Oh. I don't—I'm sorry, I am trying to think of something intelligent to say." More cringe. "I just . . . honestly? I spent this whole trip thinking about this moment. More than that, even. I have all your albums on vinyl, and I got the extended cut of *This Side of Paradise*, and my best friend and I have seen you in concert three times. And now I sound like some stalker superfan."

Benji laughs, shaking his head. "No, I love it. Though I am sorry you had to see the extended cut of *Paradise*."

"Are you kidding? It's so good."

"Agree to disagree," he says, and shrugs. "But I appreciate the support either way. So, what exactly were the *things* your not-boyfriend wanted you to talk to me about?"

I wince. "Oh, it's not . . ."

"Come on, hit me with it."

"I don't want to bore you with stuff about me."

Benji's eyes go wide and he laughs so loud people turn to look at us. "Are you kidding? I would *love* to talk about you. Do you have any idea—my entire day from when I wake up until I go to sleep is people talking to me about me. And planning to talk about me. Please, really, let's talk about you."

Before I start, though, Benji points behind me, toward a hallway. "Follow me. There's a private terrace off the master suite."

"You don't want to be, like, in the party?"

"No," he says, still smiling. "I do not want to be in the party."

We walk down the long hallway, and the large black-and-white pictures are of a random family. "Whose place is this?"

"Some random producer, I think."

"And you know where the private terrace is?"

"You should always know where the private terrace is, Teddy." He chuckles as we walk into the bedroom, and he unlocks the door. Once we're outside in the fresh air, he closes the door and the noise zips away like it's being sucked inside a vacuum. "Honestly, knowing where to find peace and privacy at a party like this is a skill I acquired early on."

This terrace is huge, unsurprisingly. It also looks over the Hudson and Jersey City, but there's a wall of shrubbery that separates it from the other terrace. Bougie outdoor furniture is set up in a square, with a fire pit in the center. We sit on the sofa, and Benji fiddles with a remote until a fire starts to cackle.

"All right, hit me."

"Well." I consider where to even start. "Sebastian has this idea. He thinks I should work on writing some of my own music. And I used to think about it, a little . . ."

Benji nods. "But?"

"I don't have, like, a unique point of view. I don't really have *things* to write about, I don't think? And when I write songs, to be honest? I think it's obvious I'm just trying to be like you."

This resonates, I think, because Benji pulls his feet up and sits crisscross on the sofa, his entire body facing me now.

"This is a tale as old as time," he says, placing his hands on his knees. "You know when I first started writing songs, I was totally inspired by other artists. My own sound didn't come for a while. Sure, some artists have that a little more naturally than others, but I don't think there's anything wrong with treating it like a muscle. The more you work it, the stronger it gets."

I lift my chin. "So, you're saying . . ."

"Just write. It doesn't have to be good. It might be, but it might not be, and that's okay. It's just for you. Just get things down. Write about whatever. Find what feels good, what feels authentic."

Considering this, I realize I could have been writing crappy songs all throughout high school. I could have been working the muscle this entire time. And now, I feel even more behind.

"You put out your first album at seventeen," I say. "Who

knows how long it's going to take me to figure out my voice?"

"It takes as long as it takes," he says. "And that's okay. I'm not going to act like there isn't a market for young blood in the music industry, but there are plenty of artists who start out in their twenties. Or even in their thirties. So, don't let fear stop you from trying."

"And what if I do this—I write to improve and to learn—and I end up in this same place? Without a story to tell?"

Benji leans in a little closer and smirks. "I'm going to let you in on a secret: people love fiction. And honestly? They're going to write their own version of your story, regardless of if you spell it out for them word for word. So, if it comes down to it, have some fun."

We laugh together, and in this light, I realize the Benji I saw inside is a different Benji. Not a fake one, necessarily, but an act, maybe. Out here, I see some acne on his forehead and there are bags under his eyes and his hair is a little greasier than I noticed before. And none of these are bad things at all, but I think I'm starting to realize, as silly as it sounds, that Benji Keaton is just a human.

"And anyway"—he leans back—"you'll have stuff to write about with time. No matter what. They say in life, nobody makes it out alive, you know? Shit happens. People will break your heart. Well, maybe—hopefully not. Sebastian seems great. But, just, as a general rule for . . . life. Things will break your heart. And you can do a million things with that. What I have found to be the best, is to feel it all. Write it down. Turn it into poetry, if you can. Take every loss and every hurt and make sure you gain something—at the very least, a lesson. At best, a song."

Immediately, I think of "Battle at the Shore." The pain in those lyrics. I know for certain, now, that was his lifeline. His way of getting through it. Turning it into poetry.

I think I'm frowning, because he pokes me in the arm. "What? Doesn't that sound fun? Inevitable heartbreak and pain? At least you're a creative. Imagine all of that and you're balancing spreadsheets or something—not entirely sure how spreadsheets go, but I imagine they need balancing."

I chuckle. "I actually have written a couple lines, but they're so depressing. I don't want to just write about heartbreak. I want to write like you did on *Seventeen Summers*. Happy, upbeat."

He pulls a face. "Why?"

"Because that's more me. That's the message I want to put out in the world. Something positive."

Benji considers this. "Well, it's not so black-and-white. You can write about heartbreak but focus on the hope that comes along with it. Your overall message can be positive. Didn't you get that from *Sunset*, even? That there's still hope?"

I nod. "Of course. But I just don't know if it's me."

Benji snaps his fingers together. "I know what this is. I've been there. You don't want to be vulnerable."

"I didn't say—"

"That's why you want to write happy songs," he says. "You think happy, upbeat pop songs project a fun image, but more importantly, they're safe. You're shielding yourself. Those lines you think are depressing—I bet you worry they're sharing too much of yourself?"

This is sort of like seeing a shrink, only maybe Benji is more of a psychic.

"I never thought of it that way," I say. "But I guess . . . Yeah. You're right. I mean, that's why I like acting, in a way. I'm able to express emotions but . . . Not as me. With my family, and my best friend, and now with Sebastian, I can be myself. But with everyone else, I . . . I don't know, it's not as easy. I want them to like me, maybe?"

It all clicks. It's probably why I need a lucky bracelet—I need something outside of myself to rely on, something else to believe in. Something to thank or to blame. That's not me.

He nods. "It's normal. Especially as a teenager, so don't beat yourself up. But if you want to be a songwriter, it's something to work through."

"I mean, I guess I could try to write a love song for Sebastian. I hadn't ever thought of—"

Benji shakes his head, wagging his finger. "Nope. Look, you can write a love song for Sebastian, nobody is going to stop you. But you know what I think? I think you need to write a song for *you*. Literally just for you. A vulnerable one. Whatever your true feelings are. It may end up being something you share, it may not, but that's where you need to start. That's where you find your voice."

"*For* me. Holy shit."

Benji nods, all knowing. "Don't worry about what other people expect from you or what you think people will like. And don't try to limit your emotions to what you think you should feel."

All this time, trying to figure out what to write about, I've always been so focused on the subjects, and they've always been external. People. Experiences. Things. I've been so focused on the opinions of people who I'd share the song with, but the answer has been here all along.

I just need to write a song for me.

"Wow," I say. "I can't believe that never occurred to me."

He adjusts, propping his feet up on the edge of the fire pit and laying his head back. "Being vulnerable isn't easy. If it were, everyone would do it. But I think you can, Teddy."

I mirror him, and when I stare up, for the first time in this city, I can see stars in the sky. And I know they've all aligned for this moment.

"Maybe one day this will be a story I tell."

"At the Grammys," Benji adds, glancing over at me. "I like the way you think."

This is how I know magic is real. And how I know this city is brimming with it. Because I am on a private terrace in Tribeca with Benji Keaton wishing on a star and imagining the moment I thank him for his life-changing advice when accepting a Grammy.

Annie is going to lose it.

"Oh," I say, brought back to earth. "Before I forget, can you sign something for my best friend?"

And optimism pays off yet again, I think, fishing Annie's bracelet out of my pocket.

"Of course. But can we just sit out here for a little bit longer? It's so calm. And you haven't told me about this first kiss yet! I am still a romantic, you know."

So, I spend a Friday night in New York City talking to Benji Keaton about kissing Sebastian and reality is suddenly far better than any of my daydreams.

Saturday

Chapter 37

You'll Be Back

It's Saturday morning, and this post-best-Friday-*ever* hangover is worse than the one that comes with going to school after a trip to Disney World.

It's softened by the fact that it happened, yet made worse by the fact that we're leaving New York in a few hours.

"That was really cool of Benji to take a selfie with us," Sebastian says, sitting on his bed and marveling at the photo on his phone. "He's way more chill than I'd expect."

I nod, watching the city out the window. "I never would have thought you'd be a Benji fanboy, but I love it."

"Let's dial it back," Sebastian says.

"I wonder if I really will meet him again one day," I say. "Honestly, when we were joking about it up there, I don't think I've ever believed one of my imaginary scenarios more."

He stands up and comes over to the window, then wraps his arms around my waist and pulls me in close, his lips meeting mine.

"I would not be surprised at all if you did," he says.

It isn't quite eclipsing this moment or this beyond amazing trip, but preparing to leave feels wrong. It feels against every instinct to zip my suitcase, with my salt and pepper shakers wrapped in T-shirts and my *Playbill* carefully laid flat at the top. It feels too heavy when I lift it off the bed and roll it over to the side of the room, like it wants to stay too.

"I don't want to leave," I say.

Sebastian nods. "I know."

"You get to come back whenever."

"I mean, not whenever."

"But you're going to be so close."

"You can come visit me and we can come into the city. And then spring semester, you can transfer or something. We'll figure it out. New York isn't going anywhere, Teddy."

I frown. "Do you promise?"

"Promise."

Once more, I look out the window down at Forty-Second Street. It honestly feels like we only spent one short day in New York City. I'm so jealous of everybody walking along the sidewalk with their briefcases and tote bags. Jealous of whoever is riding in the back of the cabs. Jealous of anybody who gets a second longer here.

"All right," I sigh. "I have one last thing I have to do."

Sebastian is folding one of his shirts now, and he stops, offering an inquisitive look. "Sounds secretive."

"It is very secretive," I agree. "No, I just have to see about the continental breakfast."

I'd looked for Eden last night, but she was nowhere to be found when we got back after midnight. Luckily, as expected, she's currently loading up on granola at the yogurt bar in a matching pink athletic set.

"There you are," I say.

"Here I am." She puts the scoop back in the canister and then looks up at me. "You seem to be in a chipper mood. Assuming you had the best night ever with Benji?"

"It was amazing." I lean up against the counter. "How was your night?"

Eden sighs, her hand hovering over the scoop in the strawberries, but she moves over to get some blueberries instead. "My mother went ballistic that I gave you my spot at the party. I mean it. Truly, she went *nuts*."

"Oh," I say. "I'm sorry, Eden."

Eden lifts her hand. "Are you joking? It was amazing. She'll get over it."

"And Briar?"

"She's *pissed*," Eden says. "It's wonderful."

I shake my head, laughing, and she piles some raspberries onto her yogurt.

"I'm glad you met Benji," she says. "But actually, I want to hear about the whole Sebastian thing."

"What whole Sebastian thing?" I try to play coy.

She sets her yogurt bowl down at the end of the station, pulling a spoon out and sticking it into the bowl. "Come on!"

Laughing, I nod. "I will tell you all about it. If you want, Annie and I are going to get tacos tomorrow night. You should come."

"Really?" Eden looks shocked.

"Yeah, really," I say. "It could be fun. Plus, I owe you one."

"Okay," she says, and with that, she gives me a smile and heads over to sit by herself, popping in her AirPods and ignoring the rest of the world in her confident, Eden Bloom way.

The drama club gathers in the lobby twenty minutes later, and I silently say goodbye to the city a million times. When the revolving door spits me out into the warm June air, and as we drive toward LaGuardia and the skyline shrinks.

I can't believe how much I learned in three days.

The truth is, maybe my song at the talent show wasn't vulnerable. Maybe I don't *always* feel like a butterfly. Maybe sometimes I even feel like the only one who will be stuck in the chrysalis while everyone flies away. But maybe Benji's right, and maybe there's still a lot of hope even in that. Because I know, in my bones, I won't be in the chrysalis forever.

This time, when we board the plane, Sebastian does the heavy lifting of asking the woman next to him if we can switch seats.

And in the clouds, I write a poem.

Graduation Day

Chapter 38

For Good

After all this time, it's somewhat exciting to get all new blocking and stage directions.

Technically that's not what they're called today. It's much simpler, and not only for the drama kids—*go up the steps, walk across the stage, accept diploma, shake hands, smile, walk offstage.*

A week ago, I was a different person. Or maybe that's dramatic—shocking, I know. Maybe I wasn't a different person at all, I just had a different perspective.

The sun will set in a couple hours, but for now the sky is clear and a perfect shade of blue. Different, somehow, from the one I remember at the top of the Brooklyn Bridge or the Empire State Building. I can't quite explain it. Maybe it's all the palm trees and the sprawling grass, the sea oats swaying on the dunes, or the sound of the waves crashing against the shore accompanied by the all-too-familiar smell of salty ocean spray. Somehow, the sky is different here, and while I can't wait to see it in New York again soon—and hopefully semi-permanently by spring semester—for now, I'm happy it is so perfectly unique.

The amphitheater is packed with all our families and friends, and the senior class is behind the fence, on the lawn, spread out on striped blankets and surf-branded beach towels or claiming one of the picnic tables.

The drama club is in a giant cluster, on a few layers of throws, quilts, and coverlets.

Annie is my walking partner, and it's a good thing, because she decided to wear heels she can't balance in to save her life. Sebastian sits with us, and Eden is just behind me, turning back to join in our conversation every so often.

It's strange, seeing everyone I've known forever in their orange caps and gowns. Every year, it sparks a debate because some people don't like wearing orange, but then they send out a newsletter and cover it on the morning news: *The Citrus Harbor High School graduates wear orange to represent their Hammerhead pride!*

Truthfully, the photos always turn out really nicely. The sun is lower, edging into golden hour, and the sky will start to turn yellow and pink and purple by the time all the last pictures are being taken. Since the amphitheater backs up to the ocean, there are plenty of good backdrops.

Annie lifts her hand to move some hair from her face

and her gown sleeve falls, revealing the blue bracelet with Benji's signature hanging from her wrist. She laughs, nodding as Sebastian goes on about what a joke Citrus High's in-school suspension is.

As I look around at the drama club kids, every emotion kicks in. It hits me, once more, that we'll never all be in a show together. We'll never try to rush off campus to get coffee or pizza before rehearsals. Never play dumb games backstage while we wait for our cues. Never scramble to come up with makeshift wardrobe fixes at the final hour. Never take ridiculous selfies in our exaggerated stage makeup. Never pile too many people into a car for the drama banquet.

I thought I'd gotten this out of my system when we had our grad barbecue. The parents put together a slideshow set to "Sign of the Times." I swear the adults think it's funny to make us all cry or something.

But I didn't get it all out of my system. I'm going to miss this. I'm going to miss them.

Eden catches my eye, and she offers up a soft smile. "I know."

I smile back, nodding.

We might never all be on the same stage again, but we'll never stop being a family.

"And also they have those weird little cherry candies, do you know the ones?"

Sebastian and Annie are doubled over laughing, and I am so grateful, because their laughter is contagious and just what I need right now.

"I thought you were, like, *going inward*," Annie says to me, pulling a face. "Had me worried for a second there."

"This is a really big day, Annie." I take a deep breath. "Right now, we are high school seniors. Safe in the comforts of our seaside bubble. Shielded from so many responsibilities, challenges, and tribulations. And when we walk across that stage—when those diplomas fall firmly into our grasp—we're no longer children. We're no longer coddled or cocooned. We're adults, entering the real world."

Sebastian and Annie exchange sideways glances, mouths agape.

"I think New York changed you," Annie says, finally. She nods. "You're so down-to-earth now."

"Left the melodramatics in Manhattan," Sebastian agrees.

I roll my eyes, and she and Sebastian are all giggles again.

"Laugh all you want, but this is a momentous day."

Annie puts her hand on my knee. "You're right. It is. I just think I am, personally, so glad for this momentous day to be nearly over. I'm ready for cauliflower pizza and vegan cake. And to crush some Twisted Tea at the party. Why not? I'm feeling wild. I damn near didn't graduate."

"The Friends of Nature Club were a bad influence," I say. "Admit it!"

Sebastian holds up his hand, leaving some space

between his thumb and index finger as if to say "maybe a *liiittle* bit."

"They have great intentions," Annie says. "The best intentions. They just need better organization and direction, I think."

"I will personally make sure you get a Twisted Tea," Sebastian says.

Annie clutches her heart like he's a white knight here to save her. "My hero."

I run my fingers down the only cords I'm wearing, for the International Thespian Society. Annie couldn't be bothered to tally up all her points and do the paperwork, but she absolutely could have been wearing some too if she'd wanted. Sebastian has way more. He's in the National Honor Society, the Science National Honor Society, and Mu Alpha Theta. I don't understand how one brain can house that much genius, but apparently, for him, it's no big deal.

He sees me eyeing them and groans. "Are you judging my nerdiness?"

"Just impressed by your brilliance," I say.

Wonder flashes across Annie's face. "Me too. I still cannot believe you are going to MIT. Do you know that's, like, a very, very big deal?"

Cheeks flushed a bright crimson, Sebastian nods. "Yes, thank you, Annie."

"Is Poe going?" Annie asks. "Please, he deserves to be with his papa."

"Papa?" Sebastian and I both stick out our tongues.

"I don't think I can have a fish in my dorm." Sebastian frowns.

"If you need a letter for your dorm, I bet the Friends of Nature Club can help somehow . . ." Annie chews on the inside of her cheek and looks to me. "It's too bad we can't do something."

Sebastian hums. "What would you guys be able to do?"

"We can do a lot. We can do plenty. We can make miracles happen, Sebastian. We are ordained," Annie says.

I nod. "It's true. It was like twenty dollars. It's an online certificate. But we figured maybe one day it will come in handy."

"Best twenty dollars we've ever spent," Annie says, then pulls a face. "Too bad it can't help keep you and Poe together, though. I think we should have done the notary thing."

Dean is blowing my phone up. We were supposed to leave them with our families, but I snuck mine in the waistband of my briefs.

DEAN:

Mom is making small talk with everyone

DEAN:

Dad is trying to hire some guy
to do a new neon sign

DEAN:

Grandma thinks her phone is hacked by spies

DEAN:

Wow this is all so much

I snap a selfie with Annie and send it to him.

ME:

DEAN:

Gotta love that Hammerhead pride

Mrs. Mackenzie hurries over as everybody starts to line up in pairs. Sebastian leans over, his hand finding my cheek and his lips meeting mine. They're soft, and the kiss is sweet, like the Cherry Coke slushie we just shared before this. It's pure magic how every kiss with him is better than the last.

"Break a leg," he says. "See you after."

He runs over to join the rest of the Science National Honor Society kids, where his walking partner is, and he gives me one last little wink, rocking back on his heels.

Clinging to me with one arm as she wobbles in her heels, Annie eyes my bare, bracelet-tanned wrist. "You're not wearing it?"

"I guess I forgot it." I smile, holding her up. "But it's okay. I'm already the luckiest guy in the world."

The music starts, and I take a deep breath.

It's showtime.

Acknowledgments

As always, I am so grateful for my family's support and love—Mom, Gabby, Reagan, Dad, and Erica—thank you for encouraging me to follow my dreams. To my grandmother Hola—thank you for your wisdom and for always inspiring me. You've always championed my creativity, and this book wouldn't be what it is without you. To my wonderful friends who make life so much more fun—Lizzy, Ashley, Kelly, Macy, Carson, Paige, Angus, and Marissa—thank you for believing in me and always being there.

A huge thank-you to all my talented author friends who continue to support me and my books: Shawn, Adam, Robbie, Jason June, Jenna, Liselle, Jamie, Phil, Adam Sass, Tobias, and many more! Thank you to the ever creative and dedicated booktokers, bookstagrammers, booktubers, and book reviewers!

We've arrived at Volume III of Why Kristy Hunter is the Perfect Agent—the multivolume leather-bound box set! Kristy, thank you forever and ever for being a sounding board and someone I can trust so fully. You're always supportive and compassionate and—if you ask me—the best at what you do! Also, thank you for being someone who will enjoy a glass of rosé and truffle fries by the water with me. I very much appreciate that.

My editor, Olivia Valcarce—where do I even begin? You helped bring this story to life in such a thoughtful and caring way. You got Teddy and Sebastian from the very beginning and had such amazing ideas and insight. Thank you for everything!

Thank you to Bess Braswell, Brittany Mitchell, Justine Sha, Kamille Carreras Pereira, and the rest of the Inkyard/HarperCollins team for all your hard work. Thank you to Ricardo Bessa and Alex Niit for the perfect cover!

And thank you, reader, for traveling with Teddy and Sebastian from Citrus Harbor, all over New York City, and back again. Wherever you are, I believe in you wholeheartedly, and I hope you'll always chase after your dreams—you've already got all the luck you need!